Los Soñadores

(The Dreamers)

Book Two ~ Retribution

G. Stephen Renfrey

ISALAN

Published by Isalan Publications
49 Seymour Crescent
Barrie, Ontario
L4N 8N4

www.isalan.com
email: isalan@live.ca

ॐॐ

ॐॐ

Cover design by G.S. Renfrey

Canadian Cataloging in Publications data

ISBN 978-0-9921699-3-0

Acknowledgements

To the muses, in all your forms...

To those committed to the advance of human consciousness...

To those committed to the welfare of our planet and all her species...

To those committed to the preservation of our remaining wild spaces...

Thank you.

Epigraph

I like to think who we are has nothing to do with where we come from or who our people are. I've never really understood why some place so much stock in what family name they carry or what their social standing is. It seems like an illusion, a form of mass delusion we're entranced to. I now believe it's because of an error in thought—that certain people because of name, lineage, or position, are somehow different from the rest of us. We attribute unfair goodness and virtue to these chosen few, and grant them privilege and power.

At the heart of it, maybe we're just trying to glimpse the best in ourselves, only it's easier to project our ideals on others than to look within. We know how imperfect we are, see our shortcomings too clearly, so maybe it's just easier to project all that is good and desirable onto a few we believe special, only it's not really fair to them or ourselves.

In times not too distant past, there were those deemed special, of greater intrinsic worth and favor by virtue of bloodlines. We called them Royals. It seems foolish now, though the fuss the media makes over the remnants of royal families to the day suggests we still want to hold up some sort of banner, some sort of icon that says "This is the best of us. This is who we can be, who we are".

Maybe we're half right in that, but perhaps we are all Royals in our own right. What would happen if we began to see the nobility within ourselves, and cultivated that potential rather than presume it to be the right f the chosen few? How would the world change if we saw ourselves and everyone else as Royalty, no one greater or lesser than another? Would we give the respect and deference to each other that we deserve, or would we fall into bitter dispute?

What I do believe is this: Each of us is born into this world with gifts and challenges, and it is what we do with those that makes us what we are. Yet regardless of where we may rise to, what we may become, we remain who we were born, a personification of the divine, no greater or lesser than the man or women next to us, for we are each of us special and sacred.

~ From the Journal of Jesse Benatar

Los Soñadores II

(The Dreamers)

Table Of Contents

Chapter 1

Consequences

> *Journal - Hook Point, CA.*
>
> *Seems to me that most of us go about our days with our heads full of meaningless bullshit; I know it's true for me. Sometimes, though, something happens that is so profoundly real and important, that it cuts through the wasteful insanity of it all and for a time, I become aware of what's really important.*
>
> *~ From the Journal of Jesse Benatar*

I turn back to Gwen, her hands to her face and looking scared. "Tell Mom I'm at the hospital."

The screen door creaks on its hinges and Mom's standing on the front porch. "Jesse?" she calls.

"I'm going into town," I yell back as I pull open the pickup door. "I'll be at the hospital."

"Jesse, what's happened?" she calls.

"I don't know. I'll call you from there."

With that, we're gone. Pete backs out of the driveway and the rear tires shoot gravel for twenty feet taking off. "So what happened," I ask.

"I don't know man, an accident," he says.

"What sort of accident, who was hurt?"

"I don't know. Michelle called from the hospital. The doctors are still checking everyone out. I think Paul got it the worse."

"Pete, slow down a little. Who was hurt and how?" I ask.

He takes a few breaths and our speed drops a notch. "Ah, let's see, there was Paul and Miranda, Michelle, Jeff, and Christine. I think that's it," he says.

"What about Lex?" I ask.

"No, she couldn't be found. I told Miranda I'd drive around and look for her, bring her out to your place. The rest left in Michelle's car. Oh, man!" he groans, and our speed picks up again.

t happened?" I ask.

...t know, dude. Car hit a tree and went into the river. Oh, man, I should have been there."

"Where?"

"Just up ahead."

I pat my pockets for my phone—empty. "You have your phone?"

"Yeah, yeah." Pete fumbles around in his overalls and hands me a cell phone as dirty as the bottom of a tool box. "She's in my contacts."

I find the number and hit 'call' just as Pete begin to slow for the red snake of backed up traffic ahead.

"Crap," he grumbles. "It was backing up when I came through."

"How'd you get through?"

"This way," he says, then he turns the wheel to the right and we drive off road, between a set of trees and onto one of the few open expanses of treeless field on River Road. The headlights shine on a set of tire marks through cut green grass and Pete follows them.

"Owner's going to love you," I say.

"They do—they're my grandparents."

I get Michelle's voice mail. "Hey, this is Jesse. I have Pete's phone and we're on our way. Give us a call."

To the left, about 100 feet away, I can see an area of road lit up like daytime in spotlights, surrounded by flashing red, blue and yellow lights. "That's where they went off," Pete says. "Stupid place to loose control. It's a long curve. How can someone loose control like that?"

The pickup bounces up onto his Grandparent's driveway and Pete guns it, spraying gravel again. We reach the road and there's a line of eastbound cars backed up as far as we can see. He floors the gas and the old pickup rattles its way down the open westbound lane. I look through the back widow at the accident scene but through all the vehicles and lights, I can barely make out a tow truck winching a dark object out of the river.

I search Pete's contacts for another number, find Jeffrey's and hit 'call'. There's no answer. I try Miranda's—she answers.

"Hello?" her distraught voice cries.

"Miranda? This is Jesse. What happened? Is everyone all right?"

"Jesse," she says and begins to cry. "He's all broken I saw him. The bone was sticking out and the blood."

"Miranda. Calm down, you're at the hospital. Everything will be okay."

"No, no, it's bad. I saw him, he's not talking, and his eyes were all..."

"You need to turn off the phone now honey," a voice says in the background. "There's oxygen here and it's not safe."

"No, I want talk to my friend, he has to know," Miranda says.

"Not now honey, your friends will here all about it later," the voice says. "The doctor's ready to see you."

"No, I..."

There's a muffled sound then the nurse comes on the phone loud and clear. "Hello, I'm sorry but this phone needs to go off now."

"Wait, can you tell..." The connection goes dead. "Fuck!" I blurt.

"What's happening man?" Pete asks.

"I don't know. Miranda's a little hysterical but it sounds like she's probably okay; the doctor is just seeing to her now. Paul might be in a bad way though."

"Shit, man!"

"Yeah, just get us there."

When we arrive, the small hospital seems quiet, as though the world hadn't turned over and wasn't crumbling around us. The people in the ER reception area are calm and smiling—it's surreal. I walk past them to their protests and a CHP officer steps out and stops me. It was all I could do to stop myself from dodging around him, when Michelle calls out from down the hall. The cop is cool about it; when he sees that I'm with the accident victims, he steps aside and waves me through.

"What happened?" I ask. Michelle and I hug briefly and I can feel that her whole body is shaking.

She looks worn out, scared, and sports what will likely be a couple of black eyes tomorrow. "We were run off the road, Jesse," she says. "Some stupid bastard just passed us on the corner and sideswiped my mom's car."

"Is everyone okay? How's Paul?" I ask.

"Paul has a broken arm. His widow was open and we rolled. It's bad, Jesse, really bad. I don't know if they're going to be able to save it." Michelle's face screws up and she begins to cry.

"Shit!" Pete blurts. "Shit, shit, shit." I hug Michelle and she sobs into my shoulder. She's still wet from the waist down, and I feel the dampness bleeding into my jeans. "Where is he," Pete asks. "Can I see him?"

Michelle pulls away, wipes her eyes, then speaks in a horse voice. "They, ah, have him in surgery now."

"I say we find that rat bastard who did this and run him off a high bridge," Pete says. He wanders down into the bowels of the ER where a nurse accosts him and orders him out. I'd been so obsessed about how my friends were since Pete told me about the accident, that I'd thought of little else. Pete's comment, however, triggers other, darker thoughts, and I suppress them.

"How are you?" I ask Michelle.

"Oh I'm fine, just got it good in the face with the air bag."

"Everyone else?" I ask.

"Ah, Jeffrey's about the same as me except he hit his knee pretty hard. He's been limping. Christine's pretty shaken up and Miranda's a basket case, but I don't think they're hurt bad."

"Rat bastard," I hear Pete say again from somewhere unseen. The thoughts I've been sitting on pop to the surface again and will not be denied.

"Michelle," I say with emphasis to get her attention. "Did you get a good look at the driver? Do you have any idea who did this?"

"No," she says, looking at the floor and shaking her head. "It happened too fast."

"Did you recognize the car? Was anything about it familiar?" I ask.

She looks at me oddly, and shakes her head. "No. It was just a car." Her eyes flit back and forth between mine searchingly.

"What color, what kind?"

"Jesse, the police are…"

"What color was it?" I repeat.

"Ah, silver. I didn't really notice what kind I was, only if wasn't big."

The image of the car passing the house, Gwen's reaction that time, and Michelle's description come together and I feel my muscles tighten. "Like a Sunfire?" I ask, knowing the answer.

"Yeah, maybe," she says. "I think I heard Jeffrey say something about sun fire when he was talking to the police officer." She knits her brow and gives me a seriously concerned look. "Tell me you're not planning on going after them or anything stupid."

"No, I don't think that would do any good." The car I'd seen passing the house just after the accident was a silver Sunfire. It was a junk car; a dime a dozen and thousands available. I suspect it's already hidden away and abandoned.

"You think it was done of purpose, don't you? You think you know who did this?" Michelle asks. I nod. "Who, who would do this?"

"Who'd you warn me about?"

Her eyes widened. "Wingate?" she whispers.

"Yeah," I say.

"Why? Why would he? It doesn't make any sense."

"It does when you start putting a few pieces together," I say. "Let's not worry about that now. Let's just make sure everyone is okay and we'll talk about it later."

Michelle's not easily swayed from asking more questions, but when her mother comes in, frantic, the inquisition stops. That leaves me free to check in with the others. I find Pete standing next to a gurney they have Christine sitting on. She's wet from head to foot. "Hey," I say. Christine looks my way, she's been crying, and it's clear from her averted eyes that she doesn't want to talk to me.

"Hey bro," I hear Jeffrey say. I turn to see him being pushed into the room in a wheel chair. They already have him in a peek-a-boo gown.

"Hey!" I reply. "You're knee?"

He gives me a confused stare for a heartbeat. "Oh, the wheelchair? No, the doc says I probably just bruised it. The chair is so that I don't fall over and sue the hospital. Any word on Paul?"

I shake my head. "So the car that did this was a silver Sunfire?"

"Yeah, driver must have been loaded. Did they catch him?" he asks.

"Not yet," I say.

Before long, the rest of the parents roll in. My mom comes and stays, and I'm glad she does because when Paul's parents arrive they're distraught... and ancient.

I never thought of old people as having kids that weren't grown and raising their own, but Paul's mom is in her 60's and his dad had to be 70. I mouth a silent question to Michelle, and she mouths a silent answer— '*Adopted.*'

To my surprise it hurts to see the two of them as upset about Paul as they were, and anger burns in me with white-hot intensity. When word comes that they've stabilized Paul and were rushing him to San Francisco for surgery, I'm out of there.

"Jesse, where are you going?" Mom asks.

"I'll be right back. I just have to... I'll be back," I say.

Chapter 2

Turmoil

The docks are only six blocks from the hospital and I make it in less than four minutes. I find Santiago standing on the deck of his boat, smoking, and starring across the water at Wingate's yacht.

"Mr. Santiago," I say. "Something's happened."

He glances at me and then nods his head to come aboard. Once there I tell him about the accident and about Paul being rushed to San Francisco. He takes it all in like old news, and when I'm done he's silent long enough to make me clench my fists.

"Do you know why you came to me that first day?" he asks.

"What? What kind of question is that?"

"A simple one."

"Didn't you hear anything I said? Those goons hurt my friends. Paul might lose his arm. Any one of them could have been killed."

"Si, I heard you. Does this hysteria of yours help them?"

"Hysteria? Who's hysterical?" He gives me a patient look. "I'm just upset," I say in a lower tone.

"And that helps them how?"

"You really are a cold bastard," I blurt.

"That is what I tell everyone," he says, returning his gaze to the yacht. My emotions lock up and I fall into a silent burn. On top of everything that's just happened, I have no idea how to deal with this man. "Things may get worse," he says finally, "Are you prepared for that?"

"No," I say.

"Get prepared."

"How?"

"Did you read the book?"

"Yes, I mean, I've read more of it."

"Read the book."

"That's it?"

"It's a start."

"It's not..."

"It's a necessary start," he says irritably. "In the meantime, do nothing rash. Do nothing to draw attention to yourself or interfere with the ones who did this."

"You expect me to sit back and do nothing?"

"Si," he says. He turns and gives me a look that's serious even for him. "Yes I do—for now." Then before I can spit out anything else, he says something that makes sense. "There are forces here that you know nothing of, Jesse. To go into battle and not know your enemy is the folly of countless dead." He takes another puff from his cigar.

I think about that. "Okay. Well, I need to get back to the hospital; my mother's probably frantic wondering where I've gone."

"Probably" he muses, not taking his eyes from the yacht.

I step from his boat. "Good night."

He nods, then says something cryptic, "Beware Mr. Benatar; a panther prowls among us now."

—— | ——

I try sleeping when we finally arrive home after 4:00 am but it's pointless. At risk of driving my mother mad, I push my bike across the lawn and onto the road, start it a few hundreds feet down the road, and ride back to town. The sky is just brightening in the east when I hide my bike behind he rusted dumpster and pull the loose sheet metal away from the warehouse wall. In the confusion after the accident, no one had thought to find Lex to let her know.

When she sees me, she doesn't say a thing. She just stares at me in the growing light of day. She looks strong, fearless, and fragile. There's something in her eyes that makes me hesitate; makes me want to stand in her gaze until the sun rises and sets. I know then that I'm falling for this girl—this crazy, beautiful, totally messed up girl.

"Something happened. There's been an accident."

———— | ————

It's early dawn and the smell of mist and earth is thick in the air. I race among the trees, fast and nimble, pick up a scent, then track it, slow and silent—it's as easily as following a newly paved highway. I hear them— chatter, laughter. I smell them—cigarette, aftershave, garlic. I see them— large, confident, armed. The engine of the backhoe clicks as it cools and they walk toward a truck. I feel the surge, linger on the urge, then strike—first the largest. He turns to see, to live a heartbeat longer, and then his body soars into the other, blood gushes from his throat. The other is lightening fast, but can't bring his gun to bear before he joins his partner on the ground. Their blood soaks slowly into the earth. Blood—rich with the odor of copper and iron.

———— | ————

The rest of the weekend is insane. Michelle, Jeffrey, and Christine are advised to get in a few days of rest and gentle exercise, but none of us can relax knowing Paul's at risk of losing his arm. It's also the height of tourist season, and with the renovations complete, The Kat draws more local patrons as well. Bill and Hilda tell the Mad Kats to stay home and recover, but the three, stiff to a person from the accident, show up anyway. They know that Bill and Hilda can't manage on their own.

Michelle and Christine both wear lightly shaded glasses, Michelle's to hide the darkening bruises around her eyes, and Christine's to hide the redness from her crying. They do their best to manage their emotions, but every so often I see waves of grief written on their faces, and soon after see them wiping their cheeks and eyes. When that happens, I take over whatever they're doing so they can pop out back for a quick cry.

Though I mostly buss tables and wash dishes, I learn to make an awesome salad, whip up a wicked cappuccino, and construct half a dozen sandwiches. It's exhausting work but it gives me focus, helps keep me from dwelling on the accident, Paul, and the lingering threat to my friends and family.

I don't know if it was planned or serendipitous, but Lex is never present when I am. In either case, it's a good thing; we all have enough on our minds without adding tension. I still haven't figured out what to do about her; I have growing feelings for her, know she wants something casual and uncomplicated, and I know how Christine must feel about it all. There's just no desirable solution, only a three-way lose. I do know I'm not ready to check out though; I feel like I'm standing on the lip of a 2000-foot cliff, teetering on the edge, and willing to take the hard fall if it comes to that.

While I work meaningless tasks, I think through how best to defend Gwen and Mom from the goons, come up with response options for home invasions, and otherwise plan the demise of fellow human beings. Then it dawns on me—that's how my father had lived. Everything I hate about the military, about his profession, I seem to be embracing, and in between stints at The Kat, I rush home to put a few ideas into place.

I watch my back carefully now—everyone does. I take side streets and backtrack to catch anyone trying to follow me, but either they've done their damage for now, or they're damn good at stalking their prey. Trying to beef up security at the house is like trying to make a fishnet waterproof. Doing it without letting Mom know what I'm up to is hopeless. Between it all I take Santiago's advice and continue to read the book, but it's not until Saturday night that I can spend any real time with it.

Gwen and I sit and read in silence for hours, making comments and discussing points as we go. Before long, my head's filled with so many details and struggling with massive implications, that I hit brain-lock and I'm not able to take in any more. It's another side of reality I'm coming to understand, so different from the one I've known, and I find myself confusing the boundary between the two.

In my mental fatigue, I recall something my old mentor, Max, had tried to teach me about learning from ancient wisdom. "The writings of the ancients are like prescriptions for how to live well," he'd said. "The challenge of using these roadmaps to a good life is that the territories we now live in have changed. We each of us, then, need to determine for ourselves, how those teachings apply to us personally, within our social landscapes."

It had only made half-sense to me back then, but now, as I'm grappling to understand ancient knowledge, I realize that I need to find my own meaning in the words and images. That's when I stop trying to understand it all, and that's when things begin to make sense. I share that with Gwen and we stay up half the night working with that.

When I finally turn in, I find myself lying in bed, longing to see Lex, to feel her again. I know she's with Christine, and I'm okay with that. She is where she wants and needs to be and I willingly remain at the edge of the emotional precipice for now.

——— | ———

It's not until late Sunday afternoon that we receive the news about Paul—he'll keep his arm but it's uncertain yet whether he'll regain full use of it. When we hear the news, Michelle and I hug while she cries in front of confused customers. Shortly after that, I receive a call on my cell. It's Lex.

"Did you hear?" she asks. Her voice was odd, throaty.

"Yeah," I say, my emotions dancing. "Great news."

"Yeah," she croaks.

"Lex?"

"Can we meet?"

"Ah, yeah, I'm done here shortly." She hangs up—there was no need to say where.

I find her squatting in the middle of the open space of her sanctuary, arms wrapped around her knees and rocking gently.

"Lex?" No response. "Lex, are you okay?" I squat down in front of her. Her face is streaked with tears. She looks up and when our eyes meet, a torrent of emotions passes between us.

"I need to be with you," she says.

I find myself mute, lost in the gray of her eyes. "Yeah," I finally say.

What happens next blows away my ideas about emotion and physicality. Lex becomes a writhing mass of flesh and feelings, weeping openly one minute, groaning the next, angry after that. She rages, clutches frantically, curses, and weeps. I know she's working through something deep and dangerous and I'm her means. It's frighteningly insane—until I surrender to it. Then, all the emotion that I've struggled to suppress for days comes out. I feel waves of hurt, anger, and desire wash over me and wipe my mind clean of thought.

The sight of Lex on top of me, wet with sweat, stirs me even further, but when she looks down and our eyes, meet, I lose—surrender—all control. I seize her by her arms, trap them against her sides, and pull her tighter to me. An overpowering desire to consume her alive surges through me, and an image of running down prey in the woods flashes through my mind. I've never before felt a need or desire to dominate anyone, find the very idea of it repulsive, but I need to take over—completely. I throw her over on her back and she goes without struggle or protest.

It scares and excites me in equal measure to take her so forcefully. A faint voice in my consciousness screams 'rape', but looking down at her, seeing her take pleasure in the surrender inflames me further, makes me mad for even more control. I'm an animal—wild—vicious—starving—and I'm feasting on my prey.

Afterward, Lex rests against my chest and coos soft words about things I had no idea she ever thought of—the smells of spring and fresh rain, the sounds owls make at night, and the feeling of rolling around by the ocean's surf. It's as though she's no longer the edgy freak I'd come to know and care for, but a normal, tame girl with ordinary thoughts and feelings. As I drift off into a peaceful sleep, I wonder whether she's been fixed or broken by the night, and I'm only vaguely haunted by thoughts I choose to dismiss.

Chapter 3

Regression

I awake to a soft keening I don't recognize. As my brain rouses, the noise becomes familiar—it's sobbing. "Lex?" I call softly. I hear another sob and sit up. I'm still on her makeshift bed in the sanctuary, but she isn't. Another sob pulls my attention to a dark corner, and I can just make her out, curled up against the wall. "Lex!"

I jump up, pad my way over, and kneel next to her. She recoils against the wall, pressing herself deeper into the corner; she's naked and holding tightly to a blanket. "No, it hurts," she cries. She sounds like a little girl.

"Lex, what's wrong?" My guts churn as I recall my madness earlier that night. "Lex?"

"No, it hurts. Stop, it hurts," she calls out. She sounds like Gwen did when she was five.

"Lexi? Alexis? Everything is okay now."

"No, it hurts."

"What hurts?

"Tell him to stop."

"Okay I will, Lexi, who do I tell."

"Them, the bad men, they hurt."

"Who hurt you Lexi?"

She bursts out in tears. "All of them, they all did," she cries.

"Lexi, can I hold your hand?" In the faint glow of the streetlight filtering through the grimy window above us I can barely see her staring at me from the darkness. "Let me hold your hand, Lexi. Everything's going to be okay."

She slowly extends her hand and I gently take it, squeeze it reassuringly, and then she starts sobbing again. "Can I sit there next to you to keep you company?" I ask. Her hand stiffens then relaxes and her head nods.

I take the edge of the blanket she's clinging to and slowly pulled it up around her so only her head is uncovered. She pulls it tightly around herself and sobs. "It's going to be alright Lexi. It's going to be okay I'll make it right," I say.

I feel her slowly lean against me and I carefully slide my arm around her shoulders. She cries softly into my side, and as she does, I tell her she'll be fine, that everything would be okay. I start telling her a story my mom once told me about a farmer and his ill wife. I get to a point where I can't recall more, but it's okay because Lex is asleep.

If it hadn't been for Dad's PTSD and Mom's gentle, healing ways, I'd have never found the words to say to Lex. I heard Dad sobbing in the night a few times—freaked me out at first. Mom knew how to talk to him, to comfort him and I'd heard that too. I think about what my dad had really been through, what the atrocity of war had done to him. My mind shifts back to Lex. She'd been hurt far worse than I'd thought, wounded deeper, and I'd opened her up and hurt her more. If there is a hell, maybe I'll burn in it for that, but for now, I know I have to make it right. I decide to stay with her as long as she needs tonight, but I know what I have to do later.

——— | ———

"You've changed," Santiago says. "Who is she?"

"What do you mean? How have I changed?" I ask.

"You're waking up," he says, squinting at me over his reading glasses. "I sense it. I can smell it. That usually means a female."

"What?"

"Señorita Ruiz?"

"Who? No, of course not."

"Ah, just so," he mumbles. He puts down my e-reader, stands, and leaves the room, I assume for the head. Waking up? a female? He has it half right anyway, but what was that about Catalina Ruiz? I hadn't thought much about her in days and now she seems like a distant dream.

Santiago's cat steps on the guitar case and jumps up onto the couch, as smooth and silent as an owl on the hunt, does a few turns to mark her spot, then plops over on her side and stares at me. I stare back. I've heard you can't win a staring contest with a cat, but I win this one—she soon loses interest in me and stretches out a paw to toy with something in front of her. It's a small square picture frame that Santiago had left on the couch.

I'm curious about what sort of picture a man like him would keep around so I get up to check it out. I can hear Santiago coughing in the head so I step across the room and pick up the frame. "Holy shit!" I mutter. It's an old color 4 by 4, back from the days before digital. It's overexposed and faded, but the two figures in it are clear; they're young, maybe eighteen or nineteen, and they stand next to an antique car, something from the 60's. They're dressed in jeans and patterned work shirts, and it looks as though whoever took the picture had taken them by surprise.

The guy in the picture is dark skinned and built like a bantamweight boxer. He's giving the camera a soft scowl, but there's something in his eyes that's joyful and alive. The woman—is my mother. She has her hair tied back tight and has a darker tan than I'm used to seeing her with, but her smile is unmistakable; it reaches through the picture-faded years and touches me as only her smile could.

It's strange, looking at a picture of my mom when she's my age. I've seen other pictures of her when she was young, but this one's different somehow. Maybe it's just so unexpected. Stranger yet, what the hell is Santiago doing with a picture of my mother, and who's the dude in it?

"Something interests you?" Santiago's voice echoes through the cabin.

I turn quickly and see him standing four feet away. His face is inscrutable as usual, but his body is tense. "Ah, yeah," I say. "What are you doing with a picture of my mother?" I don't know what to expect from him, so I steel myself for whatever.

Santiago looks down at the picture in my hand and holds his hand out for it. I glance at it again, look at the eyes of my mother, and hand it back to him. He takes it, stares at it, and gently places a finger over my mother. That bothers me. He stiffens, steps over to his table, and then places the picture in the lined box and slowly closes it. I'm unnerved.

"What are you doing with a picture of my mother?" I insist. "Did you take that?" I did the math quickly in my head. The picture would have been taken about '87 or '88 and Santiago would have been a messed up Vet long before that. "How'd you get that?"

The look he gives me is chilling. "This is my home," he says with tight intensity. "You demand nothing here."

"What are you doing with a picture of my mother?" I repeat louder.

He moves so fast I don't have time to react. I feel my right arm being twisted and pulled downward, fingers dig into my throat, and my shoulder erupts into fire. I don't have long to suffer before the room begins to spin and everything goes white. Then, as my awareness and vision return, I find myself sitting on the floor with my back against the couch. It takes me back to some of the tougher lessons Max had dealt me. I see Santiago sitting on the opposite couch, holding and petting his cat. I do a quick body scan as I pull myself up onto the couch—nothing damaged, but my shoulder hurts like hell and my head throbs.

"Owe," I complain as I rub my shoulder. "What do you call that?"

"A cat," Santiago says without emotion.

"Sarcasm," I blurt. "Heard that was the mark of a coward." Rather than anger him more, Santiago seems amused by my use of his own words against him. "So are you going to tell me how and why you have a picture of my mother?"

"You're persistence is irritating," he says.

"I know; it annoys me too. So what about the picture?" Santiago's eyes leave his cat and focus on me. There's no malice or anger there, but I feel he's studying me carefully and I hate it.

"You show bravery, Mr. Benatar," he says finally. I feel complimented until he adds, "I've known too many young men who paid with their lives for such nonsense. You have courage as well, but your bravery could be your demise with what is coming."

"What's coming? You mean with the Los Oscuros, with Wingate."

He nods his head and looks up at the ceiling. "What is it you fear most?" he asks.

I'd never thought of that. I'd always fought to confront fear whenever it reared its ugly head and I think I'd done a good job of it. "Hurting my mother I guess."

"Bullshit!" he says, shifting his eyes to me. "You dread that, yet you risk hurting her every time you place yourself in danger. Why?"

"You tell me," I say with annoyance.

Santiago's eyes narrow. "So you refuse to face life's greatest challenge. You wish me to do that for you."

Damn it, he's worse than the shrink I'd seen. "Yeah, yeah, the beast within," I grumble. "I've seen it; I've been there more times than you could know."

"No!" he snaps. "I do not speak of your inner shadows; you may confront them, perhaps you embrace them, but you refuse to acknowledge their driving force." That has me stumped. "Do you wish to truly confront what you fear most?"

"Sure," I quip. I believe anything he could show me would be nothing compared to what I'd already faced. "Let me have it."

We stare at each other for too long before Santiago finally says, "You answer like this is a game. Very well, let us see if it is a game you have the stomach for. Meet me here tomorrow morning at 10:00."

———— | ————

"Maybe we should slow down on the book thing," I say to Michelle over the phone. "It might take a little heat off."

"No way, Jesse," she says. "You might be right, maybe it was one of Wingate's people who ran us off the road. That's all the more reason to stick together and get to the bottom of it."

"Things might get worse, who knows how far they'll go next time."

"If Wingate is Los Oscuros, and I'm not convinced he is, then I don't think it would matter if we did stop at this point," she says.

I think about that. "Maybe," I concede, "We have to take more care though, watch each other's backs."

"I know," she says. "Getting the book to Santiago for the paper article was a good move."

"Yeah, in theory."

"What do you mean?" she asks.

"You guys were run off the road after the article came out. Seems it might have only stirred things up," I suggest.

"Or maybe it was something put into motion before the story."

She's right—again. "Fair enough." Silence fills the space between us as I ponder whether to tell her of my intentions.

"Hey, I think it's still a good idea to get together to talk about the book and what's happening," Michelle says.

"Pete will love that."

"Pete will be just fine with it. He was supposed to head back and work with his father tomorrow but he's determined to find the guy who did this and give payback."

I chuckle. "Pete's all talk"

"Yeah, he's sweet, but I don't know, he plastered three guys in grade nine who were picking on me."

"A real papa bear?"

"Something like that."

"Well my place is still an option." I say.

"Good to know."

"So you working tomorrow?" I ask.

"Yeah. Bill and Hilda threatened to fire us if we even show up at The Kat before Thursday, but Jeffrey and I plan to go in anyway."

"And Christine?" I ask.

"I don't think so; she exhausted herself."

"Yeah." I took a breath. "Listen, ah, you were right about Lex, Michelle."

"What do you mean?"

"I mean you were right; maybe it was wrong of me to let anything happen."

"Oh course I was right. What's done is done though," she says.

"Well, maybe things can be made right," I suggest.

There was a pause on the line. "Yeah, maybe," she says cautiously, "but you need to…"

"Is it true that Christine has a boyfriend someplace back East?"

"Who told you that, Lexi?"

"Is it true?" I ask.

"Well, yeah, sort of. It's complicated," she says.

"If you make it that way."

"What?" she asks.

"Hey, I have something going on with Santiago tomorrow. I've been ordered to report to his boat by 10:00 am. If you do pull something together with everyone, let me know where and when in case I survive the 'ol man."

"Sure, I'll leave you a message. You think Gwen would like to join us?"

"She'd love you like the big sister she never had."

"Great. I think she'll be a great help. Oh, and Jesse?"

"What?"

"Be careful, tomorrow."

"Hmm. I thought you were the one who said Santiago was safe?"

"I didn't say that, I just said he wasn't as bad as people think. He can be... extreme. Just be careful."

Chapter 4

The Right Thing

"I'll be back for dinner," I call into the house. I just throw my leg over the saddle when Mom comes out through the kitchen door.

"Jesse, where are you going?" she demands.

"Town. I need to talk with one of my friends."

She let's the kitchen door swing closed and walks toward me with a determined look on her face. *Shit!*

"You said that yesterday, that you'd be back in time for dinner," she says. I couldn't do anything but look away. "You were out all night."

"I called," I offer, but even to me it sounds lame.

"Yes, at half past midnight to say you weren't making it home. You wouldn't even tell me where you were."

"I said I was with a sick friend." It sounds like a bad line from a worse movie. "Seriously Mom. Were all upset about the accident and about Paul. I was with Christine and Lex," I half-lie. "They were both crazy upset."

"And their parents?"

"We were at Lex's," I say. Mom pauses and it's clear by the way she was biting her lower lip that she's thinking about that. She must know about Lex's mom, that she's not home much—she caves.

"Be back by dinner or I want to hear otherwise ahead of time," she says sternly.

I just reach the Shadow when a familiar sounding bike comes out of an alley a block away. "Shit!" I mutter. I wipe my face dry and toss on my helmet. I no sooner throw my leg over the saddle, when Bolin rides up on his Kawi.

He pulls his bike up close to mine, stops, and stares, no greeting. "Hey," I venture. "How's the leg?"

He glances down at it. "The leg's fine."

"So what's up?" I ask.

He looks at me in a way that I think is supposed to draw out a confession of my sins, but I have other things to deal with just then. "Man of few words, huh." I fire up the Shadow's engine.

"Your tough on the girls," he says finally. It's my turn to give the silent stare. "I saw your little friend running away in tears. Pity, she's a cute little thing."

"Yeah, a lot more than you could handle, Bolin. What do you want?"

"I'll have to see about that," he muses cryptically. That gets to me and I think he sees it because he laughs quietly to himself. "Let's ride."

"Another time. My mom's expecting me home for dinner," I say.

He laughs and points a finger. "Cute," he says. "I've got to give it to you, you do have a certain…" his manner suddenly turns threatening, "homespun style."

"Thanks," I say dismissively. I pop the bike into first gear. "Be careful out there, and watch those tight bends… they can be a bitch." I let the clutch out and pull away, keeping him in my rear view mirrors. I half expect him to follow, but he doesn't. Instead, he looks fixated on the river, and I know that was where Lex had gone.

I slow to squint at the image of her houseboat in my mirror—her boat is gone and I know it was there when I arrived. Of course, she'd use her boat—that was the one place I couldn't follow her.

I stop at the main road and turn on my phone again. I call Michelle but she doesn't answer. I leave her a message, letting her know Lex is on the river in her boat, that it's important that someone be waiting for her when she gets back, then I reluctantly start for home. I get no more than 20 feet when a sinking feeling and suspicion forces me to turn around and head back to the houseboat. Bolin was gone.

I ride up and down the streets and alleys near Lex's but there's no sign of him. I check my watch—I have to get home, but what about Lex? What if Bolin finds her? Would he hurt her? Those thoughts cause my gut to tighten, and something new—an emotion that I can't place. I've never felt this one before and it's both exciting and threatening, a low flame that begs ignition. I close my eyes and breathe to calm it down. *What's happening to me?*

I ride back and forth along any street I can find that follows the river closely looking for Lex. After 20 minutes I give up and reluctantly start for home. That's when I find her. Out by the breakwater her boat sits at idle, pointing to the open sea. I stop my bike a few hundred yards away, hidden among the cars and pedestrian traffic along the waterfront, and call Michelle.

"She's out by the breakwater," I say.

"Okay, I'll head down there now, I was just about to leave."

"Okay, I'll wait until you get here."

"Jesse, what's going on?"

"It's ah, complicated, Mich. Can we talk about it later?"

There was a pause on the other end of the line. I heard a car door slam and an engine start up. "Okay, but later Jesse."

"Promise. You driving?"

"Yeah, insurance rental."

"Hey, hurry will you? It looks like she might be contemplating a one way run to Japan."

Lex sits in the back of the runabout and she looks so alone. Another emotion erupts—anguish. *You fucked up again.*

Four minutes later, a gray Chevy parks illegally by the breakwater and Michelle pops out. She walks over to the edge of the concrete pier and I can see she's calling to get Lex's attention. A minute later, Christine shows up. They both stand at the edge of the breakwater gesturing and talking to Lex, forty feet away. Then they do something unexpected; they kick off their shoes and dive in.

Lex turns back to the engine and looks to be slipping it into gear to make the run, but Michelle and Christine are fast swimmers and in seconds, they're both hanging onto the sides of the boat. Lex was safe.

I do get home in time for dinner, which Mom is happy with, but I don't eat much, which upsets her. I change up the topic as she prepares a plate for me to take out to the Therion for later. "Hey, do you remember a picture taken of you with some Spanish dude, next to an old 60's car?"

"No, I don't recall anything like that, why?" she asks.

I decide it's time for some honesty. "I was visiting that old man today, Santiago, and he had a picture of you and some guy."

"What were you doing at Señor Santiago's?" she asks.

"Not much really," I say. "Michelle said I ought to spend some time with him, that I'd learn a lot about the town and all."

"I'd rather you not talk to him," she says. "He had a hard time with war and he's easily upset."

"You're afraid for me again," I accuse.

She nods her head. "Yes I am."

I take the plate of food out to the Therion for later at her insistence, though I don't imagine I'll eat any of it. Then I call Michelle.

"Hey, so what's going on?" I ask.

"We're here, both of us, at Christine's. I'm staying the night to keep an eye on things." She sounds worried and annoyed. "So what happened Jesse?" she asks accusingly.

"She didn't tell you?"

"No, she won't say a word. She just keeps phasing between crying uncontrollably and staring at the walls."

I feel sick. "I just did what I had to, Michelle. You were right, I shouldn't have let anything happened between us."

She doesn't respond to that for a long 10 seconds. "So you ended it?"

"Yeah."

"Just like that?"

"Yeah."

"Jerk!" she says caustically, then hangs up.

I feel my emotions threatening to erupt in the sudden silence of the cabin. I hold them off, but know they'll catch up with me later.

———— | ————

"What's wrong?" I hear the words but I don't know where they are coming from. "Jesse, what's wrong?"

I sit up, find myself in bed with Gwen sitting next to me. She looks concerned. "What?" I ask.

"What's wrong?"

"Nothing," I say. I turn and lean against the hull.

"You were crying," she says.

I wipe my face; it was wet. "Oh."

"So what's wrong?" she asks again. Her voice is soft, concerned.

"Just, stuff," I say.

"Like?"

"Stuff. What time is it?"

"A little after 10:00," she says. "Want to talk?"

"No!" I want to tell Gwen to leave, to leave me alone, but the look of concern in her brown doe eyes reminds me of the look Mom gives me too often. "No, but thanks."

"Is it that girl? Lexi?" I don't know how to answer that, but eventually nod. "Dumped ya, huh?" she asks empathetically.

"Something like that," I say.

Gwen reaches out and touches my folded knee. "I'm sorry, Jesse."

"Yeah, me too," I say. Then Gwen does some thing that a guy would never think of doing—nothing—she just sits silently with me, helping to hold the space for whatever I'm going through. After what seems like forever, I feel like talking. "You ever get tired of it all, Gwen? You ever just want to let it all go?"

Fear flashes in her eyes. "Jesse, you're not thinking…"

We stare at each other a moment as the meaning of her question permeates my fogged brain. I sit up straight. "No," I say. "Nothing like that." I can understand why someone might choose to end it all; if life sucked so bad with no hope of change, who wouldn't eventually do it? Was that how Lex feels? The recollection of the noose at the Sanctuary shoots a dose of fear through my veins.

"What's wrong?" Gwen asks.

"Oh, just worried about someone."

"Lex?"

"Yeah.'

Gwen's eyes darted about. "It was you," she says with sudden insight. "You dumped her, didn't you?"

I nod. "I had to, Gwen." I feel tears welling up. "I had to."

I roll over on my side and bury my face into my pillow, while Gwen snuggles up behind me and rocks me gently. I drift into sleep, comforted by Gwen, but the last words I remember are from another voice. "Es bueno, mi amor, es bueno. {It is good, my love, it is good}."

Chapter 5

Appointment with Destiny

Journal - Hook Point, CA

There are points in time when I'm confronted by who and what I really am, when I can no longer hide behind the facade of ego, and remain anesthetized in the mist of self-delusion. I've of heard those described as moments of truth, as though one is confronting some grand ordeal, but I've come to see them as chances to test the authenticity of my life, and when I can face my truth without shame or judgment, those points in time are moments of grace.

~ From the Journal of Jesse Benatar]

My first thoughts on awakening are of Lex; I wonder where she is just then, how she looks, and how she feels. As images drift through the mist in my mind, I feel lost in sadness and concern.

What was I thinking? If I'd only known that first night she came here that it would end so soon, so badly? *I'd never have...*

The thought was bullshit; all I feel is pain, but selfishly no regret—it sounds cliché to think it, but I feel changed by her. For her, I might have been a painful mistake, but for my part I wouldn't forego the experience being with her if I could. The look on her face before she ran haunts me without mercy, and burying my face in my pillow only makes the image stronger.

When I remember my appointment with Santiago, my anguish turns to dread. Am I up for it? Do I really want to see the old bastard?

I crawl out of bed and find a note that Gwen left:

Dear Jesse: I know we have had a really hard time lately, but I want you to know I'm here and I care. We may still have a few things to work through, but never think that I've ever stopped loving you. You're my brother and nothing will ever change that. I need you. Mom needs you. If I can ever do anything to help, please, please ask?

Love, Gee

The words are sweet and soothing. Gwen's the best. A dark thought of Wingate's goons doing something to hurt her or Mom lights a fire in my belly and I swing out of bed. Gwen's right; they both need me. Whether I want to or not, I need to meet with Santiago. There's something that draws me to him that I can't fathom, but I sense I might find answers through him, or that he can help prepare me for what's to come.

I run into Gwen halfway between the house and the boat and hug her long and hard. "Thank you Gwen. Thanks for last night and for the note," I say.

"You okay now?" she asks.

"Kind of—better anyway."

She looks happy, jubilant as we begin to walk to the house together. "So, ah, does this mean I can use your boat for a sleep over sometime?"

"No," I say.

"You're welcome," she blurts sarcastically.

"Sleep over? They still do those?"

"I don't know," she muses.

"Besides you need friends for a sleep over don't you?"

"Shut up," she complains, slapping my arm, and for a moment, it feels like things were back the way they used to be.

After breakfast I go back to the boat to grab my jacket and helmet, but when I jump on the Net, I find over 20 emails waiting for me. Most are from Tony and Michelle, but one gives me a shot of adrenaline—I open it.

'You should not have done what you did, dear boy. There are consequences... Isa.'

———— | ————

I stand on the back deck of The Revenge and watch as Santiago fiddles with something just inside the door of his war room. With his other hand he fishes into his jacket pocket and draws out a key on a fob and tosses it to me. "Go wait in my car," he orders. "Open the passenger side only and don't touch anything."

"You have a car?" I ask. I never thought of Santiago having a car. "Where is it?"

"In the marina parking lot. Where else would it be?" he says irritably.

"Huh! Sarcasm, and so early in the morning; who'd have thunk?" I say loud enough for him to hear me. "Great start," I mutter. I look at the key; it's old and worn and looks to be from a Dodge. "Well, what kind of car is it?"

"You've seen it," he says, but before I could ask another question, he turns and disappears into the interior of the boat. I take a breath and hold my tongue.

Between the marina customers, fishermen, and tourists, the parking lot is nearly full. I wander through it looking for something that stands out, something that I think Santiago would drive—a beat up pickup truck or jeep maybe. Maybe a surplus humvee?

By my second tour of the lot, I'm ready to take the key back to him and tell him where to shove it, but I spot it. In the far north corner, furthest from the gangplanks but closest to his boat, sits an old dodge. Then a flash of recognition—it's the same kind of car that was in the picture of my mom. As I walk up to it I'm certain it is the same car.

It's immaculate, detailed to perfection; the only thing that seems out of place was a small bank of LEDs beneath the center dash. The one on the far right is blinking. I reach over the try to slip the key into the ignition, but it won't fit. That's when one of the middle lights begins to flash. I half expect the car to blow up but the driver's door opens and Santiago slides in.

ᴎɪce security system," I offer. He doesn't say anything, but pushes the LEDs in a sequence I can't follow, then slides a different key into the ignition and turns the engine over. It starts on the first crank and purrs like a cougar. "So let me guess—if you didn't push those buttons in the right sequence, we'd blow up or something."

"Something," he says flatly. He puts the car in gear and we pull out of the lot and onto the street.

"This is the same kind of car in the picture," I suggest. He doesn't say anything. "Same model, same year, same paint job" He continues to drive in silence, and after a few blocks, I ask, "It's the same car, isn't it?" Of course, it was, that's what he meant when he said I'd seen it before. That meant Santiago took the picture of my mom and that guy.

"So did you know my mom back then, or were you taking the picture of the car?" I ask. He says nothing, acts as though I wasn't even in the car. I stare at him, study his face and how time and life had etched their effects on it, and then, like an optical illusion, the similarities jumped out at me. "Jesus, it was the guy," I say. "You were taking a picture of the guy. Your kid brother?" He says nothing, but he looks tenser behind the wheel. Then a thought comes out of the ozone—"Your son!" Santiago's jaw muscles tighten but that was the only thing he'd give up.

I decide that if he doesn't want to talk I'll do it for both of us. "Where is he now? How did he know my mom? They weren't dating were they, 'cause if they were, shit, you could have ended up being my grandfather, and that would really su…"

"He was not my son," Santiago breaks in irritably.

The car is suddenly silent; even the bustle outside seems muted. I stepped on something, but what? "Was? So he's dead?" he says nothing. "Who was he then?"

Santiago makes a right onto River Road and we head inland. I'm certain he isn't going to answer, when he speaks up. "No one of importance."

"Nice of you to say," I jab. "How'd he know my mother? How's he die?"

"He just did," he quips, "many years ago."

That's as much conversation as I get out of him for the next few miles. We pass the house and I see Mom unloading bags of groceries from her car. I want to stop and help her. I glance at Santiago and he's staring into the side view mirror.

"Maybe this isn't such a good idea today," I suggest. "I should probably go help my mom with her groceries." Santiago ignores me. Crap! I realize I'm in a situation I might not want to be in. "So, like, you're not taking me off someplace to do me in and dispose of the body, are you?" I ask.

He gives me a deadpan look and says, "If you are lucky."

We pull into a gravel drive about a mile past the house and follow it through a narrow ravine that opens onto a small farm nestled among grassy hills. When we pull up to the barn, a guy comes out that looks perfect for the lead in a slasher film. He's large, ugly, and his overalls are stained with blood. Christ! The thought occurs to me that I'm about to be turned into hot dogs.

Santiago steps out of the car, but I stay put just long enough for him to look back and give me the 'get the fuck out here' look. He goes on to greet slasher-dude with what passes for a smile.

The two men hug. "Carlos, my friend," I hear him say as I close the car door. "Always a pleasure." When he smiles, the twist in his face tells me he isn't everyday ugly, but has been terribly scarred, as if a truck ran over his face and someone did a bad job putting it back together.

"Good to see you again, Hector," Santiago says. "How is Sonia?"

"She is very well, thank you." Hector says. "She is at her sister's in Lodi and will be very angry she missed you." The big guy looks my way and then gestures toward me, "So, is this the one?" Santiago nods. "Ha, ha, ha," the man bellows loudly. "I will leave you to him then."

With that, Santiago motions me to follow him into a large shed next to the barn while the big guy lumbers up towards the farmhouse. I stand my ground and Santiago turns to look at me. "Are you going to stand there like a school girl or are you going to do what you came to do?" My turn—I say nothing. "Your game is not so fun now, I imagine," he says, and with that he turns and disappears into the gloom of the shed.

I don't think he's actually going to kill me, but the alarm bells going off in my head make me hesitate. Beat me to within an inch of my life—maybe. I look back down the drive; it is about a quarter-mile to the road and a mile home. I can run that in about six or seven minutes, I think to myself but turn and enter the shed.

It's a slaughterhouse—literally—and it stinks of blood and death. As my eyes grow accustomed to the darkness I see that a narrow pen, the path of death, leads from the far outside wall into a small enclave over which sits a block and tackle on a track that leads to the butcher zone. There, meat hooks hang from the rafters over stainless steel basins. One whole quarter of the place is taken up by a huge walk-in refrigerator. When Santiago gestures me towards the killing zone, my blood runs cold. *Shit! It is hot dogs.*

Chapter 6

A Harsh Lesson

I hear the grunting of a pig and Santiago begins to speak Spanish at the end of the path of death. He speaks too quickly for me to follow any of what he's saying but I slowly make my way to within five feet of him. There, at the end of the narrow, fenced in path, a large pig stands. Unable to move forward or back, it simply stands there awaiting slaughter.

"Is this what you brought me here for, to watch a pig be killed?" I ask. "You trying to get me to give up my bacon?"

Santiago gives me a look of disdain. "Still with the jokes," he says. He studies me a moment in silence. "No, I have not brought you here to watch this creature die. I have brought you here to kill it."

"Right," I say. "I'm done here." I turn to leave but fire erupts in my shoulder and I find myself yanked back and shoved against the rails of the pen. The pig goes wild.

"You are not done here until I say so," Santiago spits. Being knocked around like a helpless dummy is all too familiar, but this is different; when my old man did it, I felt enraged, wanted to kill the bastard. Now, I don't fight back—don't feel angry—only a growing fear. I feel his grip on my shoulder release. "You're a fraud, Jesse Benatar, a shadow of what you pretend."

"What are you talking about?" I say, rubbing my shoulder.

"You think yourself a tough guy, a hero, ready to kill for a just cause if you have to."

"Bullshit!" I spit.

"You hide behind a veil of righteousness when all you truly want is to vent your rage, to make someone pay."

"Fuck, you," I growl. I move to bolt from the shed but I'm thrown back against the railing. God, the old fucker is strong.

"No! Fuck you!" Santiago says with cold resolution. "I have seen too many lost souls take the dark path, it will not happen to a child of hers."

"Child of who's? You're nuts," I say.

"Si," he says with a grin, "and you are a fraud. Now take out your knife."

"What knife?"

"The one you carry in your boot, the one you think you've been ready to use." I shake my head. I'm hoping the big guy with the scarred face returns. "No? Then use mine," Santiago says. He slips his knife from his belt and flips it open in one quick movement, and buries the tip of the blade in the post next to my head. "You think you are ready to take life, then take life."

"I don't what to kill anything," I defend.

"Bullshit," Santiago spits. "You wanted to kill that shit father of yours many times. You thought about killing that shit Wingate at the dock that day…"

"But I didn't," I say. "I stopped you."

"Yet you carry the knife in case—just in case." That catches me short. I always thought of my knife as a tool, but in truth, the one I carried was more than that; it could slice flesh like butter and penetrate deep if it had to. "What? No smart comment?" he spits.

Santiago spins me around with the strength of four men and slams me against the killing pen. The pig bucks and squeals in shock and fear. He forces the handle of the knife into my right hand and clamps an iron fist over it. "Not even man enough to kill a pig. Let me help you," he says.

He forces my arm down toward the pig's side and I resist with everything I have. "What is wrong, Jesse Benatar? Do you not long to know what it is like to feel the blade punch through the skin, slip between the ribs, and cut the delicate membranes that hold the life of this animal together?"

"No," I shout. I struggle to free myself but Santiago is impossibly strong. The pig squeals again and moves back and forth the few inches the pen allows, as Santiago breathes down my neck.

"Do you not wish to feel the animal writhe in pain under your blade, then weaken and surrender itself to fate?"

My head spins as my mind fills with images of the countless gruesome deaths my father had described to me in sick detail, of the war porn he'd made me watch. My rage surges with recollections of Mom being slammed around, and my desire to kill peaks when I recall tearing into my father to defend her. "Fuck you!" I shout.

"Do it, Jesse. Just a few more inches and you will finally know what it is to take life, to know how it will have felt to kill that bastard."

"No," I shout.

"Come on, you can do it, I'll help you."

Santiago starts to force my arm into the pen further and I muster all the strength I can. I elbow him in the side of the head with my free arm, then slide down and twist out from under him. I roll to the side and I'm away, but instead to bolting out of the barn and making a dash for the highway and home, I fall to my knees.

I hear a voice scream in rage—mine but not mine, I feel blood surge through my neck and arms as I clutch the knife. A hundred memories flash through my mind in an instant, image of things that have made me want to lash out, to kill. Most are of my father, but now there's Wade, now Bolin, and a dozen others.

A firestorm of rage grows and I feel the desire to rip and devastate. Pressure builds behind my eyes, I feel my back stiffen, and the muscles in my shoulders and arms seem to swell with blood and strength. The room takes on a reddish hue, and everything slows. Sounds became amplified, and I can smell everything in the shed.

I feel as wild and powerful as I had in my dreams of being an animal on the hunt. I am an animal on the hunt. My rage to blindly destroy transforms into a white-hot point of focus—kill. The pig is only two feet in front of me, an easy reach with the blade. It bucks wildly, squeals, and throws itself against the pen, somehow sensing the mortal danger at hand. I stand over the frenzied animal, clutching the knife, poised to make the strike.

I've read about turning points, moments of truth when all that you assume to be true and important takes a large step sideways and it changes everything. One blindsided me as I stare at the doomed animal. I feel an upwelling of compassion, think of Gwen and Mom, and of Lex, and all that seems important just then is how precious life is—all life. I drop the knife.

I feel Santiago at my side and spin around faster than I thought possible and shove him away from me. To my horror, he sails, airborne, and hits the wall six feet away. He bounces off the wall, but rather than crumple into a heap as a man of his age should, he lands smoothly on his feet and stares at me.

I stand firm, but feel totally spent. "You're fucking nuts," I say.

"Si, that is what they tell me," he says calmly. He takes two slow steps toward me and I tense. "So, do you know now what you fear the most?"

"What? Is that what this was all about?" I ask. "No!"

"Not all, but it is important. Think," Santiago suggests. "Let us not have wasted time here." There is something about his eyes just then that burn into mine and I find myself thinking about the question. "The worst thing you ever experienced was seeing that man hurt your mother, the same man you once loved and looked up to."

"I never loved him," I spat.

"Of course you did," he says. "He was your father. All boys love their fathers and it takes a monstrous asshole to change that. He was a monster, el dañados una {the damaged one}, one turned to a dark path. He would have destroyed all the good that is your mother, and he may have turned you and your sister."

It fit perfectly, but a feebly protest, "That's nuts!"

"No, I am nuts—focus Jesse. Your worst nightmare is your own father and what he would say and do."

"What of it?"

"So then what is your worst fear?"

His eyes burn into mine and the answer comes. I feel weak in the knees and fight back tears. *God, no, not in front of him.*

"What is it Jesse?" he asks in a surprisingly soft voice.

My knees buckle and I fall on them. I feel a tsunami of anguish wash over me. "I swear I will never let anyone hurt someone I care about again," I blubber. "I... I promised I'd kill them first, even if I had to die trying."

I stay on my knees, sobbing like a boy, and I don't give a damn what Santiago thinks. It is truth, my truth, and I let it resonate through me. I'd known it all along at some level, but now it isn't a half-truth buried beneath years of bullshit. Buried for so long, now it seems like a pathetic promise a child makes that he can never keep.

I feel a gentle hand on my shoulder. I look up to see Santiago looking down at me with gentle compassion. *Who is he?*

Chapter 7

Family Secrets

The drive back to town is slow. There's a lot of stuff going on in my head, a lot of emotions surging through me, but as spent as I am I have questions that burn to be answered.

"What the hell happened back there?" I ask.

Santiago takes a moment to answer. "More than you can yet understand."

"Help me."

He glances at me briefly. "You learned the truth of your anger, what has made you so ready to cross that line."

"Line?"

"Of taking human life," he replies. Santiago gazes out the windshield, but with the thousand-mile stare he has going on, I doubt he even sees the road. "When you do that you never forget and you are never the same," he says finally. "It is never a good thing, and not something for you to have on your soul."

"I couldn't even kill a pig, what makes you think I could kill a person if it came to that?" I grumble.

"Because it can come to that. A terrified animal that bears you no malice can be harder to kill than a man who will harm you or your loved ones," he says.

"So the point of that is?"

"For you, to remind you where your anger comes from and what your greatest fear is. For me, to see if you would actually kill the pig."

"And?"

"You did not kill the pig." I was too spent to feel annoyed at him. "'It is a good thing,' he adds. "I think maybe I will help you now."

With what, didn't need stating. After another bend in the road, I ask, "How did I do that back there? How did I shove you that hard and how did you not get hurt? I mean you hit that wall damned hard."

"Si," he says with a wince as he adjusts himself in his seat. "I felt your strength, but that is for another day, Jesse. There is much more for you to learn."

"I'm sorry I don't think I can handle much more." A collage of all that has happened during the last month flashes through my mind. "It's been crazy since I arrived here. So many things have happened so quickly—it's just too much."

"So it must be sometimes." Santiago draws in a deep breath and breathes out slowly. "Much of what is happening has been a very long time in the making. There is much tension, like too much water behind a damn. You opened the floodgates when you arrived."

"Me? How?"

Santiago laughs quietly. "You said you'd had enough, and yet more questions."

"Yeah, forget it," I say, not really meaning it.

"Remember this well, Jesse; when those feelings come over you again, as back there, beware; the next person you shove may not walk away so easily."

When we pull into the parking lot of the marina I turn to Santiago. "So are you going to tell me about the picture?"

Santiago parks his car, kills the engine, and stares down at the dash with a heavy sigh. "She is not your mother," he says.

"Yes she is, I know my mother's smile, I know her when I see…"

"She was your mother's mother, Jesse. The woman in the picture was Esmeralda, Esmeralda Sanchez."

"Esmeralda? No, my grandmother's name was Harriet."

"Harriet McBride was not your mother's mother."

"Bullshit!"

"Evan McBride is your mother's father, but your grandmother was Esmeralda Sanchez." The way he looked at me, I knew he was telling the truth. "She was…" and he paused, "La Soñadora."

I stared at him in disbelief. "Selene and Serena Sanchez?"

"Si. Esmeralda's niece and great niece; your cousins."

I let that sink in a minute. "You mean, Mom is… Gwen is, I'm part of The Colony?"

Santiago shakes his head. "No! You have blood ties, but being a part of those people means more than blood. You can never be part of them now."

Then something else dawns on me. "It was you in that picture."

Santiago pushes the two outside LEDs under his dash and steps out of the car. "Get your ass out of there before 'something' happens," he says, and I'm out with the door closed in a heartbeat. "Knowledge is a powerful thing, and is sometimes dangerous," he says, stretching his back and rubbing his shoulder. "Be careful how you use it."

"Hey, are you alright. Did I hurt you in the shed?" I ask.

He gives me an annoyed look, then starts walking toward the gangway to the docks. I follow him in silence up to my bike, torn between the dozen questions in my head and concern that I've injured him. He stops by my bike.

"Does my mother know this?" I ask. Santiago looks down and then back at me and nods. "So why is this the first I'm hearing of it? Why didn't she tell us?"

"Your mother was an infant when she came to be raised by Evan McBride. She knows little of her legacy. I cannot speak for her as to why she did not tell you."

"But…"

He held a hand up to silence me "Too much too quickly," he says, raising his eyebrows a notch. He lit a cigar and stares out toward Wingate's yacht. "Sit with everything you have learned today, digest it thoroughly, then come see me again, but do not take too long."

"Is my family in danger?"

"His eyes bore into me intensely, but with no threat. "I will not lie to you, Jesse." He looks up in the sky and smells the air. "It is going to become very hot soon," he says, as though commenting on the weather. "There is danger to you, your family, and your friends. There is danger to us all."

"What do I do?"

"Read the book and watch your back. We will deal with the danger, the Mother willing." With that, he turns and walks to the gangplank that takes him to his boat.

Left alone with my only my thoughts for company, I feel empty and abandoned, yet all that has happened in the last hour leaves me with a sense of awareness and calm I can't begin to understand. All that I've seen and felt, all that I've heard, sits in front of me, patiently waiting my comprehension. We aren't even who we thought we were all these years. I need to be alone, but I want to be with my friends.

———— | ————

The Kat's humming with lunchtime activity when I arrive. It's the regular throng of tourists mixed with locals that I've grown used to, but they all seem different—I see people doing the daily busyness of their lives for better or worse. On the faces of the tourists, I see excitement, frustration, and hope—they're no longer mindless gorbies, but people out to break the monotony of their lives, to find a little joy or maybe something deeper. I'd always despised the lot of them for their pathetic drama and pettiness, but now, I can see their vulnerability, and how leery they are about what life has in store for them. *They're asleep; the poor bastards are all asleep.*

Clanging stoneware draws my attention to the counter and I see Michelle behind a tray of clean coffee mugs. She's staring at me, looking dogged tired… and angry. I take a step toward her and she slams the tray down on the counter hard and loud enough to attract the hushed attention of everyone within 20 feet. I stop dead and my mouth drops open but nothing comes out, then she turns and disappears into the kitchen. I make eye contact with Jeffrey and he gives me a sympathetic look.

I stroll over to him. "Not a good time, Jesse," he says as he tops up half a dozen dripping coffee filters with hot water. "I've never seen her in as a foul a mood as this before. You know what's bothering her?"

"Yeah," I mutter. I scan the crowd again.

Jeffrey slides the tray of clean mugs Michelle left under the counter. "Do I ask?"

"Probably not the best time or place," I say. "How's the knee?"

He glances down at his legs. "Better. I started riding this morning and I might be able to run again by the weekend," he says.

"That's awesome news; I'm glad for you. Any word on Paul?" I ask.

"No. Last I heard, the surgeon was still guardedly optimistic," he says, slipping a coffee to a waiting customer.

"Damn!" A loud clanging of dishes resounds from the kitchen and draws both of our attention. "Maybe I best leave before she wrecks the place." I say.

"Jesse," Jeffrey says. He waits until I make eye contact. "Is this about Lexi?"

Shit! Not here, not now. "Yeah," I finally say. "It's complicated." That doesn't seem to satisfy him: he stands resolute, ignoring an impatient customer, and his eyes tell me he's calling me on my avoidance. "Let's just say I really screwed things up," I say in a hushed tone.

Jeffrey's eyes relax and he leans over the counter. "Hey, man, we all screw up," he says in a low voice. "Despite our best intentions we sometimes hurt the people we care for, but those intentions count for something."

"Yeah, well…"

"No! Don't do that to yourself. You're one of the good ones, Jesse. I'm happy to know you and proud to consider you my friend. And I'll tell you this—we all feel that way. Whatever's happened, we'll get through it."

My emotions began to stir and threaten to breach my newfound calm. *Christ!* All I can think to do is close my eyes, force a smile, and nod. I turn my back on Jeffrey and walk out of The Kat. I keep walking, down Main and across its busy traffic.

I'm spacey, feel de-rezzed, as I make my way through the miasma of disused buildings in the old industrial zone. Somewhere, some part of me knows where I'm headed, but the rest is just along for the ride.

I stand in the middle of the floor and stare up at the pale yellow light streaming in through the grime-laden widows. Lex's sanctuary is empty,

I am empty, and the outside world no longer exist or matters. I look down at my feet, the place where Lexi and I had made out so violently, so passionately. I kneel and touch the floor. *Ecstasy to agony—how the fuck do things change so fast?* I kneel in silence, lost in the moment, then without warning I keel over on my back and let out a river of tears.

I feel detached from it all, numb inside, but my body seems to know what it needs. As my tears soak into the moisture hungry floor, my resistance slowly dissolves and the anarchy of emotion makes its way to the surface... I am lost.

I don't know how long I lay there before sleep mercifully takes over, but when I wake the light in the vaulting room is different. I roll over on my back and stare at the silent streams of yellow light. I can't recall feeling more peaceful; I no longer find myself lying on the aged floor of an old warehouse, but in a sanctuary with stained glass windows. *I get it Lex. I understand.*

Chapter 8

Cut From Different Cloth

The clink of glass against glass tells me someone's home in the boathouse. I wasn't expecting Lex to be there but after leaving the sanctuary, I felt compelled to check—sometimes I luck out. Christine must have brought her home. I take the short gangway down to the deck and knock on the side door. I hear another clink of glass then silence. I'm about to knock again, when the nob jiggles and the door slowly opens. *And sometimes I don't.*

A woman, about mid-thirties, looks out at me. She's nice looking, in a used-to-be sort of way; her eyes tell me that life has taken a heavy toll on her, and there's something familiar about her nose and lips.

"Yes?" she asks.

"Ah, is Lexi home?" I ask.

"Alexis? Who are you?" she asks gruffly.

"I'm ah, Jesse, Jesse Benatar, one of her friends. Is she home?"

My name seems to register with her and she says, "Frank's nephew."

"Yes. You must be Mrs. Anasenko."

She nods, looking me up and down, then opens the door further. "Come in."

She doesn't move from the doorframe so when I step through the doorway I have to do it sideways to stop from brushing against her. As I pass, I pick up a strong smell of booze. The door closes behind me and I turn to see Mrs. Anasenko walking over to a small table where an empty dinner plate and glass of amber fluid sit.

Her hair is long and pulled back into a pony tale that dangles half way down her narrow back. She is small, like Lex, and through her thin housecoat, I can tell she's stayed thin despite her age. She picks up the glass and turns toward me. There's something off about the way she carries herself, and I grow uncomfortable.

"So how is Alexis?" I ask. I look toward the closed door I assume to be a bedroom and then to the ladder steps. I don't sense her presence; there's an empty feeling to the place that tells me Lex isn't here. When her mom doesn't answer, I look to see her leaning against the kitchen counter, holding her drink and giving me a look that sets off an alarm of discomfort.

She looks me up and down a few times, as though deciding something, glances the other way towards the sliding door facing the river, then sips her drink. The tickle of the ice cubes cut the silence like shards of glass. I shoot a look back at the doors to the two small rooms and the ladder steps. "Alexis is fine," she finally says in a dour tone. "Alexis is always fine." She takes another sip from her glass.

Are you fucking kidding me? I take a deep breath. "I was concerned," I say, "...am concerned. The last time I saw her she was pretty upset." Her mom gives me a questioning look but says nothing. "Lex... Alexis, is hurting, Mrs. Anasenko. Something's really troubling her and..."

"So you fucking her?" she asks.

What the fuck... you shiting me? "What?"

"Are you fucking her?" she repeats, pronouncing the words slower and carefully, as though I was dim.

You're one fucked up piece of shit, I think as I stare at the woman with my mouth open. Her eyes are large like Lexi's, but what's behind them is a completely different animal. As I stare, they shift from the look of aggressive hunger, to icy satisfaction. "Huh, I thought so," she mutters. "Only one reason you'd come sniffing around."

"What the fuck?" I blurt.

That brought a smile to her face. "It won't last you know. Never does with my dear daughter."

"What the hell do you know about your daughter?" I ask.

"More than you ever will," she says, obviously amused.

"Well you're wrong about that. I've seen her. I have really 'seen' her," I say, pronouncing each word as slowly and carefully as she had. "You should try it sometime. Lex is amazing." Her eyes flash with anger then fill with amusement and she laughs. "Lex!" I shout.

"You've got some fire, kid," she says. "Don't waste it on my daughter."

"Lex!" I shout stepping toward the ladder-steps.

"She's not here," she says.

I turn to look at her. The amused look on her face has shifted to a frustrated expression. "Your daughter is amazing," I repeat. "She's funny, sweet, smart, exciting…more exciting than anyone I've ever met before."

Mrs. Anasenko gives me a bored look. "Yeah, and she fucks like a rabbit."

I feel the fire in my belly erupts into an inferno of anger and the room tints red. My senses become hyper-acute, my focus razor sharp, and for a few brief moments my mind is empty of all thought.

Mrs. Anasenko's eyes widen with a wave of what looks like fear sweeping over her face., and she straightens up against the counter, bracing herself. Then, slower than it came, the shift subsides and I stand there breathing heavily. *This piece of shit isn't worth it.*

I manage to walk to the door, muscles still shaking with adrenalin, and throw it open. I pause and look back the woman, still staring wide eyed and clearly shaken. "Your daughter's an amazing girl. You're so blessed and so fucking blind," I say. "You don't deserve her." I turn and leave and rapid footsteps are followed by the sound of the door slamming closed and the lock engaging.

"You'll never have her, not for long," Mrs. Anasenko yells from inside the houseboat. "She'll spit you out like the rest of them. You'll find out what she's really like and you'll wish you'd never met her."

It is only after I fire up the Shadow's engine that I fully come out of the spell I'd fallen under. It feels like I've awakened from a dream and that everything that happened in the last three minutes wasn't quite real. A wave of sadness passes through me when I think of Lex growing up with that as a mother—the way she is makes so much more sense now.

It only takes a stop at a corner store on the north side of town to find out where Christine lives. I find a quiet spot on a nearby side street with a view of the house; it's a small stucco, done up in a pseudo Spanish style with simple, tasteful landscaping. The large living room window looks ominously dark and is anything but inviting.

The impulse to visit with Lex after being at her Sanctuary, and the sadness I felt after seeing her shit-bag mother have both faded. I'd wanted to talk to her, to tell her that I got it, but what did I get? As much as I can relate to her pain, I'm only kidding myself to think I understand it, and I know I've added to her pain as well.

A figure passes in front of the window and my heart throttles up. A moment later, it returns and stands close to the pane—it's Christine. She looks up the street, then down, and on the return sweep her eyes seem to fall on me. I squint hard to see if she's looking at me but she steps away from the widow and a moment later, the drapes pull closed. Message received.

I'm exhausted when I arrived home. Mom is out, probably shopping for dinner, and Gwen's likely with her. In any case, it feels good to be alone. I know I ought to put in some work into the Bonneville but I'm just not up to it; so much is bouncing around in my head it feels like it'll come off. I never get headaches, but I have a good one going. I go out into the Thereon, put on some quiet music, dim the lights, and strip off.

I sit at the edge of the berth and stare down at my right boot where the tanto's clip holds the knife firm against the inside lip.

The smell of dirt and blood is cloying. The pig bucks and squeals and I feel Santiago's hot breath on my neck. My muscles strain against his impossible strength but I am helpless. 'Do it, Jesse. Just a few more inches and you will finally know what it is to take life, to know how it will have felt to kill that bastard.' A dismal groan fills the space…

I wipe my face dry and fall back onto the futon. I stare at the low deck above as thoughts and images beg attention. "Too much." I roll myself up in my blanket and slip into the darkness of sleep.

——— | ———

I awake confused, and it takes a few moments to remember where I am. I feel exhausted and sad and want to roll up tighter and escape back into the darkness, but my stomach growls and won't shut up. I glance at the red numbers of the digital clock on the other side of the room—7:48. Either Mom has planned a late dinner or they forgot about me. It's neither; when I stumble into the kitchen, I find it empty with a note on the table.

Jesse. We're having dinner with an old friend. Please join us. 1205 Manzanita Valley Road. We're eating around 6 and will be there until 8 or 9. If you don't come, I've left a plate in the fridge for you to warm up. Love, Mom.

I warm up the plate in the microwave and make myself a tea, then take my feast into the living room to watch the boob tube. I watch a bunch of nothing for a while until the phone rings.

"Hello," I answer.

"Jesse, you're home," Mom says.

"No, not really," I quip.

"I've been calling every half hour or so."

Shit! "Yeah, well I was out in the boat. I just saw your note a little bit ago."

"And you left your cell phone off," a hint of irritation in her voice.

Damn it! "Yeah, I'm thinking of getting rid of the thing, trying out life without cell for a while to see if it's survivable." It is a tease but as I say it, it sounds strangely appealing.

"As long as you come home when the street lights come on, I'm okay with that," she says.

"What?"

"So you're okay?" she asks. "Did you find your dinner?"

"Yeah, just finished it a bit ago. It was really good, Mom. Thanks."

"Your welcome."

"How's your visit? How's Gwen?" I ask.

"Good to both. So you're okay being left alone?"

"Mom!" *Not really,* I think.

"I'm only asking because we're thinking of taking in the 9:00 movie at the old Rio in town," she says.

"That old place still shows movies?"

"Yes, would you like to join us? I can swing by and pick you up if you like."

"Ah, no thanks. I'm tired, I think I'll just take it easy tonight."

Silence fills the earpiece for a few seconds. "Okay, if you're sure. We'll be home about 11:30."

"Okay."

"Love you," she says.

"Love you too Mom. Oh!"

"Yes?"

"Can we talk when you get home?" I ask.

Another silence. "What's happened?" she asks with concern.

"No, no, nothing," I assure her. "It's nothing like that, nothing bad. I just want to talk about something."

"Of course we can talk. We can talk anytime, Jesse. Are you sure you're okay."

"Yes, I'm fine Mom. Enjoy your movie."

"All right then, but if you change your mind, you can join us."

"Okay, I'll keep that in mind. Love you."

"I love you too Jesse."

I have to hang up because Mom seems never be able to hang up on me. I stretch out on the couch and flip through the channels until I find a sci-fi series I'd heard of but never seen. It's a good distraction, but it can't hold up to my fatigue, and before long I'm out.

Chapter 9

Telling Gwen

'Jesse...Jesse...' Silence. 'Jesse Benatar.' I feel something pressing down on my shoulder and open my eyes. Catalina Ruiz is kneeling next to the couch with her hand pressed against my shoulder. I sit up quickly and her large dark eyes flash surprise but she doesn't back away.

"What are you doing here?" I ask. I look at the front door, certain that it's locked.

'What is wrong?' she asks, concern in her eyes. Her accent has changed; it's not as brutal as I know it to be, and there's something different about her voice. She reaches a hand toward my face and my head moves back instinctively. She hesitates, her brow knits, then she caresses the side of my face. 'Jesse,' she says softly.

Her eyes are wide and captivating—I'm drawn into their rich darkness, the beauty of their shape, and the essence that lay behind them. 'Jesse.'

'Yes,' I say, wanting to surrender to the moment.

'Jesse? Jesse?' She puts a hand on my shoulder and shakes it. 'Jesse!'

The room changes—the color, the sound, and something intangible. Catalina's face begins to shift and her eyes begin to lighten...

I'm looking into the concern face of my mother. I levitate off the couch, and the next thing I know I'm at the other end of it. "Mom?"

"It's okay, Jesse. You're awake now," she says. She slides up and sits at the edge of the couch, but doesn't take her eyes from me. Gwen's standing behind the easy chair staring at me. "Just another hypnopomp. You'll be fine in a moment."

Hypnopomp? No way. I've had them a lot, ever since I was a kid, and the doctor my mom sent me to talked about sleep inertia and the still half asleep mind trying to make sense of the real world, but what I saw and felt was too vivid, too real. *It was real.* "Yeah, I'll be okay."

God! The feelings I'd had staring into Catalina's eyes, the longing... then seeing my mom's face? *That's fucked up.*

"Jesse?" Gwen asks. "You okay?"

I look up to see Gwen staring at me. She knows something's up that I am not talking about. I nod my head. "Yeah, I'm fine. Just like mom said," I say, but I can tell from the way she looks at me she knows better.

Mom stands. "I'll make us a tea and we can have that talk if you'd still like to."

"Ah, can we do that tomorrow, I'm really bagged." Mom gives me a discerning look. "You do look tired, Jesse. Hard day?"

"Yeah," I say rolling my eyes at the understatement. "But nothing bad, nothing for you to worry about," I add quickly. I put one hand over my heart and raise the other in stereotypic pledge fashion. "Scouts honor."

She frowns and gives me a wry smile. "You were never in the scouts," she says, but she doesn't press the issue. Instead, she makes me a hot chocolate and I carry it and my sorry ass out to the Therion.

Halfway there I remember I hadn't asked mom how her movie was. I stand frozen in indecision whether to go back or move forward, until the kitchen door creaks open and then closes. I turn to see Gwen coming my way.

"We should talk," she says.

"No shit." We head for the Therion.

"So what happened back there?" she asks.

I tell her about seeing Catalina and her transforming into Mom and being certain it wasn't just another hypnopomp. "That's weird," she says as we climb the steps. "I mean, it would be reasonable if there was some sort of connection between Mom and that girl, but there isn't."

"That may not be so true," I offer as I unlock the cabin door.

"What do you mean?" she asks. I enter the cabin and she is right on my heels—literally. "What?" she asks impatiently.

I sit her down and start telling her about my time with Santiago. I leave out the part about the pig and the knife, but when I tell her that Santiago claims Mom's mother was La Soñadora, she gets so excited she starts to vibrate.

"Oh, God, oh, God, I knew it. This is so cool, I just knew it. I knew we were connected to something like that. I felt it all my life." She stands and starts to bounce on her toes. "Everything makes sense now. My whole life makes sense…"

"Gwen!"

"All those dreams and feelings…"

"Gwen!"

"I'm not a flipping freak," she squeals.

"Yeah, you are," I counter. She has me smiling. It's amazing to see her so excited and happy and I don't want to burst her bubble.

"Oh, Jesse, this is so cool," she says wide-eyed. "We're like, part of the coolest people ever."

"Gwen! Gwen!"

She pauses wide-eyed, and looks at me. "What?" she says with mild annoyance.

"Don't get too excited, at least not yet."

"Why?"

"We're talking Santiago here," I warn. "You know, the guy everyone thinks is nuts."

"He's not nuts," she says with conviction.

If you only knew what I did. "Nuts or not, we should check out what he said before assuming anything."

"You have no faith, brother." She flops herself down on the chair again with a dismal look on her face, but it only takes a half a second for it to brighten again. "We can ask Mom… wait! Mom says you wanted to talk tonight and tried pumping me to see if I knew what it is about." I smile and nod my head. "Let me ask her," she suggests. I can go do that now and you can wait here and rest or something."

"Gwen."

"Come on, Jesse," she whines. "You don't think I'll get any sleep tonight if I don't do you?"

"I don't think you'll get any sleep even if you do," I counter. "We can ask her together, in the morning." Gwen looks crestfallen. "She may not know anything," I add, even though Santiago had said otherwise.

"Well I believe it anyway. It only makes sense; I mean your dreams, my passions, the book, Catalina, why else would it all be happening if there wasn't some connection. Besides, Mom doesn't exactly look 100% white in case you haven't noticed.

It's true; Mom's features and skin tone aren't the Celtic and Nordic combination they're supposed to be. "Gwen, my gut say's it's true, but let's just slow down with it okay. I don't want you to be too disappointed if it's not." My mind goes back to the photo of Esmeralda and Santiago. *It is the truth.*

"Too late dear brother," her eyes flick up to the ceiling and a crooked smile slides onto her face. "Isn't it exciting, Jesse? I mean, don't you just get the shivers thinking about it?"

I shake my head. "No more than if I found out our grandmother is Amish. I mean, they're nice people and all, but they're sort of backward, right; isolated, seriously low tech, and keeping to themselves like they do."

Gwen looks at me as though I'm developmentally delayed. "Oh dear brother, you really don't get it do you?"

I'm exhausted and about to fall asleep sitting up. "Maybe not. Not tonight, anyway." I get up and go the head to brush my teeth.

"Well let me fill you in while you get ready for bed. There is nothing backward about the Los Soñadores, at least not in anything that matters. They're the most advanced people on earth, maybe a couple of hundred years ahead of the rest of us.

"Really," I say, accidentally spitting toothpaste foam on the mirror. *Shit!*

"Yes! You've read the book. They've been a part of the driving force behind our philosophical and spiritual development since our beginnings. They've played a major part in advancing our consciousness and countering our corruption."

I spit in the sink. "Well if you ask me, they need to work a little harder at it. Maybe being plugged in to the Net might help them get the message out."

"The Net's lost, Jesse. A hundred million sites trying to sell one thing or another."

Gwen is smart and I agree with her, but I don't like to hear her being cynical; I do that enough for the whole family. "You're right, Gee," I say, splashing water on my face. "Maybe they are important, maybe the most important group of crazies in the world, but I don't see how their isolation is helping the rest of us out here"

I reenter the cabin and strip off my t-shirt. "Sitting back in the hills contemplating their navels while Rome burns doesn't seem so effective to me."

"They have to do that, buffle-brain. You read about the Spanish Inquisition and their escape to here."

I was about to say 'that was then and this is now', but it occurs to me that there are far more subtle and dangerous threats to their society today than the Spanish Inquisition. "Right. So we talk to Mom in the morning, right?"

Gwen gives me a peeved look. "Okay," she says eventually. "You're giving me the bum's rush and I haven't even told you about what I discovered in the book."

"Ah, yeah well I'm going to fall over here in a minute."

"Won't be the first time," she says.

I take hold of my pants zipper threateningly. "Won't be the first time I've seen that either," she says. I give her a questioning look then pull it down with emphasis. She pops up off her chair. "Just kidding," she says, mockingly shielding her eyes and making for the door. "Just in case you're interested, the Los Soñadores lost something that I think the Los Oscuros would really like to get their hands on."

That makes me pause before pulling off my jeans. "What?"

Gwen smiles triumphantly. "And I suspect Wingate may be after it. Sleep well, dear brother." With that, she slips out of the cabin and closes the door.

I stand there frozen between going outside and calling after her and falling back into bed. Bed wins, but the thought of what she might have discovered follows me there.

Chapter 10

Gwen Spills It

When I enter the kitchen for breakfast, I know something's gone sideways. Gwen's sitting at the far end of the table without anything to eat in front of her, and she's smiling uncomfortably. My breakfast is sitting at the other end waiting. Messed up eggs, overdone toast, something that is, I think, supposed to be skillet vegetables from two dinners ago. Clearly, Gwen has made me breakfast.

I sit down in front of the offering and sip the coffee. I didn't think anything could be as bad as gas station coffee but I'm wrong. I swallow, set the mug down, and clear my throat. "So what happened?"

"What? What do you mean?" she asks guiltily. Gwen is as guileless as they come and it only takes a short stare from me to make her confess everything. "I asked Mom."

"Gwen!" I blurt. I push my chair back and stand up.

"I'm sorry, Jesse," she adds quickly. Then she becomes sheepish. "It just sort of came out."

"When?" She looks up at me as I pace. "When?" I repeat more angrily.

"Um, what do you mean?"

"What do you mean, 'what do you mean?'"

"Last night," she blurts.

"Gwen! You didn't even make it to morning?"

"Yeah I know, I'm sorry."

"How…"

"It's just that she came into my room last night to talk and, well, it just seemed to come out."

"Where is she now?" I ask as I make my way toward the living room swing door.

"In town," Gwen says. "She left a note."

"What did it say?"

"That she's gone to town and she'll be back later this morning."

"What did you tell her?"

"Just that you'd been talking to Mr. Santiago and he said that she's the daughter of a woman from the colony named Esmeralda. Then I asked her if it was true."

I sit my ass at the table and stare down at the eggs. "So what did she say?"

"Ah, not much, really," Gwen says.

"Not much. You drop a bomb on her like that and she doesn't say much?"

"No," Gwen said shaking her head quickly. She rolls her eyes up to the left then right, then left again. "Ah, she just said that it was something she'd talk to you and me about tonight."

"So she didn't deny it?" I ask.

"Nope! She didn't admit to it either, despite my begging her."

"You begged her?" I ask.

Gwen looks like she's been caught with her hand in the cookie jar. "Well, a little anyway. I mean, it was late and I was in bed and I didn't think I could wait a whole day to hear about it. I mean, come on Jesse, this changes everything, right?"

"No," I grumble. I poke at the eggs with my fork. "You sleep well after that?"

"No, not at all. I was too excited to sleep."

"Good!"

"You don't have to be mean about it," she says.

"You know something else," I prompt after trying the eggs. Gwen pauses for the answer.

"These eggs suck."

Gwen nods her head. "Yeah, I know."

———— | ————

I try calling Michelle at home and then on her cell—no answer to either. Then I place a call to The Kat—Christine answers.

"Mad Kat," she says in a subdued tone.

"Hey, it's Jesse…" *click!* I stare at the far wall of my cabin in the Therion, jolted by the rebuff. "Damn," I say, closing the phone. I sit the phone down on the table and my attention slides to the folded lockblade sitting there, waiting for me to clip it to the inside of my boot.

I pick the knife up and squeeze it, feel its cold firmness, and recall the sense of protection it always provided. Now, it brings the memory of the shed and the pig, and a feeling of disgust at the thought of taking life. The whole sick thing with Santiago seems unreal, like some mad dream, only I know it was all too real.

Holding the tanto feels different, and the thought of clipping it to the inside of my boot feels wrong. Perhaps it would be different in a life and death struggle; maybe I could use it then, but chances are I'll never have to find that out anyway. That I'd wanted to use it against the man who hurt us, seems like a distant nightmare that I'm finally waking up from.

I unlock my kit box and place the knife in the slot I made for it. It had been a near constant companion to me for two years, and it feels as though I'm abandoning an old friend. I run my finger along its backbone of steel. "Thank you." I close the box, lock it, and slide it under the shelves.

Chapter 11

Exiled

Journal - Hook Point, CA

From what I've seen, most of us avoid our truth when we can. I suppose it does take courage and faith to really look at yourself—perhaps the greatest challenge we each face in this lifetime is the willingness to witness our naked truth, but I see no benefit from avoidance. Doing so only delays the inevitable for we all face the final moment of truth at the time of our death. I've come to believe that the most important moment of our lives is that of the last conscious breath, when we face the truth of what we have done with the precious few years we are gifted. Whether we experience the anguish of regret or the joy of knowing a journey well traveled may all come down to how we've used or avoided those little opportunities to face our truth that life gifts us—those moments of truth.

Gwen runs out of the house and flags me down as I ride the shadow around the back of it on my way out.

"What?" I ask.

"You still mad?" she asks anxiously.

I roll my eyes. "Gwen!" As a running start to my reply—it doesn't lead anywhere.

"Please, Jesse," she pleads. "I'm sorry. I can't stand it if you're mad at me."

"I'm ticked, Gwen," I say glaring at her. A long pause ensues and I can see the tension build on her face as she squirms. As much as I am ticked, I can't let her suffer. "No!" I blurt. I'm not mad, just… disappointed." Gwen looks shocked and then her face screws up as though she's going to cry; my being disappointed in her is clearly worse than being mad. "But, not that disappointed," I add quickly. "I guess I can't blame you too much.'

"I'm sorry," she repeats contritely.

"Yeah, I know."

"Are we okay then?"

I look at her and have to answer honestly. "Of course we are, Gee. Nothing will change that."

A huge smile grows on her face and she bounces in place. "Then I have to tell you." I sit in the saddle quietly and she waits for me to ask her what she has to tell me. A look of disappointment briefly flashes across her face. "Fine!" she says. "The thing I discovered yesterday, the thing the Colonials lost?"

"Oh, right, I forgot about that," I say.

My renewed interest makes Gwen beam. "Well, it appears they lost something very ancient, super important, some time after arriving here in California."

"What sort of thing?"

"I don't know, the passage doesn't say, but it does say that if the People of Darkness were to ever destroy it, then the Enlightened Ones, would cease to be."

"Shit!" I mutter.

"Yeah," Gwen blurts, "serious shit!"

The ride into town is a mixture of relaxed bliss and nagging discomfort. Despite everything going on, I feel more at peace than I have since I was five, and at each bend in the road, the Shadow and I lean into it like graceful dancers, a flesh and steel ballet.

I roll into town and head straight for The Kat, but then turn early and head for the docks. A few minutes later I find myself sitting across from Santiago on The Revenge.

"So you are here to learn of your mother?" he says. "Why?"

The question throws me. "She's my mother," I say redundantly. "I, ah, want to know about her. I want to know about my family."

"Your family. Ah! And why is that important to you?" he asks.

It's such an unexpected question, one that you'd think wouldn't need asking, that I have to think about it. "It's part of where I came from, who I am," I say finally.

"What part would that be?" he asks.

Fuck! Twenty questions again? I grasp at a thread of understanding floating through my consciousness. I catch it, expand on it, and provide an answer that I think he'll be impressed with. "My lineage. I'm the result of all the dreams, intentions, and actions of my ancestors," I say. Santiago raises an eyebrow. "Well, not just me, but I'm one result of all that they were and strived for."

He's silent for an uncomfortable few seconds. He strokes his cat curled up beside him, and she starts to purr. "And how will knowing your lineage help you today?" he asks.

"Um, well, it'll help me find purpose," I squeeze out. I'm not sure where that came from or if I even believe it. It seems to strike a chord with Santiago though; he squints and knits his brow slightly.

I feel agitated and pop up on my feet. I pace a few steps back and forth, as I gather my thoughts. I feel emotions well up inside me and thoughts stream into my head from somewhere deep. I can't say why but I just start spewing them out. "I've never wanted to be me. I've always wanted to be... to be anything but... but related to him."

"You are your father's son," Santiago interrupts.

Fuck no! I quell my anger. "But I'm also my mother's son. I've spent so much time not wanting to be his that I forgot I am also hers." I stop pacing and sit down with fisted hands. "I want to change that. If I know more about my mother's people, maybe I'll feel I finally belong somewhere."

Santiago's demeanor never shifts but his cat stands up on all fours, stretches, and then disappears into the forward chambers. Then his voice takes on a more menacing tone. "You want to run away from one part of yourself to escape into another."

That sinks in and hits home. "He's not part of me," I say angrily. I ignore the warning flags waving somewhere in the back of my mind. "I don't want anything part of him. I'm me—I choose to be who and what I want. I…" I feel like I've been hit in the face with cold water as my own words snap back at me.

I look up at Santiago with wet eyes, expecting to see derision on his face. Instead, I see a vague shadow of kindness. "So choose your own path," he says, nodding. "Just so." He pauses for just long enough to make me wonder where this is leading. "Would it not be better to start clean, to be free of the weight of paternal and maternal lines?"

"I guess," I say, tentatively. "I've always believed that, until now anyway. That's why I never paid much attention to Mom's family either."

"What has changed?"

"Me," I say too quickly. "Or maybe it's this place."

"Or perhaps Catalina," he says.

I have to think about that. "Maybe! No! I don't know. What if it is?"

"What indeed?" He stands and gestures with a tilt of his head. "Come." I reluctantly stand and follow him through the chart room, up into the wheelhouse, and out onto the rear deck. He walks to the transom, leans against it, and lights one of his small cigars. After a few moments he speaks.

"I am not an educated man, and I am considered by most to be loco, but for what it is worth I do not believe we are prisoners of our ancestors." He draws in some smoke and blows it toward the sun, and mumbles something in Spanish in its direction. "But they do leave us with a legacy."

"A curse," I mutter.

Santiago looks either displeased or amused, I can't tell. "Sometimes," he concedes, "and sometimes a wondrous gift. In any case it can be very hard to overcome if one is so inclined." He shifts on his feet and seems lost in thought for a few moments. "I know of a woman who left her people when she was very young, a few years younger than you. It was a time of war and rebellion and she had become infected with the desire to swim into that dangerous current.

"She was La Soñadora and very innocent, a blessed one with the gift of vision. She knew nothing of what awaited her out here and her lineage had not prepared her for what she encountered." Santiago looks down at the deck and a pained expression washes over his face. "A pure and innocent among the dogs, an un-inoculated child among the diseased. She did not have a chance."

"She was killed?" I ask.

"Perhaps that would have been better. No! Her body survived the brutality of the streets—the drugs, the beatings, the rapes—but her mind fared less well. Today she wanders about, babbling of visions no one believes in."

That sounds like the crazy lady at Graylings. "Maureen Lopez!" Santiago does not react to the name—he doesn't have to. "You're talking about the old woman at Graylings, aren't you?"

"She is not so old as she looks," he says. "Her struggles have done that to her."

"If she is La Soñadora, why don't her people take her back and help her?"

"She is no longer La Soñadora. Such is not a birthright; it is a way of being, something acquired. Once tainted by the outside world, she would have been a disease among the un-inoculated, or so they believe."

"That really sucks," I say passionately.

I see Santiago smile for the first time. It is slight and brief but he gently nods his head and seems genuinely amused. Then it occurs to me that we're way off track. "What does this have to do with lineage?" I ask.

"There is a teaching in Ms Lopez' fate that you would be well advised to heed," he answers.

"What?"

"When she walked away from her people to try a new life, she could use few of the teachings her people had given her. She grew up in one world then tried to live in another." I suppose it's obvious that I'm clueless to his point, so he adds, "Is that not a truly clean start, one with nothing carried into life from either parent?"

Bingo! He sees my understanding. "Whether you care for it or not, Jesse, your father and your mother have given you many teachings about life. Some good, some not so good, and certainly some on what not to do, but they are part of your road map in this ailing world. Do not throw them away."

I think about that. How will I ever not reject my father's ways, I don't know. "I don't want to throw my mother's away. I want to learn more; that's why I'm here," I say.

"Do you think you can ignore half of who came before you? Do you think all of your paternal ancestors were like your father? Do they not deserve respect for their struggles?"

I have no answer to that. He's right, but I don't want him to be. It makes sense but I still want no claim on my father's line. He lets me stew on this for a while. As I do, I watch him smoking his cigar and squinting up at the sun.

In that moment I am humbled; this crazy, dangerous old man has suddenly transformed into someone gentle, understanding, and wise. Then, out of left field an idea pops into my head. "You're El Soñadoro," I say.

Santiago misses a breath. He gives no other sign of reaction until he says, "No. I am not that."

"You were," I press. "Just like Maureen, you were but you left your people."

He looks to be staring into oblivion. "Soy un caido {I am a fallen}," is all he says.

"What does that mean?" I ask, but he doesn't answer. "Was that why the war messed…?" I cut myself off.

"Messed me up?" he completes. There is a distinct edge of anger in his voice and my heart begins to race. He squints up at the sun and then closes his eyes as though silently pleading. "To take one so innocent and place him in that hell…" He looks down at the deck again and suddenly appears tired and old. "All I wanted to do was fly, to ride in a helicopter."

"I'm sorry, Mr. Santiago," I say, feeling genuine sorrow for him.

"For what? You did nothing."

"For you, for what you went through," I say.

"What do you know of it? Do you think that excuses me for the terrible things I have done?"

I want to say it does but I can't. "I don't know," I confess, "but you didn't ask for what they did to you, what they made you do."

"A man is responsible for his actions," he says tensely. "No man truly surrenders all of his power to another."

"How could you know that then, you were a kid?" He says nothing. "What choice did you really have when you found yourself there?"

"You know nothing of it," he repeats.

It was true; all I know is what I've heard from men like Max and what I can imagine of myself being caught up in a lose-lose situation. "Well, I hope you don't condemn Maureen as badly as you condemn yourself."

"Maureen has not stained her soul with blood."

"What about therapy?" I ask, and then quickly regret it.

Santiago holds his hands up to the sky and laughs. It's a quiet, mad laugh that sends shivers up my spine. "There is no redemption for what I have done. You will best remember that." Then he looks at me with the same dead, intense stare he gave Wade. "You go now."

"But?"

"You go now," he repeats intensely.

I nod, stick my hands in my jacket pockets, and look down at the deck. I slowly turn and take two steps, then turn back to face him. "You know, you helped me yesterday," I shared. He says nothing in reply. "I've seen you, just as I see you now." He gives me a hurt and threatening look. I swallow hard. "You're not crazy Mr. Santiago, but I think you're full of it!" That draws a reaction from him I can't interpret.

I take half a side step away from him without realizing it. "I think you've copped out, given up on yourself. If you had the courage to face your truth the way you made me face mine yesterday, the way you pushed me to do it again today, then maybe you'd find your redemption." I turn, step down the short gangway to the dock, and walk away.

I expect something dramatic, at least harsh words, but nothing happens. When I walk back up the gangway from the floating docks, I look back toward Santiago's and squint hard. I can just make him out leaning against the boat's gunwale where I'd left him. I learned nothing of my mother or her family, but I learned a hell off a lot about Santiago, and maybe myself.

Chapter 12

Christine's Ire

Hilda Carter lets me know that Michele and Jeffrey aren't scheduled to work until the afternoon, but that Christine's in the back room on break. When I gesture towards the back and ask if I can talk to her, she widens her eyes and holds up her hands as though to say, "you can always try."

I find her sitting on a sack of green beans, texting on her phone, but when she catches sight of me she immediately stands and pockets it. She starts toward the kitchen door, ignoring my presence, when I do something that surprises me—I step into Christine's path and block her way.

Her eyes flash fire and she tries to scoot around me. I step into her and pin her against the wall with my body. *Shit!* I've stepped over a line I didn't think I'd ever cross and I know I could probably be arrested for what I'm doing, but it's as though someone or some thing has taken me over. "We need to talk," I insist in a hushed voice.

Rather than a fist in the face or a cry for help, Christine closes her eyes and the anger on her face slowly melts. She nods and I step away. Without a word, we walk through the storage room, out the back door into the alley, and close it behind us. We stand there in silence and she glares at me until I find words. "So what can I do? How do I make this right?"

Christine huffs and shakes her head. "This isn't just some broken machine you can fix, Jesse. You're talking about people; people with feelings and lives you've messed around with."

"I know, I'm sorry, I..."

"Sorry doesn't cut it," she flames. I'd not heard Christine speak so passionately before; I'm seeing a whole other side of her. "It doesn't undo what you've done," she says.

I feel pressure build up inside my head, behind my eyes—not good. *Jesus no. Not here.*

"You can't just mess with people's lives," she says.

"I never meant to do that," I say, detaching from the pressure as best I can. How can I explain how torn I was when Lex came on to me? How can I convince her that I am not a total creep, a predator without bringing Lex's part in it up? "I never meant to hurt you. I wouldn't have…"

Christine rolls her eyes. "God! This isn't about me; this is about Lexi. Do you have any idea what you did to her?"

What we did to each other, I think defensively. "It isn't like that, I never used her, it wasn't that for me," I pleaded with more emotion than I cared to show, "but once I saw how she was affected by it, I put a stop to it."

"No, no, no!" she blurts, waving her hands. "You just don't get it do you? Where did you come from?"

I throw my coffee against the whitewashed wall and it burst into a splat of steaming brown. "What?" I shout. "What do you want me to say? What do you want from me?"

Christine looks shocked, maybe a little scared, but she recovers quickly. "I want you to get it, Jesse. I want you to know what you've done and what you're doing."

"What's not to get? You've all made it perfectly clear, I fucked up and Lex got hurt. I took advantage of her and she got hurt. I get it. I've told her we can't get together anymore and I've apologized up the ying-yang, what else can I do."

Christine raises her hands in my direction, fingers tense like claws as though to rip my head off. "Ugh! You, stupid, fraking shit." That's a new one on me and it distracts me from my own anger and frustration. "Jesse," Christine blurts as though exhausted. "You didn't take advantage of her."

"What?"

"No, that's just it." Christine looks to be suddenly flushed with emotion and turns her back on me. "Don't you see, you weren't just another fuck for her, another guy to play out her shit with."

The silence that follows is probably only a few seconds long, but it seems endless. Christine wanders over to one of the recycling receptacles and leans against it. I wander over and stand near her.

"You weren't like the others," she says, not looking at me. "It hurt to see her do that to herself, to let them do what they did do, but she got a charge out of it. She would make a guy want her and then fuck with him; it made her feel in control, only she wasn't really. They'd give in to her, and sometimes she'd actually fuck them, but then she'd mess with their heads, and some of them would hurt her back, physically."

Christine looks up at the sky, tears dripping from her face. "She hated them for that. Maybe I tolerated it, hoping that she'd remember who really cares. Then afterward, hell, the nightmares of her stepfather and her mother's boyfriends." She closes her eyes, and fat tears drip onto her legs.

Christine shakes her head. "God, so many dark days, always watching her to make sure she didn't hurt herself. Half the time she'd disappear somewhere and I'd spend hours, sometimes days hunting for her, scared that she'd finally gone too far."

Lex told the truth; Christine doesn't know about her sanctuary and I'm tempted to tell her about it. "Must have been hard," I say.

"Huh! More than you can know," she says ruefully. "Way I dealt was asking her not to tell me anything about it. Always knew something had happened afterward though." She looks up and catches my eyes. "You were different, Jesse; with you I could tell she was into you before she visited you that first night."

"You knew about that?" I ask.

She nods. "I keep close tabs on her Jesse; I've had to."

"I meant it when I said I didn't mean for…"

"Yeah I know. Thing is, she never gave off the vibe she normally does after the two of you were together, none of the moodiness or rage. She was happier than usual and I didn't want to mess with that. I thought maybe, she finally…" Her pained, watering eyes meet mine. "She gave herself to you, Jesse. Whatever you did or said, she opened up to you and that was the first time she's ever done that with a guy."

"Fuck!" I mutter.

"Yeah, huge, fraking, fuck," she says. "I think she thought she finally worked all that crap out of her system; here was a guy she liked and respected, someone who liked and respected her back, and there was no regret or anger. Then…then you drop the bomb on her and rip her guts out. A knife would have been easier on her, and that, dear cowboy, is what I'm pissed at you about."

Eyes closed, my head spins wildly as everything about myself, Lex, and the chaos around us reorganizes. "Oh, fuck!" I say, finally. "I had no idea."

"Yeah!" Christine says with an edge of sarcasm. I lean my backside against the bin next to Christine's and the two of us remain silent and still. After a few minutes, Christine breaks the silence.

"I don't blame you, Jesse," she says. I look at her confused. "Oh, I'm still pissed at you," she clarifies with intensity; then in a softer voice, she says, "I just don't blame you for letting happen what did. Lexi has a way, a gift or curse I suppose; she can slice through resolve and make you crazy with desire."

"Yeah," I acknowledge. "It doesn't excuse it though. I felt like shit around you, Michele and Jeffrey, like I was betraying everyone. I couldn't deal with the secrecy but I didn't want to give up what we'd…"

"You're a good guy Jesse. I can see why Lexi is drawn to you."

Just then the back door opens and Hilda sticks her head out with a questioning look. Christine nods. "Coming," she shouts.

"Any suggestions about what I should do? You think I should talk to Lex, explain things to her."

Christine nods. "I don't know if she's ready for that yet, but yup! Watch her right hook though; it's nasty."

Lex isn't at Christine's where she is supposed to be, and she isn't at her sanctuary or the houseboat where I also find her little skiff tied up. As Christine said—Lex disappears.

I swing by Graylings to see if Michelle is there doing her volunteer thing, only to be surprised by who I find standing near the front steps talking to Maureen Lopez—it's Mom.

Chapter 13

Somos Del Lobo

I ride past the Victorian, park my bike on the next side street, and then hoof it back to Graylings, a dozen questions running through my head. Mom is just leaving and I almost call out to her; instead, I stand behind a telephone pole to obscure her view of me. I watch her cross the road and walk up a side street, and a minute later, her car appears and turns toward River Road.

I continue up the street and through the gate into Graylings. I find Ms. Lopez sitting in the garden, smiling to herself as she stares at the flowers. She looks peaceful, happy, almost normal. She catches sight of me as I approach and her expression changes, first to shock, then to fear, then sadness. She makes no attempt to move nor does she verbally accost me as she had before.

"Señora Lopez. Perdón por favor," I began. "Ah, ¿Habla Inglés {Speak English}?"

She looks up at me with sad eyes and then looks down at the lawn. I've busted her good mood and almost feel bad about it. She nods. "Un poco {a little}," she says at last.

I sit down on the grass about six feet from her. "You were talking to my mother a few minutes ago." She gives me a confused look. "Mrs. Benatar—Jennifer," I say pointing back toward the stairs, "She's my mother." Ms. Lopez looks down at the grass and nods, but I'm not sure where to go with that. "What was she doing here?" I ask. No good.

"Ah, how do you know her? Are you related? Familia?" She flashes me a quick look, then nods. "So we're like relatives?" I ask, alternating a finger between her and I, which she doesn't seem to like.

Ms Lopez shakes her head. "No blood," she says. She waves a hand in front of her in the air. "En el espíritu," she says.

"In spirit? We're related in spirit?"

She looks at me dourly. "Si. You are hermano menor?"

"Hermano menor? ¿Qué es hermano menor?"

"Like young brother," she says.

"But not by blood?" I ask. She shakes her head. "Ah, then it's like a clan," I suggest.

She ponders this and shrugs only partially satisfied. "Like clan."

"So, then what are we?" She gives me another dour look. "I mean, what sort of clan is it? Eagle, hawk, or do you—we—even use animals?" Then a thought comes to me. "It's mountain lion or some other big cat, isn't it?"

Ms Lopez looks disturbed by what I've said, then angry. "Mantenerse alejado de la niña{Stay away from the girl}," she says threateningly.

"What?" *Shit, not again.* "Michelle and I are good friends. I would never do anything to hurt her."

She squints at me, "No Michee." She rolls her eyes to the sky with a look of frustration, "La Madre nos proteja {Mother protect us}." She turns her black orbs back on me. "Stay away Señorita Ruiz," she spits.

"Señorita Ruiz? Catalina Ruiz?"

"Si! Stay away or bad thing happen."

"I don't understand. How will bad things happen?"

Maureen stands and walks in circles a moment with increasing agitation. "I see," she says. "Like before, like always. ¿Por qué esta maldición de la oscuridad {Why this curse of darkness}?" she asks the sky. She turns to me with an anguished look. "Like tu abuela, like Señora Sanchez."

"Esmeralda Sanchez, my grandmother?"

"Si! It happen her, it happen Señorita Ruiz."

"I don't…"

"They kill her," she spits. "Murder for who and what she be."

"What does that have to do with Catalina and me?"

"Señora Sanchez go outside colonia, find mate outside. Señorita Ruiz same. That dangerous, always danger, always…" she struggles a second, "…many time great price."

"So, you're saying that Catalina is really into me?" She gives me a questioning look. "Catalina likes me."

"Si, she to you, ah instinto {instinct}," she say gesturing with her hands, "to mate with one outside." She points at my chest, where the cougar's tooth hangs beneath my shirt. "You relación her kind. She to you—la pasión del fuego. El deseo de La Madre {the passion of fire. The desire of the mother}."

I am trying to translate—fire and passion, maybe, something to do with a mother. "Well, I do like her but..."

"Stay away!" she scolds. She muy importante, she come one time, siete generaciones {seven generations}," she says holding up seven fingers. You, her..." she makes a circle of her thumb and forefinger with one hand and poked the forefinger of her other hand in and out of it, an obvious gesture of sex. "...muy malo {very bad}. You her..." she repeated the gesture, "...you like Señor Santiago, tu corazón sabrá dolor {your heart will know pain}."

"What do you mean? What about Señor Santiago?"

"Ella era su amada {She was his beloved}," she fumbles for the words. "Lovers," she ventured.

"Holy shit," I mutter as it comes together for me. The picture of he and Esmeralda, what he named his boat, it all makes sense. Damn, he might have been my grandfather if things had gone differently.

"He want her. No other, he want her." Señora Lopez made claws of her fingers and gestured as though holding something between them. "She want him—Que eran amantes {They were lovers}. She pull to mate outside—very sad—hearts break," she throw her hands open as though resigned to something, "Then dead. Now he suffer. You and Señorita Ruiz..." she repeats the sex gesture, "... all suffer."

"All suffer? Everyone?" She seems to think about that a moment then nods. It sounds stupid and lame. "So what if I stay way from her?" That seems to confuse her. I gesture with one hand, naming it Catalina, and the other me, then pull them apart. She smiles and nods. "What if she goes ahead and mates, ah marries someone else from the outside?" I make hand gestures to illustrate that as best I can.

A subtle smile creeps onto Señora Lopez' face and she shakes a raised finger at me. "No! She importante, destino importante. She no go outside, only you she go outside."

"How do you know?" I raise my hands in a questioning gesture.

"I see," she says flatly, tapping her head with the fingers of both hands.

"So why me, then? ¿Por qué yo?"

Señora Lopez gives me a curious look and shakes her head slowly. "You importante also. You have fate. She to you." She falls silent and stares down at my chest. "Ustedes dos están conectados, pero no puedo ver cómo {The two of you are connected, but I cannot see how}."

"What fate? What conectados?"

"Usted tendrá que descubrir tu destino {You will have to discover your destiny}," she blurts, then pauses. "You find fate.

"Okay, Si. But what relation do I have with Catalina? Are we like, mountain lion?" She struggles with that. I point a finger to my chest. "Mountain lion? Cougar?"

"Ah, si," she says, looking at my chest where the tooth lay beneath my shirt. "Puma."

I draw the tooth out from under my t-shirt and point to it and then to me. "¿Puma? ¿Soy un puma?"

She scrunches up her nose and looks at me like I'm crazy, shakes her head. "No! La Señorita Ruiz es de la pantera." She gives me a hard look and I can see something vaguely familiar in her eyes, and feels like it had a couple of times with Santiago—me looking at her looking at me. Then she says, "Somos del lobo {We are wolf}." With that, she turns on her heels and scurries across the lawn and into the manor.

I only half understand what she's said and have lost most of the context. I reach into my jacket pocket and remove my iPod. I turn off the recording mode and try playing it. It's muffled but I can make out our voices just enough; Gwen and I will be able to piece it all together. I set out to find Lex, not knowing then that it will be a fruitless venture.

Chapter 14

Esmeralda's Daughter

Gwen and I sit on the couch, facing Mom in the easy chair. She'd insisted on waiting until after dinner to talk to us about the family secret, and it had been a tense and silent meal. Gwen's so anxious she's vibrating again and I'm restless myself. "So?" I ask.

Mom sits with her legs together, her hands folded on her lap, and stares down at the floor. She looks to be gathering her thoughts but in those quiet moments, my perceptions shift and I see something different in her—a calm dignity, something stately in her manner, and it begs respect.

"Mom?" Gwen whines anxiously.

Our questions shatter the silence but not Mom's composure. She clears her throat and begins. "Jesse, what Señor Santiago told you is true: my mother, your grandmother, was Esmeralda Sanchez."

"Yes!" shouts Gwen. She jumps up and does a little dance on the carpet like some football thug after a touchdown. "Shit, shit, shit this is so cool."

"Gwen!" Mom scolds. The tone of her voice brings an abrupt halt to Gwen's celebration.

"Sorry, just slipped out," Gwen says. She flops herself back onto the couch, contrite but still pulsing with excitement.

The knit between Mom's brows fades and she takes a breath and continues. "She and your grandfather, Ethan, were…" she looks away quickly and then to me, "…well, they fell in love."

"Oh, Mom, you mean they…" Gwen interrupts but shuts up when I slap the side of her leg a little too hard. "Ouch."

"They became involved with each other," she continues, "and, well, I'm the result." What follows is an awkward silence.

"So then what?" I ask. "Did she leave the colony?"

"Did you grow up there?" Gwen asks.

Mom raises her hand for us to stop. She draws in a deep breath and looks up at the ceiling as though searching for her words. "They couldn't be together, not in the normal way," she finally says. "It may be hard for you to understand, I don't myself—not completely, but my mother stayed in the colony while your grandfather remained here."

"So you did grow up there," Gwen says excitedly, "at the colony."

"Only until I was 8 months," she says softly.

"And then?" Gwen asks. I realize that Gwen doesn't know what happened to Esmeralda Sanchez, I hadn't had time to tell her.

"She died," I say, saving Mom the discomfort. Mom looks at me questioningly. "Gram Sanchez was um, killed."

"What? How?" Gwen asks, eyes blazing wide.

"Los Oscuros," I say. Now Mom's eyes widen. "Santiago told me," I say.

"Jesse I don't want you involved…" Mom begins.

"I am involved," I blurt. I stand and start to pace. "You're involved, Gwen's involved—we all are. Things are happening around us and there is no way to avoid it…" I catch sight of Gwen sitting silently with her head bowed. "Gwen, I'm sorry, I never had a chance to tell you about Esmeralda's… our grandmother's…" I sit back down next to her.

"They killed her?" she sobs. "They just killed her?"

"Gwen I'm sorry," Mom says. "I never wanted you to know that."

"But she was my grandmother," Gwen says.

Mom looks at Gwen and tilts her head slightly to the side. "You're right. I should have told you a long time ago. I'm sorry." She picks herself up and sits on the other side of Gwen and places her arm around her. "I'm so sorry, Sweetie," she soothed. She strokes her hair.

Gwen takes in a breath and her body tightens. "So what now?" she asks, reddened eyes courageously searching for truth. Mom hesitates, and Gwen pleads. "Please!"

She nods. "Okay, Sweetie." She strokes Gwen's hair again and I can see she has been fighting back tears herself. "Well, I came to live with your grandfather."

"Why? Why not stay at the colony?" I ask.

Mom looks down at the carpet, her face a mask of sadness. She shakes her head gently. "I don't know, but the elders decided it best that I was raised by my father."

"Part of the danger, the price," I mutter recalling Maureen's warning.

"What was that?" Mom asks.

I shake my head. "Nothing. Just something Señora Lopez said about women from the colony getting together with outsiders. It is dangerous."

"When did you talk to her?" Mom asks.

"Today, right after you left her. And what's up with you talking to her today anyway?"

"We're getting off track," Gwen sobs.

"You're right," Mom says.

"So you were raised by grandpa then?" Gwen asks and Mom nods. "What about Gram McBride? Didn't she have something to say about that?"

"She wasn't around, Gwen. She'd left your grandfather a year or more before that?"

"Because of him and your mom?" I ask.

Mom looks saddened again. "I don't know. When I was first told who my mother was, I was nine, I confronted dad but he denied everything, said Señora Lopez wasn't right in the head. Then he told me not to speak of it again to anyone and I knew the story was true.

I started asking questions of other people around town and when your grandfather found out he hit me. It was the first and only time he ever did that. I didn't realize it then, but he was only trying to protect me."

"From what?" Gwen asks.

"From the town's people, from my own friends. Even then there was animosity toward the colony and he was afraid that I'd be picked on if people knew."

"And he wanted to protect you from your mother's killers," I suggest.

Mom gives me a pained look and shrugs. "I don't know. I don't know if he knew much about that."

"But where were people supposed to think you came from then?" asks Gwen.

"The story your grandfather told others was that your grandmother was unknowingly pregnant when she left him, and had a hard time caring for me alone so she gave me over to him."

"Did he ever confess to the truth? To you I mean?" I ask.

"Oh, yes," she says with a smile and nods. "He was able to keep me stifled until I hit Gwen's age, then he had no choice but tell me."

"So that's where I get that from," I jest.

She gives me an enigmatic look "And from your father."

"So, like, then what? Did you ever think of going back to the colony?" Gwen asks.

Mom gives Gwen a sad smile. "I did think of it. When you're that age, your age, the rebellious search for truth can be overpowering, even when the truth is right in front of you."

"And?" Gwen asks

"I wasn't allowed, Gwen," she says.

"What? Why?" Gwen asks incredulously.

"They have a long tradition of rules that protect them," Mom replies.

"From you? From one of their own?" Gwen asks.

"I wasn't one of their own," Mom says with a shade of sadness. "I was raised on the outside so my connection with them was broken."

"Well that's stupid," Gwen says angrily. "The Dark Ones, their mortal enemies, kill your mother and they cast you out."

"No, no, Gwen, it wasn't like that," Mom reassures her. "I felt that way once, I admit, but not anymore. I knew nothing of the Dark Ones, not until I took the book from your room and began to read about them, but for a long time I believed I'd been abandoned by my mother's people." Mom paused and bit her lower lip. "It made me do some stupid things…"

Like marrying dad, I thought.

"…but it wasn't like that," she says.

"So then how was it?" Gwen asks.

Mom begins to tear up and seeing that, makes me want to as well. "My father loved my mother, loved her deeply…" tears slid down my mother's high cheeks. "…and he loved me too." She sniffs and looks up at the ceiling. "The elders decided I would best grow up in his care because of the depth of his love for me, not because they did not care." Mom's tears flowed steadily now and Gwen began to openly weep.

"Um," I say for no reason at all. Mom makes eye contact with me and I can see a gentle invitation in them. "You found that out just today, didn't you?" Her face became a picture of joyous anguish and she nods. *Señora López*. I'm fighting back my own tears, using an imagined scene of some goon killing my grandmother to fuel anger instead.

"Don't do that Jesse," Mom says. "It's okay to cry."

"Ah…"

"It's okay," she says standing. Gwen stands and hugs Mom, crying into her chest. "It's okay."

She holds out an inviting arm and I find myself standing. When I hug her, I feel the soft comfort of her warmth and smell, something opens inside and all the shit of the last few weeks bubbles up and over. Part of me is mortified by it all, but the rest of me feels relieved.

Afterward, Gwen doesn't want to leave Mom's side but I need space. I go out back and shower. It's still light out but the sky is clear and the air is chilly. Washing the day from my skin feels poetic, and vibrantly real. I feel clean, light, and tell the voice in my head that complains of being a wuss for crying to go fuck itself.

I dry off and saunter back to the Therion. I feel like being alone and I feel like connecting to the world. I open my laptop to find a dozen emails, and at the bottom is one from an unrecognized eddress. The tag line reads 'She who shall not be found.' *Lex?*

"Beware dear friend, there is a Judas in your midst. Don't know who yet but will advise. Please don't reply—They might intercept my messages! Isa.

Chapter 15

A Moment of Truth

> *Journal - Fort Carson, CO.*
>
> *Home! What the hell! How can it be the source of so much pain, and at the same time so much happiness? Some days I want out and other days I can't get enough of it. Can a family be so flawed, so dysfucktional that the best option is to leave it and never look back? Some days I think so, and then something happens, something my mom or sister says or does that reels my heart back in and, for a while anyway, things seem right.*
>
> *~ From the Journal of Jesse Benatar*

"I have such a hangover," Gwen says as she rubs her face and brushes the hair from her eyes.

"A what?" I ask.

"What?" she whines, looking at me through bleary eyes. "Don't smirk at me." She makes a lame attempt to kick me with one of the legs she has dangling over the dock's side, then flops down on her back on the deck. "Agh!"

"You're funny," I say.

"You wouldn't say that if you were inside my head right now,"

"So you into the nail polish remover again this morning?"

"Oh, shut up, that was only that one time and I was six."

"So what's given you this hangover then?" I ask, staring out over the rising sun's beams on the river.

"Me, thinking; I couldn't get to sleep last night."

"It is a lot to think about," I muse. I think of telling her about the message from Isa the night before but decide to wait until she's better equipped to take it in. Was it just a mind fuck from whoever Isa is? I couldn't think up a better one if I tried; I lost sleep myself thinking about it.

"What's up with you?" Gwen asks. "You seem more dreary than usual."

"What, me dreary?" I ask with mock surprise.

"That's right keister-head." Gwen falls silent and the wry smile that's on her face fades. A pained expression sweeps over it and she sits up quickly and stares down into the slowly flowing water. "He wasn't very nice sometimes," she offers.

"No," I answer. I feel my heart sink into the muddy bottom of the river.

"I know how he hurt you, Jesse," she says softly. "I don't want... I mean I..."

"Hey, it's okay Gwen,"

"No it's not," she says in a tone that makes me think she's starting to cry again, only she doesn't. "It's not okay, Jesse. It scared me, and he hurt Mom too. I'm the only one he didn't knock around."

"Well, that's one good thing."

"No, it's not. He hurt me too Jesse, inside, just knowing what he was doing to you and Mom, how you'd try to protect her and how he'd... I thought he'd killed you one time and I lost it."

"When? I don't remember that."

She looks at me with a wry smirk. "Yeah, you were out cold. I couldn't wake you up. Mom couldn't wake you up. Dad picked you up and rushed you off somewhere in the truck, leaving Mom and I in hysterics."

"So, like what happened? Did I die?"

"Shut up!" she says, punching me on the arm. "This is serious."

"Sorry," I say. Gwen sits silently for a moment then scoots closer to me and buries her face in my shoulder. I put my arm around her and she leans into me. "I'm sorry Gee."

"Yeah, me too," she says. "He was a bastard," she sniffles, "but I still loved him."

I didn't say a thing for fear of shattering Gwen's moment of truth. I hear Mom calling from the front porch and I look to see her waving us in for breakfast.

"Hey! Chow time," I say.

"Yeah, I hear."

We get up and make our way back toward the house. Gwen walks a little unsteady. "So what time did you get to sleep?" I ask.

"I didn't yet."

"So you're running on zero."

"Yeah," she groans.

"Well," I say as we prepare to dash across the road. "Could be an improvement."

"Shut up again," Gwen says.

We cross after a milk truck passes, and in the distance, the single beam of a motorcycle headlight comes around the far bend. I stop and watch it pass, a touring Beemer, and it dawns on me who the Judas was that Isa mentioned. "Not much of a surprise there," I mutter.

"What?" Gwen says, turning and walking backwards.

"Nada!"

Breakfast is... anticlimactic. After the tearful closeness of the night before, things feel pretty much like they always do at breakfast. I pull out my iPod and begin playing back what Maureen Lopez had said.

Mom listens carefully, and glances uncomfortably toward Gwen when the old woman refers to sex. "So?" I ask after the recording has played.

Mom purses her lips, glances at Gwen and stands from the table. "We can talk about this later, Jesse."

"Mom!" Gwen groans. "I get most of it, I've had almost seven years of Spanish in school." Mom gives her a contemplative look. "I'm not a child," Gwen says."

"I've looked up most of it on Google Translate," I tell her, "and I get the parts about me having to find my own destiny and all, but what did she mean by the passion of the fire and the mother's will?"

"Jesse, I…" Mom begins.

"It means that Catalina Ruiz is driven to mate with you," Gwen pipes up. "Sometimes La Soñadora have an instinctive need to find a partner outside of the colony and have his child—sometimes," she continues.

Mom looks stunned but doesn't interrupt her. "It's a tradition, sometimes, but I think it's to make sure the gene pool stays strong." She looks up at Mom, who is staring at her. "What? I'm not a child anymore."

"No, I suppose you're not," Mom says. She looks at Gwen with a mixture of what looks to be pride and sadness.

"So I can see why a small group that keeps to itself would want to inject new DNA into the pool once in a while," I say, "but this sounds like a compulsion, like some sort of human pon farr, and what's the deal with the will of the mother."

"I don't know much about it, Jesse," Mom says apologetically. "Some of the elders took me aside when I discovered the truth and told me enough of my heritage to explain why I couldn't rejoin them and that I had best hide that side of me from others, but I know little more than that."

"But you read the book," Gwen says.

Mom shakes her head. "No, Sweetie, I only had enough time to read the first few sections before you found it in my room. I'm sorry I took it from you."

"Want it back?" Gwen asks, quietly. Mom gives her a puzzled look. "I thought you gave it to Señor Santiago?"

"I made copies," Gwen beams. "I'll put one on your phone for you."

"So the stuff about the mother's will?" I ask before the two of them can fall into another love fest.

"That one's simple," Gwen says. "The Mother is what they call the earth. They have a special connection with nature, their beliefs revolve around it, and they see the earth as the mother of us all."

"Like a lot of indigenous people," I say, my mind kicks into hyper-drive.

"Yeah, only different somehow, I mean, really different," Gwen says.

"I might be able to help with that," Mom says.

The morning paper arrives at the front door with a thud and Gwen goes to fetch it. It leaves me alone with Mom, who seems sad and quiet. "You okay, Mom?" I ask. She looks and nods but her eyes belie something else I've seen too often.

"We're okay," I assure her. "Nothing bad will happen, promise." I'm about to make a joking remark about her not looking convinced when Gwen burst into the kitchen, nearly popping the swing door off it's pivots.

"Holy," she says. "Not going to believe this." She's holding the front page of the paper in front of her, staring at it. She sets it down on the table and Mom and I crowd in to see what's triggered her excitement.

When I see the headline, my heart skips—*Hiker's Dog Finds Dead Guards and Buried Car*. When I see the photo of a tow truck with a dirt encrusted Sunfire attached to its winch, my heart stops—it is the exact scene in my dream of attacking the two men.

Chapter 16

Mei

A quick call to Christine gets me nowhere—she hasn't seen Lex all night and has no idea where she's gone. She's worried and I promise to let her know if I find anything out. A quick call to Michelle gets me nowhere faster—no answer at all. Jeffrey's off the grid as well and I know Miranda is in the city visiting Paul.

My first stop in town is the houseboat and then the sanctuary. There was no sign of Lex or her mother at the boathouse but Lex had been at the Sanctuary; an empty coffee cup from The Kat and a bag from some burger joint I've never heard of sits by her books. I leave her a note and hit the road again. Half way to The Kat, I see a girl walking that way and pull up next to her and match her speed.

"Hi, Mei," I say.

Mei Ling flashes me a nervous glance but keeps walking. "Hi," she finally says.

"You heading to The Kat?" I ask over the low throb of the engine. She gives me a questioning look. "The Kat," I repeat. "The Mad Kat."

Her eyes brighten and her head nods slightly in recognition. "Yes," she says. She gives my bike and I a quick look over. "You work there," she observes, finally recognizing me.

"Me? No, I was just working there for a few days." She continues walking but her eyes dart nervously between me and where she is walking. "Hey, listen, do you know Lex, Alexis," I ask.

Her brow knits and she flashes a puzzled look. "What?"

"Lexi?" I repeat. "Alexis Anasenko, do you know her?"

Mei stops and faces me and I brake the bike. Her eyes shine a stunning gold in the morning sunlight. "No," she says. "I don't think so."

I remind myself to be cautious. This is Bolin's sister, and she might be as caught up with Wingate as he is. "She's about this high," I say, gesturing with my free hand. "Blond, short hair, cute, kinda intense."

"She lives down at the floating houses?" Mei asks.

"Yes, that's her," I say. "Have you seen her around?"

"She's a friend of yours?" Mei asks.

"Yes," I say, "A very good friend. Have you seen her around?"

She looks down and bites her lip, then gives me a look that I can't interpret. "I think she might be the girl I saw with my brother."

My stomach churns, my heart races, and I feel my face flush with heat. "She's with your brother, Bolin?" I force out past the lump in my throat. Mei nods. The look she gives me is apologetic, and it seems genuine. "Where? When?" I ask too intensely.

Her eyes widen and she pulls her head back a little. "Yesterday," she says. "I saw the two of them together on his bike."

The image of Lex on the back of Bolin's bike burns white hot in my mind. The empty bag from the burger place I'd not heard of—he's taken her there. Then I recall Bolin's subtle threat to 'check her out' and my mind races.

"Are you all right?" she asks.

"Yes, I'm fine," I blurt. "What time was that? Where were they heading?"

"Late afternoon," she says. "I saw them pass the restaurant heading toward the highway."

"And after that, did you see him last night?"

Mei drops her eyes again and shakes her head lightly. "No, he was suppose to help close up last night but did not come home."

"Fuck!" I mutter.

"She's your girlfriend?" Mei asks cautiously.

Our eyes meet. "Ah, no, not really."

"I think 'not really' maybe means yes," she suggests.

"Ah, well it's complicated." She looks at the ground and then at me again, but says nothing. "You're brother…" I can't end the question without sounding like I'm accusing him of being the creep I know he is.

"He is not bad," Mei says defensively.

"You two sound so different," I say quickly. "I mean, you have this really cool Chinese-British accent going on and he sounds like Mr. America."

She smiles slightly. "Bolin is my half brother," she says.

"Same father?"

She shakes her head. "Same mother."

Thoughts of Lex and Bolin yank at my heart again and I shove back. "You grew up apart then?"

She nods. "My brother was raised here by relatives. I grew up in Hong Kong."

"So the accent." I can't keep my mind off of Lex and Bolin and Mei must have picked up on my loss of focus.

"I should go," she says, gesturing with her eyes toward Main Street.

"Sure," I mutter. "Thank you for talking."

She nods. "You're welcome." She looks about to resume her walk but hesitates. "If I see your friend, should I say you are asking about her?"

I nod. "Yes, please, and tell her Christine is worried as well."

"Okay," she says. Her eyes flash gold between me and the ground a few times and she nods ever so slightly, then turns to leave.

"Oh!" I say. She stops and looks back. "What exactly does your brother do here, if I can ask you that?"

"He works for Mr. Wingate," she says.

"He doesn't work at the restaurant?"

"Yes, he's supposed to but he's absent often, doing other things," she said.

"Like?"

She shrugs. "Whatever Mr. Wingate has him do."

"Your father doesn't mind that?"

Mei Ling hesitates. "He doesn't like it but he has no choice," she says finally.

"I don't understand," I say.

She hesitates then says, "Mr. Wingate is my father's business partner; he owns the restaurant."

Chapter 17

Trap

I call Christine and tell her what Mei had said, and she says she'll get the word out to keep an eye open for both Lex and Bolin. Four hours and a half-tank of gas later, however, I've not seen or heard anything of either, nor has anyone I'd talked to. My mind races with thoughts and images that eat me up and I fight an impulse to detach from i 'to hell with Lex', and by mid-afternoon I'm spent.

When I lumber into The Kat, Jeffrey gives me a somber nod. "Christine and Michelle are still out looking," he says. He leans in close. "Hey, man, we tend to underestimate Lexi. When it comes down to it, in a pinch, I think she can take better care of herself than any of us."

"Yeah, you're probably right," I say. I know what he says is true, but I also know something about Bolin that Jeffrey doesn't. "Thanks."

"You hear about the bodies they dug up near that car?" Jeffrey asks in a hushed tone.

I had nothing except Lex on my mind all day, and the question triggers a recall-rush. "Yeah, anything new on that?"

"Nope, but it has a lot of people talking, and I overheard a few regulars talking about rogue colonists being responsible," Jeffery says.

"What?"

Jeffrey stands upright and shifts his attention away from me. "Hi, can I get you something?"

I turn to see a couple of tourists behind me looking impatient. Jeffrey takes their order and gives them a number. "That's crazy," I say after they leave to find seats, and Jeffrey starts throwing their order together. "Anyone who knows anything about them knows…"

"I know, I know, but you're preaching to the choir here," he says. "People like to believe what they want to believe. Want to know something that may be just as crazy?" I nod. "I think the car they pulled out of the pit is the same one that ran us off the road."

I feel my face flush. "No way," I say, trying to act surprised.

"Way! Christine thinks so too. I had a gut feeling as soon as I saw the picture in the paper, and Christine pointed out that the trunk hatch was darker silver than the rest of the car, same as the one that night. I hadn't even remembered that until she pointed it out."

"Well if it is, the cops may be able to match the paint with the scrapes left on Michelle's car."

"Those guys are Black Knight Security, Jesse. That means Wingate was responsible to the accident and for what happened to Paul."

Another set of customers come in and Jeffrey takes their order. As he's explaining the difference between items on the menu, I hear a bike engine and spot Bolin Ling passing by on his bike—alone. "Hey, later," I shout back to Jeffrey, and I'm out the door before he has a chance to reply.

I'm on my bike and into traffic of Main Street before Bolin disappears down the road that will take him back to Ling's. He doesn't stop at the restaurant though; he passes it by and turns right onto a narrow crossroad I've never been on. I turn onto it myself just in time to see him turning up an alley between two old warehouses. I follow him up there—big mistake.

The alley dead-ends into a courtyard surrounded on four sides by walls and sealed delivery doors. Bolin's bike is leaning over on its side-stand at the far end of the court and I have to do a near 180 look around to notice that he's now standing between me and the only way out.

I hit the kill switch and lean the Shadow over on her side-stand. As I dismount and remove my helmet, Bolin approaches to within five feet of me.

"You looking for someone here or you just exploring the underbelly of this little shitburgh?" Bolin asks.

"Just slummin with the trash I guess," I say. Bolin is there for trouble and I have the good sense to know he can probably dish out a lot more than I can handle.

"Cute," he says coming two steps closer. He raises his hand and shakes a finger at me. "That kind of talk costs."

"Where is she, Bolin?"

He hesitates a moment, then a glimmer of understanding passes over his features. "Ah, your little friend," he says with a smirk. "The cute blond."

"You know who I'm talking about, Where is she."

"Wild little minx, that one," he continues with a smugness that I want to wipe off his face. "Great little body that won't quit, but a little heavy on the attitude."

He is trying to provoke me and it is beginning to work. The focused determination that I'd felt all day is giving way to surges of anger and some other irrationality that I can't get a grip on. "This isn't a joke, Bolin. Lex isn't like other girls..."

"Oh, is that love talking?" he sneers.

"That's not what I mean." I don't want to tell him anythin Lex, about her vulnerability, and that leaves me stuck for words.

"Yeah," Bolin says. He steps to within two feet of me, setting off my alarms. "Your little skank's been taking care of, Benatar. If I were you, I'd worry about your own skin."

A surge of rage hits me like a rogue wave and I nearly lose it on him. From the glimmer of satisfaction on his face, he knows it and likes it; if I'm not careful, I'll play right into his game.

I take a long slow breath and let the wave pass beneath me, but I feel pressure behind my eyes as a firestorm grows within—the way it had with Santiago in the killing shed.

"Nice control," Bolin says. "Won't do you any good, though; you see, Mr. Benatar," he says, poking a finger into my chest, "you've messed with the wrong people, people who don't forget and never forgive."

"You make them sound like exactly the right people to mess with," I say. "Maybe you don't know who you're really dealing with, Bolin."

"What? You?" he says with amusement.

"No, I'm talking about Wingate. Being one of his tools may cost you in ways you can't imagine." Bolin doesn't like that; the smugness melts from his face, replaced by anger and something deeply sinister. So this was what it is to be a corrupted one.

"Unimaginable costs are what your little slag has paid, what your bitch of a mother and that kid-sis…"

The firestorm erupts too quickly to contain; the surge of energy runs through my spine and out my limbs like a flash of lightening. Bolin sails through the air and hits the concrete wall eight feet away so hard I know he'll go down and not get up—only I am wrong. Bolin bounces from the wall, lands on his feet, and is on me in a blink.

When he makes contact it feels like a freight train hitting me and it's my turn to fly. I land on my back and see his foot coming at my head just in time to turn away from it. Energy surges through me as I roll and make ready to counter attack, but pain erupts from my side and I find myself tumbling. I just come to a stop and Bolin is on me and has my throat in a vice-grip hold.

I can't breath and it feels as though my throat is being ripped open. My vision begins to blur, but not before making out Bolin's face glaring down at me with a grimace of murderous rage. Before everything goes white, I hear a girl's voice calling out. It sounds like Mei, then transforms into two other voices. They're speaking in Spanish and I can't understand the words but the meanings somehow penetrate my mind…

… *"Has he passed?"*

"No!"

"He came very close."

"Yes."

"What now?"

"He must be told."

"Is he ready?"

"No."

"The risk…"

"It cannot be helped."

"And the other?"

"Not yet."

"When?"

"Soon, let us hope."

"You place much on hope."

"As it must be…as it has always been."

"It is up to you then."

"No, it is up to him…and the other."

"With the Mother's blessings…"

"Jesse! Jesse! Wake up, Jesse. Wake up…"

…My head feels as though it's been busted open. I crack open an eye and a blurred face floats above me. "Jesse!" The voice is female, and familiar. "Jesse!"

I roll over on my side, then force myself up on my hands and knees. I kneel there, unsteady, head pounding, throat feeling as though it's been ripped out. "I'm up," I rasp. It hurts like hell to try to talk. "I'm up," I repeat. I sit back on my heels and open my eyes again, only to find myself alone in the courtyard.

I drag my sorry ass up and over to my bike. My throat is painful to touch, to swallow, even to breathe. My mind races in circles with a dozen questions, but I focus on just one—where's Lex? If Bolin hurt her… I look at the wall I sent Bolin flying into. Where his head had hit, there's a red smudge. There's only one place I can think to go.

Chapter 18

Chastised

"You look like shit!" Santiago says as he inspects my throat. It hurts too much to talk so I keep my comeback to myself. He frowns. "Come below."

We leave the back deck of the Revenge and as soon as I settle on his couch, his cat jumps up and starts rubbing up to me. "I need your help," I rasp.

"I know," Santiago replies from his galley. I hear the tinkling of glass and steel and he turns and hands me a small glass of greenish fluid. "Drink this. It will help."

"This guy in town, one of Wingate's goons, he's…" My throat seizes and I can't finish the sentence.

"Drink it!" he reminds me.

I take a sip and nearly spit it out. "Agh! What is it?"

"Drink it," he repeats. He goes to the small galley fridge and takes out a small bag of frozen peas. I do as he says and nearly gag getting the stuff down. It tastes like a sewer smells and I swear I detect ammonia in it, but almost immediately my throat begins to feel better. He takes the empty glass and hands me the peas. "Hold this against your throat."

"Oh, man!" I rasp as the cold pack and fowl fluid work their magic on my throat.

"You came close. I told you to be careful," he chastises as he sits across from me.

"I didn't have a choice…" I squeak.

"Wrong! You always have choice," he says.

…ah but this guy's done something to Lex, I had to find out where she was," I rasp.

"And you know this how?" he asks.

"No one has seen her in days and she was seen with this guy. He told me…"

"What he knew would anger you," Santiago interrupts. "You blundered into his trap and were caught."

"I had to do something," I retorted with a wince.

"Of course you did, it is our way, but you act bravely and that is the stupidity that can get you killed. How you escaped that fate this time I don't know."

"Mei," I say, recalling hearing her voice. Then I recalled hearing other voices.

"My?"

"Mei Ling, Bolin's…this guy's sister. Just as I was passing out I heard her voice… shouting at her brother." The memory of the other voices taunts me but I cann't recall the words or the understanding I'd had at the time. "I don't remember anything after that."

Santiago sits back and studies me as I adjust the sack of peas. Finally, he says, "The girl saved you then. She is not like her brother."

"Not like her… no one is like that guy," I say. "That thing happened again, like with you in the shed. I had this surge of strength and I sent him flying. He hit the wall so hard he left blood where his head hit." Santiago didn't seem surprised at that.

"It didn't seem to faze him at all. He landed on his feet like a cat and hit me so fast and hard, I didn't have a chance to react." Santiago stares at me and I feel something stirring in the back of my mind. "So what's with that? How could I do what I did and how could he?"

Santiago sighs and draws himself up to standing. He steps back into his galley and begins filling two glasses with water. "I mean, I've heard of people performing feats of strength in a crisis, but this was different, it was… I don't know," I say.

He returns and hands me one of the glasses and resumes his seat, he leans back and takes a long slow drink in silence. He can be damned intolerable. "Not so different," he says finally.

"What?"

"Not so different from those who gain strength in a time of need."

"No, you had to have been there," I say. "To see this guy move." I involuntarily put my hand up to my neck. "If you'd felt his strength."

"I have felt such strength," Santiago says. "More than once."

"Not like this," I argue.

"Do you want to know of this or would you prefer to continue to tell me what I have and have not experienced?" he asks irritably.

"You're right. Sorry." I lean back on the couch and keep the sack of thawing peas in place. It's giving me a headache, but my throat feels better.

"What do you know of Berserkers?' Santiago asks.

"Berserkers? As in the Norse warriors?"

"Si."

"Not much. They're supposed to have gone into battle with uncontrollable blood lust and have…" I sat straighter. Santiago gives me a knowing look. "… they were said to have had superhuman strength and speed."

"So the story goes," he says.

"But that's myth, it's not real right?" I ask.

"You tell me." Santiago looks dead serious.

"So you're saying Bolin is some kind of Berserker? That I am?"

"Some kind," he answers cryptically.

"No, no. Berserkers are supposed to have taken drugs or worked themselves into a blood lust or something. I didn't do any of that."

"Those are only attempts by rational minds to explain something not so rational," he says. "The truth is not so simple."

"So what is the truth?"

Chapter 19

Los Lobos

Journal - Fort Carson, CO

I remember a quote attributed to Einstein that stated, 'Reality is merely an illusion, albeit a very persistent one.' That made me laugh when I first heard it, and I decided Einie had a sense of humor, but then it began to puzzle me—was he serious? It sent me on a jag of contemplation, which for me is often a matter of jerking off between the ears, but in this case it was the start of questioning everything.

Last night I drank some Tequila with Tony up in the mountains, and I had an epiphany—if the physical reality of our bodies is constrained by the laws of physics, but the metaphysical reality of our minds is not, and if matter and thought are all just forms of energy and information and there is no meaningful distinction between mind and body, then is our physical being really a prisoner of the laws of physics, or is that an illusion? I thought it profound at the time, Tony thought it was funny, but even in the sobering light of day, it has me wondering.

~ From the Journal of Jesse Benatar

Santiago gives me a long hard stare, and just when I think he's forgotten my question, he speaks. "You did not read the book." He accuses. I'm about to explain how I read most of it but he cuts me short with a wave of his hand.

"The truth is simple—we live in two realities, all of us," he begins. "The reality of the physical world, and the reality of the metaphysical, that of thought and spirit. Do you understand this?"

"Ah, I think so, yeah," I reply.

"Do you accept it?"

"Ah, as in believe it?" My mind races back to a quote I once read from Einstein—*Reality is merely an illusion, albeit a very persistent one.* "I don't know. I like to keep an open mind but not too open... know what I mean?"

"Fair enough. Keep your mind open a little longer and learn." Santiago leans back into the couch and sips his water. His cat jumps up and settles down next to him. "We go about our business during the day in the physical world, and sometimes we go about our business during sleep in the other."

"Like in dreaming," I suggest, "and the whole spirit travel thing. Okay, that I get. Not sure I…"

"So which is real?"

"You're kidding, right? This one." Santiago frowns. "Both?"

Santiago nods. "There are laws that govern both realities. They are similar but different, just as the worlds are similar yet different. So if you dream of visiting Paris, are you in Paris?"

"No, of course not," I answer, but Santiago only stares at me in silence. "Uh, yes?" Silence. "Okay, how about maybe?"

Santiago clears his throat. "Sometimes yes, sometimes no."

"So sometimes a dream is just a dream, and sometimes it's a real journey of sorts," I offer.

"Si; just so. It is something all people do. Most never know the difference between a dream and a journey, but some come to recognize the difference and some go on to learn to journey at will."

I thought about that. A month ago I would have chalked it up to new age bullshit, but since arriving in Hook Point my sense of what's real and what isn't has done a few summersaults and I have to accept some truth to it. "Okay, so how does this relate to what I did to you in the shed, and with what happened today with Bolin? We were all awake."

"Some people by birth or training, can experience both realities at the same time. When this happens, both sets of rules can apply." I must have looked as blank as I felt because he adds. "Then, sometimes the impossible of the physical world, becomes the possible."

"Like incredible speed and strength? Like the Berserkers?" I ask, while Santiago sips his water. "So I'm one of those? Can I learn to control it?"

"The latter remains to be seen."

"So then Bolin is one as well?"

"Si. I warned you that there is a new panther among us."

Another thought comes to me. "Wait, you're talking about shape-shifting, changing into an animal." I recall the junk I read about it on the 'ou can't be serious?" Santiago says nothing. "You can't really believe in that crap about changing into an animal."

Santiago takes a deep breath and sighs. He holds up two fingers as he stares at the ceiling. "Two realities," I say. "You're saying that one of those possible impossibilities is changing into an animal?"

"No," he says, "not in the way you are thinking. The blurring of realities is never so complete. The rules bend as they mingle, but they do not break."

"So you don't believe people actually change into birds and wolves and all that," I ask, half joking.

"You watch too many movies," Santiago quips.

I remembered how it struck me as odd that so many cultures had a tradition of shape shifting and that shifting into animal forms was almost universe. "So why animals?" I asked. "Why not trees or rocks."

"What would you do as a rock?" he asked.

"Ah, yeah, okay, maybe not a rock, but…"

"The ability goes back to the earliest days of our species. Why it is so, I do not know. Perhaps it began with hunters studying and honoring the ways of great hunters, like the wolves, the cats, and the hawks. Somewhere along the way, people so inclined developed a special connection with one or more animals."

"Like the clan systems of American Indians," I suggest.

Santiago thinks about this and shrugs. "Si… similar, but different also," he says. "Most who have this connection experience it only in the metaphysical plain. Dreams of flying, of running wild with the pack…" Santiago takes on a far away look and an almost-smile creeps onto his face as he stares at nothing.

"Señora Lopez says we're wolf, her and I. Is that what she means?" Santiago nods. "So I'm like a werewolf or something."

"Something," Santiago says.

Then a thought comes to me. "You are too." He nods. "So you and I are like brothers, even though you might well have ended up being my grandfather."

"I could never have been that, Jesse, as much as I might have wanted…" his words faded into the silence of the room.

"Señora Sanchez?" I ask, but he doesn't bother answering. "So what changes then when I do the shift thing? How can I learn to control it?"

"The rules change. Some of the limitations, nothing more," he says.

"So, I don't change my appearance?"

"No, except to one who can see such things. Some are so gifted."

"How would I look to them?"

"Perhaps like your cinematic werewolf to some, but usually just a distortion of form that radiates the animal essence," he says. "They might see a shift, but mostly they will feel it."

"So that's where the legends come from," I suggest.

Santiago nods. "Only a few can see the shift, but that combined with the extraordinary things we can sometimes do planted the seeds of legends."

"So does it take a silver bullet to take me out when I'm that way?"

"No," he says blandly, "a regular one will do just fine."

"And Bolin, he shifts into a panther?"

"Si! Very cunning and hard to defeat. They make dangerous foes."

"Sounds as though you speak from experience." Santiago doesn't react to that. "So how did Wingate get hold of a panther? For that matter, what does it make Wingate?"

"That one is different. He is El Oscuro, a Dark One."

"Wait a minute, Señora Lopez said that Catalina Ruiz was Pantera, a panther. Is she connected to Bolin some how?"

"Yes, but not in any way that matters to us," he replies.

"What about my sister? Is she a shifter? And my mother?"

Santiago shakes his head. "Not your mother; she is gifted with other abilities that she may not be aware of, but your sister is a different matter. I do not know if she is like us, but I believe there is something very special about her."

I realize just then that I'm about to piss my pants. "Ah, can I use the head?" Santiago nods and gestures toward the front of the boat with his eyes. On the way I take the near thawed bag of peas back to the galley and put them back in Santiago's fridge.

I don't know what was in the drink but it and the icing helped more than I would have thought possible. In the bathroom I catch sight of myself in the mirror. *Fuck me!* I'm in deep shit—my neck is one big blue and red bruise—no way I'll be able to hide this from Mom.

I stare at myself while the day's events and Santiago's words sink in. I don't know what to make of it all, not yet, but I decide to reserve judgment and let the truth show itself. I wash up and as I clean the dirt from my face, another thought comes to me. I dry off and rejoin Santiago.

"So, is there supposed to be any sort of special connection between people like us? I mean, some sort of telepathy?" Santiago gives me a puzzled look. "Is it possible that you can see things as I do and vice versa."

"Why do you ask?" he asks suspiciously.

"Because the first time I visited you here, there was a split second when I thought I was seeing me through your eyes. It came and went in a flash but..." I shrug. Santiago looks to ponder what I am saying. "Then there is the time I escaped from the goons in the cannery and you picked me up at the jetty just when I needed you to."

My mind shifts to a darker thought. "And not long after that, I dreamed that I attacked that same goon in the cannery and he ends up dead. Then the two goons that ran my friends off the road..."

Santiago gives me a grave look. "Oh, shit! You killed those guys. You really killed those guys and somehow I saw it." My head begins to spin and I sit down hard on the couch.

"Jesse," he begins. "I was taken as a boy your age and trained to kill who I was told were the enemies of my country. I learned that those they called enemies were not such at all, and I've never forgotten that lie, but I have also never forgotten how and why to kill a true enemy."

"But, two days ago, the shed, the whole 'thou shalt not kill' thing. Was that all bullshit? Didn't that mean anything to you?"

Santiago's eyes blaze with pain and anger. "It means everything to me," he says.

"But..."

"Do you wish to be a monster like me? Sparing you that means everything to me."

An uncomfortable silence falls over the cabin. Santiago's c against me again and I stroke her. There's something abou cat... "Well I would never call you a monster."

"But that is exactly what I am. I do what must me done, what others dare not or cannot do," he says.

"And that makes you a monster?" I challenge.

"Yes! Yes it does and do not forget that."

"That's not fair," I say.

"Don't speak to me about fair. Life is not fair."

"Maybe not, but we should never trying to make it so." I stand up and make ready to leave. "I need to find my friend."

"Si. This you must do."

I make it to the curtain that divides his war room with his living space, and turn back. "Bolin made a threat against my mother and sister," I say. "I don't know if he is just pulling my chain or if it is serious..."

"Nothing will happen to them," Santiago says darkly.

"Well, that's just it. I don't want you taking him or anyone else out. We can get the police involved." Santiago brakes into a soft laugh. "I'm serious. I have enough on Bolin to have him arrested now for assault. We can get a restraining order." Santiago laughs louder. There is a chilling madness in his laughter. "I want you to promise."

Santiago's laughter trails off into silence. "I have made my only promise to you," he says. "As I made it to her I make it to you."

"Her?" That drew nothing from him. His small tabby hops up next to Santiago and begins rubbing up against him. He begins to pet her and the darkness that surrounds him seems to lessen. "Esmeralda Sanchez," I mutter. Of course—this man had vowed to protect her child after they had killed her. "Who killed my grandmother?"

Santiago stops petting his cat and clenches his fist, then relaxes it and resumes petting the purring tabby. "Who killed her?" I repeat.

"This you already know," he says.

"Wingate," I offer. "No, that can't be true. Unless he's an old man with a young family, he'd have been too young. His father then."

"Uncles," Santiago says. "His two uncles. His father was in South America at the time, but he passed too soon after."

"Passed, as in you killed him as well," I suggest. He says nothing. "It has to stop sometime, this killing."

"Let us hope," is all he says.

There is so much more I want to ask him about, want to say, but I have to find Lex, and I have to warn Mom and Gwen about Bolin. I zip my jacket all the way up so that the collar covers my neck. A pang of discomfort, perhaps guilt holds me back from leaving.

"Thank you," I say. "Thank you for doing what has to be done. Maybe we can do something to make it all stop now." That evokes no response from him, and I reluctantly leave the man, alone with his cat.

Chapter 20

Right Hook

A churning emptiness in my stomach reminds me that I haven't eaten since breakfast and it's almost dinnertime. I call Christine right away and tell her about what Bolin had said, then call home but get no answer. I decide against all hope to try Lex's again and ride that way on the side street that takes me by her sanctuary. As luck would have it, a block away, I see a familiar figure walking toward houseboat row.

She's dressed in faded blues and her 'Powered by Estrogen" t-shirt and she looks to be okay from a distance. She must have recognized the sound of the Shadow's engine because she glances over her shoulder and picks up her pace.

"Lex," I shout when I pull up next to her. She stares straight ahead with fierce determination. "Lex, we need to talk." She gives back nothing but icy air. I pull ahead by 50 feet and kill the engine, dismount, and remove my helmet. I ready myself to intercept her, but she takes a quick turn to the right and goes up a narrow alley between two disused buildings. I grab the keys from the bike and dart after her.

"Lex!" I shout. "Please we need to talk." I grab her by an arm and pull her to a stop. She swings around so fast I don't know if I could have blocked the punch if I'd tried. It catches me square on the side of my face and my eyesight flashes a starry void and my knees wobble. If it wasn't for an old 40-gallon drum in the alley I am able to grab hold of, I would have gone down. By the time I recover enough to go after her, she's a dozen steps ahead.

I catch up and yank her around again. Rather than another crack in the side of the head, she angrily pushes me away. "Fuckin leave me alone!" she shouts.

"No," I retort, grabbing her again. She spins around to shove me away and I grab her by the forearms and hold tight. She tries to knee me in the groin but I am ready for that one. "Lex, stop please. You have everyone worried about you."

"Fuck everyone and fuck you," she shouts.

"No, fuck you!" I shout, shoving her hard against the closest wall. The wall had a four-inch pipe running along its length that makes contact with her upper back. To my alarm, she grunts and winces with pain when she hits, and her arms relax.

I begin to release my grip, but she tries to break free and I shove her against the wall again. This time tears come to her eyes when she grimaces and her whole body wilts.

I'm horrified by what I've done and release her arms. "God, Lex, I'm sorry, I'm so sorry," I say. "I didn't mean to..." Wham!

That one I deserve. My legs buckle and I fall back on my butt against the facing wall. I open my eyes just in time to see Lex disappear down an intersecting alley. I can't believe what I'd done to her; I'd never gotten physical with a girl out of anger like that, not even Gwen in her most devilish of moments. Pushing Christine at the back of the Kat had been bad enough, and now this. What next?

I settle myself against the wall, pull out my cell phone, and place a call. At least Lex is okay, at least... "Hey, it's me. I found her..."

"Where? Is she alright?" Christine asks.

I am too aware of the throbbing pain that used to be the side of my face. "Yeah, she's alive and kicking. She's heading home I think." I don't know that for certain but I'm not ready to give up the secret of her sanctuary just yet.

"I'm still with Michelle. We'll head down there now," she says.

"Good idea. She'll probably be in a bad mood. That's my fault."

"What happened?" she asks.

"Something that should never have happened…"

"Jesse?"

"Ah, nothing. Whatever she says about me though, it's probably true."

"Jesse, are you alright?"

"Yeah, peachy. Listen, if she's not at home, give me a call right away, okay. I think I'll be able to find her again."

"Where?" she asks.

"Not my place to say. Just get down there and talk to her okay?"

"Yeah, we're on our way."

I close the phone and shove it in my pocket, then unzip my jacket to cool off and breathe easier. I tap the back of my head against the cinder block wall, and then in a stupid act of castigation, I whack it harder while kicking at an empty roof sealant bucket. "Agh!" My head explodes as the bucket hits the far wall and goes spinning down the alley. "Fuck!" I close my eyes to help the pain subside. "Asshole!"

"Damn straight you are," a familiar voice says.

I open my eyes to see Lex looking down at me from the junction with the connecting alley. "I usually get that one right," I say.

"You really are you know," she says.

"Yeah, I know already."

She takes another step into the alleyway. "You were talking to Christine just now?"

"Yeah. She and Michelle are on their way to your place."

"You aren't going to tell her about the Sanctuary," she says stepping deeper into the alley, but no closer.

"No, of course not. I may be an asshole, but I know how to respect a secret."

She takes another step closer. "Well, I do apprec… Holy fuck! What happened to you?" she asks with alarm.

"What?" I look to see her wide eyed, staring at my neck.

"Your neck!" she says. "I didn't do that. I didn't hit you there," she says much as question as statement.

"No, you wish," I say.

"What the hell... you look like someone tried to strangle you."

"And you'd know that how?"

She gives me a 'you dumb ass' look. "I've been there."

Shit! "Sorry."

"What..."

"Your buddy is what happened," I blurt.

"Who?"

"Your buddy, Bolin. Nearly tore my throat out."

"Jesse, you need to stay away from him. He's serious trouble." I do my best to give her my own 'you dumb ass' look but it hurts too much. "No, I mean it. There's something really wrong with that guy," she says.

"No shit! So that's why you hang out with him?" A look of shock crosses her face and she appears ready to bolt. "No, no, I didn't mean it that way, Lex. I mean, why the hell are you hanging with him?"

"None of your damn business," she says angrily. "And who says I'm hanging out with him anyway?"

"Someone saw you riding on the back of his bike," I say.

"Oh, and that means I'm hanging out with him? I suppose it means I'm fucking him too?"

I catch myself short of asking if she is. I look down at the filth of the ground beneath me and shake my head. "Lex, I was just worried. We all were."

"Oh, there it goes again—crazy..."

"He told me two days ago that he was going to check you out," I said too loudly, "and I don't mean in a good way. Then you disappear for two days and when I catch up with him, he does this," I say gesturing to my throat. "He said he'd hurt you."

That brought her to stillness. "Well, he didn't, okay."

"Fine! Thank you for keeping everyone in the loop," I say. Lex stands about six feet away, staring down at me as though torn between running and saying something. "Lex, people care..."

"They shouldn't," she blurts. "I told you Jesse, I'm not who you think I am, not who anyone thinks I am."

"Yes, you are, and more..."

"You hurt me!" she blurts, anger and hurt dancing across her face.

"I know, I'm sorry, I didn't mean to do that—I don't... the day's been nuts and I lost control." She stares at me incredulously. "Look, if you want to have me charged I'll plead guilty, I..."

"Not that you dumb shit," she shouts, pointing to where I shoved her against the wall. "Hell, my mother does worse than that."

Then I realize the hurt she's referring to. "I know, I know. I thought I was doing the right thing..."

"Right thing? You ripped my heart out, you fu..."

"Lex, I'm so sorry," I say through forming tears. "I didn't want to. I only did what I did because I thought it best for you."

Lex's eyes water up and unspoken words move her lips. She shakes her head slowly. "It wasn't, Jesse," she says finally 'It wasn't.'

With that, she turns and disappears down the other alley. I try to get up to follow, but my body won't obey. I lean against the wall and let the shit of the day drain into the ground beneath me.

Chapter 21

Bum Surfing

"Hey, what's with not coming in for dinner? Mom's getting the feeling you're hiding out here; she's ..." Gwen takes in a sharp breath, covers her mouth and nose with her hands, and stares wide-eyed at my neck.

"It's not as bad as it looks," I lie. I'm sitting at my table with my laptop and e-reader. I'd heard Gwen calling me in to eat twice so I'd sent her a text message, asking her to come out to the boat.

"Jesse?" Gwen breathes through her hands.

"I had a run in with Bolin," I say, while opening up a web page I saved. "You're not going to believe what I was told today."

Believe it she did—more or less; she finished the book and is nearly finished her second reading of it, so she'd read all about what The Dreamers had to say about shape shifting. The only part she has trouble accepting is that I might be one myself.

In mid-discussion, we hear the kitchen door close. "Mom!" she says with alarm.

"Get out before she gets here," I say, grabbing my jacket. "She'll freak if she sees me like this."

"What do I tell her?" Gwen whispers as she makes for the companionway door.

"Just tell her I'm online with Tony."

"I can't lie to her, you know that," she complains.

"Then tell her I'm busy looking something up on the Net and I want to eat my dinner out here."

Gwen nods and opens the door. She steps through just as Mom calls out our names. "Be right there," she calls back. She ducks her head back in the cabin. "Dinner. Anything else?"

"No," I say. "Yeah, a bag of frozen peas or corn if we have any."

"Right," she says. She ducks out, closes the door, and I hear her talking to Mom as she runs down the stairs from the deck.

I put on my jacket and zip it up to cover my neck in case Gwen's diversion doesn't work. It does. About five minutes later, she returns with a plate of hot food. "I'll have to get the peas when Mom's out of the kitchen." She sets the plate down with a cutlery set. "I gave you extra tofu sausages 'cause I know you like them."

"And the mashed turnip?" I say, eyeing the foul tasting veggie.

"Oh, well, that's good for you. Mix them with your carrots; it tastes better that way." Gwen turns to go but spins back, "Oh, and Mom says to tell you that Hilda Carter called and wants you to call her or Bill as soon as you can."

"What do they want?" I ask. She shrugs and turns again to leave. "Hey!" She stops and looks back expectantly. "Thanks Gee."

"Thank me later," she says. "Eat up, I'll be back before you finish your turnip. You're going to tell me everything."

And that's exactly what I do, everything—even loosing it on Lex and shoving her against the wall in the alley. Gwen's a little shocked at that part but not as shocked as I'd feared.

"Well if you are a shifter, you need to be careful," she says. "From what I've read, shifters have to learn to control themselves when they're in that form."

"You really believe that stuff?" I ask, shifting the bag of frozen corn on my neck.

"Well, sort of," she says. "I mean, I don't think people actually change into animals, but their etheric body might."

"Yeah, Santiago said something about that. Two realities, two sets of rules that blend."

"Exactly," Gwen says. She's clearly enjoying talking about this stuff. I'd always made fun of her interest in the esoteric and occult. "Oh," she blurts. "If you are, and I doubt it dear brother, then maybe I am too." The thought seems to excite her. "Maybe Mom is."

"No," I say. "Santiago says she isn't, that she has other gifts. He doesn't know about you though."

"I want to meet him," she says. "Maybe he'd be able to tell."

"So why don't you think I'm a shifter?" I say out of curiosity.

She opens her mouth, as though to answer, then gives me a cautious look. "Well, shifters are supposed to be different—I mean you are different from the rest of us, but they're supposed to be strange different—not that you're not strange."

"Thanks," I say.

"You know what I mean?" she asks earnestly.

"No, but I'm good," I assure her.

"No, seriously," she persists. "They can feel really different to be around, they can be moody and do weird things unexpectedly, and sometimes they have odd hair growth, stuff like that." Except for the hair part, from what I'd seen of him anyway, that fits Santiago.

We discuss everything Santiago told me—even the part about him killing Wingate's goons—and everything I've experienced. We weave that together with everything she's read on the subject. What we ended up concluding is that shifters may well exist but they're nothing like their pop-culture counterparts, and that most never develop conscious control over the change. Many may not even be aware of it.

When we're done, it isn't that late but we're both bleary eyed. Gwen looks about to crawl back to the house and hit the sack, when I recall the teasing she dished out the other night. "So what is this thing that The Dreamers lost that Wingate wants to find?"

"Oh, that, yeah," she says, perking up as though jolted with an instant refill. "There's something they brought over from Spain, something they call 'La Talfar'."

"La Talfar? What's that mean?"

Gwen shrugs. "The Talfar. There's no real translation of the word that makes any sense, but it's older than dirt and buku important. How'd that go," she asked herself, "'El corazón y el alma de Los Iluminados'—their heart and soul. Anyway, the thing is so important their prophecies warn that if the Dark Ones destroy it, all will be lost."

"Sounds like something out of a bad movie," I muse.

"Seriously, Jesse," she says. "It went something like, 'Si Los Oscuros destruyen esto, estamos todos perdidos,' or 'If the Dark Ones destroy it, we are all lost,' or something like that."

"If you want me to take it serious, that doesn't help," I say.

Gwen closes her eyes to muster more patience. "Well, whether it's true or not, they believe it is and so Wingate might as well."

"Okay, so let's say that part of the book is factual, and they brought this Talfar over here. So what happened to it?"

Gwen rocks her head back and forth gently as she does when she thinks sometimes. "It disappeared sometime around the mid-1700s as best as I can make out."

"Really? Their heart and soul and they loose it? I thought I was bad," I say.

"Jesse, you need some sleep," Gwen says with obvious annoyance. She's right, I get punchy when I'm tired and my sarcasm is getting the better of me.

"You're right, sorry, but how can they just lose it? I mean, they have all this consciousness and they come half way around the world to preserve their way of life, and then they just lose their heart and soul?"

"Well they didn't just misplace it or lose it out of carelessness. Something happened, something big, and it was lost to them," she says.

"Did they try to get it back?"

Gwen scrunches up her nose. "Well that's the part that doesn't make sense to me; it seems they decided to leave it where it was, like they maybe knew where it was but thought it too hard to get."

"Well, yet another one for the book of mysteries," I say.

It is obvious that her surge of energy is short lived and she's spent. She closes her eyes and teeters in her chair. "Yup," she says.

"Go to bed, Gee," I say.

"How's your neck?" she asks.

"It's better. It's good."

She cracks open an eye and aims it at my throat. "You lie bad."

"Maybe, but get to bed."

She stands and shuffles to the door. "Oh, that stuff about the Mother's will—not that complicated. Like I say, they believe the earth is the mother of all life, but Mom said it's more like they believe it's one big living organism and we're all part of it."

"Like the Gaia principle," I suggest.

"Yeah, maybe, I don't know much about that, but the Mother's will is like the right path or nature's desire," Gwen said. "It has something to do with destiny… I don't know Jesse, I'm head dead."

"You look it," I tease. "Hey, you didn't sleep last night," I recall aloud.

"Nope!"

"Get to bed" Gwen doesn't move. "Want me to carry you?"

"Please?" she moans, leaning against the companionway.

"No," I say, as I check my email.

"Creep!" she complains.

"Yup! That's why you love me."

Gwen frowns and leaves without another word. I see I have an email from Hilda or Bill Carter but go straight to the one from Christine. I just had time to read her request for me to call, when I hear and feel a loud rumbling on the steps from the boat. "Gwen?" I shout. I'm out of the cabin and down the steps before Gwen realizes what's happened to her. "Gwen are you okay?" I ask.

"Ow!' she moans, sitting up. She had taken a tumble down the stairs, something she did more than once before when over-tired.

"No, no, sit still, I'll get Mom," I say.

"No!" she blurts. "I'm okay. If Mom sees you like that…" I'd removed my jacket and now my bruised throat was glaringly obvious.

"Just sit still a minute, okay," I ask. "Did you hit your head?" I asked, gently probing the back of her head with my fingertips.

"No," she says, brushing my hand away as though it were an annoying bug.

"Your arms—can you move them?"

"Yes!" she says, irritably.

"Let me see." She gives me a pissed look and moves her arms around. "How about your wrists?" At that she twists to her side and pulls her legs up to stand. "Gwen!"

"I'm okay," she says. "I just hurt my bum." She stands and brushing it off.

"You bounced down the stairs on your bum?" My fears begin to subside, seeing she can stand and cop attitude. A smile must have started to form on my lips because she glances at my face and slaps my chest.

"Not funny!" she blurts. I say nothing, only stare at her and wait. After a few seconds a resisted smile forms on her face. "Okay it's a little funny," she admits. "But it hurt."

"I know Gee. Let's get you in the house." We walked toward the house, Gwen with a slow troubled gate and me staying close to her side.

"Thanks for not making fun of me," she said when we were half way across the yard.

"You mean like the time you bum surfed the stairs at that motel in New Mexico?"

"Shut up!" she blurts, half laughing. "Ow! Don't make me laugh; it hurts."

"Sorry."

"It's going to hurt to walk tomorrow," she complains.

"Don't worry, I'll carry you around." That earns me a slap on the arm and another complaint of pain.

From the blue flicker from the living room, we know Mom is up watching a movie, so when we get to the kitchen door, Gwen stops. "Okay, go," she says. "Mom can't see you like this."

"You going to make it up the stairs?"

"Yes!"

"Gwen, is that you?" Mom's voice calls from the living room.

"Go," she whispers more emphatically.

"Okay, if you need anything, call my cell."

"If you turn it on I might," she says.

———— | ————

Back and the boat, I turn my cell on, and the message on my laptop reminds me to make a call.

"Hello?" Christine says.

"Hey, it's me, Jesse."

"Hey Jesse. Thanks for calling."

"How's Lex? You still with her?"

"She's okay I guess. She's out in the tub with Michelle; I just stepped in to take your call."

"You're at Michelle's?"

"Yeah. Lexi's mom came home for the night. She had a little too much to drink and well..."

"So she's okay then, Lex I mean? She says anything about where she's been for two days or what's happened?" I ask.

"No, she never talks about what she does when she disappears. She is hurt though."

"How?" I ask. I feel a surge of anger and concern.

"She won't say, but she has a couple of really bad bruises across her back, like someone hit her with a baseball bat."

My heart sinks. She'd been hurt all right…by me.

"She won't admit it was Bolin," she continues, *"but we know it hads to be. Michelle and I are thinking of going out and looking for him."*

"No, you don't want to do that," I say. "He's…not right. He's dangerous." My mind races, trying to find a way to tell Christine that I did that to Lex, without it sounding unforgivable.

"Yeah, that's what we decided. It was a sweet thought though."

"Did she tell you about our argument?" I ask.

"No, wouldn't talk about it. Michelle and I both assume it was heated."

"Yeah, it was…, I um…"

"Hey, Lexi's out of the tub and looks like she's about to do cartwheels across the lawn again."

I hear Lex's voice in the background. It sounds as though she is in one of her more jazzed moods. "Sounds like she's in a good mood."

"Yeah, that's the problem. Michelle's neighbors are really conservative and they have two pubescent boys who've been trying to catch a glimpse since we went out there."

"So… oh, she's in her birthday suit."

"Yeah, we don't usually wear bathing suits in hot tubs around here Jesse. I'd better get out there and help Michelle."

"Sure."

"I just want to tell you she is okay, and thank you for finding her and letting us know," Christine says.

"Of course. No problem," I say. "Thanks for letting me know."

"Bye."

"Yeah." The phone goes dead on the other end, and I sink back into my chair. Thoughts about what they'll think and do when they find out it was me who bruised Lex begin their long night of haunting me.

Chapter 22

Festival

> **Journal - Hook Point, CA.**
>
> *After some deeper contemplations on life, my mind hit a wall and gave up the task. That's when it struck me that we are intimate companions with all of life—every plant, animal—and if the Gaia Principle is correct—with the physical earth herself. In this, even in the darkest times, our loneliest moments, we are never alone, no one is any less connected than another, and none of our lives is really more important or meaningful than another's. Maybe if we open ourselves to that idea, something inside can change, and then maybe we can find more room for love, compassion, and profound belonging.*
>
> *~ From the Journal of Jesse Benatar*

The bruise was noticeably fainter in the morning. I don't bruise easy to start with and they fade quickly, but this is unusually fast. My first though is that maybe this shifting thing gives me super healing power, but then I think that's just wishful thinking, the stuff of comic books. I decide it was Santiago's concoction and the icing.

I check in with Gwen on my way out; she complains of a sore backside and how it's going to ruin her day at the beach with Kalie and Kalie's mom. The good thing is, I'm able to get out of the house without Mom catching a glimpse of my neck—even with my leather jacket zipped all the way up and the tube collar snapped into place, Mom's keen eyes could well have spotted the bruise.

As I ride into town, I rehearse three ways to tell everyone about losing control and shoving Lex against the alley wall. None of them end good. Lex hadn't said anything but I know the truth has to come out. Problem is, I can explain shoving her once and not realizing the pipe was there—it doesn't excuse it but it might pass their creep detectors—but the second time I can't explain away. Hell, I don't even get it.

I glance out over the river that beams with morning sunlight. It promises to be a hot one and I'm not sure how I'm going to keep my neck hidden all day, but I can't hide away at home. I decide to wing it.

I roll into town and I'm struck by how busy Main Street is. A series of banners over the road announcing the summer festival reminds me that tonight is the big kickoff and the whole town will be crawling with tourists for nine days.

As it is, the street looks like a colony of ants has taken it over; dozens of people busy themselves with putting on the town's best. I spot Jeffrey and Michelle walking along Main in front of Carver's, dressed for running and carrying Kat coffees.

They see me and wave and I gesture to the nearest side street. When I pull into it, I have to ride halfway to the docks before finding space to park my bike. I dismount and lock my helmet as they wander down towards me.

When I turn and step up onto the sidewalk, I almost bump into her—Catalina. She's standing at the edge of the road wearing her jeans, checkered shirt, and a shy smile that catches me off guard. She has her hair pulled back, revealing her black eyes and dark oval face in all its beauty.

"Hello, Jesse Benatar," she says in her thick accent.

I reach out and give her a little poke just below her right collarbone with a fingertip. She is real and so is the puzzled look she gives me. "Just checking," I say. She cocks her head a little to the side and knits her brow. Then her eyes drop to my collar and her expression changes.

"Jesse?" Michelle says. She and Jeffrey both have questioning expressions as they walk up to us.

"Hey, ah, Catalina, these are friends of mine, Michelle and Jeffrey," I say. "Guys, this is Catalina."

They trade their hellos in Spanish, and then all three look to me expectantly. "I'm, ah, surprised to see you. What brings you into town today?" I ask Catalina.

"We make cabina at festival," she says, self-consciously. Michelle and Jeffrey exchange concerned glances.

"Is that safe?" I ask. "I mean, with all the bad feelings in town..." How can I tell her in a way that she'll understand but not be offended?

She seems to understand though. "We know this. We sell only honey, muñecas...ah, dolls you say, baratijas, ah how you say?" she says looking to Michelle.

"Trinkets," Jeffrey answers. "Bracelets, necklaces, rings" It's obvious he's into talking with Catalina and more than a little charmed.

"Si!" she says with a bright smile. "This only we sell. No trouble." She looks satisfied, like that settles things, but we know it doesn't.

"Catalina!" a woman's voice calls out. I look to see the stern figure of her grandmother, Señora Ruiz, about 60 feet away looking our way. I wave but she only frowns in return.

"Yo vengo," Catalina calls back. She turns back to me and smiles widely. "Nice to see you again, Jesse Benatar." There is something in the way she says my full name that makes it sound like the coolest name in the world. She turns to Michelle and Jeffrey. "Nice to meet you," she says in a near flawless American English. She's clearly practiced.

"El placer es mío," Jeffrey says.

"Vaya con a Madre," Michelle says.

Catalina hesitates long enough for me to see that she's studying Michelle, and I can't tell if she's pleased or pissed with what she's said. Then she closes her eyes and bows her head slightly. "Vaya con a Madre," she says. She gives my neck a surreptitious glance as she turns and begins to walk down the hill toward Señora Sanchez. She looks over her shoulder once. "Bye!" she says.

I wave in return, and when she is about 15 feet away, Michelle says, "That girl seriously likes you." I begin to say something to blow off the comment but cut myself short when I see the look Michelle is giving me; it's both a question and an accusation. "Catalina Ruiz is the girl you told me about?"

"Ah, yeah," I say.

"No wonder you wouldn't say who it was," she says, eyes flitting around my buttoned up collar.

Then it dawns on me where she's going with that. "Hey if you think there's something going on between Catalina and I..."

'Isn't there?' she asks with her eyes.

"Well, it's nothing like you're thinking," I say.

"Well there was definitely some serious vibe going on there," Jeffrey says, "but hey, let's not get into that now; we have some serious stuff to ponder, like figuring out how to make sure no one stirs up trouble at the colonist's booth."

"Yeah," I say, grateful for the refocus. "Maybe Uncle Frank can help with that. He's supposed to be coming home this weekend."

"We're off for a morning bike and run," Jeffrey says, casting his gaze toward Catalina as she joins Señora Sanchez and a group of 20 something men from the colony. Michelle remains silent but her eyes continue to flit back and forth between mine and my neck, clearly aware that something is amiss. "We'll be back by 1:00 or so," Jeffrey adds.

"Any word on Paul?" I ask.

"He has another exam by the neurologist this morning." Jeffrey says. "Miranda said she'll call as soon as she finds anything out."

I become lost in the thought of Paul in the hospital with Miranda and his elderly parents by his side, and the silence moments that follow tells me we all have. "And Lex, she still with Christine?"

Michelle gives me the start of an irritated look but Jeffrey answers before it can wind up. "Yeah. Bill and Hilda have her helping out at the Kat this week. She's there with Christine now. They were asking if you're available to help this week as well."

I only then remember that Hilda had called the house and that I have an unread email message from her or Bill in my Inbox. "Well, I hope that works out. Might be good for her to stay busy."

"It will. Hopefully it works out better than the last time they tried hiring her." That created a few images for me but I decided not to ask. "We start at 2:00 and 4:00 and I'm closing tonight, but we should get together, all of us, talk about things," Jeffrey suggests.

"Definitely," I say. A twinge of anxiety strikes as I realize my tussle with Lex might come up in the conversation. "I'll pop in later, join the madness."

"And mad it's going to be—all week long," Jeffrey replies.

"Is this festival really a big deal?" I ask.

"As big as things get around here anyway," Michelle says, breaking her silence. "Last year over 30,000 people visited over the nine days. Traffic and parking are a nightmare so you might want to consider dusting off your mountain bike for getting around." With that they're off.

I leave the Shadow where it is and make my way to The Kat. I'm leery of creating a scene so I peak through the front window—it's busy and Lex is nowhere in sight. Christine is just coming out of the kitchen area as I enter and grows wide-eyed at the sight of me. I nod and mouth 'I know' to convey I am aware that Lex is working there.

Two blinks later, Hilda bounds out of the kitchen. She spots me right away and beams me a bright smile. "Jesse, I'm so glad you could make it." Christine and I wince at the same time. Hilda waves me over to the counter, and not hearing any breaking dishes or other disturbances from the back, I venture over to talk to her. "You got our messages then. When can you start?"

"I um," I begin.

"We're open from 7:00 am to midnight until next Saturday night. We can give you four to eight hour shifts almost any day you want."

"I'm ah..."

"We can put you in the kitchen, in the back, or you can bus tables—whatever you'd like." A ding at the kitchen window sends her that way to pick up a couple of food orders. "You can even help out up front," she says over her shoulder. "You did really well last time."

Just then, someone slaps my butt. "Move that cute thing will you?" I turn just as Lex squeezes by me carrying a tray full of plates and cups in one arm, and guiding herself around the end of the counter with the other.

"Hey!" I blurt.

"Hey yourself," she says as she carries the tray around to the back of the counter. She slips by Hilda as Christine and I exchange questioning glances.

"So when can you start?" Hilda asks.

Chapter 23

Training Begins

"That's the best news ever," I say.

"I know. They're keeping ... there another week and then he's co... home," Michelle says. The reception is mediocre and her voice cracks and fades.

"We'll have to do something special for him," I say, picturing Paul sitting with a cast on, surrounded by the tribe.

"Yeah. He won't be up... too much; he's on heavy hitter pai... eds and he'll be going back and forth ... trauma center for treatments for months," she says. *"We'll do some... ecial for him though. Say, where are ... Your signal is terri..."*

"Yeah, I'm up the highway a ways." I have a load of questions that beg aswers but none step up. That's followed by a long silence before she speaks again.

"So, Hilda tells ...'re starting work here tonight."

"Ah, yeah, she sort of talked me into it. I'll stick to shifts Lex isn't working though."

"Yeah, sh... with it, but ...be best if you do. ...ybe we can talk ...ight."

"Talk tonight, sure."

"How's ... oat?"

"What?"

"How is ... throat?"

"You saw it then?"

"... heard about it."

"It's fine. A little sore but it's the bruise that's the real prpblem."

"What's that?"

"The bruise. I don't know how I'm going to cover it up at the Kat. I can't exactly wear my jacket all night."

"I'll ... to Jeffrey about it. ... think he has something tha... ight help."

"See you at 6:00 then," I say. I lose the signal so I shut off my phone and stare down at the ocean far below. I don't I know how long I'd sat there at the cliff's edge before the call, and I lose track afterward, but a lot of thoughts come and go like the surge and surf below. I write a few down on my notepad, but I feel too antsy to make it poetic. At the end of the vigil, only one thought remains: I have to talk to Santiago.

——— | ———

I no sooner reach Santiago's boat than he waves me into his Zodiac. I'd arrived just in time not to miss him—or he'd been waiting for me. Within minutes, we've passed through the busy channel and beneath the

Main Street bridge, and we're moving lazily past the row of riverside businesses that are seeing a slow renaissance.

When we pass by Ling's, Santiago takes on a 1000-mile stare in its direction, then seemingly satisfied by something, redirects his eyes to the river ahead. He looks as he usually does—somber, determined, and darkly intimidating, and I wonder if I'll look that way some day.

When we pass houseboat row, it's my turn to take on a reflective stare. The few closest to the Italian restaurant are new, large, and seriously middle class. At the far end, their counterparts are old, small, and worse for wear. Between the two extremes sits two older house boats that look to be owned by artists who either have a thing for flamboyance, or they're completely nuts; they sit like guardians, the only things that stands in the way of gentrification sweeping over the rest of the flotilla. Lex's home is the saddest of the lot, but it's where she lives and that makes it the best of them.

Santiago opens up the throttle a little and after we pass the last of the town buildings, he opens it up full and we jet along the river at a dizzying speed. We're the recipients of a lot of glares from fisherman along the way, but Santiago doesn't seem to notice or care.

When we pass Uncle Frank's dock, I wonder how far up we're going. I told him I need to be back before 6:00 and I only hope he has a better sense of time than I do. After another 15 minutes or so, we slow and head toward the north shore. He motors between two tall willows whose branches dip into the water and I grip the gunwale, expecting we'll hit the shore hard, but we enter a narrow channel that was completely hidden from the river. On both sides of the channel, signs declare "No Public Access".

Santiago throws some switches and the back of the boat comes alive with whirring and clicking. I go back to see that the blades to main the outboards are tilted out of the water. A smaller sounding engine begins to grumble and the telltale white plume and a hydro-jet shoots out the stern and we nudge forward.

"Nice set up," I say, taking my seat next to him at the controls. "Prop main and a water jet secondary." He nods but says nothing. "This rig cost a fortune. You rob a bank or something?"

"Something," he says dispassionately.

"Something like…"

He gives me a deadpan glance. "A gift from a friend."

"Hey, hook me up, I'd like a friend like that," I say.

"No you wouldn't," he says. "What we went through to forge it you would not want."

I recall Michelle mentioning that Santiago has a few close friends in high places, men who's lives he'd saved in Vietnam. "Right, well, it's nice of you to share." No response. "So just how far are we going?"

"Not much farther."

Knowing I'd get nothing more from him, I sit back and take in the scenery. The tributary is slow moving, narrow, and so shallow in most places you can clearly make out the rock and sand bottom. After we pass beneath River Road, the sides become choked by trees and brush so thick I don't think we could have gone ashore if we'd wanted to. It's pristine, nature at its best. When we round a bend, I see a large sign has been erected in the river itself—so much for being unspoiled. When we draw closer I see it is a warning:

Warning! Private preserve. Dangerous wild animals likely present. Turn back now.

I am wondering what sort of jerks would put up a sign like that when another thought came to me. "We're on colony land, aren't we?"

Santiago nods.

"Aren't you concerned? I mean, I know you used to be one of them and all, but they don't exactly like outsiders around."

"We have an understanding," he answers flatly.

A few minutes later, we come to a section of the river bordered by an open meadow and Santiago guides the zodiac into the shore. Boat secured. He leads me to the middle of the meadow. I'm certain I've never been here before but there's something about the way it feels that's familiar. "What is this place?"

"A classroom," he says, stretching and warming up his limbs.

"For what?"

"You," he says. "You and others like us."

"So the wild animals the sign warned about?"

"Us," he says, and with that the strangest and most profound lesson of my life begins.

Chapter 24

A New Threat

"You want me to wear this?" I ask, holding up the turtleneck dickie. "It's so…"

"Gay?" Jeffrey asks.

"Well, yeah," I admit. I hadn't meant anything to do with homosexuality but I let Jeffrey run with it.

"Well, if the dickie fits, baby duck," he says with a perfect effeminate lilt.

"You scare me sometimes," I say, pulling off my t-shirt. "I…"

"Hell, Jesse," Jeffrey exclaims, staring wide-eyed at my torso. "You look beaten to hell—I thought Bolin just bruised your throat."

We are in the small bathroom used by Kat employees. I look down at my chest and then scope out my back in the mirror. I look like black and blue camo. "Ha! I didn't feel any of that," I mutter.

"What?"

"I guess he got me worse than I thought," I say. There was no way I wanted to explain that it was my lesson with Santiago that accounted for most of the bruises. "I'm good though." I put on the t-shirt and check it out. "Damn!"

"Yeah, just don't say it."

"It's true," I mutter, withholding the comment.

"Well, that will have to do you for now," he says, as he opens the door and takes a step into the storeroom. "I have something else for you for next time if you can't manage on your own." He turns toward the storeroom. "Oh, hi!" he says.

I look to see Bill Carter standing about ten feet away staring at us. I mumble something to prime-up an explanation, but he holds up his hands to stop me. "Not my place to judge, boys," then he turns and enters the kitchen.

"Oh man!" I whine.

Jeffrey looks about to burst out laughing. "Well, it's official now, dude. Welcome to the club."

Tourists had started trickling in during the afternoon and by 8:00 that night they drove, rode, and walked through town by the horde. There's nothing quite so inviting as the warm glow of a café at the end of a long drive, so the Kat's a hot spot and we're kept busier than bees. Most of the time I don't have time to think, which is probably a good thing. The scary part—it's the least busy night of the festival.

Michelle and I never do get to have that talk and after helping Jeffrey close up for the night, I offer to give him a ride home on the Shadow.

"No way, man," he says. "Those things are dangerous." Funny coming from a guy who routinely hits 30 mph on crowded roads riding an 18-pound bicycle.

I don't have to start until afternoon the next day so I decide to check out the festival on foot. It's past midnight and cars continue to roll down the hill into town, but most of the attractions are shut down for the night. Even so, the atmosphere is festive—people explore the town, buy junk food at the few venders still open, or drink too much at the beer garden set up at the marina parking lot.

I grab a flyer and read about the week's events. They have a little of everything; demos and contests of every sort including surfing, fishing, lumberjacking, and a dozen baking competitions; wine, beer, and cheese tasting; Shakespeare in the park, yada, yada. There's even a carnival set up by the beach.

It is more than I'd expected from Hook Point or even a town twice its size. It seems as though every square inch of space the place has to offer is staked out for one thing or another, every part but the cannery anyway. Between the pier, parking area, and building itself, the cannery has as much usable concrete as a football field, and yet it sits dark and empty. You'd think if Wingate wanted to gain more favor in town, he'd have be smart to open it up for free parking.

As I walk back to The Kat to get my bike, I scan the narrow harbor and see his yacht is gone again. It occurs to me that I haven't seen anything of Wade or his gang of goons in days. That makes me wonder what they're up to. I think about that as I ride past Lex's house to find it dark and quiet, and past her sanctuary to find it has too many cars parked around it and people milling about to dare an entry. I decide to head home.

Three roads led from that part of town to the main highway and I took the one furthest from Lings'. I learned a lot from Santiago that day, and though I feel I tapped deeper into my abilities, the most important thing I learned was just how dangerous it all was. I knew I'd have to pick my battles wisely and that I couldn't hope to be a match for Bolin any time soon.

———— | ————

When I get home, I go straight to the boat and find a bag on my bed with a note pinned to it.

Jesse! I found this at a booth today in town. Thought it might help keep your neck covered if you tighten the strings a little. Mom wants to talk to you when you get in. So do I. Message me.

I open the bag and pull out a black lightweight hoodie. I put it on and check it out in the mirror. With the buttons done all the way up and the hoodie down but tied, it does a reasonable job of covering my throat. "Way to go, Gwendolyn," I say. I start to text her when I hear footsteps on the stairs. They are light but they don't sound like Gwen's.

There is a knock on the cabin door. "Jesse?" Mom's voice calls out.

"Right there mom," I shout. I do a quick adjustment to the hoodie, check it from left to right in the mirror, then answer the door. "Hey, Mom. Haven't seen you in a couple of days." I say. She smiles. "Come on in, or would you prefer me to come out to the house?"

"Here is just fine, Jesse," she says, then waits.

"Oh, come in, please." She does and I clear a place on the table and pull out a chair for her.

"How is your day at work?" she asks, taking the chair I offer her. She gives my hoodie a good looking over.

"Ah, it's crazy busy. I had no idea there were that many people who even knew Hook Point exists."

She nods. "The festival's always had a big draw, even when I was a child. New shirt?"

"Um, yeah. Gwen picked it up for me today when she was in town. Kinda sweet of her you think? How is Gwen?"

"She's fine, but I had to send her to bed early tonight," she replies.

"On a Friday night. You must have had a fight on your hands."

"Not too much. She's not been sleeping well."

I have a sense that Mom is leading somewhere and it's probably some place I don't want to go. "I guess with everything that's been happening, she's just really excited."

"That's one of the things I want to talk to you about," she says.

Here it is.

"I think moving here's been a little too much for her," she says.

"I don't think so. We talk a lot Mom, maybe even more than before. She loves it here."

"I know you two are working things out and I can't tell you how happy that makes me, Jesse, but I have to think of what is in the best interest of both of you."

"What are you talking about?"

"I think it might be best to move back east," she says.

"What?" I stand up, alarming her. "Where? You can't."

"Jesse, there's…"

"How can you even think about that?" I yell, waving my arms. "We just moved here, I'm just getting to know Uncle Frank, and I'm making some real friends for a change."

"Sit down please," she says in a controlled voice.

I reluctantly sit down and kick a box of undistributed junk I have under the table. Mom flinches and despite attempts to look calm, I realize she's nervous, maybe even frightened. "Mom, are you okay?"

"Yes, I'm fine Jesse," she says in words, but everything else about her says otherwise. I'd seen that look a hundred times—whenever dad was in a mood and working himself up.

"Mom, I'm sorry. I just got a little angry, just blowing off a little steam."

"I know," she says.

"I'm not even that angry, just scared." Her eyes meet mine and seem to relax. "Mom, I really, truly think that moving here is the best thing that's happened to me. It's not just the friends I've met, it's something a lot deeper. It's family, and roots and, something I can't even explain."

Mom sits forward and takes one of my hands in hers. "I know, Jesse," she says. "That's what scares me."

"Mom, everything is going to be okay."

"I wish I could be sure of that," she says, "but it's up to me now to make sure you and Gwen are safe."

"No, no it's not," I say. "It's up to you, me, Gwen, Uncle Frank, Señor Santiago, the town, the colony, everyone. It's not just up to you. And what about the other night? You can't tell me it wasn't something special when you talked about your mother, father, and the colony. You think that would have ever happened if we'd moved to Pittsburgh?"

Mom's eyes shifted their gaze to the bare surface of the tabletop. "Mom, Gwen and I are connecting to something real here, something that may be more important than anything else we may get involved with…ever. Please don't take that away from us."

She shifts her eyes back to mine and I see something different in them. Perhaps it's always been there, but a child has a hard time seeing it in a parent—uncertainty. "I'll think about it, Jesse. I can't promise anything but I'll think about it." She looks tired. "I want to you promise me one thing though."

"Sure, anything," I blunder.

"I want you to promise me you'll stay away from Señor Santiago."

"Ah, why? He's really not crazy and he has a lot to… share, you know, about life and Hook Point."

"Just promise me," she asks.

A silence grows between us and I know if I speak the truth, it may sway her toward moving away. Finally, I let it out apologetically. "I can't, Mom." How can I explain it. "I can't." By the way she tenses and the fear returns to her eyes, I guess Santiago is somewhere near the heart of her fears.

She stands and smoothes her blouse and pants with her palms. "I feared as much, Jesse. You're too old to forbid you to see someone, though heaven knows I want to."

"Why?"

"Because of what's happening around here, and what is going to happen. Because if you associate with Señor Santiago, you'll likely end up in the middle of it."

"Sometimes the middle is the safest place to be," I say. That doesn't have the desired affect. "Like with a hurricane," I add hopefully—no change. "Look, how about if I promise not to do anything stupid or anything you'll be ashamed of me for?"

She thinks about that, or seems to, and then her expression changes. "It's a start," she says. "It's late, Sweetheart. Get some sleep."

"Yeah," I say as she makes for the companionway door. "So when is Uncle Frank coming home. I don't see his truck out there tonight."

"He'll be here in the morning," she says somberly. "Now go to bed," and with that she's gone.

My mind spins so fast I stand there gapping like some burnout. She'd decided, I saw it in her eyes—we're moving and if I know Mom, it'll be before the end of summer. I have to come up with a plan to change her mind. I pace the cabin and think of a dozen things that will never work. I decide that if I have to, I'll emancipate myself and stay here with Uncle Frank or out on my own. That option fades in the image of Mom and Gwen living alone somewhere.

Facing the prospect of leaving Hook Point, forces me to realize just how important to me this crummy town has become. I can't go back to... being alone. I boot up my laptop and message Gwen. I scan the inbox, find nothing there I want to reply to, and send a quick email to Michelle, Christine, Jeffrey, and Pete.

What I write sounds like a plea for help and it's probably as incoherent as I feel. I look at the eddress Isa has last left and I'm tempted to send a message there as well, but I remember her plea not to. Who the hell is she and who's watching her?

Gwen doesn't get back to me right away so I figure she must be out cold. I don't see any point in disturbing her, poor kid. She's sensitive, impossibly caring, and always thinks and worries too much about things; a good night sleep will do her good. Maybe Mom's right though, maybe being here with all that is happening isn't a good thing for her. My head races with nonsense and it promises to be my night to stay up thinking.

ıpter 25

Peligrosa Belleza

> ### Journal - Hook Point, CA.
>
> *Someone incredibly special pointed something out to me the other day and it has haunted me since and in the best of ways. We are intimate companions with all of life—every plant, animal—and if the Gaia Principle is correct—with the physical earth herself. In this, even in the darkest times, our loneliest moments, we are never alone, no one is any less connected than another, and none of our lives is really more important or meaningful than another's. Maybe if we open ourselves to that idea, something inside can change, and then maybe we can find more room for love, compassion, and profound belonging.*
>
> *~ From the Journal of Jesse Benatar*

I decide to shower off the day, and I know if the water's cold enough it'll help me get out of my head and back into my body. I grab a towel and make my way out across the yard to the shower.

In the pale light of night, my arms, chest and belly are mottled with bruises, like shadows through trees, and they're sore to the touch. My muscles and joints ache but not near as much as I'd expect with the workout Santiago put me through. I'd never experienced anything like it before and I look forward to the next one. I'm not sure when that will be, but he did tell me not to plan anything for Sunday.

I stand naked beneath the oversized showerhead, and pull the chain. The initial downpour is the cold water sitting in the exposed pipe from the holding tank, and it shocks me fully into the world of the physical—for those few moments, nothing else exists but the sensations radiating from my skin. The experience shifts to soothing warmth as water in the tank, heated by two days of sun, makes its way to me.

The rain-like stream lulls me into a feeling that all is well in the world. Sometimes focusing on the pleasures of life can be as centering as pain, only a lot more pleasant. After I've rinsed, I stand and let the water pour over me for the pure enjoyment of it, then I sit beneath the gentle downpour and let the sound and sensations carry me away...

I soar on a stream of pure energy where time and place have no meaning, nor do I. That clean and simple experience, the peace, is disturbed by the sense that something is out of place, and I am roused into opening an eye. Through falling droplets and darkness, I see a figure standing at the far end of the enclosure.

"Hey," I complain, covering myself with one hand while trying to keep the downpour out of my eyes. "Gwen?" The figure takes a step closer as I pop up on my feet and step out of the stream of water. Shaking my head and wiping the water from my face, I find myself staring at the robed figure of Catalina Ruiz. "What are you... ah, toss me my towel will you?" She laughs her soft chortle. "Catalina!"

"I no think you shy," she says mirthfully. "You shy."

Keeping my essentials covered, I step over to where I've hung my clothes and towel and she steps to block me. She notices the bruises on my torso and is taken back for two or three heartbeats, then her eyes move up to mine and she gives me a wicked smile that I'd not have thought her capable of. "And I never thought you were so... such a pest," I say.

She laughs again. "I help you more comfort," she says, and her cloak drops to the ground around her ankles.

My first impulse is to look away—but I can't; I've never been one to stare or ogle, but the sight of Catalina Ruiz, standing naked in the pale evening light is the stuff of fantasies. My eyes find a new boldness and slowly take her in from head to toe and back. Every line and curve of her body etches itself in my consciousness. When my eyes meet hers again, I see something in them that is killer wicked. "Catalina, I..."

She reaches out to touch my chest and I take her wrists into my hands to stop her. Her skin feels warm and soft to the touch, and a sensation of pleasure travels through my hands and up my arms. She looks down to see my excitement and smiles.

"Shit," I mutter, letting go of her wrists. I reach around her and grab my towel, then cover up my embarrassment as best I can. "You're worse than my brat sister."

Catalina leans against the wall with her hands folded behind her and stares at me expectantly. "You're really something, you know that," I say picking her cloak up off the ground. "You're so shy and reserved when I see you in town, and here you're a regular... femme fatale.

I don't think she catches half of what I say; she just leans against the wall and stares at me in a way the makes me want to do bad things—amazingly, wonderful bad things.

I hold the cloak out for her to take. She stares at me a moment longer, then steps away from the wall and slowly turns her back to me. She is so close I can smell her hair, almost taste her skin, and I feel an urge to grab her and push her up against the wall… she turns her head to one side and looks down over her shoulder. "Catalina," I say. My hands shake as they drape the cloak over her shoulders. "Please don't."

She lowers her head and secures the cloak around her, then turns to face me. I expect a look of embarrassment or anger, but she looks totally, completely content. The cryo-magnet draw and sexual intensity have lifted, as though she's thrown some switch, and now she is the demure girl again. "This good?" she asks.

"Yes," I answer. "This good." I begin to dry off and dress. "I'm sorry, I just… there's just… You know, you're amazing." She leans herself against the wall, and watches me and listens quietly. I feel compelled to fill the silence. "Believe it or not I saw you on the first day I rode into town. You were in that old yellow pickup and I only saw you for seconds, but the image has never left me. I still see it in my head all the time."

Catalina looks radiantly peaceful and content. "Hell, you won't understand most of this, which is probably a good thing come to think of it," I rambled. "I felt something that day, something I still don't understand."

I finish dressing and then squat down with my back against the wall opposite Catalina. She moves herself to within two feet of me and gracefully lowers herself to sitting. We sit facing each other a moment, then she says. "I feel same."

"What, you understood all that?"

She nods. "Most. Understand more, talk little…talk much hard."

I'll have to remember that. "Yeah, well I still feel this thing between us, but, hell, everything has changed so much for me, and things are crazy."

"Yes."

"So, you and I… We can't…"

"You like other girl?"

"Who, Michelle, the one you met? No. Well, I like her but not that way."

"No! Other girl." She made a gesture with her hands that conveyed a sense of intensity.

"Oh, Lex. Well, yes, I guess so. We're not really seeing each other, but I have these feelings and I just…"

"What trouble heart much bad, Jesse Benatar?"

I see a look of concern in her eyes, exactly like what I've seen in Mom's countless times, and I want to tell her everything. I open my mouth to say something but nothing comes out. Where to start? "I um… Did you know my mother is from your people?" I ask using hand gestures.

Her lips move as she translates. "Sí. Señora Sanchez-McBride."

"Huh! Well, wouldn't that be, McBride-Sanchez? Or I guess it would be McBride-Benatar now." I thought briefly about my dad—how alone he must have felt, heart and soul bunkered away by his PTSD and whatever else his problems were.

"No," she says. "Girl, one name, same like mother," she says holding up one finger. Then she holds up two. "Two name, same like father one name. Boys…" she holds one hand over the other and turns them over. "Other way. No change. Even marry no change. This our way."

I nod. "I like that." That would make me what—Jesse Benatar-Sanchez by her way of thinking. "So, yeah, I just found this out three days ago, and I know that doesn't make me a part of your people or anything, but I have this good feeling about it, like it's been something missing that I didn't know was lost, but that I've found now." Catalina listens quietly, and I have a feeling that she understands me. "So that's a good thing, and so are the friends I've made. You know, like Michelle and Jeffrey you met today."

"And other girl," she adds. She does understand.

"Yeah, and Lex. I like them all—actually, I'm coming to love them all. And then there's Señor Santiago; he may be one crazy old dude, but I think he's the most amazing man I've ever met." I hold back mentioning anything about shifting; I am not certain myself what to make of that and have no idea how to bring that up or talk about it.

"You happy here," Catalina suggests.

"Yes, yes I am, and for the first time since forever I feel I belong someplace."

"Is good," she says.

"Yes, is very good."

"Why sad heart?" she asks.

I cross my legs and sit up straighter. "I found out tonight that my mom plans to move us away from here." A brief look of concern passes over Catalina's face. "She thinks it's too dangerous for me here, and for my sister, Gwen. Thing is, she might be right."

"You madre come today, speak to Old Ones," Catalina says.

"What, the colony? Today? What did she talk about, what did they say?"

Catalina shrugs. "No se, not know. But not happy when go."

So that's it. Mom went to the colony and whatever it is she heard there, convinced her to leave town. I lean closer to Catalina and she leans a little closer to me. "Can you find out what they talked about and what was said... for me I mean?"

She draws her head back quickly. "No," she says. "No good. Talk to Old Ones very big, sagrado..." she seems to struggle for a word "Is mu privado. No talk about."

"Okay, okay, sorry." Catalina is perturbed by the suggestion so I know I've stepped on something I don't understand. I have to ask Mom about it, and come up with an explanation how I know she'd talked to them.

"This what trouble you?" she asks.

"Yes, this is what troubles me very much. This is where I want to be, where I need to be, here." Catalina smiles and nods gently. "I don't know how to explain it, but I have a feeling that... this place isn't just important for me, I'm also needed here for something."

"Si, es tan," she says.

"You know something about that, what it might be?" I ask.

Catalina smiles. "You no fear. You no go away."

"I wish I can be as sure of that as you sound."

"You no go away, Jesse Benatar."

"How can you be so sure?"

"Some thing just know, long time."

"Ah..."

"What fear you most?" she asks. An image of Santiago and the killing shed flickers on and off at the question. "You go, mother take away, what fear most?"

"Oh, um..." the question stirs an uncomfortable feeling in my heart and my mind takes me to a sad place. "Loosing everything, I guess; the people I've grown to love, people I haven't met yet, it may sound odd but your people as well, even this lousy little town. I belong here." A wave of sadness threatens to submerge me. "I've spent so much time on the outside looking in, I don't want *to do alone anymore." The lump in my throat prevents me from saying any more.*

Catalina reaches forward and brushes my hair back from my forehead and smiles softly. It's the same smile as moms—different, but the same. "You not alone, always not alone," she says.

"Oh, yes," I say. "A lot."

"No," she says, with a gentle shake of her head. She says it with such simple conviction, as though it's an accepted truth, that my own perceptions falter. "No people alone. No thing alone." Our eyes held contact in the darkness.

"Like water in river—one. We go life together. Past people down river," she says pointing to one side. "Now people here," she says laying her lands on her lap. "Tomorrow people there," she says, pointing the other way. She holds her hands apart, then brings them together over her lap. "All same river, together."

It makes sense with a wide lens and an Einsteinian view of time, but not from the perspective we live in. "Well, okay, sure, but…"

She lightly holds a finger to my lips and let it linger there. "All life this way, bird, tree, fish—all together, not apart, not alone. Look alone, feel alone, but not alone. Always Mother hold close," she says, looking down at the ground beneath us and caressing it gently with both palms. "This you see?"

I do. The connectedness I feel with life, when I am in nature, grounded, and at peace; I've felt that—briefly. I've never thought of it so broadly though, and can only imagine what it will be like to feel that belonging 24/7. "That's totally beautiful, Catalina."

"Si," she says. Her teeth and the whites of her eyes seem to blaze in the dim light. "You not forget."

"No, I not forget."

Catalina stands. "I go now."

I pop to my feet. "Do you have to?"

"Si, I am called," she says, brushing off her cloak.

"Called? Called by whom?" I ask looking around.

"Old Ones call. I go."

"Who are these old ones?" I ask.

"Sleep well, Jesse Benatar, you no have heavy heart now." She turns to leave.

y. I suddenly feel dizzy and look down at the ground and take in
eady myself. When I look up, she is gone. "Catalina?"

:yes as the water rains down on me in gentle droplets. I sit
alone under the shower, with the sounds of the night and pattering
water calling me back to now.

Chapter 26

Tag Team

"Good morning," Uncle Frank says. I'd found him in the shed
inspecting the little bit of work I'd done on the Bonnie.

"Morning," I say, leaning again the shed doorframe, holding my first
mug of coffee. I'd slept in until 9:00 and by the time I got to the house
for breakfast, everyone had finished and Mom was up getting ready to
go and help out at the festival. Gwen was nowhere to be found.

The bruise is nearly gone, but I adjust the top of the hoodie to make
certain it's well covered. "I guess I didn't get a lot done on the Bonnie,"
I begin.

Rather than being annoyed, he shrugs his shoulders and smiles.
"Well, I haven't exactly been here to help out," he says. He looks more
tanned than usual, and appears happier. His expression becomes
marginally more serious. "I've been away, but I've kept up on what's
been happening—you've had your head and hands full."

"You've been talking to Mom," I guess.

"Of course, almost every day, but she's not my only source," he says
mysteriously. He wipes some grease from his hands and lays the rag
back over the bike frame. "Nice work there, by the way."

"So you know she's thinking to move away from here?"

That catches him off guard. "No, I didn't know that, Jesse."

"You can't let her do it," I say.

Frank's brow knits. "Jesse. If it's what your mother wants to do, it's
not my place to try and stop her even if I could."

"You want us to go?"

"Of course not. I want nothing more than for the three of you to make Hook Point your permanent home. You're family."

"So help me do something, at least help convince her that Hook Point isn't a dangerous place for us," I ask.

"I'll do my best with that," he says. "I'm just getting to know my sister again, getting to really know you and Gwen for the first time." He puts down what he's doing and walks over to me. "We're family and we've spent a lot of years apart, and I've...," he falters.

"Spent a lot of years alone?" I suggest.

He nods. "Yeah! Not entirely alone mind you, but enough to know the value of being with loved ones." He motions for us to return to the house and closes the shed door and locks it.

"So what's the plan then? You take her high and I'll take her low?"

He chuckles. "I don't know. Your mother use to pack a mean right hook, I don't know if I want to deal with that half."

"Seriously?" Uncle Frank stops and points to a faint scar over his right eye. "No way—she did that?"

"Yup," he says as he resumes walking. "Well, to be more precise the metal frame I ran my head into trying to avoid one of your mom's punches did it, but she likes to hold the bragging rights."

"Okay, I've got her high then," I say, entering the kitchen.

"Got who high," Mom asks. She's packing a cooler with sandwiches and fruit but shoots me the glance.

"Oh, nothing, just an expression," I say. "Morning." I walk up to her and stand there while Frank goes upstairs.

"Good morning," she says suspiciously. "What do you want?"

"Just a hug," I say.

She stops what she's doing and gives me a long, soft hug, and when she's done, she asks, "Are you okay, Jesse?"

"Yeah, always."

"So then what are you up to?"

I'm tempted to tell her exactly what I am up to but intuition sends me in a different direction. "Well, you know how you are thinking it might be best so move away from here?"

"Yeah" she says suspiciously.

"Well, I know you decided last night that we would, but you don't have to worry about that now," I say.

She gives me a sideways glance, "How did you... and why don't I have to worry about that?"

"Because it's not going to happen," I say matter-of-factly.

"And you know this how?" she asks, resuming her cooler packing.

"Last night I had a vision or dream or whatever you call it, and I was told we wouldn't be moving."

"Oh, I see," she says, a smile forming on her lips.

Before I let her have too much fun with it I add, "Yeah, I was told about your trip to see the Old Ones yesterday and that you were told something that scared you, and that's why you're fearful for us, but you don't have to worry."

Mom gives me a serious, questioning look. "Who told you that?" she asks.

"Like I said, it was a vision or dream. Any who, we won't be moving away because our staying here has been known for a long time and, well, you can't buck fate right?"

Mom stands there staring at me with an expression of disbelief mixed with concern. She says nothing for at least 15 seconds and I begin to think I chose exactly the wrong thing to be up front about. Frank bounds down the stairs and into the kitchen.

"So I'll be gone all day," he says. "These the sandwiches?" Mom nods yes and he gives her a second look. "You didn't start on her without me did you?" he asks.

"No, not intentionally," I say. It looks like Mom is growing angry. "So you're working at the Festival?" I ask quickly.

"Every year," he says, slipping a couple of cold beers into the cooler. He pauses a moment, then slips in two more.

"What will you be doing?" I ask.

"A lot of everything usually, but today I start by helping set up the real booth and display for the colony." He checks his pockets, pulls out his wallet and checks the contents.

"A real booth? They have a fake one?" I ask as Mom leaves the kitchen without a word.

"Well they did until last night. A little idea I came up with on the road. Set up a sham booth put together from bits of nothing on the first night, then replace what's left of it in the morning."

"Brilliant, but what about tonight and the next night and the one after that? I ask.

"We've arranged that someone will be watching things 24/7. Last night Sam Jorgensen had his van parked near the site. Had surveillance cameras on it waiting to catch the culprits on film."

Go Jorgensen! "Did he?"

"Yup!" he says triumphantly. "Shane Grady, Mitch Williams, and Harold Thoms. There were a couple of younger fellows helping them as well, mostly keeping watch, but they did some damage."

"Anyone I know?" I ask, thinking I knew already.

"Eddy Thoms and Frankie Harris," he replies.

"Have they been arrested yet?"

"Ha! That would be a trick. Local law enforcement needs an overhaul and the tapes just might bring this about. So far, they've refused to press charges, which we expected, but an inspector from the department headquarters is paying a quiet visit to look over how they're handling the issue. We might catch two birds with one trap on this one."

"You've been busy when you were away." I say.

"Yes I have, and not just on the windmill project," he says.

"Want some help today? I start work at The Kat at 4:00 but I'm good 'til then."

"Sure," he says. "Why don't you take this stuff out to my truck; I need to have a few words with your mom."

I grab the cooler and have second thoughts. "Hey, there's something I need to do around here this morning, how about if I join you in town in an hour or two?"

"What ever works for you, Jesse," he replies from the kitchen door.

"Thanks. Oh, have you seen Gwen this morning?" I ask.

"Ah, yeah, she said she was going to go out and get you up right after breakfast," he replies. "She didn't do that?"

I shake my head. "Don't worry, I think I know where she is."

Chapter 27

Disenchantment

I was right; as I walk down the wooded hillside to the meadow, I spot Gwen sitting on the rock, leaning back into the natural chair it forms. She looks to be sleeping.

Hey!" I say from ten feet away.

"Ah!" she shouts. "Jeez, Jesse, you scared me," she complains.

"Sorry!" I say holding up my hands in appeasement.

"Jerk," she mutters as she rearranges herself on the rock.

"You meditating or something?"

She cast me an annoying glance. "No! Well, maybe, why?"

"Just wondering is all; I didn't think you were into that."

She gives me a peevish look. "Well, I thought I'd try it," she says.

I lean a hip against the rock. "So what's up?" I ask. She gives me a puzzled look. "Your mood? You seem, I don't know, off?"

Gwen stares down at the tall grass and wild flowers that fill the meadow. She frowns, rolls her eyes, knits her brow, then takes in and slowly blows out a long breath. "I'm jealous," she says, as though confessing a crime.

"Jealous, you? Jealous of who?" I ask.

She drops her head slightly. "You," she mutters.

"Me?" I blurt. "You... huh? Why, what is there to be jealous about with me?"

"Oh, come on Jesse, don't play dumb," she says.

"I don't need to; it comes natural." That doesn't cheer her. "So talk to me; what are you jealous about?" She stares down at the meadow, then looks away. "Gee, don't gap on me here."

She quickly turns her head to me. "You're special," she blurts.

"Well that is what they said in school, even had a special class…"

"Will you be serious for once!" she complains.

"Sorry. So how am I special and how are you not?"

"Well think about it," she says. "You're at the center of everything that's been going on here. The book was left for you, not me. You're the one having these amazing night journeys, and now you end up being a shape shifter. Come on, what's not special about that?"

"Gwen, it's not special, I don't feel special. I feel like crap with most of it."

"Really?" she blurts sarcastically. "Really Jesse? You want crap try being me for a day." She slides of the rock and steps out in to the meadow, facing it. "I'm the weirdo little sister," she yells to the world. "I'm the baby of the family. My mother won't even talk about sex around me. I'm thirteen and I haven't even started my period yet."

At that she stops dead and stands still. After a long silence she turns around, head to the ground and comes back to the rock. "I didn't mean to say that one. Too much information, right?"

"Definitely!" I answer. "Feel better?"

"No," she pouts. "Well, maybe a little."

"Gwen, listen to me." I took a step closer to her. "You are special."

"Don't patronize me," she complains.

"I'm not, seriously. When all this started happening you were the one I turned to for help."

"That's me, Gwendolyn the peon."

"Will you shut up and listen for a minute." Gwen looks a little shocked but she becomes still and listens. "You have a real talent, Gwen. What you know, and I'm not just talking about what you read, it's how you seem to be able to sense what's real and what's crap. I think you have a gift of intuition." Gwen seems to ponder what I am saying and her glumness lifts slightly. "Even Señor Santiago says there is something special about you, only he doesn't know what it is yet."

"You're just telling me that," she says hopefully.

"No, really. It was when I asked if you and Mom were shifters and he said Mom wasn't but he wasn't sure of you, but he was sure that there was something special about you. In fact, he said 'very special'."

She stands still a moment and then climbs back up on the rock, looking moderately pleased with herself. "So what are you back here for," she asks.

"Well, two reasons really. To find you because I thought you'd be back here, and to do my exercises."

"Exercises?"

"Yeah," I say. I began to take my hoodie off. "Santiago took me out to… someplace yesterday and put me through this training."

"Holy shit Jesse, what happened to you, to your…" Gwen shouts, staring wide-eyed at my torso.

"Oh, yeah. Like I said, it's crap most of the time."

"Did Señor Santiago do this to you? Did he beat you?"

"No," I say. "Well, there was some contact, but most of this is me misjudging things; running into trees, tripping over my own feet… there's a learning curve to all this you know."

"Oh, if Mom finds out…"

"I know, that's why she's not going to," I say. "So… wanna try something?"

Chapter 28

Cousin Serena

Getting to town is crazy; being there is crazier. I can never figure out why people flock to public attractions; between the crowds, parking problems, and overpriced bad food, you'd think it'd be enough to repel anyone. Thirty minutes to get to the town limits—clearly not.

The only place I can find to rest my bike is the loading area behind The Kat. I leave her there and make my way over to where most of the display booths are set up. It takes a while but I find the booth the colony has set up.

It's simple but it makes an impression. There is an interesting display about the history of the colony and Señor Juan Alba is all diplomat and charm as he fields questions from people. There are booths on either side of the display; one is selling food and the other is selling trinkets, dolls, and other hand made items.

The dresses and robes on display draw a lot of attention and it's easy to see why; they're simple, elegant, and unique; the perfect catch for a tourist on the prowl for something special to take home. I'd wondered why the colonists bothered with the festival—they don't seem to want much to do with outsiders and they really don't need our money—but seeing the interest the crowd shows, I get it. The enjoyment on the faces of the people means the colonists are sending good memories and good will home with each of them.

I finally find Uncle Frank sitting at a picnic table behind the booth. He's caught up in a spirited conversation with one of the colonial women who has her back to me, and he seems happier than I've ever seen him before. When he catches sight of me, he waves me over, and the woman turns her head to me—it's Señora Selene Sanchez.

"Buenos Tardes, Jesse," she says, joyfully. It's obvious she's getting off on the conversation as much as Frank is. *Go Uncle Frank.*

"Buenos Tardes, Señora Sanchez," I reply. "Sorry I got here so late, Uncle Frank. Gwen and I got involved in something."

"No worries, Jesse," he says mirthfully. "Well, there's still plenty of work around here if you're so inclined."

I'm physically tired from the exercises Santiago had given me to practice, and it promises to be a busy night at The Kat, but my mind is sharp and cruising in high gear. "Sure, I'm good for it," I say.

Frank gives Señora Sanchez a nod and she calls toward one of the booths, "Serena!" A moment later, Serena Sanchez pokes her head out from the booth's cloth backdrop and flashes her brilliant smile. Something non-verbal passes between the two of them, and Serena looks at me, then her mother, and becomes excited. She disappears back into the booth and then emerges carrying a small bandolier bag.

"Serena has been dying to visit the Mad Kat," Frank says.

"You would not mind taking her?" Selene asks.

"She's there," I say. "I'll even get her a job there if she wants one."

"Oh, the tour will do just fine," Selene says with mock annoyance.

"Hi Jesse," Serena says, smiling. "Nice to see you again."

It dawns on me just then that I have no idea whether Uncle Frank knows who Mom's real mother is, that I'm blood related to Señora Sanchez and Serena. "Nice seeing you too, Serena. You set to go?" She nods and we we're off, but not before Frank has me promise to have her back in an hour.

 We slowly make our way through the crowd that has gathered in and around the colony booths. I notice right away that Serena waits for gaps between people before moving, and know we'll never make it to The Kat if I don't do something. "This way," I say, taking her by the hand.

I gently nuzzle my way through the crowd, excusing myself as I go, bringing Serena with me. She seems a little disturbed by it all so when we clear the throng and are walking side-by-side, I ask her, "Are you okay?"

"Yes," she says unconvincingly, then adds, "We do not do that."

"What, walk through crowds?" I ask.

"Yes, not like that. It is considered… bold," she says uncomfortably.

I don't detect judgment from her, just a statement of fact. "Well, you might want to learn to be a little bolder if you want to attend more events like this. It's normal and expected here, as long as you're polite about it."

I lead her along a few less traveled streets as we make our way towards the bridge that will take us over the river and to The Kat. We talk non-stop; she wants to know everything about living in Colorado and what it's like for me living in Hook Point, and I want to know everything about living at the colony.

She talks freely about day-to-day life there, how amazing it is but also how isolated she feels. She'd spent almost all of her life living abroad, mostly in France, Spain, and Norway, but also in Turkey, India, China, and New Zealand. Living within the placid confines of the colony is an adjustment for her. That explains her near perfect English but another question dawns on me.

"I thought you couldn't move back to the colony if you grew up outside of it, or spent too much time away," I ask.

She nods and frowns. "This is so, most of the time, but it is different sometimes." It doesn't sound like she is going to add to that so I patiently wait. "Some of our people are chosen to have contact with the outside. My mother was chosen to visit the others, to learn of their healing and teach them of ours, then share it back and forth. She has traveled like this since I was born, six months or a year here, a few years there."

"Sounds like my life growing up on army bases, only not as exciting. So who are the others?" Serena looks down at the ground and bites her lip. "Are there other colonies like yours?" I ask.

She looks at me apologetically. "I cannot talk of this," she says. "I am sorry."

"Oh that's cool," I say. "I can respect a secret. I won't tell you about my secret life as a heroic crime fighter though, or what my secret power is." She gives me a searching look, and then brakes into a delightful laughter. "What, you think that's funny?" I jest. "You don't think I have a secret power?"

"I know all about your secret power," she says. "It is the heroic part I find funny."

Serena was sharp, aware, and damn fun. "Did you know we're related?" I ask without thinking?

She smiles widely and nudges her shoulder into mine. "Yes!" she says. "I did not know if you knew so I did not say anything."

"Yeah, me too." Damn! I'm walking over the bridge with my awesome new cousin, a cousin I never knew I had until a few days ago.

"So where's your dad?" I ask. This has an unexpected effect on Serena; her smile fades and she becomes quiet. "Sorry, if I'm prying, you don't have to answer that," I say. "I just want to learn as much as I can about your side of my family."

She nods and smiles unconvincingly. "It is alright," she says. "You are not prying." She hesitates a moment and says, "My father left when I was born. I don't remember anything about him."

"No way."

She gives me a look that is one part annoyance and one part anger. "I am not lying," she says.

"No, no. I mean, no way, I don't... well it's just an expression. It means 'that's too much', 'that sucks', that sort of thing. She nods her head. "I suppose that must have been hard," I say, scrambling to save the mood.

"I would not know that; I have nothing to measure it to, but I sometimes feel sadness when I see other girls with their fathers." She grows silent and thoughtful, and I do nothing to interrupt. "I have known many good men where we lived, each like an uncle, each cared for me. In our way, we have one father, one mother, but many parents."

"Sounds nice," I say, thinking about what it might be like growing up in a community where people really look out for each other

"It is," she says. Her white teeth flash in the sun with a quick smile, but her mouth shifts and she looks sullen. "I heard about your father. I am sorry for your loss."

"I'm not," I mutter, and for the first time ever the words didn't quite fit.

"What?" she asks, surprised.

"Oh, it's just that my dad was not like those good men who helped raise you. He was in the army and was hurt, hurt in the head, and he wasn't a nice man sometimes."

"But you still loved him," she suggests.

That one stopped me dead on the crowded sidewalk. I feel tears trying to form in my eyes and I fight against them until I can finally say something. "Yeah, I guess I did." We resumed walking and Serena did the sweetest thing—she gently takes my hand and holds it in one of hers and holds my arm with the other as we walk.

"Are all your people as caring as you?" I ask.

She nods. "Mostly, yes. Some say I have my mother's way, the way of the healers, like her mother, like your grandmother, but kindness is at the heart of who we are."

We reach The Kat and I see right away that it'll be a wait. I check my watch. I could sneak her in back, but I have a feeling that Serena wants to get the full Mad Kat experience. "After you," I say as we enter.

The lineup is almost to the door but I begin telling Serena about The Kat, Bill and Hilda, and the friends I know who work here pointing out Christine and Michelle behind the counter. When Michelle catches sight

of me, she gestures with her head for me to come beh
and looks puzzled when I wave the suggestion off.

I catch sight of a head of blond hair as Lex pushes h
the crowd, busing tables. By the time we're next up, she's
and back with a full tray, but I don't think she's seen u.. As we stand
waiting for the couple in front of us, I catch Christine throwing me a
concerned stare. Her eyes shift between me and Serena and widen as if
to ask, 'what the fuck?'

When Michelle sees Serena and me together, she gives a stare that
could cut titanium. Then just as we're stepping up to order, I hear a
rattle of cups and then feel a sharp jab in my kidneys that nearly sends
me into the counter.

"Excuse me please," Lex's voice blurts.

I recover just in time to see Lex make her way around the end of the
counter carrying a tray of mugs. Christine and Michelle both look
alarmed and Serena looks shocked. "Are you okay?" Serena asks,
keeping a concerned eye on Lex.

"Yeah, that's just one of many sore spots." I look up at Michelle and
Christine who are both giving me 'what the hell do you think you're
doing' looks. That's when I drop the bomb. "Serena, this is Michelle and
Christine, and the one in a big rush is Alexis. Guys, this is Señorita
Serena Sanchez, my cousin."

Lex stops dead in her tracks and the look on all three faces is
priceless. "Hello," Serena says with a bright smile.

I don't let anyone recover though, and roll into our order. "We'll
have a double French roast with room for cream, and a Chai Latte,
whole milk, to go, please," I say with as much nonchalance as I can
muster. All three just stand there staring for about three seconds.

"What?" Michelle asks. I repeat the order. "No, no, your what?"

I start to play dumb, but Serena steps in to help. "Cousin," she says.
"I am Jesse's second cousin." I have a hard time keeping the grin ff my
face.

"Ah... oh, jeez sorry, hi," Michelle says, recovering. "Happy to meet
you."

"Me also," Serena says.

A guy behind us clears his throat and makes some comment to someone just loud enough to be overheard, about country service, which doesn't bother me a bit. Christine and Michelle start to get our order ready, but Lex just stands behind the counter looking back and forth between Serena and me.

"You'll have to excuse our confusion, Serena," Lex says. "We have a communication problem around here. Sometimes people don't tell other people what they should and things get terribly mystified."

"Yeah, and sometimes people only find things out like a few days ago," I say.

The order is placed on the counter in front of us and when I try to lay down a five, Michelle says, "We got it." She has a mischievous smirk on her face. "You're starting at 4:00 today right?"

"Yeah," I say.

"I cannot wait," she says, with a mischievous smirk.

I hand Serena her cup, wave to Christine, and flash wide eyes at Lex, who flashes wide, wild eyes back.

"Your friends," Serena begins when we exit The Kat, "they did not know you have ties with us?"

I motion for us to walk down toward the docks. "They do now. I only found out a few days ago myself, Serena."

"The small one, Alexis—she is angry with you," she says.

"Ah, well, for the moment anyway. She thought maybe you and I..."

"She is your girlfriend?" she asks.

"No. We were hanging out but that's over," I say.

"Maybe for you," Serena says, sipping her tea. "Ah, this is very nice."

"You think Lex still likes me?" I ask.

"Oh, yes, but she is also very angry. I think maybe you hurt her?"

"Not intentionally," I say. "Say, how do you know this?" She gestures to her eyes and ears and smiles.

I take Serena along the docks before heading back to the main strip. It's busy with tourists, boaters, and fisherman's booths, and the beer garden. We chat mostly about the places she's lived, and I lead her up a less used street to get away from the crowds.

Half way to the main drag, a commotion in an adjacent alley draws our attention. Two young guys are standing in the alley looking unsure of themselves, and a third guy, a little older, stands facing the two of them. The younger guys start fishing through their pockets.

"What are you looking at, fagot," the older guy shouts at me.

"Just keep walking," I say.

"What is happening there?" Serena asks.

"You don't want to know."

"Yes I do. It is one of the things I must do," she says.

"What do you mean?"

"Like my mother, I will travel a great deal in my work, and I must be prepared."

"Huh! Well, if you must know, that was a drug deal. First one I've seen go down around here."

"Ha! I have heard of that," she says with a little pride.

"Well, hear this, it's best to stay clear of people dealing drugs because they're messed up in the head, have nothing to live for, and they like to carry guns."

"I've heard of that also," she says more somberly.

I'm only 10 minutes late getting Serena back, but no one seems to notice. She thanks me for taking her to The Kat and for the tea and I suggest that she get her mother to bring her to the house sometime to meet Gwen. We no sooner exchanged intentions to stay in contact when she's pulled away to work the booth.

Uncle Frank and Señora Sanchez are nowhere to be seen so I wander around to the colony's main display and look it over. It tells the story of how the colonists came to California from Spain in 1703 and landed in the protected cove of what is now Hook Point two years later.

It tells of establishing their first settlement where Hook Point sits today and living a peaceful co-existence with the aboriginals, then moving to their current location in 1711. Then the display goes on to convey that 'La Colonia de Los Soñadores' had diligently preserved the lands they'd held stewardship over ever since. It addresses their simple way of life and the contributions they've made to the State of California, most of which I'm surprised to hear about.

Chapter 29

Gwen's Folly

The last thing I want to do is bus tables for 8 hours, but it's time to report for duty at The Kat.

"So dish it out, Jesse," Michelle demands from the other side of the bathroom door as I'm washing up.

"No time," I call back. "I need to finish washing up." The door swings open and Michelle steps in and closed it behind her. It isn't uncommon for several of us to use the bathroom at the same time, but her forcefulness surprises me.

"Here, you need to wear this anyway," she says tossing me a Mad Kat t-shirt.

"Ah, I can't; you know that," I say.

"Just wear it over your hoodie, you'll be fine."

"Yeah and dehydrate from sweating all night."

"So cut the whining and dish out? What's this about Serena Sanchez being your cousin and why didn't you tell anyone before?"

I splash water on my face. "I only found out Tuesday from Santiago; my mother's lineage has been a family secret since her birth."

"That's incredible," she says as I towel my face dry. "So your mother's related how?"

"That's the killer. My grandmother, my real grandmother, was Esmeralda Sanchez, as in 'Esmeralda's Revenge'," I stress.

"Holy shit," Michelle sighs.

"Yeah. Santiago and her were really into each other but she was compelled to get it on with my grandfather instead," I say, slipping the t-shirt over my hoodie. Peligrosa Belleza

"Una belleza peligrosa," Michelle mutters.

"We need a rabies shot up here," we hear Jeffrey calling from a distance, our signal that they are being swamped up front.

"Right, well, some Los Oscuros, two of Wingate's uncles, killed her when my mom was an infant, so she was sent to live with her father, only the official story is my grandfather's estranged wife, my supposed to be grandmother, had abandoned her."

"And they kept it a secret…"

"To protect her," I answer.

"Wow, this is huge, Jesse. I mean, really… it puts a whole different spin on things—Santiago, your involvement with everything—everything."

"Yeah, I know. I haven't digested it all myself yet." I haven't told her the strangest part, about being a shifter, and can't imagine where to start with that one, but I do plan to fill her in on the Talfar and it's importance. "There's something else we need to talk about if we get a chance. So how do I look?"

Michelle frowns, "Like you're going to die in that."

"Well, It's as good a day as any," I say, motioning us to leave.

Michelle opens the door and we both stepped out to face Bill Carter. Before I say anything, he just **raises** up his hands, "Not my place to judge," he says with a smile on his face.

———— | ————

I finally catch up with Gwen when I roll home at 12:30 in the morning. I do a quick rinse out back, twice spooking myself enough to look over my shoulder, half expecting to see Catalina. I towel off and go back to the boat. Gwen's waiting for me in the dark on the back deck. "You're still up?" I ask.

"Yeah, I can't sleep," she says.

We enter the cabin and I duck into the head and put on a fresh t-shirt and a set of light cotton khakis then rejoined her. "I think I sweated a small…" I begin, '…hey, what's… you look terrible."

Her face is beet-red and she looks tired, spacey, and to be in pain. "I think I hurt myself," she says.

"How?" I ask sitting down at the table next to her. "What happened?"

"Well, you know that exercise Mr. Santiago taught you and how it didn't work for me this morning?"

"Yeah, of course. You got so frustrated."

"I was," she said. "Well, I went back after you left and did it again."

"Did it work?"

"No, not exactly, but I had this idea of adding something that I already do." She stops dead and I wait.

"And?" I ask finally.

"I don't know, I just went someplace, kinda like a dream. It was… crazy, strange, I wasn't even aware of myself." Her face takes on a scared look and she starts to cry. "It was scary, Jesse. I didn't know where I was and didn't know if I'd find my way home again."

Oh shit! "Hey, hey, it's okay, Gwen." I say, taking her hand in mine and squeezing it lightly. "You made it, you're here now."

"But it was so scary," she repeats, "and when I woke up, I was lying on the rock in the field. I'd been gone for hours."

"So all this is sunburn?" I ask, gesturing to my own face. Gwen has never had a sunburn as far back as I can remember.

"Yeah, I, ah, was just laying there the whole time I guess," she says. "So what happened to me? That's not what happens to you is it?"

"No, totally different. I have no idea what happened, but I'm going to take a run to town to ask Santiago." I say, grabbing my jacket.

"No, no, don't," she says. "I'm okay. I waited all day for you, please don't go."

I thought about that a second, then set the jacket on it's hook. "You sure you're okay?"

"Yeah, I'm just scared to go to sleep," she says.

"Yeah, I guess you would be," I say. "Well, I'm seeing Santiago again tomorrow, I'll ask him about it."

"Okay," she says in a soft voice. She falls into a dazed stare; similar to how my dad looked when he was gapping.

"Gwen!" I say. "Hey, look at me." She does. "Don't go back there. How's your face?"

"Hurts," she says. "Mom put some stuff on it and it helped, but it still hurts."

"What d'you tell her?"

"Just that I fell asleep in the sun out in the field." The truth—with Gwen it is always the truth, or at least most of it.

"Well, whatever you do, don't mess with any of this stuff again, at least until we figure out what happened."

"No way," she says, then gives me a pleading look. "Jesse, can I stay here tonight?"

"Of course, but won't you feel better being near Mom?" I ask.

"No, I can't talk to her about what I did; she won't understand."

"Sure, no problem. I'll make up the other bunk for you."

Gwen and I talked for a short time before crashing. I told her about spending time with our cousin, Serena, and that up-shifted her mood a few notches.

"Night Gwen," I say when I kill the lights.

"Night," she says. She sounds anxious.

"Hey, you're here, you won't go back there when you fall asleep."

"Are you sure?" she asks.

"Yes," I lied. "Everything's going to be okay."

It takes a while, but the change in Gwen's breathing tells me she's finally fallen asleep. Now I have to manage the same.

Chapter 30

Vampires Among Us

Journal - Hook Point, CA.

Solzhenitsyn said something profound about the dividing line between good an evil cutting through the heart of each of us. I'd come to believe that, that we're all angels and demons, gods and monsters, and our acts of terror and benevolence are just opposites on the continuum of human potential. It made sense to me then that 'The Beast' of folk lore and religion, 'the enemy', the 'evil empire'... were only projections of the evil within us all and that we'd been looking in all the wrong places to conquer it.

> *What I've been learning these past few weeks makes me question whether it's as simple as that: maybe there are those who have embraced the dark side of their potential so tightly that they have become... Evil!*
>
> ~ *From the Journal of Jesse Benatar*

I awake with a start. Gwen is lying on the other bunk asleep, breathing slow and steady. I slip out of bed and pad over to the cabin door, quietly opening it, and go out onto the back deck. It feels like somewhere between 2:00 and 3:00 am, the dead hour—all is so still and quiet, but I can't shake a haunting, creepy feeling I have.

I do a 360 around the boat but nothing's out of place, and nothing stirs amid the dappled moonlight filtering through the trees. I turn to go back inside and the hairs stand up on the back of my neck, I turn—sixty feet away a robed figure stands alone among the trees.

I make my way over there and she moves further from the boat. "Why am I not surprised?" I say, when I reach her. "This is getting to be a regular thing with us."

"You no like?" Catalina asks. She's wearing the blue-black robe she had on the other night.

"Yeah, I do. It would be nice to meet someplace in the day is all."

She gives me a sly look. "You no like me in day; muy shy."

"No, I like you day or night, Catalina," she smiles widely at that—that wickedly enchanting smile. "Do you know anything about shifting?" I ask, quickly.

"Shifting?" she asks.

"You know, shape shifting, as in, yo soy un hombre lobo."

"Ah, si, I know. Usted es un hombre lobo," she says nodding, as if it were no big deal.

"Well, I have this problem. Señor Santiago is teaching me to control it, what to do with it." I stop and wait for her to translate.

"Si, is good," she says.

"Well I showed some to my sister, Gwen." I tell her what Santiago instructed me to do and then Gwen tried to do it herself."

"No! No good," Catalina says, looking uncomfortable. "Not for her. Must not do."

"*Yeah we found that out. Is she in any danger? Is Gwen going to be alright?*"

Catalina closes her eyes and looks to be concentrating on something, then opens them. She good, danger no more."

"*So what happened to her? She says she went some place and got lost.*"

"*Sister have gift to see, travel far. Must learn good or danger. What you tell her no good, not for her.*"

"*Travel far? See? I don't understand,*" *I say.*

"*Like this,*" *she says gesturing between us,* "*but more, much more… more far, more… tiempo.*"

"*Time? As is telling the future?*"

Catalina moves her hands in a gesture of uncertainty. "*Tal vez, ah maybe little…*"

"*Huh, wait until she hears this.*" *Catalina gives me a questioning look.* "*Nothing,*" *I say.*

She walks closer to me and speaks softly. "*Sister good. You, Jesse Benatar— you good?*" *She stops about a foot from me and looks up into my eyes. What I see there, what I feel… She seems to know the effect it's having on me because she gives me that wicked knowing look of hers.*

"*Catalina, didn't we talk about this.*"

"*Talk much not good,*" *she says leaning closer.*

"*Talk not enough even worse,*" *I say stepping back* "*Do you know what the Talfar is?*" *I ask on impulse.*

She gives me a curious look. "*Si. Talfar is heart of people. Is our way.*"

"*Well I know you've lost it, we read that in the book,*" *I say.*

Catalina smiles. "*No lost, have always.*"

"*You may think it's safe were it is, but Adam Wingate knows about it and is trying to find it.*" *At the mention of Wingate's name, Catalina lowers her eyes, turns away from me and steps into the shadows. It is as though his very name is hurtful to her.*

"*He is destroyer, all he do make bad.*" *I can't see the expression on her face as she speaks from the shadows but her voice conveys sadness.*

"*A dark one,*" *I suggest.* "*El Oscuro.*"

She turns to me and steps back into the moonlight filtering through the bows above us; it lights her face with a ghostly glow and the whites of her eyes shine with a bluish radiance. She's so beautiful and looks so—I don't know—sad and vulnerable. Once again, I'm drawn to her, compelled to reach out and touch her.

"Si!" she says softly. The expression on her face shifts from sadness to puzzlement, as though searching for words to express her thoughts. "He is dark one... make people want be with, control people—town—take life slow, like ..." She looks frustrated and makes a gesture of slashing her wrist and of blood dripping, then sucks at her wrist. "Drink life slow."

It was an odd way to talk about Wingate and the Dark Ones. If the book is right, they are the prime negative force of humanity, the counterbalance of her people, evil if you believe in that sort of thing, but she's talking about him as though her were a monster from a bad movie. "You talk about him as like he's a vampire," I tease.

Her face lights up a little. She looks at me with her large black eyes that I swear don't blink until she opens her mouth and says, "Si, he is vampire."

I feel my mouth drop open and then the corners of my lips turn up. She has to be joking... only she isn't smiling. "Seriously though," I say. Catalina continues to give me a serious, expectant look. She mustn't have known what I meant. "No such thing," I say to clarify. "Vampires aren't real."

"Si, Jesse Benatar, vampire real, pero no how you think—they more bad, mucho peor."

She looks so earnest and speaks with such conviction I feel myself believing her. I shake myself to sensibility. "So let's get real here. You're saying Adam Wingate is a blood drinking, undead, Bela Lugosi?"

She hesitates. "No conozco a 'Bela Lugosi', pero no, he live, he no dead, no drink blood."

"But..."

"I see you live...un poco...little," she says as she begins to stroll lazily into a larger patch of moonlight. "I see two vampire movie. 'Underworld', one name," she says with a distasteful look on her face. She shakes her head. "No like," she says. "No beauty."

"That's my favorite," I blurt.

She flashes me a cynical look, "Mui violento—violent no good, poison, poison all people, harm all we do," she says with a touch of delightful passion. "I see 'Twilight', she says.

"Twilight? That was so lame," I blurt.

Her lips repeat my words silently, and the she shakes her head as though dismissing what I've said. She looks up at the moon through the redwood bows and smiles. "Muy romántico."

I thought the film was a drama dump but I made a note to watch it again. Seeing the blissful look on her face as she stares up at the moon, I feel another strong urge to take hold of her. I shake it off. "So, like, this is the sort of vampire Wingate is supposed to be?" I ask.

She laughs her sinfully nice laugh. It isn't high and giggly like a lot of girls, but gentle and sonorous—bewitching. "No!" she says with humor. "Eso es lo que yo digo... such thing es, how you say ...metaphora?"

"Metaphor" I suggest.

"Si, apenas tan. Such thing es metaphor, only story de real maligno."

It makes sense—I often think of vampires, werewolves, and the Frankenstein monster as projections of our own inner demons. I read up on it once, when I was going through a dark pseudo-nihilist phase. If werewolves are real but not the things of pop-culture, why not vampires? "But don't we all have that darkness? What makes Wingate so bad?"

Her eyes turn to me and as she translates my words, a mixture of surprise and pleasure form on her face. "Si! You understand... little. All have darkness. Hold darkness close, live darkness strong... muy mal... big bad."

She paces back and forth, excitedly and I remain silent to let her catch her thoughts. I become aware of the compelling draw to her again; she is una belleza peligrosa to be sure, but what is her lure—her looks, her manner? Definitely, but it is something else as well.

She waves her hands through the air. "All have darkness. You say 'I not have', es no good, bad. You hold darkness close to heart, live darkness strong? Very bad. You see darkness inside, know darkness..." she struggles with the next words and then rattles her thoughts off in Spanish, "pero no lo abrazan... let sleep, e no feed... you live good..." Her face shows the strain of trying to find her words, and then as though frustration has won out, she rattles off in Spanish again. "Tal vez usted va a conocer la gracia de algún día." She gives me an expectant look then, seeing I am dumfounded, tries another translation. "You no feed darkness, some day ... maybe you have gracia?"

"Gracia... thankful, grateful?" I offer. She shakes her head, stands tall, then slowly stretches out her arms as though welcoming a cherished guest. She is, at

this moment the epitome of … "Grace!" I usually only think of grace as something religious relatives make you say at the dinner table.

"Si… yes! You have grace, you be at joy," she says holding both hands up as though to feel a gentle rain, "to have corazón pacífico." She says the last part with a tender smile that would have made the Mon Lisa look pissed in comparison. It's radiant in a way that has to come from…then I understood.

"A peaceful heart," I mutter.

Catalina looks at me, the soft aura of peace still lingering on her face, in her eyes. Before I have time to stop myself, I step into her space, and pull her in tight to me. 'What the fuck are you doing Jesse?' I think. "Catalina," I gasp breathlessly.

She says nothing, but lets her body press into mine as she continues to gaze sublimely up at me. 'What does it matter?' I ask myself. 'This is only a dream. A mad wonderful, crazy dream but only a dream.'

The feel of her, the smell, is consuming and I feel myself becoming excited and she knows it. Her serenity slowly transforms into something earthy and carnal, and the fires of unbridled desire brake out within me. The feeling is similar to how I felt in the Sanctuary with Lex, and just as overpowering, but it's different somehow, and even more powerful.

My mind flits between the sight of this perfect willing creature in my clutches and the images of Lex and I together, until my body takes over and I hold her even tighter and bite down into her shoulder. I want to consume her and I'm alarmed—excited by the thought of tearing flesh from her body.

Catalina relaxes even more, the muscle of her shoulder yielding to my teeth, and she lets out a groan that expresses both pleasure and pain. That is when a voice from some place deep brakes through the fire. Maybe it's only a dream, but what I choose to do or not do is still important—somehow.

I release Catalina and carefully pull her robe back to expose the muscle at the top of her shoulder; it looks discolored even in the darkness—she'll have one hell of a bruise. I cover her shoulder back up and step back. She looks perturbed, a tad anxious. "I, ah…" Catalina turns quickly, pulling herself away from me, and takes two steps. "Catalina, I'm sorry…"

"Why you like crazy girl?" she spits in her brutal accent.

"How'd you… Crazy girl? How do you know about Lex anyway?"

She turns and her eyes and teeth flash bluish in the moonlight. "You like crazy girl. No good para you," she say angrily. She catches her breath and falls silent, staring down at the ground. I'm caught between feeling bad and feeling angry and stand there with my flap zipped. "Lo siento," she says contritely. "Yo estaba perdido." She turns to walk away.

"Catalina, please," I say. "I'm sorry. Lo siento. I'm just confused, kinda messed up right now."

She looks over her shoulder and says, "Is good, Jesse Benatar," then she slips into the darkness of the foliage.

I hit myself in the head. "Catalina, wait," I call out. I dash in to the trees disappeared into and find nothing but darkness and silence. "Catalina?" I whisper.

Chapter 31

Respect

Gwen is still asleep when I wake just after 9:00. I quietly check my email, then sneak out and pad over to the house to grab a coffee and a bite. The kitchen is deserted but a note from Mom sits on the table.

Jesse / Gwen – I've stepped out to run an errand and will be back by 10 or so. There are leftovers in the fridge for breakfast or you can make something fresh. If you need me for anything, call my cell.

Gwen – Kalie called this morning to ask if you wanted to go to the festival with her. I'll be going later this morning so you can join her there if you like.

Jesse – The coffee is fresh but I turned the warmer off so it won't burn. Don't let Gwen have any though. Can't recall if you're working today. If not, please come to the festival with us.

Love – Mom.

There is an added note below that…

Your Uncle Frank just called – apologizes to you, Jesse, for disappearing yesterday ??? Said if you want to help today, he'll be at the same place.

I pour a coffee and pop it into the microwave, and then dish out a couple of plates of cold lasagna while it's heating. I grab the Sunday paper from the front porch and flip through it while I am drinking my first coffee.

Uncle Frank had canceled his subscription to the rag, but it continues to be delivered. In fact, every household in the area is being given a free month-long subscription, thanks to a generous donation by Wingate Enterprises.

Amid articles about upcoming festivities, and an editorial declaring the festival an immediate and unprecedented success, there's a front-page article about the 'controversial' decision to allow the people of the colony to set up a booth, despite ongoing investigations into the serious health concerns about their food products. It ends by declaring a hope that '…no one comes to any serious harm in the wake of this questionable decision.'

"Wingate," I swear under my breath. I think about what Catalina has said, that he is a true vampire, the sort of real human predator that the myths are built around. It fits! So many look up to him as a mover and a shaker, someone to save them from their fears and bring prosperity. That's how he gains control. He's sucking the very life out of the community, and people support him, do violence for him, and cheer him on in the process. It makes sense—Wingate is a vampire, and he is far worse than his fictional counterpart.

The kitchen door opens and Gwen steps in, looking disheveled and bleary-eyed. "Where were you?" she complains. "I woke up all alone."

"Sorry, Gee. I didn't want to disturb you. This is from Mom." I slide the note toward her and she sits at the table as I get up to get her breakfast. "Want your lasagna warm or cold?"

She scrunches up her nose and starts reading the letter. "Cold."

I set her plate down in front of her and as we eat, I tell her about the visitation with Catalina, and the reassurance that she'll be fine. "I don't feel fine," she grumbles.

"Well you will be," I say, "but she warned me that you shouldn't do whatever it was you did again. It's dangerous." Gwen gives me a feeble 'no kidding' look through bloodshot eyes. "Oh, and…" I begin, waiting until I have her full attention. "She says you have a gift, a very special gift."

Gwen reluctantly perks up a bit. "Yeah?" she softens.

"Yeah, totally yeah. It might make anything that I can do look lame."

She stares at me as I eat. Finally, she asks, "So, what is it?"

"What?"

"Oh shut up—what is it?"

"Well, as best I can make out, it's something like these night journeys I have, but way more?"

"Seriously? She said that?" she asks, three notches more excited.

"Yeah. She said you can do it much father and says something about time as well."

Gwen takes in a sharp breath, "No way."

"Way, only when I asked if she meant seeing the future she became uncertain." Gwen's eyes bug out as she stares at the ceiling. "So don't bother trying to predict winning lottery numbers just yet."

"No, no, that's not what it's about," she says, resuming her starry eyed look.

"Then what is it?" She doesn't answer. "Okay, while you decide what it is or isn't, I've gotta get ready. Santiago's picking me up at the dock in about 20 minutes."

I'd received an email from him this morning—I'm not certain I'm up for more training but I am determined to be ready at the dock for him because he's to arrive about the same time Mom's expected home.

I leave Gwen to her daydreaming and I dash out to the boat to get ready. Ten minutes later, I'm back in the kitchen. I take a cup of coffee from Gwen, mid sip, chug most of it down, then dump the rest down the sink. "Mom's orders," I say, expecting her to bitch. She doesn't; she's so lost in the world of possibilities that I could have squirted ketchup in her hair and she probably wouldn't care.

"So listen. Tell Mom you don't know where I am—because you won't—but that I'll come to the festival this afternoon."

"Okay," she says. She goes over to the coffee pot and begins to pour herself another.

"Hey, no coffee for you," I said, taking the cup from her.

"What's with you?" she complains.

"Mom's orders," I dump the coffee and put the cup in the sink. "And remember, don't mess with that..."

"Yeah, yeah, I know," she blurts peevishly.

"Okay, then, enjoy the day." As I go through the kitchen's swing door, I hear the coffee carafe slide off the warming plate. That put a smile on my face that lasted to the edge of River Road.

The traffic is the heaviest I'd seen yet, with a steady line of cars heading to town. Once at the dock, I start to pace. It's a waiting game and I hate waiting. I can't let Mom see Santiago at the dock or me leaving with him. I sit to calm down, but at 10:01, I'm pacing again.

A high drone grabs my attention and rivets it to the downstream bend in the river. To my relief, Santiago's zodiac comes cruising into view. It slows as it approaches the dock, and as though orchestrated, so does the traffic on River Road behind me. I look to see Mom slowing with her signal light on to turn into the driveway. I duck into a squat. "Perfect freaking timing," I mutter. My only hope is that Mom is to occupied driving to see me.

Santiago brings the zodiac up the dock and I make ready to leap into it for a quick getaway, but he tosses me a line. "What are you doing, I'm good to go." I say.

"Secure me," is all he says. I catch the determined look on his face and know it'll do no good to argue. Once secure, he cuts the engine and steps out on to the dock.

"Aren't we going?" I ask.

"Si, but first I must talk to your mother," he says stepping by me.

"Um, I don't think you want to do that," I suggest. He says nothing and continues up to the road. He holds out his hands like a traffic cop and the traffic in both directions slows to a stop as he crosses the road.

I sit down on the dock and think about what to do—I decide to face the unpleasantness taking part at the house. I spot Mom and Santiago talking next to her car, but have to wait for a break in the traffic. She nods and then the two of them walk together toward the back of the house. By the time I get there, it is clear they are strolling the property and talking—peacefully.

"Best leave that alone," I mutter. I sit on the steps up to the kitchen and wait.

"What's happening?" Gwen asks. I turn to see her standing on the other side of the screen door.

"I think I'm in the process of getting in shit," I say.

"Jesse, what did you do?" she asks, suddenly alarmed.

The conversation is becoming more animated now, with Mom walking faster and using her arms expressively. "Nothing, it's just... Mom asked me not to see Santiago again and I refused."

"Well, you can't, you have to learn from him," she replied in an unexpected vote of support for rebellion.

"Yeah, but she doesn't know about the other or about what he's trying to do for me," I say. "I think if she did, she'd pack us up and move us tomorrow."

"Move? Who says we're moving?" Gwen asks.

Mom raises her voice but they are over by the boat and I can't tell if it is in anger or distress. I stand and call to her. "Mom?" She doesn't react, but Santiago cast me a 'back off' glance. By now, Gwen's standing next to me.

Mom sat herself down on the steps to the Therion's deck—she's crying. "Mom!" I shout. I run towards the two of them, but she catches sight of me and waves me back. She stands and the two of them make their way toward the house.

"Are you okay Mom?" Gwen asks as they come within conversation distance. She's still conversing quietly with Santiago but looks up and nods.

Santiago faces my mother and bows slightly. "Con las bendiciones, Señora Sanchez," then says, "Time to go," as he walks past me.

I don't move. "Mom?"

She looks up at me and nods, "Go, Jesse," she says with barely contained emotion.

"Mom?" I persist.

"Just go," she says. "We'll talk about this later." There is an edge to her voice—her distress is shifting to anger.

"Mom, if you..."

"Go!" she says. It's anger now, and even Gwen is taken back.

When Santiago and I are out on the river at speed, I break the silence that has separated us since we left the dock. "So what the hell was that about back there," I ask.

He keeps his eyes on the river and acts as though he hasn't heard my question. I am coming to know that Santiago answers questions in his own sweet time—I wait. "Respect," he finally says. I try pumping him for more but he tells me I'm old enough to figure that out for myself.

I ponder this for a nano-second, but have too much to talk to him about. "So Gwen tried some of those exercises you gave me." He frowns but keeps his eyes on the river. "It didn't work for her but she mixed it with a few other things she does…"

I'm cut off by Santiago throttling down the zodiac. He puts the engine in neutral and lets it idle, mid-river, then turns and faces me. "What sort of things?" he asks.

"I don't know, the sort of things she's into," I say.

"I told you what you were doing was powerful and not to be trifled with," he says angrily.

"Yeah, but…"

"And so you decided to share it with your little sister?"

"She's not that little," I protest. "She knows a lot more about this stuff than I do—she has a real knack for it."

"What happened?" he demands.

I told him exactly what Gwen told me and he looks deeply dismayed. He sits in silent contemplation as the zodiac drifts with the current. "Catalina Ruiz says she is going to be alright, though."

"Señorita Ruiz?" he asks.

"Yeah, I had another visit from her last night." Saying that, and seeing the puzzled look on his face, I realize I haven't talked to him much about her visitations. I tell him about the last two visits from Catalina, minus the seductive parts, that Catalina said Gwen will be okay, and that she has a powerful gift herself, something related to spirit travel but more somehow."

"Prescience," Santiago mutters.

"What?"

"Have you warned her not to do anything so foolish again?" he asks.

"Yeah, big time. I even shared with her what Catalina told me— about the dangers and her gift."

Santiago thinks about this a moment, then turns back to the controls of the Zodiac and kicks it into gear. "Tell me about these visits from Señorita Ruiz."

Chapter 32

Resistance Softens

I watch the zodiac disappear around the bend on its way back to town, then stand on the dock and stare in to the river. So damn much to absorb, my head's numb and my body aches—everywhere. The training was different this time, an exploration of speed and endurance, and I hadn't been battered up much other than when I took a tumble in the forest. The long soak in the cold stream Santiago had me endure at the end had been both shock and bliss.

I wander up to the house and find it empty. I used to love empty—it meant peace. Now it just leaves me with a sad, hollow feeling. I make my way over to the Therion to suit up for town. The moment I strip off, my fatigue hits me like a landside and I'm compelled to roll into my bunk. "Just one minute, that's all," I promise.

I sink into the mattress and my whole body applauds. I'm so freaking tired, sore, and hungry—5000 calories or more is what he said—a lot to use up in a few hours.

I start to run over the lessons in my head, the dozens of things he's told me as he pushed me harder than I thought possible. I felt like Luke Skywalker being trained by Yoda, only my Yoda was one scary dude when displeased. He reminds me of the Zen Masters I read about, only he never hits me with a stick when I stray from the path—he assails me with his eyes and words—I would have preferred the stick.

I feel myself sliding down the slope, slipping fast, I struggle to resist it, but my body wins out. My last thoughts are of our conversation about the Talfar, and his warning to stay clear of Wingate and anything or anyone associated with him. Then all is darkness.

When I wake, it's dark. Pulling the tangled sheet off my face only lightens things a little. My body feels heavy, but I manage to lift my face off the mattress enough to glance at the clock. "Huh!" 7:57—I slept for over 5 hours.

I roll out of bed, dress, turn on my cell, and call Mom right away. "Hey it's me."

"Jesse, where are you?" she asks. There's an edge of anxiety in her voice.

"I'm at home. I crashed when I got back and just woke up," I say.

"Are you all right?"

"Yes. I'm fine, Mom, great. How about you—you okay?" is the best conversation I can manage.

"I'm fine Jesse. I didn't hear from you."

"Yeah, I'm sorry Mom, I hadn't intended to sleep all afternoon, it just happened."

"I know, Sweetheart. Señor Santiago said you'd probably sleep for a few hours."

"When did you talk to him?" I ask.

"He came and talked to me after he dropped you off."

"Mom, don't worry. What he's teaching me will keep me safe," I assured her. "I'm really learning some things that… well, I know I've taken some stupid chances before but, I don't know, I think that's all changing."

"We can talk about that later, Jesse. Have you eaten?"

"No," I say.

"You must be starving, Are you coming to town?"

"Yeah, I was hoping to."

"Meet me down at the colony exhibit. I'll have a meal ready for you."

"Great, I'll be there in about 15 minutes—oh, and Mom?"

"Yes?"

"You're the best. I really mean the best." Silence. "I love you."

"I love you too Sweetheart."

I hang up, dress, and quickly check my email. I have notes from Michelle, Jeffrey, Christine, Pete, and even Miranda, commenting or asking questions about my connection with the colony. I flag them to be answered later and then send a quick response to Tony to apologize for not getting back to him on any of his seven earlier emails. I promise to fill him in soon. Then, as I'm checking off a bunch of junk mail for deletion, I catch sight of a tag line among them—*This is Isa.*

"He's coming now, coming himself, and you're in danger. If I say much more and he finds out, I don't know what he'll do. Please be careful, and please, please don't respond to this. I'll try to get away long enough to call you. Isa."

"Call me? Jeez, Isa, what am I suppose to do with this?" I close down my laptop and check the battery on my cell. It is charged enough to leave on at least until I get back home.

The ride into town has a surreal feel; the serenity of the twilight sky through boughs of the trees contrasts against the impatient intensity of the white snake of headlights that fills the oncoming lane. Things are winding down for the night in town, giving it a tired and sleepy feel, and I'm able to find a spot close to the exhibit to park my bike.

No one is standing at the exhibit, and I don't recognize any of the colonists tending to the dwindling crowd at the booths. I wander behind the setup and spot Mom standing by the old yellow pickup that's parked there. She's talking to three older women, one of whom is Señora Marianna Sanchez.

She spots me as well and, rather than invite me to join them, motions me toward the picnic table were a large foil covered plate sits. Beneath the foil, I find a hot meal of roasted honey-cinnamon sweet potatoes, a serving of wild-rice, sliced avocado and tomatoes, and a couple of char broiled pork chops. The chops are a little surprising because Mom isn't big on eating meat, but they're exactly what my body seems to crave. I dig in like a hungry... wolf.

I glance up between mouthfuls to see all four women watching me eat as they talk. Mom looks uneasy, two of the women smile, but Señora Marianna Sanchez glowers. I feel a sudden wave of self-consciousness and try to recall how I'd been eating. *Shit! I was probably eating like a pig.*

Their conversation ends and the three women disappear as Mom strolls over to the bench and sits down. "So what was that about?" I ask, digging back into the food.

"How's your dinner?" she asks.

"Totally amazing," I say as I wolf down another chunk of meat. She gives me a curious look and I become self-conscious again. "So what's with the pork chops anyway? I mean, it's exactly what I was craving but you're not into the whole meat thing."

"Well, you can thank Señor Santiago. He suggested them," she replies.

"Huh! So what did you two talk about anyway?"

She shakes her head just perceptibly, as though telling herself not to talk about it. She looks down at the tabletop and knits her brow. "Just what we had to," was all she says.

"Mom?"

"Jesse," she urges uncomfortably, "I know about what's happening with you. It is one of the things the elders warned me about when I visited them at your age. They knew, if I had a son, that he might have that ability. It's one of the reasons I hesitated coming back here."

"How could they know that, I wasn't even born yet?"

She smiled gently and shrugs. "The ability runs strong in some of their families."

"Don't forget they're your people too Mom," I say.

"No, Jesse..."

"Yes!" I insist. "I saw you standing over there talking to them— you're one of them. Whether they want to accept it or not, you're a part of them and none of their fracked up rules can change that." Mom turns her head away and raises a hand to hide her mouth; she's smiling or about to cry, or maybe both. "Mom, I'm..."

"You reminded me so much of him just then," she says, turning emotional filled eyes back to me.

"Who?" She says nothing in reply. "Oh, no way." There it is, my worse nightmare—I remind Mom of Fuckhead.

"He was always so determined, never let anything get in his way, once he set his mind to it," she says. "It was one of the things I loved about your father."

I try to remind myself that this was not just my mother but a grieving widow as well, and harsh words about the man she lost have no place here. "Yeah," was all I could muster.

"Your father was a lot of things, Jesse, and many of them were good; I hope you'll see that some day."

I stare at my plate. "Why did you choose him?" I ask before I can stop myself. "I mean, were you aware of his other side? Did you... sorry, don't answer that."

"I saw his dark side, Jesse. He'd always had it and I s?
fought so hard against it. I thought I could help him with th'
he saw, things he did in that war... he lost the fight. It had been ...
foolish fantasy that lead me to choose him, but I'm not sorry for it." She
catches some expression on my face because she adds, "You and Gwen
would never have been born were it not for your father."

What do you say to that? 'Gee, Mom, wish you'd picked better for
yourself; I know someone else would have been born instead of me, but
hey, I'd have preferred that'? It was new on me that Dad had always had
a dark side but it made sense; I've know a lot of vets with PTSD and
none of them were anything like my dad. Now I realized that his PTSD
just made what he'd always struggled with, worse.

"Eat up, Jesse, your dinner's getting cold," she says.

I stare at the remaining food on my plate, and despite the emptiness
in my belly, I've lost my appetite. "I remember when Dad went out that
Christmas morning to buy batteries for those games you bought Gwen
and I. He was gone over two hours and never complained about it." It
was a small thing, perhaps, but it was an act of a father trying to make
his kids happy.

Mom smiles. "He did a lot of things like that." Her face saddens.
"Not so much after the second gulf war started."

Mom's phone rings. "Hello?" she answers... "Where are you now?
... Who's there? ... Well... How will you get home? ... Well, okay, but
if anything changes, you call me right away.... There's no... Well how
are you calling me now? ... Alright, Sweetie, enjoy yourself and stay
safe."

"Gwen?"

Mom nods. "She wants to know if she can stay with her cousin
Serena for the night."

"What? Where?"

"At the colony?"

"No way, they allow that? How'd she get to be there anyway?"

Mom nods. "They occasionally allow visitors. Señora Marianna
Sanchez suggested that she go along when your Uncle Frank drove
Serena and her mother back to the colony."

"So, does that mean Uncle Frank is staying there too?

"Perhaps, or he's planning to drive back over there in the morning."

"Huh! Go Uncle Frank," I mumble.

"What was that?" Mom asks.

"Oh, nothing, but now that we're on the topic of Gwen, did the elders tell you anything about her, or what she might be gifted or cursed with?"

She doesn't answer that right away. "I was told about a few possibilities," she says finally. "It's one of the reasons that I let her explore all the things she's been drawn to over the years."

"Huh!" I am taken back by the realization that she's kept that knowledge to herself, watching, waiting, helping us along as best she could. "Well, she has a gift, Mom. I don't know what it is exactly but it's supposed to be special." Mom looks down at a piece of waste paper teasing her foot in the gentle evening breeze. "And so do you," I add.

She looks at me questioningly, then gives me a wry smile. "No, Jesse, I don't. I hoped I had at one time, back when I was your age; when I first learned of such things I wanted to be special in some way."

"But... you are!" I say incredulously. *Doesn't she see it?*

She shakes her head. "I gave up such ideas when I moved away. It's no longer something I want, Jesse. I just want you and your sister to be safe and happy."

"We will be Mom, we are, but that doesn't mean you don't have your own life to live, your own dreams to fulfill."

One of the two older women Mom had been talking to poked her head out from behind the booth's back curtain. "Perdon, Señora, puede usted por favor nos ayude aquí?"

"Si, por supuesto," Mom replies. She turns back to me. "Jesse, there is so much we need to talk about." I nod. "Try not to get home too late tonight."

"Okay, Mom."

She stands from the table. "Finish your dinner," she says and begins to walk away.

I look down at my plate. "Mom!" I call. She stops and faces me. "I love you."

She gives me that smile of hers. "I love you too, Jesse."

Chapter 33

Alley Chat

The streets are busy for a late Sunday night; people wander about looking for a final entertainment fix or bite to eat. I make my way towards The Kat, which I know is just closing. I think about going in to help out, but when I see Lex wiping down tables, I think better of it.

I stand away from the widow and watch her a while; I don't know what it is about her, I hate complications and drama and Lex has proven far too much or both, but watching her there—I want to be with her.

"Jesse Benatar?" I hear a girl's voice ask. I turn to see the Mei Ling standing about six feet away. "We can talk?"

"Mei! Yes, of course." I look around. "Here?"

She shakes her head and gestures toward the side street. "It is not good here. Can you meet me behind this place?"

"What The Kat, in the alley? Yeah, sure." She nods and makes an about face and walks down the street and makes a turn down the first side street. I turn to take one more look at Lex—she's gone.

The back of The Kat is dark and quiet, and for two seconds I think I've blundered into a trap. Then Mei Ling moves quietly into view from the alley. In the light of the small dim bulb above the alcove, she looks austere and intimidating.

"Hey," I say. She says nothing in return, only walks up to me and stops about four feet away. "I want to thank you for what you did the other day, saving me from your brother."

That seems to surprise her. "You were aware?"

"Barely. The last thing I remember was you calling your brother's name." She looks uncomfortable with that. "So thank you," I repeat.

She nods. "My brother is dangerous." Her eyes convey anxiety and hesitation. "He is not like other people, he is different," she says at last.

"I know," I say.

"No, no you don't, he's…"

"I know," I repeat. "I know what he is, what he does."

She looks searchingly into my eyes and sees something that convinces her. "Then if you know, you must leave here."

"Leave here, leave Hook Point? Why? I can't just leave—this is my home."

"You do not understand. Something is going to happen here, happen soon," she says anxiously.

"What? What's going to happen?"

"I do not know. I only know that my brother has been very busy preparing for something, and I overheard some of his conversations on the phone. I think he and the men he works with plan to hurt a lot of people, and I heard your name mentioned many times."

"Anyone else, my mom, my sister?"

"No names that I can remember."

"So why are you telling me this?"

"Because I love my mother and father and it will hurt them terribly if my brother does this," she says.

That makes no sense to me; if what she's saying is true, then even if I do get out of town for a while, he'll still hurt others. "Okay, so what's the real reason?" She searches my face with darting eyes. "Mei, I don't know what you're holding back but if you want us to get anywhere here, you need to trust me a little."

She looks down at the ground and turns her back to me. "I have dreams," she says. "I see things sometimes… and sometimes they come true… sometimes."

"Prescience?" I think aloud.

She turns and faces me. "You believe me?"

"Mei, prophetic dreams are not the strangest thing I've had to accept this summer."

"Then please accept that you must leave here, for a time," she says with heartfelt concern.

"What will happen if I don't?" Mei opens her mouth but her eyes do all the talking—something terrible will happen. "That bad?" I ask. She nods. "To me?" I ask.

She shrugs. "Maybe."

"To your mother, then?"

"I don't know," she says agitated. "All I know is that if you face my brother again, something terrible is going to happen."

Right away, I think of my mother. Will she lose her son after losing her husband? "Mei, will you be willing to talk to someone I know?"

She shakes her head. "No. Talking now is already too dangerous. If my brother finds out I spoke to you he will become angry and reckless, and Mr. Wingate might do something to punish my parents as well."

"What? Mei, that sounds like something out of the third world."

"No, it is the world I live in, his world."

What she says, and the fearful look in her eyes, makes me angry. I imagine Adam Wingate and the rest of the Los Oscuros holding the lives of Mei Ling and countless others in their hands. This is true terrorism and it is happening here and now—so much for Homeland Security.

"Frack!" I blurt. I feel my wave of anger transform into a single-point focus of mind, body, and instinct as Santiago has taught me to do. I let it drain from me as fast as it's building, and soon the wave passes. The whole thing only lasted maybe three or four seconds, but when I look at Mei, it's obvious she noticed something; she stares at me as though I just grew two heads.

"Mei, I…"

"You! You too," she says. "I saw…"

"You saw that? How?" Then I remember that some people are able to see the shift in the aura. "Mei, it's okay, I'm not like your brother."

"Yes, you are," she says taking a step back.

"Damn it, Mei, I'm not, believe me I'm not. If anything I'm exactly the opposite of your brother, or might be anyway."

"This must be why he wants you out of the way," she says, still not taking her eyes from me.

"Mei, I'm no threat to your brother, believe me…"

"No, not my brother—Mr. Wingate wants you out of the way."

"Wingate? Why?"

"I do not know, I'm sorry."

"Mei, will you please come with me and talk to my friend and tell him this. His name is Carlos Santiago and he's…"

"Santiago," she blurts. "That is another name that is mentioned. I think Mr. Wingate has something special planned for him."

"Mei, you have to come with me to tell him that."

"No, I'm sorry," she says. "Please don't tell anyone what I've told you."

With that, she turns and runs back up the alley. I call the number Santiago gave me to make a secure, scrambled call to him. I fill him in on what Mei has told me; his reaction is simply to remind me to stay away from Bolin and to meet him at his boat Wednesday morning. "Jeez, you're welcome," I say, closing the phone.

"What are you doing here?" a familiar voice asks.

I turn to see Lex standing in the doorway next to the loading bay. She is holding a sack of trash. "Oh, I am just hanging out."

"Really?" she asks doubtfully.

"Yeah, no, well actually I am just back here having a clandestine talk with someone who told me that Wingate has it in for me."

"Now that I believe," she says as she carries the sack over to the trash bins. "You could have half the town gunning for you without even trying."

"Okay, I guess I deserve that."

"You do," she says lifting the lid and dropping in the sack. Rather than march back into the back of The Kat, she stands by the trash bin and folds her arms.

"How've you been, Lex?"

"Peaches," she says sharply.

"Lex, I…"

"…am a jerk, a dick, an asshole?"

"Sure, if that's what makes you happy," I say.

"What do you care what makes me happy?"

"Will you just shut up and get over yourself for a minute." Lex looks as though I slapped her across the face. Her features shift, her eyes dart, and I expect her to go ballistic.

"Fine, okay," she says. Rather than bolt, she simply stares at me.

I have no idea where to start, so I just jump in. "Everyone is pissed off at me, telling me how irresponsible I am being with you." Lex doesn't react to that. "I hated the secrecy of it all and when that was broken, it just got worse."

"Glad I am such a pain to you," she says in a hurt way.

"You are supposed to shut up. I thought you said you'd shut up." She makes a wide-eyed gesture of zipping her mouth closed. "I ended up not caring as much about that as about you." I take a step closer to her, and she tenses. "You and your crazy messed up ways got to me Lex, and I was willing to put everything on the line."

"But? There's always a but."

"But when I saw your reaction that last night we were together, after we made out so... violently—Lex, I thought I'd really hurt you, and then what the others had said, I figured they were right after all."

"So you decided to ditch me," she says.

"Well, I wouldn't put it that way." She stares at me, daring me to put it another way. "I decided I wasn't good for you."

"Now there's something true," she mutters.

"Lex, I'm..."

"Oh don't go saying you're sorry again. I've heard that way too much in my life." Lex turns and walks three steps, then turns back. "It's all for best anyway, Colorado. I must have been off my gourd in the first place, I mean, you're seriously not my type anyway, so thank you for ending it." With that, she storms back into the back of The Kat and slams the door.

: **34**

Shark Bait

The talk I have with Mom that night is nothing short of profound. Other than the details of my relationship with Lex and the visitations from Catalina, I don't hold much back. Mom, in turn, tells me about the visits to the colony an a teen, and the things she'd been told by the elders. I have a feeling that she's holding back a few things, but that's fair enough seeing that I've not been completely open. When we're done, it is near 1:00 am and we're both bushed.

Other than Gwen coming home with enviable tales about her stay at the colony and what she did with Serena and a few other cousins she'd met, not much happened over the next two days. Even my sleep was devoid of dreams and visitations by Catalina.

The horde at the Festival is considerably less than it was on the weekend but it's still hard to get around. I see a good number of kids around my age at The Kat and elsewhere in town, and I begin recognizing who the locals are. For the most part, they seem normal enough, meaning dull, and I feel fortunate that I hooked up with the tribe as quickly as I did.

I arrive at Santiago's boat at just past 9:00 am Wednesday morning. I toss my pack into the zodiac, jump aboard, and we're off, only this time we don't head up river; we make for open water.

The sun's dazzling in the east and the sky above is the richest blue I've seen in years, but miles off shore, a band of gray-white fog stands like the wall of a massive fortress. It sits, waiting, for the sun to warm the land and draw it in from offshore. When it does the 70's air on shore will drop to a damp 55 degrees in seconds.

As we pass through the breakwater, I can hear the noise from the beach and carnival to the north, but when we clear the water traffic, it all disappears from my mind. Santiago points the prowl of the zodiac for the wall of fog and opens the engine full.

"Do you trust me," he shouts above the roaring engine and wind.

"No," I shout back.

He seems amused by that. "Do you trust yourself?" he shouts.

"Most of the time," I shout back.

"Today, you must learn to do both, but mostly you must learn to trust yourself."

That sounds ominous enough, but when we enter the fog bank—the bone chilling air and muted light—an oppressive anxiety hits home. Santiago tosses a towel over the gimbaled compass and then goes through a series of wild and unpredictable maneuvers. Like a compass, I always seem to know which way is north, but after a few minutes of that, I've completely lost my bearings.

Santiago cuts the engine. "Okay, strip," he says flatly.

"What?"

"Strip. You'll not want to swim in those clothes."

I look at the gently rolling water around us. It is slate gray in the fog, and looks cold and forbidding. "Yeah, I don't think so."

"You're afraid," he suggests.

"Yes, I am most definitely afraid."

"Good," he says, lighting one of his cigarillos.

"Look, I'm not a strong swimmer to start with and we're out in the middle of nowhere. If you lose sight of me in the fog, which is pretty damn likely, I'll drown."

Santiago leans back against his seat and gives me an inscrutable look. "Would you?" he finally asks.

"Well, yeah, of course. It's miles back to shore and I'm good for maybe half a mile if I'm lucky."

"Are you?" he asks. He stares at me, but there is nothing intimidating in it; he's evaluating.

"You're not really serious?" I ask.

The water's colder than I imagine. The plunge in would have taken my breath away had I not been holding onto it for dear life. Sensations of cold scream from every square inch of my skin and a part of my mind reacts with panic. When I bob to the surface, I look to see Santiago smiling down at me.

"You're one mean old man," I gasp at him.

He nods and smiles wider. "Si," he says.

"Ugh," I blurt. "Now what?"

"Now you learn," he says. He starts the zodiac's water-jet engine and lets is settle to a low purr. It triggers a surge of anxiety and I impulsively take a stroke toward the boat. "Is the light on the transponder still blinking?" he asks.

I glance at the small rectangular box secured to my right wrist. A small green LED blinks slowly in response to the signal sent out by the transceiver on the boat. "Yeah," I reply. By then, the zodiac is pulling away. "Hey!" I take a few strokes toward it, only to realize how futile it is. If Santiago doesn't want me in the boat, there's nothing I'd be able to do about it. "So what am I supposed to do, swim after you?"

"No!" he shouts back. "Swim back." With that he guns the engine and all traces of him disappear in to the fog before I finished cursing him out.

 I gulp in a mouthful of water and cough it out; anxiety sweeps over me, causing me to stiffen and breathe shallow, and that makes it difficult to keep my head above water. *Shit, shit, shit, what's he thinking? I can't do this; I'll never make it. I don't even know which way to swim.*

A barrage of thoughts scream through my mind at warp speed. "Santiago!" I shout. "Santiago," *Gulp—cough—cough.* "Santiago!" Nothing but the sound of my own flailing arms on the water break the deathly gray silence. Even the engine noise has died.

Slow down, fucking slow down. He's not going to let you die out here. I take in a full breath of air and lean back, using slow movements of my arms and legs to keep me floating on my back. I reassure myself that Santiago is sitting nearby in the fog, tracking me with his transceiver.

I'm comforted by the image of him sitting back, smoking his little cigar, and smiling sadistically at the small blip on the screen that tells him exactly where I am. "You can do this man. He's not going to make you swim all the way," I say to myself, but even as I say it, doubt creeps into my mind. "Yeah, you would you bastard."

I look around to get my bearings. If I can only make it out of the oppressive gray of the fog, I'll be able to see where I'm going, maybe even attract the attention of another boat. On the other hand, I know that the sight of land so far away could cause a surge of panic and that could kill me. It's just then that I notice the light on the transponder has stopped blinking.

"Fuck!" I don't know if he's shut off the transceiver or if the transponder has malfunctioned, but either way, I'm on my own and no one, not even Santiago knows where I am. "Santiago!" Nothing but the austere silence of the sea answers me. "Santiago!"

In a surge of panic, I start swimming madly, blindly, even while a part of me knows it's a deadly mistake. After 10 or 15 strokes, I'm breathless and have to stop. *Get a grip! Get a grip! Get a grip!* I force myself back onto my back and to take long slow breaths. I stare up at the gray ceiling of mist and breathe, just breathe. I focus on the sensation of the cold water against my skin and breathe. My mind slows and what emerges from the chaos is one word—trust.

If this is about learning trust, did it mean I have to trust Santiago not to abandon me, to find me before I drown? Do I have to trust myself to get back on my own? Then it dawns on me—I have to begin trusting myself. I look around.

The sea is gentle; 2-foot rollers, stretched out a good distance apart, pass around me with clockwork regularity, punctuated every dozen or so by a larger set of three waves, maybe 3 to 4 feet at most. The fog above drifts around me. Under different circumstances, I would find it all serene, a sought after experience.

I begin to feel chilled and have to start moving, but which way? Then logic kicks in—the way the waves are heading—toward shore.

I begin a slow, easy breaststroke. Though slow, I know I can keep it up for some time, and when I tire, I can roll over on my back and gently kick towards shore. I might not make it all the way, but if I get out of this fog, someone, perhaps even Santiago, might spot me and pick me up.

As I swim, I keep my mind focused on one thing, the next stroke, the next breath, and the feel of the water. Movement is my meditation, and every time a thought drifts into my mind—Mom identifying my drowned body, a great white circling slowly beneath me, preparing to strike—I shift my mind back to the next stroke. In this solitary focus, I find a strange peace, a comfort in the now, that is perfect and unshakable—I have found what I can truly trust.

I lose track of time, and there are brief moments when I feel a shimmer of joy pass over me. I grasp at it the first few times, but find that it quickly disappears and that leads to despair. I recall what Max told me—grasping and evading are the roots of all human suffering. I never really understood that until just now.

I keep my mind centered on the task, the sensations, and the breath. After an indiscernible time, the shroud of fog seems to grow brighter, thinner, and after a while longer, the disk of the sun shines through the gray overhead.

I'm careful to not get excited, to remain on task, but when the gray gives way to a bluish haze and then blue sky, I can't suppress my elation. I roll over on my back and rest, gazing up at the indistinct blue-gray boundary I just crossed over. I felt... amazing... whole.

It's more than a good feeling after having achieved something—it's a sense of mastery. I don't fool myself into thinking I attained mastery over the sea—no human ever has or will do that—but I have, on this occasion, mastered my fear and the instinctive impulses that would have killed me. It's a sweet feeling.

I still have a long way to go, at least four miles, and I know I might still succumb to the task on my own, but I feel blissfully detached from the concern and give myself a rest. When I'm done, I roll back over on my stomach and there, floating just outside the fog bank, about 50 yards distance, sits the zodiac. Santiago is watching me and I swear the old shit is smiling. Odder still, I feel a little disappointed that I'll not get to face the task alone.

Turns out, I didn't have to swim in after all. Santiago motors over to me and tosses over an oversize knotted rope for me to pull myself aboard. When I flop onto the floor, I lay still a moment, then sit up. Santiago hands me a mug of hot coffee. It's only when I drink greedily of it that I realize I'm chilled to the bone.

"How long?" I ask.

"Thirty seven minutes," he replies.

"Jeez," I mutter. It felt a lot longer, so much in so little time. "Well, your tracking system crapped out. Did you even think about that possibility?" I felt my irritation smothering my serenity.

"It didn't fail," he said. He leans back to let me glance at the tracking screen. There I am, blinking red, dead center.

I look at the unit on my wrist—the light is dead. "You rigged it." I accuse him. "Man, you don't miss a trick."

"If you think I am sitting in the fog watching over you, you might have just floated around and waited for me to get bored."

I smiled. "I thought about it."

"Si."

Chapter 35

The Good Side of Bad

I arrive at The Kat for work at 1:00. I expected to be dead exhausted, but the swim spooled me up higher than I can remember being in a long time. I feel on top of the world, the master of my own fate, and ready for anything that might come my way. When I step into the back of The Kat from the alley, my confidence slips a few notches—Lex is standing there with a look on her face that I can't read.

"Lex, you're off today!" I say stupidly.

"Jesse…" she begins awkwardly.

The door from the kitchen bursts open. "Jesse," Michelle says. "Where have you been?" She sounds agitated but looks concerned.

"Ah, swimming. What's up, I'm not supposed to get here until now. I'm even two minutes early."

"Your mother called here about an hour ago looking for you," she says striding up to me. She's definitely flustered.

Fuck! "What did she want?" I ask.

"Something happened," she blurts, "but I think everything's okay."

Jesus fuck! "When? What happened?" I ask mindlessly as I pull out my phone and turn it on. *Why is this off?* I give her a questioning stare as I listen to the phone ringing on the other end.

"It's Gwen," Michelle says—my stomach turns over.

"Jesse, where have you been, I've been trying to get a hold of you," Mom says.

"What happened? Where's Gwen's?" I blurt. My voice sounds odd—shaky and unfamiliar.

"She's fine, she's shaken up a little but she's here in the living room, watching Harry Potter."

A wave of relief washes over me. Harry Potter movies are Gwen's great escape. Whenever she's stressed, she watches one or two and it always brings her out of it. "What happened?"

"I'd best let you talk to her, hold on," Mom says. A moment later, Gwen's voice comes on, She sounds as though she's ten again. *"Hi,"* is all she says.

"Gwen, what happened?" There's a pause.

"I drowned," she says. It sounds like she's starting to cry.

"It's okay, Gee, you're okay. Just look at the TV screen and tell me what happened," I say.

"Kalie talked me into trying surfing with her this morning," she begins. I pictured what likely happened—Gwen's a lousy swimmer. *"The beach was so crowded and there were too many people out trying to surf."* I picture that in my mind as she speaks wall-to-wall surfers with no place to go but down. *"We were okay for a while and I really got used to just sitting on the board, floating around, but then these large waves came in and we tried to catch them."* She goes silent.

"What happened then?" I ask, though I'm certain I know.

"My board caught the wave but I was too scared to stand up and just hung on, but then the board flipped and I was pushed down by the wave." Pause. *"When I came to the surface another board from somewhere hit me in the back of the head."* Bingo!

"And then…"

"Nothing," she says. Then her voice cracks and is strained with emotion. *"Then I drowned, everything went black. Next thing I know I was lying on someone's board and someone was giving me CPR."*

"How are your lungs, do they hurt?" I suspect that Gwen didn't drown but had only passed out.

"No, but my head still hurts," she says.

"The hospital?"

"Yeah, I went and mom's friend checked me over. It wasn't a bad bump and he thinks I was just stunned, but it still hurts."

"I am just glad you're okay. Next time you want to try surfing, let me know."

"What, so we can drown together, I've seen you trying to surf."

That brought a smile to me. She's right—I suck at it. "Yeah, exactly. Saves on the funeral expenses." That gets a reluctant snicker out of her. "So you're okay now?" I ask.

"Yeah, I'm okay," there's another pause. *"I just keep thinking about what might have happened if I hadn't been pulled out of the water when I was."*

"Well don't think about that. It didn't happen so don't create it in your head. We just have someone to thank for being there."

"Yeah, that's the part I didn't tell you about yet."

"What?"

"It was Wade Wingate." The world stops for a moment as I drift into the Twilight Zone. *"Jesse?"*

"Ah, Yeah, I'm here. Um, you sure, I mean, you sure it was Wingate? Maybe it was someone who looks like him." I suggested, hoping.

"No, I didn't even know what he looked like until I saw him looking down at me."

"Then how do you…"

"The lifeguard called him by name, then other people started talking to him. It was him."

"Jeez." Of all the people to save my kid sister, it had to be him.

"I know," Gwen says, sounding as confused as I am. *"I guess it goes to show you."*

"Yeah." I don't know what it shows me but it complicates my impression of Wade; it's easier to think of him as just plain bad. "So you're okay then?"

"Yeah, I'm okay. It was scary, but I'm okay."

"Want me to bring you anything home?"

There is a pause, then Gwen says, "Well, one of those sticky buns would be nice."

"Done. I'll see you when I get home. Does mom want to talk to me?" I hear mumbling on the line.

"No," Gwen says at last. *"She just says to keep your phone on and call if you're going to be late."*

"Right!" I am about the close the connection… "Oh, Gwen?"

"Yeah?"

Now it was my turn to be silent. "Ah, I'm really glad you're okay."

"I love you too, Jesse," she says, and then hangs up.

I look up to see Michelle staring at me wide eyed and see Lex disappearing through the kitchen door. "Can you believe it?" Michelle says. "I guess Wade's not a total creep."

"Well, you dated him so I guess that's true."

"Well I didn't really date him… not really, but seriously though; after all that's been happening and what his father's involved with."

"I know, right?" I say.

"So you want me to take your shift?" she asks.

"Ah, no I'm good. You've been working like mad as it is. Besides, I'm only on until 7:00." I look toward the door that leads to The Kat's front end, and then lower my voice. "What's Lex doing here? I thought she was off?"

"Jeffrey called in," she says.

"He sick?"

"No, just had an unexpected visitor from the city last night," she says knowingly.

"Visitor? Like who?" Michelle smiles and raises her eyebrows. "Really, he has, like, a guy friend?"

She nods her head and lifts her eyes to the ceiling. "Well, sort of. Nothing steady, just someone he's involved with sometimes."

That got me thinking. "So what's this guy like? I mean…"

"Jesse, are you jealous?" she asks with a huge smile.

"What?" I blurt. "No, nothing like… hell no. Jeffrey's a nice guy is all, don't want to see him hooking up with some loser."

"Well, my, my, you do have a few surprises up your sleeve Mr. Benatar." Michelle turns to leave, then turns back. "Hey, I'd like to drive out to see your sister. You think she's up for it?"

"Hell yeah, if you don't mind watching Harry Potter with her. She does that when she's upset."

"Not at all. So what does she want you to bring home to her?"

"Oh, a sticky bun. We still have some, don't we?" I ask.

"Yeah, a few, but they're usually gone by three. I'll take a few out for her, and I'll tell her I'm hand delivering them for her doting brother."

"That'll be great, except for the doting part."

Michelle leaves with two of the largest, gooiest sticky buns remaining, and I get to work. With Jeffrey gone, Lex and I have to share the load of helping Hilda up front, Bill in the kitchen, and bussing tables. It's tense for a few hours and that doesn't go unnoticed by Hilda and Bill.

"The tension between you and Alexis is thicker than my stew," Bill says at one point. "Not my place to interfere, but taking a few minutes to sort things out might make your day go by a little more pleasantly."

A few minutes, try a few years. I think. Then later, Hilda leans close to me and says, "You know, waiting on a dirty diaper isn't usually a good idea."

"Um… what?"

She is a short woman with a large but gentle presence, and when she shoots me a conspiratorial look with her light blue eyes, it arrests my attention. "It doesn't get any better, Jesse, just messier and tougher to deal with when you get around it."

Just when I think she's finally lost her marbles over the constant stream of customers, she flicks her eyes toward Lex as she brings in another tray of cups and plates. When I look back to Hilda, she's already helping another customer.

It isn't for another hour until I can pull Lex aside. "Hey, can we talk later?"

She gives me a questioning look. "Yeah, I guess," she says. Her voice is low and soft and her gray eyes dart between the floor and my own.

"Good," I feel compelled to say more, a lot more, and we both seem to feel the awkwardness of the moment. "Ah, how about right after work then?"

"I said I'd stay a little longer tonight to help out Christine," she says.

"Okay then maybe…"

"Maybe we can take a few minutes out back when you're done."

"Perfect!" I say.

"How's Gwen?" she asks.

"Gwen's fine. She's shaken up, but I think she's even more freaked by the fact that it was Wade who rescued her." I pause as Lex nods. "I am a little myself."

"Yeah, go figure."

At 7:15, we are both standing in the loading area off the alley. I stare at her and she at me for a good three minutes before either one of us is willing to speak. "Look, Lex, I promise I won't say I'm sorry again, but we've got to find a way around this."

She ambles lazily across the breadth of the loading area, staring down at the ground. "Yeah," she says. "It seems to be getting everyone's bun hole twisted."

"So how do we do this?" I ask.

She turns and faces me and then shrugs. "I don't know," she says shaking her head. "We just do it I guess."

"Okay, we just do." I stuff my hands in my pockets and stand there stupidly. "Any rules, boundaries, things like that?"

Lex rolls her eyes. "Guys can't do anything without rules, can you?"

"Well, if there are no rules, there'd be nothing to break, no getting in trouble—no fun in that."

The mood lifts about 4 notches and we both seem to breathe easier. "Okay, well only one rule for me," she says. She lifts a finger and points it threateningly. "You don't try anything with me again, you don't touch me, make sexual comments, you don't even look at my ass."

"Jeez, Lex, I can't even look?"

"No! Especially no looking."

"Well like that's possible," I mutter.

"What?"

"That's completely possible," I say louder and clearly. "No problem, you're invisible."

"Then see that I stay that way," she says.

Chapter 36

Safe

> ### Journal - Hook Point, CA.
>
> *Maybe Solzhenitsyn did have it right after all, maybe each of us has the equal potential for good and evil, but it's clear to me now that we have a choice. We can become angels, demons, or remain a confusion of mixed potential. Maybe it all comes down to what we set out to be, what side of our potential we cultivate, and what our world helps shape us into.*
>
> *When I look around and see the hostility that's so quick to arise between us all, I can't help but think the cause is whatever system we live in; does it support cooperation and sharing, or competition and greed? Which side of our potential does it feed?. Though we may have choice despite whatever system we live in, I suspect too few people are conscious or evolved enough to transcend their conditioning, and like rats in a Skinner box they will do as they have been trained to do. If that is the case, then what's the answer? How are we going to survive into the centuries to come? Fuck if I know, but if some day we wake up and adopt an ethic that brings out the best in us, perhaps then, at last, we will enjoy true peace.*
>
> *~ From the Journal of Jesse Benatar*

It's Gwen's turn to be watched over during the night. I find her stretched out on the living room couch, dressed in her comfy clothes and surrounded by books, DVD's, and accompanied by the stuffed Tiger she's had since she was three. She wants me to check out the bump at the base of her skull; it's clear she'd been hit by a soft board as there's only a slight swelling and mild discoloration of a bruise, but I play it up a little for her.

I wolf down a dinner plate Mom has reheated for me then rejoin Gwen in the living room while Mom leaves to make a quick run into town. Rather than watch a movie, she relay's the whole scene to me twice, reliving the fright and pondering the "what ifs".

I'm used to near disasters as I've routinely thrown myself into them since I was five, but Gwen has always been the coddled one, the protected princess, and though not exactly risk averse, she doesn't get off on the prospect of danger either. She's still shaken by the incident but also a little proud that she'd flirted with death and survived. That isn't what's troubling her most though.

"Do you know what this means?" she asks after retelling how she awoke to see Wade looking down at her. I shrug my shoulders and shake my head. "He kissed me!" she blurts. "He put his lips on mine… My first kiss and it was him?"

"Gwen, CPR isn't exactly kissing."

"Close enough, Agh! The thought of it," she says sourly.

"Any new thoughts about the Talfar?" I ask, trying to change the subject.

"No," she says halfheartedly. She picks up her iPod from the couch and stares at it. "I haven't really thought about it much."

"Not surprising Gee. Too much happening," I say.

"Yeah, but…" she says, trailing off to nothing.

I'd not given the matter much thought myself. Between finding out I'm a shifter, training with Santiago, the confusion I feel about Lex and Catalina, the epic clash of the Los Soñadores and the Los Oscuros, and the future of humanity presumably hanging in the balance—well, it just hasn't seemed too pressing somehow.

"Want to hear something ironic?" I ask. "We both had an ordeal out there today." I go on the tell Gwen about my training that day.

"He left you out there alone?" she asks, wide-eyed. Her breathing is fast and shallow and I know her anxiety is escalating.

"Yeah, well, no, not really," I backtrack a little. "He was somewhere in the fog tracking me, but I thought I was alone and had to rescue myself. That was the point."

"Gwen gives me a scared look. "Jesse, you could have drowned," she says. "What if a shark attacked you?"

I don't know how to answer that one. When I threw that question at Santiago, he simply said he promised my mother and my grandmother that he'd watch over me, that he has only broken one promise in his life and would never do it again.

"Well, the point is, I didn't, and neither did you," I say. "No point in either of us tormenting ourselves about what could have happened." Gwen nods slightly as she ponders that.

I feel for my kid sister. She's always been bookish, not much one for flirting with danger, and now, she's had two nasty ventures in less that a week. "We're good, Gwen. Home and safe," I assure her.

———— | ————

I'm swimming through the fog bank and feel something big and heavy bump into my side. I know it's a shark, testing out a prospective meal—I panic and start swimming mindlessly as fast as I can. When I sense it coming at me from below, however, my fear changes to anger, and I dive after it.

Prey becomes the hunter as I swim down to meet the surfacing giant. My aggression causes it to veer off, but not before I shove a hand into one of it's gill slits and seize as much flesh as I can manage.

The shark goes wild, and drags my through the water at lightening speeds, twisting and breaching, trying to shake me off, but my grip just digs deeper into its flesh. I feel the shark's tissues tear, see blood streaming from the gill slit, and the shark's frenzy grows wilder.

I'm determined to tear the beast apart and reach to shove my other hand into a gill slit when the animal breaches again, catapulting both of us six feet into fresh air. I feel an iron grip on the back of my neck and then I'm pulled away from my prey. Then, I'm sitting in the bottom of the zodiac with Santiago smiling down at me.

I awake to see Gwen sleeping peacefully on the couch, and then I rearrange myself in the easy chair and drift back to sleep.

———— | ————

I wake up early with the morning's light streaming into the living room, and leave Gwen sleeping. I find a near full pot of coffee in the carafe and I don't have to taste the thinly brown fluid to know Uncle Frank's home. I remake the coffee with some Mad Kat 'Katacomb' blend I brought home, then set out to find him—coffee in hand. He's in the work shed, stooped over the Bonneville.

"Morning," I say.

He looks up, excited as all hell. "Hey, Jesse," he says exuberantly. "How's Gwen?"

"She's okay. Still sleeping but I don't think she had any trouble during the night."

"Good! A bump on the head by a board can be nasty." He casually raises his right hand and rubs the back of his head. "She was lucky."

"Yeah! Lucky Wade Wingate was there to pull her out before she took in any water." Frank stares off vacantly into a dark corner of the shed, then nods. "Go figure, huh?"

Frank rouses from wherever he'd gapped to, then gives me a wry smile. "Well it's not entirely unexpected, Jesse. Wade's father may be a serious piece of work, but his son is his own person."

"Well, from what I've seen, he's not falling far from the tree."

"Maybe so, but even the darkest heart has a light spot," he says. "Bottom line is he did the right thing."

"You think he regrets it?" I ask.

Frank chuckles. "No, I don't imagine he does." He gives me a discerning look. "I suspect even Adam Wingate, as corrupt and malevolent as he is, has a good streak."

That rankles me. It's easy to marginalize Wingate and his breed as evil and not deserving of kindness or respect; it's hard to accept them as people not fundamentally different from myself or my loved ones. What is it that Solzhenitsyn said, something about the line dividing good and evil running through the hearts of us all? I know it's true—I've seen my own dark side.

"Yeah, I suppose," I concede, then drop one for shock value. "So, you and Selene Sanchez have been hanging out?" I ask. He smiles but doesn't say anything, and returns his attention to the bike. "Anything coming of that?"

He pulls the last bolt-able piece from the frame and stands back. "Now we can get it x-rayed for cracks."

Chapter 37

Hunting Lesson

"What?" Michelle asks as we moved along the crowded walkway at the beach.

"I'll be right back," I repeat. "Give me a second." I resume my pace toward the crowd of teens hanging out near one of the shower stations. Wade is standing there amid his goons, and when one of them catches sight of my approach, he says something and the gang turns in unison to face me.

The goons take up positions on either side of him like bodyguards in a gangster movie, and the girls stand back, faces thick with anticipation. They all look hungry for a little drama—except for the girl I saw that day in front of the hardware store, the one that looked at me sadly. She's a little older than Gwen and a little younger than me and she gives me a worried look this time.

Wade faces me, dripping wet from the shower, the top of his wetsuit pulled down around his waist. I come to within six feet of him and stop; he says nothing. The pleasant looking girl gestures to say something but looks down and doesn't.

"I heard about what you did the other day," I say.

"And what is that?" Wade asks, his shit-eating attitude matching his shit-eating grin.

"You saved my sister from drowning," I say. It wasn't as hard to force out as I'd expected it to be.

"That was your sister?" Wade asks.

Didn't know it was her—that explains it. "Yeah, that was my sister." I say. That stimulates a round of stupid comments by his cronies and the nice looking girl looks embarrassed. Even Wade doesn't look too pleased. "Anyway, I want to thank you for that," I say.

"What do you want me to do, take a bow?" he asks.

"Not a damned thing," I say, "just wanted to thank you." As I turn and begin walking away I see Michelle is approaching apprehensively.

"Benatar!" Wade calls out. I turn and wait as he walks up to within a foot of me. "We're even now," he says in a lowered voice.

"How so?" I ask.

"Shanks told me what old Santiago wanted to do with me that day by the docks." I recall having laid Wade out cold and Santiago wanting to toss him in the harbor. "He says you stopped him."

"Yeah, but I don't..."

"So the score's even," he says and then returns to his gang.

"Seems the gloves are still off," I mutter.

"What's that?" Michelle asks as I rejoin her.

"Nothing really?" I say looking back at the group.

"What is that all about?" she asks.

"Just thanking him for saving Gwen," I say.

"How'd that go over," she asks.

"Surprisingly well," I say. "So who's that girl near Wade, the younger one with the purple bikini?" As if picking up on the vibe, the girl looks at the two of us and doesn't look away immediately.

"That's Sarin—Wade's sister," she reply's.

"Wade has a sister?"

"Yeah, and a mother and a father and even an older brother from what I hear," Michelle says.

We turn and resume our walk. "Imagine that," I mumble. I look back once to see Sarin staring at me. Her expression is somber but otherwise unreadable—sad, hurt, sympathetic? It's Michelle's voice carrying on her half of the conversation that finally pulls my eyes away from Sarin's.

After that, the rest of the day and night go by without incident and we're all so beat from working The Kat that no one wants to hit Redline Beach as we'd planned. Friday comes, and with it, an ever increasing number of tourists hitting the last and busiest weekend of the festival. I planned to go home right after my shift at The Kat, but Santiago calls and tells me to meet him at his boat when I get off.

"So what's the plan tonight, shark wrestling, sky diving without a parachute?" I ask when I plop myself down on his couch.

"Shark hunting is a close guess," he says. I see Santiago securing a small holster to his lower leg and then roll his pant leg down over it.

"You have a permit for that thing?" I ask. It's a stupid question but I've heard it so many times in movies that it just popped out. I grew up around guns and heard gunfire on target ranges almost every day, but the sight of guns repulses me—so much irreversible damage with a moment's careless or angry use.

He straightens himself and then fixes his shirt collar. "Tonight you learn to tune your senses to that which you would find, and hunt it down." With that, he makes for the companionway to the back deck and

I follow. Before long, we're strolling the back streets of Hook Point with barely a word between us.

Finally, as we approach the same alley that I saw the drug deal go down the other day, Santiago speaks. "Do you feel anything here?" he asks. I look around. "I asked about what you feel not what you see," he says.

I stop walking and close my eyes. *Here we go.* Thoughts race through my head. "Yeah, stupid." That earns me a quick but surprisingly gentle slap up the back of my head.

"What do you smell?"

That's something I can focus on. I breathe slow and steady, concentrating on my sense of smell and I'm suddenly hit with a hundred scents, each subtly or not so subtly different from the next. "Damn," I mutter. "There's just too much. Does the world always smell this... complicated?"

"Si," he replies. "Find the most repugnant smell you can discern."

Between the smell of urine wafting from a dark recess between buildings, rotting food in a large dumpster, and the odor of burned diesel fuel coming up from somewhere near or on the river, it's a toss up, but then I become aware of another smell, something sharp, bitter, and almost imperceptible. Zeroing in on that, it seems to grow stronger and I feel a bit queasy. "You smell it," Santiago suggests.

"Jeez, what is that?" I ask.

"The stench of corruption, the reek of decaying spirit," he replies.

"It smells like something left dead in a sewer for too long."

"Si,"

"This is what you want me to learn tonight?" I ask. "If so, got it, let's go."

Santiago stretches and looks to the night sky. "Study the odor a while longer. You do not want to forget it."

"No worry there," I mutter. I do study it and the dozens of other smells that fill the night air. I recall a meditation Max had me do once; he had me focus on one small part of my body, and after a couple of intolerable hours of doing that I became aware of the countless sensations streaming from it, sensations that my brain usually filtered out. This was similar, but even more potent. "Man this is incredible. Do you smell things like this all the time?"

"When I have to," Santiago says. "Come, let us walk, but remain aware of changes in that odor and its intensity."

As we walk I notice it increase and decrease depending on where we go. On the main drag, a car passes and soon after that the odor hits me hard and heavy. Santiago notices it and he watches as the car turns down a side street that heads toward Lex's Sanctuary. He leads us that way. The streets are still busy with people and the odors coming from them are like listening to a large marching band that's trying to tune up but can't quite get there.

I detect things I've never smelled before and once, as I pass a woman who's holding on to her boyfriend or husband like she doesn't want to lose him, I felt aroused. I glance back at the couple and Santiago says, "She's ovulating."

Seriously dude? It makes me think about Catalina, how I feel so drawn to her. Is that the secret of the dangerous beauties? "Did you lose the scent?" Santiago asks.

"The scent? Ah…" *Damn!*

"Do not lose focus. The scent is everywhere but some places more than others," he says. "Where does it seem stronger?"

I stop and do a slow 360. The odor seems stronger in the direction the car had gone. I point that out and Santiago seems pleased. We cross the street and soon after we pass a lone man walking in the other direction. The smell he exudes is similar but it has a distinct sharpness to it. "Do not be distracted," Santiago says.

"But that's…"

"Different. He is one who has carnal interests in children."

"You mean, as in molest them?" I ask.

"Si," Santiago replies dispassionately. I stop dead in my tracks and look back at the guy. He seems like any normal Joe, like someone who you see working at a corner store. "I told you not to be distracted," Santiago censures.

"Shouldn't we do something about him?" I ask, refusing to continue.

"Such as?" Santiago asks. "Would you have us kill him or call the police?"

"I don't know," I defend. "You're the expert here."

"Correct," he says. He resumes his walking and I catch up. "Know this, Jesse—what you smell there is his corrupt and selfish desire, not his intention. For all you know, he has never acted on that desire and may never act on it. Would you condemn him if that were the case?"

I have no answer for that. I pick up the target scent again, this time quicker. It's tricky to track, like detecting the direction a sound with one ear closed. It takes us down the side street toward Lex's, and it's crowded with parked cars and people strolling. It's a Friday night away from the city for many people and they have no desire to turn in early like I do.

I momentarily lose the scent in a buffeting breeze, but catch it again when it dies down. At the first cross street the scent shifts again and we go right, down a narrow, unfamiliar road. It is a dead end but several alleys run off it.

The odor is strongest in the direction of a lane that runs between a dead winch repair shop and an even deader barrel maker. Once I've identified it, Santiago motions for me to be still. I look around as he closes his eyes in concentration; except for a few cars parked on the side of the street, it's the most lifeless strip in town I've seen yet. None of the buildings are occupied and half the streetlights are burnt out.

Santiago motions me to follow and then moves into the alley. About 50 feet in, an alcove opens between the buildings and there, sitting empty in the dark, sits the car that carried the odor. Santiago stays in the shadows and gestures towards a small glass globe on the wall near the back entrance of the building. Surveillance—whatever's going on in there, they don't want unexpected visitors. Santiago gestures again and we retrace our steps out of the alley.

"What did you sense back there?" he asks as we start back towards the docks.

"It's, ah, creepy. It feels... I feel... queasy, kind of sick, and something else... danger I think, like some disease infests the place."

"Just so, that is exactly what it is. Remember it well and know to stay clear."

"So what's going on there?" He doesn't answer, but even before asking I think I know. During the rest of the walk, Santiago talks to me about what I just did. It really has more to do with intuition and sensing energies than anything, but this can be channeled through the sense of smell with the result—I can track people down based on what energy they give off.

"You will say nothing of this to anyone," Santiago commands. "Go home and forget what you saw, but do not forget what you learned."

"Aye, Aye, Yoda sir," I say, donning my helmet. I'm bushed and too tired even to give Santiago a hard time. The incident has been bizarre and I'll think more about it tomorrow—all I want to see now is the business side of a pillow.

Chapter 38

Las Hadas

> ### Journal - Hook Point, CA.
>
> *I've seen and felt things these past few weeks that have completely changed by view of reality. There are stranger things than I'd ever dreamed of to be sure, but the other night... I learned that magic, and the things of fairy tales are real... They're real!*
>
> *~ From the Journal of Jesse Benatar*

I ride home, managing not to hit anything or anyone on the way, and find a note from Mom on the table.

Dear Jesse. How was your day? Gwen and I are back in the meadow. There is Boysenberry pie in the fridge if you're hungry. Love ~ Mom.

"Huh," I mutter. I cut myself a slice of pie and for something that has no fat or added sugar it's amazing. I wolf it down and make my way to the Therion, dreaming of that pillow again, but as I climb the steps to the deck my curiosity gets the best of me. "The meadow?"

I make my weary way up through the woods and over the hillside, torn between the pillow and the question, but when I start down the gentle slope to the meadow, my mind and senses rally—there's something in the air, something... happy... serene, and it smells fresher than ocean air, and carries the delicate scent of flowers.

I slowly descended the hill, studying the smell, feeling my reactions to it, and fully aware that my gut is telling me to take it slow; it's like reaching out to a chickadee that you suddenly find sitting on a branch a few feet from your face. As I approach the bottom of the hill, I catch a glimpse of the meadow through the bows and I'm surprised to see the soft light of fireflies.

I stop at the edge of the trees and watch in amazement as dozens of tiny blue lights float above the grass, slowly revolving around the rock. Sixty feet away, Mom is sitting on the rock with her back against it, and Gwen is sitting between her legs, leaning back against her. They're quiet and unmoving, as though sleeping. Watching them sit under a canopy of brilliant stars and the fireflies floating around them lulls me into a sense of peace—all is perfect and good in the world.

Three thoughts ruffle my tranquility at the same time. Fireflies give off green light, not blue; they blink and are not steady; and I don't think they have them in California. The lights seem to react to the disturbance in my thinking, subtly moving away from my direction. I feel disappointment, loss, and refocus on how peaceful Mom and Gwen look. *Do they even know what's going on around them?*

I squat on my heels, leery of breaking the magic of the moment, and watch as the tiny blue lights gently drift over the meadow, and make their way around the rock. Occasionally one will dart after another and the other reacts as though playing a game. I close my eyes and focus on what I am feeling. I find myself going deep, following the subtle thread that connects my conscious mind with something boundless.

"What is happening here?" I ask. "What are they?"

"Las Hadas," a feminine voice replies. I open my eyes and see Catalina Ruiz sitting on the ground next to me. "Las Hadas favorecen tu madre y tu hermana."

"Catalina," I say, surprised. She gives me a tranquil smile then returns her attention to the dancing lights. "What does what?"

"Las Hadas favorecen tu madre y tu hermana," she repeats.

The Hadas favorecen... favour?" She nods. "Something favors my mother and sister?" She nods. "What? What are 'las hadas'? ¿Qué es las hadas?"

"Las Hadas estan... espiritus," she says.

"Spirits? Like ghosts?" I ask.

"Espiritus de La Tierra, de La Madre," she replies with a sublime look on her face and her arms open to the meadow, as if greeting them.

"Spirits of The Earth, of The Mother," I translate.

"Si," she says.

I gaze out at the meadow and notice that a group of them have drawn nearer. Catalina keeps her arms out in a welcoming gesture and as one intrepid spirit draws near, she opens the palm of one hand. The blue light drifts in and floats just above it. The others join in and I find us surrounded by pinpoints of soft blue light, and with that comes a sense of peace. One comes within a foot of my face, and when I raise my hand, it darts back to Catalina. "They're like… fairies."

Catalina giggles. "Si, some name that."

We sit there for a while longer and then Catalina whispers something I can't hear and they move back into the meadow. One holds back and comes close to my face again. I want to hold up my hand again but think better of it, and then it moves off to join its kin.

"She favor you," Catalina says.

"Whoa!" I say. "Fairies, freaking fairies."

"You rest now," Catalina says.

My fatigue hits me again and I want to curl up on the ground and sleep right here. "I, ah, just need to watch over my mom and sister."

Catalina giggles again. "You no need watch." She gestures to the meadow and when I look I see the lights—spirits—moving gently around them.

"Well, their all fine and pretty, but I don't see how…"

"They safe, Jesse Benatar," she says. "Protect strong. No danger."

"Catalina, I don't think I can sleep knowing they are out here alone."

"They no alone," she says. She struggles to find words. "For them," she says apologetically.

"For them?"

She nods. She gestures to the meadow. "For them," she says, emphasizing 'them'.

Then it dawns on me. "Oh, this is for them, as in I'm not supposed to be here."

Catalina nods. "Si. For them. You no fear. I stay, I watch."

"Thank you Catalina. Gracias, but who's going to watch you? Besides, you're not real. I mean, you're not really here are you."

She smiles her serene smile again. "What real, Jesse Benatar?" That is the question that I expect will taunt me for years to come. What is real? Spirit travel, shape shifting, and now fairies? The world is a lot more interesting and reality much more vague than I have ever thought.

"If danger come—it no come—pero come, I come to you," she assures me. Then she rolls over on her hands and knees so that her face is directly in front of mine. "Go now, Jesse Benatar," she says, then she kisses me. It is a soft, gentle kiss that warms me from the inside out.

When I open my eyes, I am sitting at the edge of the meadow and the tiny blue lights are floating around Mom and Gwen. They seem asleep, at peace and safe, and I make a decision to trust my gut feelings and leave for home.

Chapter 39

Falling-Out

"Good morning," I say, stumbling into the kitchen. It's past 10:00 and Mom's there, drinking coffee and reading the paper. I pour myself one. "Kind of a late breakfast for you isn't it?"

She smiles up at me. "Uh, huh."

"So, you look all sparkly today," I say. "Have an enlightening night?" She gives me a curious look, obviously not getting my puns. "The meadow," I prompt. "It must have been amazing for you and Gwen."

"It was, Jesse, it was..." she nods her head, "...amazing." She looks at me like something's still missing in our conversation. "How did you know about that?" she finally asks.

"I was there, well, for a few minutes, after I got home. When I saw you and Gwen surrounded by all those lights and looking all blissed out on the rock, I came back home and crashed."

"Huh," she says, then sips her coffee. She doesn't look entirely comfortable with what I just told her.

"Well, I was only there a few minutes and it looked like a private party so I left the two of you alone." She nods and smiles. "So, like was it...private?"

"Yes," she says.

I feel a sudden and completely stupid pang of jealousy or one of its close cousins. It's great that Mom and Gwen had a special moment together, so why would that bother me? "Oh, that's cool. So, where's Uncle Frank?" I ask.

"He's in town at the festival."

"And Gwen?"

"With him. She's spending the day with her cousins."

"So what are you up to today?"

Mom rolls her eyes and smiles. "I have no idea," she says.

"Wow," I mutter, reflecting on the pivotal importance of the statement. "It's about time."

Getting to town is crazier than crazy. I'm not one to ride the ditches and zip in and out of traffic, but there's no way I am sitting still on the skinny parking lot that River road had become—I brake just about every rule of the road getting to work.

The Hook is even worse. I thought it was as busy as it could get the weekend before, but they may as well have closed the roads and turned the whole place into a walking mall. There must have been 30,000 people in a town of built for 7,000.

The main street is completely blocked but when a sheriff's cruiser and ambulance lay on the sirens, they manage to push a hole through the chaos and I'm right on their tale. The cruiser and ambulance turn left, toward Lex's Sanctuary, and I turn right next to The Kat. Even that short strip along the side of The Kat to the back alley is blocked by irate drivers in cars that can't move, as throngs of people swarm around them like ants.

I eventually make it to the loading area behind The Kat and find Bill Carter arguing with a rough looking character near a 60's yellow Volkswagen bug that's parked in the middle of it. I park my bike and join Bill just as the other guy squeezes his massive frame into the bug and with a flurry of curses, crawls off into the jammed streets.

"Some people's children," Bill mumbles.

"Giving you a hard time?" I ask.

"Hey there, Jesse," he says with a forced smile. "You can't really blame people for wanting to find a place to park, but assuming you can just block someone's loading area?"

"We have deliveries coming today?" I ask.

Bill frowns. "No, that's the part I'm having trouble with. I feel like a dog in a manger. If only he'd been polite about it and asked. Well, let's get to work," he says.

To work, we got. The lineup stretches out into the sidewalk all morning and then things get busier around lunchtime. On top of that, it seems that every police cruiser in the county sirens it's way through the madness at one point or another. It's totally nuts, and when Christine and Lex finally arrived to help out, Bill and Hilda ask if Michelle would stay for a second shift.

As harried as it all is, I love every minute of it; it's as if we have a near impossible mission to complete and are working together like a well-oiled machine. A shared challenge is a rush.

I catch Lex giving me odd looks every once in a while, and catch Christine catching Lex, and a few times catch Michelle catching me catching them. It isn't a case of drama though; it is more a case of curiosity and concern. I'm thinking about this as I walk into the back room to take a toilet break, when I hear Bill talking on his cell.

"You're kidding… No… No… Really… No kidding." He went on like that until after I finished my business in the bathroom. When I pass him again, he's staring down at the floor with a concerned look on his face.

"Bad news?" I ask.

He gives me a blank stare, obviously not quite processing my question, then quickly says, "Yes, it seems Hook Point has had it's first major drug bust. People were killed."

I have a sick feeling when I hear that and it lingers all afternoon as news of the drug bust and killings spread through the locals like a plague. 'Gang warfare' and 'street shootings' are phrases that stand out from the constant people-buzz that fills the air.

According to the gossip, the drugs found run the gamut: marijuana, cocaine, amphetamines, heroine, Oxys… . The place where it all went down is variously identified as a grow-op, a storehouse, and a crystal-meth lab, and the number dead ranges from one to more than ten.

I noticed that it's the regulars and other locals who are doing all the gossiping. This is something big for them, something that took place in their own backyard. The tourists seem to ignore it all as though it's yesterday's news.

One question burns in my mind that I can't get a clear answer to, at least not until Jeffrey arrives for his shift. "It's crazy out there," he says in the back room after arriving. "Mad enough with the festival, but with the big bust and all the cops…"

"You see anything of it?" I ask.

"What the bust?" he asks. "Yeah, had to pass near it to get here."

"Where is it?" I ask.

"Not far, really, far south side. Ghost town we call it," he replies, pulling on his Mad Kat t-shirt.

"Where?" I ask.

Jeffrey gives me a curious look. "Over at the old barrel works," he replies. "Why? Are you okay?" he asks with concern. "Jesse?"

"Yeah, I'm fine," I lie. "It, ah, just really sucks."

The night before with Santiago—hunting he called it—plagues my thoughts over and over. I try to work but keep messing up. For all I know, it was a gang hit, part of a drug war that's made its way to Hook Point, but I keep coming back to Santiago; the way he talked about what was going on in that place, and the controlled anger I'd sensed boiling beneath the surface as he spoke about it.

Despite the busyness, Bill Carter turns on the small TV he has in the kitchen during the dinnertime news. What comes at me over the airwaves is like watching a manifesting nightmare. A good looking woman from a Bay Area news station stands on the very side street my senses had taken Santiago and I down the night before.

In the background, the street's filled with squad cars, two police panel vans, and a gang of cops in uniform and suits going in and out of the building I'd tracked the scent to. Despite the noise around me, I only heard the words the young woman speaks.

"Carefree summer celebrations merge with violent death as the biggest annual festival in this coastal California town has been trumped by the biggest drug bust in the region's history, and by what has been described as gruesome gang style killings.

Officially, police remain tight lipped as they continue their investigation, but an inside source has revealed that the police, responding to an anonymous tip, found substantial quantities of cocaine, meth-amphetamines, and the highly abused prescription opiate, oxy-contin, along with a cache of automatic weapons and hand guns. More disturbing, however, is that among the weapons and drugs were the bodies of four men and a woman.

Though unconfirmed at this time, this reporter was informed that some of the victims were mutilated. Police are unwilling to confirm it just yet, but the killings have the hallmark of a gang-style hit. This, just a few short weeks after the murder of two local security guards shocked this sleepy coastal town…

The woman rambles on about how traumatized Hook Point is by it all and interviews on-lookers. I don't listen to any of that, I can't. All I can think about is Santiago and what he'd made me a party to.

I tell Bill Carter that I have to take care of an important piece of business and leave before he can protest. I find Santiago on The Revenge, playing his guitar with his cat sleeping by his side. There's an unearthly, inhuman calm about him that makes me think, once again, that he might really be insane.

"What did you do?" I demand when I enter. "You killed those people, didn't you?"

"If I did then the whole marina knows about it now," he says dryly. He continues to play a serene piece on his guitar.

"Why?" I demand. "How could you do that?" I ask in a quieter tone. "You just, just killed them and a woman too?"

He gives me a tired look. "A woman can be as corrupt and as deadly as a man. It is not one's gender that should elicit compassion and mercy, but one's heart and deeds."

"And you can see into their hearts, know their deeds?" I challenge.

Santiago looks at me as if I asked about the obvious. "Si!" he says as he strokes his cat. "You glimpsed the hearts and deeds of those people last night, smelled their corruption. In time, you will come to see such with profound clarity."

"I don't want that," I say, "and it doesn't matter what they did, you didn't have the right to kill them."

"And if you knew that they would bring your family to harm?" he asks. "If they came knocking at your front door and you knew they would maim or kill your mother and sister?"

I can't help but imagine the scene. "That's a bullshit question. A cheap dodge," I say finally.

"They were a clear and present danger," he says, citing the same crap the government uses to stifle inconvenient free speech. "I sent them back to the creator. Perhaps they will be returned in a better state."

I have no idea what he's talking about, and don't care. "That's it? You can justify killing…"

"I justify nothing," he interrupts angrily. "You know what those people were, you know the toll in human life and misery they levy."

"It doesn't matter. There are laws and rights and …" Santiago breaks into a chuckling laugh. "… such things as a trial," I continue.

That elicits a deeper laugh from the old man and for a few seconds, there seems nothing sinister about him. Finally his laughter subsides. "I follow a higher law," he says. "One where there is no escaping accountability."

"That makes you damned too," I chide.

"Oh, si, I am among the most damned of all, only there is no hell but that which we make for ourselves."

"And you know this how?" I ask.

"I live there." He begins playing the guitar again, and his small tabby gets up, stretches, and hops off the couch to greet me.

"I can't do this," I say.

"Do what?" he asks.

"This," I say, gesturing to air. "None of this. You've killed eight people since I've known you, and implicated me in five of them." An image flashes in my mind of me being lead out into a courtroom in an orange jumpsuit while my mother cries in the corner.

"I have implicated you in nothing. You were not there, you had no knowledge of it."

"But I know now." I say. I don't know where to go with that and Santiago stops playing his guitar and simply looks at me. I know I can never tell on him, and I know if it ever came to it, I'd lie for the man, and that makes it all a deal breaker. "I'm done here," I say. I turn to leave. "I'm done with you. I'm sorry, but I can't be a part of anything like this."

"Si, it is good, Jesse," he says. "You are learning well."

"No you don't get it," I say turning back to face him. "I am done here!" I say emphasizing every syllable. "Done, finished, see you later." He doesn't respond to that and I turn and storm out of the cabin. Up on the back deck of the revenge, I hear his guitar again; it's a sweat melody.

Chapter 47

Gestalt

I wander along the dock, numb to the noise and festivities surrounding me. I've been a part of the murder of five people! Mom was right about Santiago—he's dangerous and I should never have fallen under his influence. I meander through the beer garden in the marina parking lot and head for the bridge to the other side of town. The Kat, my job, none of it holds any meaning to me now.

In time I find myself standing in front of the display and booths set up by the colonists. Señor Alba is addressing a large crowd of people, while women of the colony stand behind their booths, cheerfully engaging eager buyers. I yearn for the peace and simplicity of their lives; it had been mine to embrace—until last night. I feel an overwhelming need to do just one thing.

I make my way to the area behind the booths but Mom isn't there. I catch sight of Serena talking to her grandmother and when she glances my way, I gesture for her to come over. She says something to her grandmother and then bounces over to me with a wide smile.

"Hello, Jesse," she says, beaming.

"Hey! Listen, do you know where my mom is?" I ask.

My abruptness takes her smile down a few notches. "Yes, she and Gwendolyn left to pick up more dresses from home, from the colony. They are selling very…"

"You know when they'll be back?" I ask.

"Should be very soon now," she says, looking concerned. "Jesse, what is wrong?"

"Wrong?"

"You are worried about something. I can see it on your face."

"Oh, nothing, I'm, ah, just late getting back to The Kat from my break," I lie. "Don't bother telling her I was here asking for her when she gets back, okay? I'll talk to her later."

"Okay," she says uncertainly.

Before she can ask any more questions, I turn and duck into the crowd in front of the booths. I think of calling Mom by cell but decide against it. After all, what would I say? I mindlessly wander over to where Señor Alba is keeping the large crowd entertained.

He stands slightly elevated on a platform and looks the quintessential spokesperson he is. He fields questions and makes the history of the colony seem like something out of a great adventure movie. Few in the crowd can guess it is likely the most important adventure in human history.

Then an elderly man identifies himself as an ancient ship enthusiast and asks him what had become of La Soñadora the one that brought them there. "Ah, that is an interesting chapter in our history," Señor Alba begins. "The ship, La Soñadora, was anchored for many years in this very harbor next to us. For 55 years she was carefully maintained by our shipwrights should we once again need her, but she was destined to never sail the open sea again. On the night of April 17, 1760, a fire inexplicably broke out on her and it spread like a demon, so fast, in fact, that in a desperate effort to save what we could of her, she was scuttled."

"They didn't raise her later then," the old man offers.

Señor Alba shrugs his shoulders. "That is another part of the mystery. For reasons of their own, the elders of the community decided to let the good ship La Soñadora remain at rest."

"Is the precise location of her resting place known?" the old man asks. "I know some people who might be willing to excavate her."

"Ah, well that is an unfortunate unlikelihood. She sits at the end of the inlet, somewhere beneath the old cannery you see there today."

I step away from the crowd and walk slowly in the direction of the cannery at the far end of the harbor. At this distance, its monolithic gray can pass as a massive rusting tombstone. Pieces fall into place one at a time until a near whole picture forms for me. "Huh!"

I make my way back through the crowd toward the booth Serena's now working. I catch her attention and motion for her to meet me in the back. She does a quick scan of the crowd around the booth and the other colonists working it, then nods. I slip around behind the booth and a moment later Serena joins me and gives me a questioning look.

"Listen, I need to ask you something and it's very important you tell me," I say.

She nods. "Yes?"

"Do you know what the Talfar is?" She looks perturbed by the question and hesitates. "I know it's important. My sister and I have been reading Del Baca's book, *The Cave of the Prophesies*, and I know it's something you've lost." Serena's eyes grow wider as I speak, and she makes furtive glances around as if to check if anyone else is listening. "I, we, think the Los Oscuros are after it and I think I just figured out where it is."

"Jesse, it is not good to talk about such things like this," she says, gesturing to the openness around us.

"But this is important, Serena. Señor Carlos Santiago has been urging me to read the book, says there are things happening around us that we need to be prepared for, dangerous things, and I think the Talfar might have a lot to do with it."

Serena gives me an anxious look. "I cannot talk of it now, not here."

"Later then," I ask.

She glances around again, thinks about it, then nods. "Okay," she says with clear uncertainty.

"Where? When?" I ask.

"I do not know. Maybe later, someplace not so open."

It isn't a clear answer but it's all I have. "Okay, I'll check back later and see," I say. She nods then returns to the booth. She gives me a quick, anxious glance just before disappearing behind the curtain. The one person I feel a strong urge to tell is someone I've decided not to talk to again. Santiago would want to know what I suspect, but he'll have to learn of it from someone else.

I cross back over the river and wander down to the docks, and then sit at the end staring at the cannery, imagining what the place looked like 250 years ago. I imagine the ship sitting at anchor in the shallows at the end of the inlet with perhaps only a rudimentary dock nearby. No roads, no town, just a ship anchored by itself, and manned by a skeleton crew, if by anyone.

Then the fire—was it lightening, an accident, or arson? I imagine a small group of men desperately trying to save her, making that fatal decision to pull the sea cocks, and perhaps trying to pull the burning hull out into deeper water while it filled, and finally the ship settling in the muddy bottom while its masts still burn in the air above. What I can't imagine is letting her remain in her watery tomb.

Then I notice something that's been sitting in front of me for the hour or so I'd sat there—the cannery looks completely deserted. For weeks there'd been at least one ominous Black Knight security vehicle parked by it 24/7, but now the lot is empty.

I go back to The Kat for my bike, then ride up the hill of Highway One as it curves around the back of the cannery, and stop on the side of the road high above it. Looking down from that perspective, it's confirmed for me; there's no sign of Black Knight security or any one else around the place. After being so well guarded, why nothing now? Was it the three agents Santiago killed, the festival, or something else?

My mind temporarily relieved of its angst about the killings, I decide to go back to The Kat, collect my things, and apologize to Bill Carter for disappearing on him and the crew. I plan to tell him I'll not collect any pay for the days I'd worked that week to make up for it.

Chapter 41

Late Chat

"I still say he should have fired your ass," Lex says, pulling back on a beer. She flops herself down on the couch in Jeffrey's living room next to Christine, who looks to be falling asleep sitting up.

"He was pretty upset that you took off," Christine says through half open eyes, "but I think he was more worried about you than anything." She yawns, slumps to one side, and rests her head on Lex's shoulder.

"Bill and Hilda still want you to work there, Jesse," Michelle says. "He likes you."

"Go figure," Lex grumbles.

I shoot Lex a look and she looks away, knowing she's crossing the line of reasonable taste. "Yeah, he's a great guy," I say.

"So you going to stick with us?" Jeffrey asks, sitting on the arm of the easy chair Michelle is stretched out on. His parents are up the coast in Mendocino to avoid the chaos of festival, and his guest had returned to the city, so he has the house to himself. It's a large Victorian, immaculately decorated and furnished to give it elegance. Jeffrey hands Michelle a glass of chilled white wine and takes a sip of his own. I take a drink of my seltzer.

"Hey, well, I'll always stick with you," I say," but I'm not sure I can work at The Kat."

"Always is a long time," Lex says, staring at me. She raises her eyebrows and takes another pull on her beer.

"So what's up?" Michelle asks me. She gives me that concerned look of hers but it's tweaked by something else—frustration, or maybe it's just fatigue. "You seemed worried about something all day."

"It's nothing," I lie. How can I tell them I'm an accessory to murder, or have at least been complicit with it. "A lot's been happening and I think it's catching up with me."

"'Bout time," Lex mumbles.

Michelle gives Lex an annoyed stare. Lex stares right back at her with her own version of an annoyed stare, then looks at me in a way that I know she doesn't believe me. "So then what's this about?" she asks gesturing to the circle of us.

I'd urged everyone to get together after The Kat closed and Jeffrey offered his place. It's exactly 12:30 am and we are all dreaming of our beds. "Okay, so I know some of you have to get up early for the morning shift, so I'll keep this short."

I go on to tell them about what I heard Señor Alba say about the scuttling of the colony's ship, *La Soñadora*, and about the connections I made between that and the things we've read about the Talfar. Jeffrey's excitement rises as he makes the same connections as I speak, and Michelle looks pensive.

"So you think the Talfar is on the ship and sank with it in the harbor, and that's why Wingate is excavating below the cannery," Jeffrey suggests.

"Exactly, and he may have already found it; the place looks deserted now," I say.

"Or they just stopped the work until after the festival," Michelle suggests.

"Yeah, maybe. Let's hope," I say.

"So what's the big deal about this Talfar?" Lex asks. "How important can something called a Talfar be?"

"The Talfar is some sort of sacred object the Enlightened Ones have guarded for thousands of years. The people from the colony brought it here for protection, and the prophecies say that it will be the end of things for them if the Dark Ones ever destroy it. "

"So what, Wingate gets it, destroys it, and then The Dreamers disappear?" Jeffrey poses.

"Yeah, I don't know," I admit. "Said that way it doesn't make sense, but the book's warning is ominous, and if I'm right, Wingate is taking it serious. Serious enough to kill for," I add, recalling the homeless guy found dead after visiting the cannery.

"So what do we do?" Jeffrey asks.

"Have you told Santiago?" Michelle asks.

"I shake my head. "No, we've, ah, had a falling-out." Michelle gives me another questioning look. "But I think it's a good idea. Maybe you can let him know, like soon."

"So, what are we going to do about it?" Jeffrey repeats.

I look down at the floor and run through an idea that's begun to form. Michelle, in her uncanny perceptiveness, widens her eyes at me and tilts her head. "You're not thinking of going back in there," she says. I'm not certain if it's a question or a command, but I just let it go.

"That would be crazy," Jeffrey says, giving me a questioning look.

"Crazy," Lex mutters, looking up at the ceiling.

"Well, it's an option," I say, "one way to find out if that's what he's been doing in the cannery."

"Forget it Jesse," Michelle says. "You know what happened to that homeless guy and what almost happened to you."

"So we just sit back and do nothing?" I ask.

"Nothing," Lex mutters in the background.

"I'm not asking any of you to go in there with me," I say.

"You're not going in there at all," Michelle demands. "If I were to tell your mother…"

"What's with you, the cannery, and snitching on me?" I ask angrily, recalling that she snitched on me nine years earlier.

"Snitch," Lex mumbles.

"Shut up," Michelle and I tell Lex in unison. That wakes up Christine but makes us all shut up and in those few moments of silence, we begin to grin, then laugh.

"Oh, man, too much work and too little sleep," Jeffrey says.

"Right," I say. "We're all punchy."

"Punchy," Lex says to herself.

"Okay, look," I begin, "I won't go into the cannery without letting you guys know about it. In the meantime, I'm going to talk to my cousin about this."

"Serena?" Michelle asks.

"Yeah. She's staying at the house tonight with Gwen."

"Wow, that's different," Michelle says. "First time I've ever heard of any colony kids staying with outsiders." Her eyes widen. "Not that you're entirely outsiders," she adds. "Oh, my head's asleep."

"So you think you can get word to Santiago?" I ask Michelle.

"Yeah, sure," she says through drooping eyes.

"So let's check in tomorrow to report on anything new," I suggest.

"One more thing," Jeffrey says. "I think we all need to be a lot more careful poking around anything Wingate has his hands in, especially after the killings last night."

My heart races and my throat goes dry. "What's the connection?" I ask, barely containing the quiver in my voice.

"Such a newb," Lex says quietly, then holds her hands up near her face a though to ward off blows.

"Some of us think Wingate's involved with the increase in street drugs we've had here over the past two years," he replies.

"Responsible, more like," Michelle adds.

"No shit," I say.

"No shit," Jeffrey responds, "and if that was one of his operations, he'll be doubly pissed and out for vengeance."

The ride home is an anti-treat. I've said I can fall asleep anywhere doing anything, but when I wake up just as the Shadow and I are about to drive straight into the river on a bend, I surprise myself. It's just past 1:00 am when I pull into the drive and the house is dark except for a dim light coming from the living room.

When I lock the Shadow by the Therion I notice that the living room light has been doused, but a dim one glows from Mom's bedroom—she'd waited up until I arrived home. It's too late to talk to Serena and I only hope I'll be able to get up in time to talk in the morning before they leave for the festival.

I fire up my laptop to type Gwen a quick message, but find one from Isa by way of yet another email address waiting for me.

'He's really pissed now. He believes the old man killed those people and now he's ordered him killed. Stay away from the old man, Jesse. Please stay away from him. Isa

'PS... Please, please don't reply.'

"Damn you Isa, who are you?" I'm tempted to reply, but instead fire off a quick email to Michelle asking her to warn Santiago about the threat on his life. I nod off for a few seconds sitting up, but manage to type my note to Gwen.

I tell her what I think I've sorted out about the Talfar, and ask that she and Serena talk to me in the morning. Then I strip off and flop onto the bed without as much as washing my face. Sleep will not come easy, however—thoughts and images torment me—four men and a women. I toss around, unable to deal with it rationally, unable to escape into sleep.

Chapter 42

Workout

'Jesse. Tried to call you but guess whose phone was off!!! Imagine that. So what happened between you and Mr. Santiago? Where did you hear about the threat against him? Was it Isa again?

'I'll head down to his boat this morning before work. So tired I could sleep on a bed of nails.

'Take good care of yourself and stay away from the cannery. M'

'I sit and stare at the screen and yawn. 9:13 and I feel like shit. I turn my attention to the email from Gwen.

'Gross! I was just one step ahead enough to prevent our cousin from being traumatized. You said to talk to you before we left but when we got to the boat you didn't answer... I went in only to find your naked ass sprawled out in the berth. Gross! WEAR SOMETHING TO BED! You owe me so big.

'Lucky I turned around just in time to stop Serena from entering. Can you imagine how she'd react, what her mother would think? She'd never be allowed around here again. Anywhile, I yelled at you but you only grumbled some shit and buried your head under your pillow. Sometimes you're just gross!

'So here's the deal, though I don't know why I'm telling you this. Serena doesn't know a lot about the Talfar, other than it's very old, very sacred, and holds the heart of the people. I think some of the colonists are more deeply studied in their traditions. Serena has chosen a healing path. What we want is someone from a spirit path, a true spirit walker. Sorry best translation I can make from Serena's description. But guess what? Your friendly midnight visitor, Catalina Ruiz, is just one such animal.

'Crap... gotta bounce. Can we catch up later?

'Love (most of the time),

'Gwen'

I twist my stiff neck and turn an eye reluctantly to my bed; dang, I'd only wrapped up in a thin sheet last night and that was twisted into a knot in the corner. I almost flushed with embarrassment. I'm going to have to remember to lock the cabin door at night.

I stretch and yawn and pop a cup of water into the microwave. Instant coffee will have to do since there's no way I want to crawl to the house just yet. The cabin's getting warm in the morning sunlight that hits it through the trees, so I push open the door and breathe in the freshness of the new day. Then, from somewhere in my latent genius, an idea springs to life.

I stumble to the table and type out an urgent message to Tony. If he's still able to use the computer he'd hacked into at the Colorado Department of Education, I have a use for it. I smile at recalling how Tony thought he'd hacked into the school records data-base in the hope of graduating himself three years early and with straight A's. In fact, he only managed to hack into an account used by some maintenance department.

I send the message and then set about creating a new email account with a bogus name and Denver address. With that done, I have but two things on my mind—breakfast and a decent cup of coffee. After that, who knew what the day had in store.

———— | ————

The meadow's unnaturally quiet; in the bright morning light, when you expect it to be abuzz with life, an eerie silence hangs over the place. I stood in a soundproof chamber once, during a school tour of a military research lab; the complete lack of sound had felt like a gentle vacuum pulling at my eardrums and I'd felt spacey. Except for the muted crunch of my own footfalls and the faint hiss of my legs moving through the tall grass, it sounded the same, with the same effect.

"Why am I here?" I ask, breaking the silence. I came with a vague plan to workout, to practice what Santiago had taught me; I might have decided to kick him out of my life, but I'll never forget the what he's taught me or stop my sessions. What I'd learned was profound, perilously important, and a serious buzz. Standing in the middle of the meadow, however, I'm not certain where to start. Vacillation is mind cancer, so I start at the beginning—I run.

I make a circuit around the perimeter of the meadow to warm up. Santiago had driven that lesson home a dozen times; using your body in extraordinary ways means extraordinary stresses—tearing muscles, ripping tendons from their inserts, and breaking bones are not unheard of. Everything depends on properly preparing the body and then mindfully slipping into the twilight world between the physical and metaphysical realities.

He'd warned me that a crisis could propel me into that zone, and without the needed preparations, that would make me vulnerable to injuring myself. It was something I had to learn to control, which at first was supposed to be as hard as trying to stop a cough half way through it. Harder yet, was bringing it on intentionally with a full, calm, presence of mind.

Warmed up and stretched out, I fall into an easy trot around the perimeter of the meadow. I half close my eyes to the narrow trail I've made in the grass, and focus on my breathing, the movement of bone and muscle, and the feel of the earth under each footfall.

With Santiago's knowing presence, I'd been able to stay focused, certain that what I was doing was right or it would be corrected. On my own, I'm taunted by doubt. I begin to feel centered—the sweet spot—only to have it disrupted by thoughts of failure. I hadn't failed before, I'd done things I have thought impossible, but that had been with the old man there.

Frustrated, I use the trick I stumbled on that day in the shed with him. He warned me not to use it unless necessary because the mind grows on what it's fed—*'feed it darkness, it becomes a thing of darkness'*.

I imagine a gang of Wingate's goons breaking into the house with Mom and Gwen there. They're armed and intending to kill us after some cruel fun and there's only me standing in their way. My mind races, my heartbeat follows, and I feel the now familiar dis-reality taking over my senses and perceptions.

In a burst of focused rage, I bolt from the meadow and I'm over the next hillside before I gain control again. Throttling down, I run, leap, climb trees, and bound off boulders. I don't know where I am or how far I've traveled when my senses tell me there's something amiss up the hillside to my left.

I glance in that direction and spot two people in the distance—hikers or birdwatchers maybe—but one is pointing in my direction and the other is bringing a set of binoculars up to his face. I kick in the afterburners and cook out of there, hopefully before either can get a good look at me.

It was stupid to have practiced in a public space and I realize why Santiago had been so meticulous in selecting my training grounds. If those people got a good enough look at me or worse still, filmed me as I ran across the field at a good 35 mph, it would hit the web, even the news, then it could all turn into a shit-fest.

I run a solid clip until my heart, lungs, and legs want to give out. Santiago warned me about overtaxing the body as the limits of physical reality are loosened, not eliminated. Men and women have killed themselves exerting supernatural effort for too long.

When I come to a narrow riparian gully, I stop to rest. I stumble down to a small stream that has dried in the summer heat to a narrow path of damp earth and scattered puddles. It's quiet there—not the deafening sounds vacuum of the meadow, but a peacefulness of birds, bugs, and breeze in the tree tops—normalcy. I sit in a patch of dry sand on the dry creek bottom.

I've heard it said that spending a few quiet moments in nature every day is a critical ingredient to a happy life. Thoreau or maybe some anonymous tree-hugger said it, but I know it's true. I'd learned that in Colorado where the wilds were the only place I could find peace.

I feel so tranquil sitting there that I don't sense the volcano until it's too late. My exhausted bliss suddenly gives way to a well of emotions I'd kept contained. Love, fear, passion, and anger coalesced into a surge that throws me over on my back and makes me cry out uncontrollably. All the shit that's taken place since I'd come to California flashes through my mind in no particular order, ending with an image of my mother and sister, both vulnerable and scared by something unseen.

I have an alarming thought that this is what Santiago warned me about—using images Mom and Gwen in danger to trigger reflexive rage. They seem embedded in my mind, as though they actually took place—a created memory of something I didn't want to think about.

I don't know how long I'm in that state, but when I finally roll over and sit up, I'm spent. The sun streaming down through the treetops suggests it's sometime close to noon. I stand and my legs shake and wobble underneath me from fatigue. Now I only have to figure out where I am and somehow make my way home.

Chapter 43

End of Festival

'Hey, I hope you remember me... this is Jasmine. If you're who I think you are, we met two years ago. I can't believe I might have found you after all this time.

'I've totally moved since we last spoke and I knew you'd never be able to find me, even online... bet you couldn't even now if you tried, lol. So anyway I thought I'd hunt you down. If it's not you, please delete my apologetic ass.

'So what's up? Anything interesting happening to or around you these days? For my part, so much has changed, so much new stuff going. Playing it smart and all, but, hey, you can't live life too safe, right? My 'ol man and I, you remember him... thinks he's freaking St. James half the time. Well, we aren't talking right now and I guess I'm feeling a little unfocused because of it, but you know how that is. So hey, any insight or suggestions, I'm all ears.

'So write me... talk, talk, talk... tell all.

'Hugs... Jazz.

'PS. If this is you, where are you these days? Any way for you to hook up with a girl living in the middle of nowhere? JB'

I stare at the message and read it over twice. "Does that sound like Gwen?" I want it to sound like a young girl writing. "What the hell." Send.

I stare at the screen for a couple of minutes to see if the message goes through or bounces back. Nothing happens. If it works, and Isa figures out it's me, she might be able to reply without placing herself in danger. I stand and rip off my sweat soaked t-shirt and kick off my damp jeans. I'm about to take a dash to the outdoor shower when a new message pops in.

"That's quick," I mutter, returning to my laptop. It isn't Isa.

Mishee: 'Jesse, turn on your phone please.'

'Sure!' Send. 30 seconds later the phone rings and I answer. "What's up?"

"Jesse, this is Hilda Carter. Can you come in this afternoon for a shift, we can really use your help."

The Kat is mad to be sure, and by 2:30 I'm caught up in the middle of it. Lex hasn't shown for work and Christine wants to go look for her; she bounces as soon I walk in.

In the chaos that follows that afternoon, there's no time to chat with Michelle or Jeffrey, but when I take a break out back, Pete comes out through the back door.

"There you are. Michelle said you were back here," he says.

"Hey! What's up, The Carters have you working as well?" I ask.

"Huh, right," he says, wide eyed and sits on the recycling bin next to me. It groans under his weight and he stands and leans against the wall instead. "Too much work already," he adds. "Helping my dad and uncles is tough enough."

"You're a girl," I chide.

He quickly raises both hands to his chest and cups his pecs. "Oh, damn," he says, giving them a squeeze. "Don't get me excited like that." We both have a laugh and then Pete shifts subjects. "So Mishee says you think Wingate is after something under the cannery, something important."

"Yeah," I say, suspiciously. "She send you out here to talk me out of checking it out?"

"Hell no," Pete says. "I'm here to sign up. I wanna give it to that rat bastard any way I can, for Paul I mean."

In the few minutes before Michelle comes out to call me back to duty, we form a plan; Tuesday night we'll steal into the cannery and find out what we can.

The grand finale of the festival takes place between 2:00 and 3:00 in the afternoon. By 4:00 the street begins to thin noticeably and it seems like everyone leaving town wants coffee for the road. By 8:00 the streets are almost back to normal.

Ten o'clock finally comes and we close the doors to The Kat. A tired hush falls over the empty tables and chairs and the five of us, the Carters, Jeffrey, Michelle, and myself, stand in a rough circle and stare at each other.

"Do you hear that?" Bill finally asks with a finger pointing to the air and a mischievous smile on his face. I listen but only heard the muted sound of traffic out on the street, the sound of someone trying the locked door to The Kat, and the low whirring of the glass fronted cooler behind the counter. I shake my head, but Michelle nods and Jeffrey smiles. "That's the sound of the end of festival," he says with a tired smile, "and the sound of well deserved time off and bonuses."

He and Hilda go on to express their heartfelt thanks for our hard work over the past week, something that triggers a twinge of guilt in me, and then they suggest that the three of us go home and leave the clean-up to them. No one argues and before we know it, we're standing outside of The Kat on the sidewalk.

We must have looked like a trio of stoners, standing shakily on the sidewalk with no place to go and half stooped. "Well, this is an anticlimax," Jeffrey says.

"Yeah," I say. "Seems wrong to end it all with a flat."

"Anyone up for wine and hot tubing, the folks are gone until tomorrow," he suggest.

"I think I need to just get home and crash," Michelle says. "I'm beater than a blender."

"What?" I ask. "Beater than ..."

"Oh shut up," she says with mock annoyance. "You know what I mean."

"Yeah, I guess I should get home and see how things are," I say. With the busyness of the day over, the deaths of the five come back to haunt me. I couldn't have relaxed with my friends even if we'd had the energy. "Another time though, like maybe this week sometime... or the weekend."

"Absolutely," Jeffrey says.

"Any word from Christine or Lex?" I ask.

"She can't find her," Michelle says. "She gave up for the night and went home."

"Well, on that cue..." I say.

"Hey!" Michelle says, grabbing my arm. "You're not planning to break into the cannery again are you Jesse? Please tell me you're not."

"Okay, I'm not," I lie.

She detects my insincerity and knits her brow. "Don't make me have to call the cops on you again."

"Well, if you come up with a better plan, let me know," I say, then turn and walk down the sidewalk toward the back of The Kat where my bike is.

"Jesse!" Michelle calls out.

"Goodnight, Michelle." I say. "Later, Jeffrey."

I swing by the Lex's sanctuary on the way home. It's deserted, which is probably a good thing because I don't know what I would have done if she'd been there. The tension between us isn't as thick as it had been but it's still there—both anger and desire, a volatile combination.

At home, Mom's up reading and Gwen, it turns out, is with her cousins again at the colony.

"That's getting to be a regular thing," I say to mom.

She puts down her book and gives me a curious look. "Twice isn't exactly regular, Jesse."

I feel stupid. Am I being jealous again? "Well, with them it's unusual for it to happen at all, right?"

"Yeah, it is that," she says. "Are you bothered by Gwen being there with her cousins?"

I sit down on the arm of the couch and Mom frowns so I slide down onto the cushion. "No, not really, a bit I guess. I don't know."

"What's wrong?" she asks. She gives me the look and I feel myself melting under it.

"Nothing," I say, but she knows I'm holding back. What can I possibly tell her? "Where's Uncle Frank, at the colony?"

"No, he had to get back to the project up the coast. Left this afternoon."

I stand and make my way toward the kitchen door. "I'm really beat. Need to go to bed," I say.

"Okay," Mom says.

I stop at the door and think about Uncle Frank. "Mom? You think Uncle Frank and Selene Sanchez will get together?"

She puts her book down on her lap and thinks thoughtfully, staring at the ceiling. "It will mean her leaving her home, ending the work she's been doing," she says doubtfully. Then a smile crosses her lips. "I think maybe yes."

"Yeah, me too. It would be nice, nice for both of them," I suggest. Mom nods in agreement. "Well, goodnight, Mom."

"Goodnight Sweetheart."

Back in the boat, the first thing I do is check my email. There, waiting for me, is a return reply from Isa.

'Jazz, of course I remember you. We met in Florida two years ago. I can't believe you found me... I'm so excited I nearly peed myself. How have you been? Big changes huh? New friends, romances, adventures? Tell me everything.

'Nothing much happening on this end. Staying off the grid is so awesome. You're way lucky... I'm so connected up it's almost impossible to sneeze without people knowing about it. Safety and security are a little overrated, don't you think?

'So you're staying out of trouble I hope. I wish I could say the same for myself. Sometimes I think I need a whole team of people watching over me.

'Speaking of teams, you were right about the Harry Potter movie we bet on, your team did end up with the snitch. Tricky things those snitches... hard to see and harder to catch, but well, you did win so I owe you on the bet.

'Would love to pay up in person but I'm on the West Coast these days. Unless you have flue powder and can transport yourself out here, it's unlikely. Still, I'll see if I can get away for a short trip out there sometime soon.

'Take good care,

'I.'

"Message received, Isa. You are definitely a girl and somewhere around my age. Huh! Seems you're being watched as well. But by who?" I type out a quick response, trying to imagine what Gwen might write.

'It is you. If you could only hear me scream. Hah! We did have the snitch, the bowling one, and you do owe me big on that. I want to collect on it too... soon! Maybe I can come out your way, if you can send me directions?

'Hugs to you...

'Jazz.

'PS... Can you chat or Skype anytime soon? Let me know how to make this more personal okay?'

To anyone familiar with the Harry Potter books, the banter about snitches wouldn't make sense, but I am gambling any adult intercepting it wouldn't be. I hope Isa will confirm or dis-confirm that Bolin is the informant she's been warning me about.

The email sent, I flop myself back on the bed and I'm gone before my head hits. Despite my fatigue, however, I must have awakened a dozen times during the night, with vague images of bodies I've been dreaming of and a sick feeling of guilt and doom.

Chapter 44

Mindful Morning

Morning brings a full bag of email: two are from Michelle warning me again to stay away from the cannery, and one is from Christine reporting in that Lex showed up at her place in the middle of the night so all is well.

Pete emailed me, which is a first, wanting to firm up the plans for Tuesday night. I think about Isa's concerns about emails being intercepted and I write him back, suggesting we keep the plans between the two of us and discuss them only in person, and that we meet for lunch today at Pandora's. Tony writes, asking how the deception worked, but best of all there was a quick note from Miranda stating that Paul moved his figures yesterday. There's nothing from Isa.

Mom isn't in the house but her car's in the driveway. Everything looks to be normal, including the half pot of fresh coffee in the kitchen, and I sense—smell—no danger, so I assume she's upstairs. I take a cup of coffee out to the front porch, and settle into the old sofa.

I sit a while and watch the cars roll buy and the flow of the river. The air has a refreshing chill to it and carries the scent of the trees, grasses, flowers, and the river itself. I wonder whether my sense of smell is more acute now, or if I'm simply taking the time to notice.

It's the first time I've sat on the porch to watch life go by since I arrived. There's nothing in my head that I have to do, no place I feel I have to be, and rather than being bored to distraction, I felt at peace.

Just after finishing my second cup of coffee, I hear the back door to the kitchen creak open then shut, and a moment later footsteps in the living room. The screen door creaks open and there's Mom.

She's dressed in cut-off jeans and an un-tucked white cotton shirt, and I snag another image of my mom as a teenager in the 80s. "Morning Mom," I say. "The coffee's great."

"Good morning Sweetheart," she says stepping over to the railing and looking out at the river. "And thank you." She turns to face me, then leans against the railing. I'm impressed again by the thought that my mom must have been a serious babe as a teen. Hell, she still is. Even the slight hump on the bridge of her nose where dad broke it twice only adds something to her looks.

"Did I just hear you come in through the kitchen?" I ask.

"Uh huh. I was out for a walk out back," she says, gesturing over her shoulder. Over her shoulder was actually pointing to the river but I let her messed up sense of direction slide without a tease.

"Out back?" An alarm goes off in my head. "You mean you went out to the meadow on your own?"

Mom's mouth drops open a notch and she looks puzzled. "Uh, yes I did," she says with a smile, "just like I did when I was half your age."

"Yeah, but things were different then," I say, then cringe at the words I so often poke fun of, the hallmark of the over protective parent. "I mean, with everything happening and all, Wingate's goons, the accident, I just don't think you should go anywhere by yourself... anywhere isolated I mean."

"Well, listen to you," she says, smiling. "You've become quite the protector."

It is a good-natured dig that I deserve, given I've caused her enough concern to turn her hair gray twice. I hold up my hands in a gesture of surrender. "Fine, you got me. But seriously, I think we should all be careful. Even Santiago says you and Gwen are in danger."

Mom gives me a pensive look and bites her lower lip, a sure sign she's problem solving. "He says he'll make sure nothing happens to the two of you," I add, "but I still think you both should be careful."

"And you?" she asks.

A moment of revelation? How much should I tell her? "I'm more like Santiago; it's my job to protect you." I say with a smile.

To my surprise, Mom stares at me thoughtfully then smiles. "The first step in that is to take care of you, keep yourself safe."

ᴄʜᴀpᴛer 45

Sedition

"So what's the plan?" Pete asls, leaning over the table conspiratorially. Pete's big, as in solid and beefy, and he comes off as a serious redneck. The buzz-cut and Toronto Blue Jays cap he always wares doesn't help the image, but to know him is to realize he doesn't fit any stereotypes. He's exactly the guy you want watching your back in a pinch, and I'm confident about our venture.

After being crowded out by tourists for the week of festival, the locals have packed Pandora's and I have no idea who might be listening. I go over the plan I've devised, avoiding direct mention of the cannery or anything else that would clue what we're up to. In the process I realize just how vague my plan is—get in through the vent cap again and… what? Pete doesn't notice; he's all optimism and excitement.

"Awesome," he says. "What do you think we'll find?" he asks as the server slides our pizza onto the table.

"Hot pizza for two hot guys," she says, but her attention is entirely on Pete. She's a little older than us, maybe 19 or 20, and hometown cute. The dance of her eyes and her coy smile tell me she is into Pete, only he doesn't seem to notice. When she's done trying to flirt with him, she leaves disappointed.

"She's into you," I say, scooping up a slice.

Pete pauses, shoots her retreating backside a glance, then gives me a questioning look. "Alicia? Really?"

"Yeah, really," I say.

"Man, she's like 20," he says with disbelieving interest, "a woman." Just then she turns and looks back out way and Pete spins his head back to the tabletop so fast he could give himself whiplash. She notices and flashes a quick smile.

"Yup! You have a woman who's interested," I say. "So now that you have something to live for after all, you still in?"

"Yeah, like Flint," he mumbles glancing back her way.

Before we're done, Alicia comes back to the table four times to ask if there's anything else she can get us. Watching Pete fumble over his words each time is vicariously painful. "You need to just ask her out," I suggest finally.

"I'm thinking about it," he says defensively.

"You're funny," I muse.

"What? I've just got to think it through," he defends.

"You flirt with Lex shamelessly, and you have to think about asking a girl out who is obviously interested?

"Woman," he reminds me. "Alicia's a grown woman. Besides, Lexi's... safe. She's more like a sister."

"So you flirt with your sister?"

"Shut up!"

We agreed to meet behind The Kat at 10:00 pm Tuesday night and part ways. I wander the streets a while, trying to flesh out the plan but the killings continue to haunt me at every corner. Focusing on the scheme gives me an escape, but every passing face is a sick reminder of what's been done; the town's just too busy. I jump on the Shadow and ride to a place I might find quiet.

I stand in the center of the empty floor space of Lex's sanctuary and stare up. This is where she comes for solitude, this is where we made out and shared time. Rather than helping me focus on the mission, my thoughts are divide further.

I make my way up to the second floor loft were Lex reads and sleeps, and I'm surprised to find a crystal vase containing a dozen perfect peach roses. They're fresh, and the water in the vase is full, so I know she, or someone, has put them there recently. I have no idea what peach roses are supposed to mean, but they smell like trouble.

Bolin? An image of Lex and Bolin making out triggers a rush of jealousy. "Christine," I tell myself. "She'd buy Lex flowers to calm her down." That might even be true, but I'm not pacified. I sit in the loft a while and do nothing but breathe. Though it settles most of the chaos in my head, thoughts of Bolin and Lex, and of the killings, refuse to give way.

After an hour or so, I leave for home, but when I arrive, the place is deserted. As much as it would have been nice to spend time alone with my thoughts, the prospect feels intolerable. I jump back on the Shadow, and at the end of the driveway I head east. I figure I'd been tranced out on the ride because after steering onto the narrow road, into the woods, and past the warning signs, I'm surprised to realize where I am—it's like waking up during a long trip to find yourself someplace unexpected.

The wall of trees and the simple gatehouse are just as I remember them, as is the ancient who stands in the middle of the road, baring my passage. I stop the bike about ten feet from him and he stares at me in a way that makes my skin crawl. It isn't exactly a staring match, but it feels like a standoff and I begin to feel stupid. *What am I doing here?* I think. *I'm not welcome.*

I remove my helmet and the old man tilts his head downward and crouches slightly, then juts his head forward in my direction. For a blink, I find myself looking at shimmering visage surrounding his face; it's vaguely wolf-like—he's a shifter, and he's somehow showing himself to me. I feel a jolt of adrenaline and my spine tingles from base to stem. I know then why this solitary old man is the road's guardian; should someone refuse his order to turn and leave, and if he is anything like Santiago, they live to regret it… or not.

"Ah, nice trick. I haven't learned to do that," I say. I have no idea whether he can recognize me as a fellow shifter. Santiago had said the experienced one's can see that, and a lot more.

The old man walks slow and easy until he is three feet away, and no longer baring passage. Maybe it's self-delusion but I sense kinship; he feels like I imagine a great uncle would feel. He gives the bike a once over, then bores his eyes into mine. "You will," he says, then turns and wanders toward the shack.

"Does this mean I can pass?" I call to him. A briefly waived hand over his right shoulder is the only answer I receive. "Okay," I mutter to myself.

I stop at the same hub of activity that Uncle Frank and I did when we visited. Other than a fascinated stare from a young guy Gwen's age, no one takes much notice of me and I find that seriously odd—these people keep to themselves, keep the world at a distance, yet they pay no never mind to me.

That's when I begin to feel awkward. I have no idea what I'm doing here. Finally, a woman in her 20s takes notice and approaches. "You must be Jesse Benatar," she says, with a French accent. The question surprises me because I don't recall seeing her before. *How do you know me?*

"Ah, yeah," I say stupidly.

"The bike," she says, "and you do look a little like your mother, the cheeks and nose, I think. She has a pleasant look about her, a subtle, wholesome beauty. She has blond hair, which, from what I've seen, is very rare in the colony, a robust build like you might expect from someone who does a lot of heavy physical work, and a healthy glow that screams 'outdoors girl'. "I'm Jocelyne Rosseau," she beams.

"Hi, I…" can't think of another thing to say. "You're French," I say, and then feel my face flush.

"Oui, vous parlez français?" she asks excitedly?

"Ah, no. Sorry"

"Not to worry, French is not common here," she says graciously.

"France or Canada?" I ask, feeling more relaxed in the glow of her accent and charm.

"France," she says. "From a little village in the Pyrénées that almost no one has heard of."

"Sounds mysterious," I say.

She frowns. "Not as mysterious as one might think," she says. "It is very beautiful though. Are you here to see your mother and sister?" she asks.

"No," I find myself saying. "I'm looking for Señorita Ruiz."

"I take you," a young male voice calls out before I have a chance to let what I've said sink in. I turn to see the kid who's watched me pull in. He's dark skinned, bright eyed, and displays an excited smile of white teeth. "I know, I take you," he says, staring at my bike.

Chapter 46

The Narrow Path

Journal - Sierra Nevadas, CA.

> *I hiked along a ridge today, and came across a section that was worn away on both sides for about 80 feet. The surface was a jumble of loose and irregular rock as little as a foot wide in places, and the drop off was 400 feet on either side. The smart thing to do would have been to turn around, which, dumb fuck I am, I didn't.*
>
> *I nearly bought it a half dozen times, once because of bad footing, but the rest because I'd let my mind wander from the path to the drop off. It was only by staying focused on where I wanted to go and not on where I feared that I'd made it.*
>
> ~ *From the Journal of Jesse Benatar*

"Left or right?" I shout back to Alejandro as we approach a fork in the dirt road. Until I finally got him to sit still behind me, his moving around excitedly nearly caused me to dump the bike a half dozen times. At the ten mph I'm keeping the speed to, there's no real nee to wear a helmet, but he wants to so bad I let him wear mine.

"Right," he says in his thick accent.

Another half mile down the dirt road that undulates gently through the thick forest and we come to a small clearing, in the middle of which is a sizable building made from rough hewn logs. It's as far as the road goes so I pull the bike up to it and stop. "Wow, how old is this place?" I ask.

Alejandro pulls the unfastened helmet from his head. "Two hundred eighty two years," he replies. "Almost first building made."

I flip out the kickstand and motion that I want to lay the bike over but realize he doesn't get it. "Pile off," I say with a tilt of my head. After a moment of hesitation, he slides off the seat.

"I wait and show you way back," he says hopefully.

"Of course," I say. "I wouldn't have you walk all the way back." That elicits a confused look on his face and I remember that the colonials walk everywhere they go and it's probably nothing for him to hoof the mile and a half back to the hub. It's a single road, no way to get lost on my return, but I say, "Besides, I might end up somewhere I'm not supposed to be."

Alejandro smiles brightly. "You wait, I tell Catalina you want talk, yes?" he says, and then bounds up to the building and disappears inside. I'm not the swiftest when it comes to social subtleties or protocols, but I have the distinct impression that the building is not a place I'd be welcome in.

A few moments later he comes out with a disappointed and somewhat strained look on his face. He saunters back me. "She is at ceremony, ah, at end of camino sagrado," he says, gesturing toward the forest behind the building.

"Can we go there?" I ask.

Alejandro's eyes widened in alarm at the question, "No, no, we not…"

"¿Por qué quieres caminar por la senda sagrada?" another voice asks. We both look toward the source and there, a dozen paces away, stands an ancient that makes most old people look adolescent.

She is about 4 foot nothing; has a mass of wrinkles for a face; thick hair as white as snow pulled back tight, and wares a white and yellow cotton dress that covers her from neck to feet. What seriously stands out is the clarity and strength of her voice, and the aliveness of her pale green eyes. How she crept up on us is a mystery because there's no place but the woods or the building that she could have come from, and both of those are 40 plus feet away.

Alejandro's eyes widen at the sight of her and he closes his eyes and bows. "Abuela," he says.

I thought Santiago had presence, but this old woman's a show stopper. She takes a few steps closer, not taking her eyes from me, then repeats her question, this time pointing an age-bent finger at me. "¿Por qué quieres caminar por la senda sagrada?" she asks.

"She ask, why you want walk sacred path," Alejandro translates.

"Um, I want to see Catalina, Señorita Ruiz," I say. Alejandro translates, clearly flustered by the old woman.

She takes a few steps closer and I notice how steady and erect she moves, not bent over and feeble. Perhaps she isn't as old as her face looks—I hear the sun will do that and California has plenty of sun. She stops and places both hands over her stomach, one over the other, and stares.

I don't know what else to say but Alejandro's bowing silence suggested it might be best to stay quiet. Then something begins to happen in my head—my vision blurs, I feel dizzy, and I can't think straight. It feels exactly like one of my hypnopompic states—between sleep and awake—yet I'm still standing. As quickly as it comes, it leaves and I find myself staring into the old woman's green eyes again.

She nods slightly. "No alejarse de la ruta," she says.

Alejandro looks up at the old woman and then smiles at me excitedly. "She say you no leave path. She let us go."

"¡No, nieto!" the old woman says to him, and immediately, his shoulders, fall. The old woman smiles. "Usted no está listo." The old woman then turns and begins to walk away, toward the building.

"So who's that?" I ask quietly.

"Abuela. She is grandmother," he replies.

"She's your grandmother?" I ask, surprised, she seems to hold Alejandro in affectionate regard enough, but she is way too old to be his grandmother.

"No, she big Grandmother, first Grandmother," he says. My puzzled look is not lost on him. "She is most elder, most old of all, leader of ah…" his face betrays effort to translate what he wants to say, or reluctance.

"Los buscadores de la luz," I guess.

He flashes me an uncertain look then nod. "Si."

"Jeez! How old is she?" I say looking back towards her, only to find her gone.

"Some say ah… ciento ocho años," he says.

"That's ah, what… a hundred and eight?" I ask.

He hesitates and then nods his head. "Si, one hundred eight, but uncle say she lie. He say she ciento veinte años. One hundred ah…"

"Twenty!" I suggest and he nod. "One Hundred and twenty?" He nods again.

I find the narrow footpath where Alejandro said it would be, and I'm quickly swallowed by the mid-day darkness of the forest. It meanders through towering redwoods and its spongy surface, a product of millennia of falling redwood bark and needles, absorb the sound and weight of each step.

The air is heavy with the primal scents of moist earth and plants, and something else I can't place—something so faint I'm barely aware of it, but I find it intoxicating. As I walk, the smells, trees, and palpable silence work at me until I feel a deep sense of peace, and my mind clears of its usual cacophony of thoughts.

I follow the path for a quarter mile or more, each step lulling me into a deeper state of calm awareness. I become so immersed in the moment that I have to remind myself why I am here—Catalina. I want the path to go on forever, for the journey to never end, and I imagine a forest 10,000 miles deep with uncountable secrets to discover. *If this is what it is the live in the colony…*

I catch movement in the corner of my left eye, but when I look, I see only the towering branchless trunks of the redwoods separated by the undulating forest floor. There's sparse undergrowth in the mature forest of giants and the open space between the trees is inviting. *'Do not stray from the path'* the old woman had said. "What if I do?" I mutter.

There's something out there, I can sense it, but I feel no threat, just curiosity. I watch for movement for a few minutes, then walk further until the path dips into a hollow. At the bottom I quickly drop down on my haunches, and after few moments I peek up over the edge, hoping to spot whatever or whomever I'd caught a glimpse of—nothing but the silence of the forest greets me. "Huh! Playing tricks on yourself again," I say.

I continue my trek and after a few hundred yards, I slip back into the state of bliss with little thought. Then I see, or think I see something out of the corner of my right eye. A dark patch disappears behind a tree before I can set my full vision on it. Unlike the other, this one makes the hair stand up on my arms and I feel a prickling travel up my spine. Something stirs deep within, that part that surfaces when I shift.

My vision narrows and I feel my body tense and crouch. The smell of the air seems to unfold into dozens of scents, each distinct and familiar. I take a step toward the edge of the path. *'Do not stray from the path'* the words repeat. I look down at the border between the trail, where countless footfalls have made their impression over the years, and the forest floor, perfectly undisturbed, as though no human foot had ever touched it.

I feel a sudden urge to move on—flight winning over fight. I move along the path at a quicker pace and almost immediately catch a glimpse of a figure to my left. I stop and see nothing, but don't linger as I had before. I pick up my pace and feel an urge to run but resist. My eyes focus on the path and the distance ahead, searching for any sign I'm getting closer to the end.

Movement to my left again—I glance without stopping. The forest and whatever's out there is inviting, it piques my interest, and I nearly veer off the path. *'Do not stray from the path!'* Movement on the right again—dark and threatening. Without looking, my pace increases to a jog, and I feel the now familiar stirring deep within.

Movement to my left—closer. Movement to my right—dark and fast. I look and see nothing and then search ahead for someone, anything familiar. The peace of the forest has morphed into something dark and primal, something that stirs my fear—maybe this is why people flock to cities and light them up at night. I brake into a run.

More movement on the right, only a few paces away now. I want to bolt left, into the inviting expanse. *'Do not stray from the path!'* More movement on my left—glance—nothing—look ahead—movement to the right and left. The push and pull I feel draws me closer to the edge of the path. *'Do not stray from the path!'* One side feels like certain death, annihilation; the other feels intriguing, safe, but as I look down at the path beneath my feet, only it feels… right.

In an act of courage, faith, or foolishness, I slow to a trot, a walk, and then I stop and kneel. I touch the path and feel its cool moistness and a sense of comfort moves up my arm and radiates into my body.

I slowly stand and face the left, hear the lingering thoughts of danger in my mind and feel the desire to escape into its expanse, then close my eyes and bow slightly. "No thank you," I say. "Not today."

I turn to the right and feel pure, revolting menace. I nearly feel the shift happen, once, then again as I face the unseen threat but manage to keep it at bay. Against a voice crying out from within, I close my eyes and bow. I have to quell repeated surges of fear, breathing deeply into each, until they subsided. "Not today," I say.

When I open my eyes and look around, the forest is once again beautiful and serene. "Damn," I mutter. I feel familiar with this part of the forest, and wondered if Santiago had brought me along this way in my training. A quick calculation in my head ensures me we'd not come within miles of this place.

I continue my walk, slow and peaceful again, aware of things inside and out. A rocky outcropping in the forest to my left haunts me. *I know you.* The tree to the left of the path ahead looks vaguely familiar, as well. *I've been here before.* Then, after I pass the tree and continue down the sloping path it comes back—the dream I had during my first night in Hook Point, where I ran down a robed figure at the bottom of the slope—Catalina.

I continue down the grade, and as I reach it the point where the path veers behind a redwood, Catalina Ruiz walks into view. She's alone, and dressed in the dark, hooded robe she wore in that first dream, the one she always wears when she visits. She stops in the middle of the path and looks at me as though I've been expected.

"Catalina," I say. I walk up to her and feel the same awkwardness between us that's always there when we met in the flesh. She looks at me expectantly and I realize I have no idea why I am here. I rode to the Colony on impulse, stated that I was there to see Catalina on intuition, but now what? Rather than open my mouth and jabber about nothing, I stand in silence.

She smiles. "I see you now, Jesse Benatar," she says.

Chapter 47

By Flickering Light

I sit at my laptop, reading the message…

'Hey Jazz, I'm not good for chat or Skype right now. Maybe soon. I'd love to get together if that were possible, but you being there and me here, difficult huh? I'm Mad enough to bust free and visit you someplace secluded, like in Florida. Remember the time we snuck away and we hung out in that alley, you know, the one with all the Cats. That was cool.

'Hey, sorry, but I have to jet—way too busy here. Looking forward to hump-day when I get a break. Well, not much of a break really, just a doctors appointment, and at 10:30 in the freaking morning. I swear if she makes me wait ten minutes again, I'll leave. Hey, I'm complaining here…sorry. Well, write and let me know if you'll ever be out this way anytime soon. I suspect we'll be moving back to Florida sometime soon. Sucks to be me sometimes.

'Oh, and not to intrude and all, but you should talk to your dad. I don't always get along with mine, but, hey, these old guys sometimes know what they're talking about.

'Stay smart!'

I translate several possible meanings behind her inane reply. The best I can come up with is 'meet me at the back of the Mad Kat on Wednesday at 10:40.' "Game on, whoever you are." I think of Santiago and immediately dismiss the idea, but it pops back into my head several times as I type out my reply.

'Hey, I'm so glad you got my message. Thank you for writing back…'

I stop typing and read the line. Is this what Gwen would say? No! She and mom are up in the house, probably waiting for me by now, so I can't run and get her to write the message. "Oh, hell!" I mutter, as I change it.

'Hey, you. Yeah, I remember that time in the alley. It was awesome. Let's agree to get together there again someday. I'll hitch-hike there if I have to… you know me—Mad as a hatter as they say.'

Damn, talk about vague. Will she get it? Will someone else guess the message?

'Sorry to say, no romances in my cards, so maybe I should gamble right? lol. I am enjoying my anonymity these days, too many people knowing too much gets to be a drag. Facebook really sucks for that, if you ask me. Well, I'm late myself. I'm so jazzed about getting together with you… get it? Jazzed! lol… For now, tell me more, more, more!

'Hugs… Jazz.

'PS… Doctors are such a drag… I'd leave too.'

Send. Now I just have to wait. Wednesday seems a long way off, especially with the plan to break into the cannery tomorrow, but I'm looking forward to finally discovering who Isa is.

Mom and Gwen are waiting for me with a thermos of hot chocolate, a basket of snacks, and an old hurricane lantern from Frank's shed. We go to the far east side of the property, to where a hollow is filled with water half the year and is never used for anything because of that, then sit down on an old log and light the lantern; there's a ban on open fires, being summer, so it has to do as a substitute.

Rather than sitting together in the flickering light of the TV, we sit in the flickering light of the lantern and are soon so absorbed with each other that the cars on River Road pass unnoticed. Gwen talks excitedly about her time with her cousins at the colony, and how happy and together they all are, despite living without the benefits of most modern conveniences.

"And they're so aware of what's going on in the world," she says passionately. "They want to talk about things I have no clue are happening out there," she says. "Important things, things that really matter."

"But almost no knowledge of pop culture," I suggest, sharing what I noticed talking to Serena.

"I know, right. They're clueless," she says. "And uninterested," she adds.

What surprises me is they have dance nights. "Really? To what, fiddle?" I ask.

"No, to real music," she says. "Since Uncle Frank helped them install windmills, they have dances twice a week. They love to dance."

"So much for no pop culture," I muse. I think about what Catalina told me that night, that she's seen two vampire movies.

"But that's just it," Gwen says. "They'll dance to all sorts of music but they don't know or care what it's called or who the artists are. They just like dance to it."

The more I learn about the people of The Colony, the more I realize how complex they are—advanced beyond the rest of us in some ways, downright primitive in others. Enigma meets paradox.

Gwen and I tag-team Mom about her time there but she only speaks vaguely about connecting with relatives. She's clearly holding back because press as we might, she never reveals much more then the dullest of details, and it isn't long before she redirects our attention to my visit.

I talk about my journey there and what happened. The importance of us talking about our connections with the colony is not lost on me, but I'm leery about sharing some of my experiences, especially some of the things Catalina and I talked about. The possibility of Mom hauling our butts away from Hook Point is still all too real.

Mom raises an eyebrow when I let it slip that I went there to see Catalina Ruiz. That puts me on guard and I think she realizes it. When I mention the old woman, and that Alejandro referred to her as The Grandmother, Mom and Gwen both look alarmed.

"What?" I ask in response to their wide-eyed stares.

"Are you sure he said 'The Grandmother'?" Mom asks.

"What did you say?" Gwen asks anxiously before I can answer Mom. "You didn't call her an ancient did you? She's like, as close to being their Sovereign as you can get."

"Yes, and no," I reply. "It was cool. She's old as dirt and I think a little batty," I say to taunt Gwen, "but I think she likes me." I know I overplayed it with the last line because Mom smiles slightly and Gwen gives me her 'yeah right' look.

I tell them about the walk through the woods, and even mention feeling torn between my attraction to one side of the path and my aversion to the other. I have to reassure Gwen that I hadn't strayed from the path, and then go on to tell them about meeting Catalina. I manage not to say much about our conversation, other than her not being concerned about the Talfar, at which point Gwen and I have to bring Mom up to date on our concerns about it.

When done, we turn out the lantern and make out way back to the house. Gwen accompanies me back to the boat for a quick catch up. "I can't believe you met The Grandmother," she says, "that she actually talked to you."

"What's the big deal," I say. "Sure she's old and respected and all, but she's just a person like anyone else," I say.

Gwen closes her eyes and lifts her hands up near her face as though to stop a volleyball. "Oh, my god, can you hear yourself," she says.

"Yeah, loud and clear," I say. "Can you? Listen, why don't we save the whole Jesse might have embarrassed and condemned the family line for another time." Before Gwen can object, I ask, "So what's all the concern whether or not I stray from the path about? Would I have been eaten or something?"

Gwen rolls her eyes. "Jesse, they're not like that; they're not into the whole punishment and damnation thing. That's one of the things they came here to escape from."

"So what, then?" I ask.

"I was told about that path by Serena, and that walking it is one of their sacred rites," Gwen says, looking to me for a reaction. I guess I don't give her the one she wants because she says, "Jesse, only people deemed ready are ever allowed to walk it. Why you?"

I sit on the steps up to the Therion. "Ah, like why did they allow a no count peon such as myself to…"

"No I didn't mean it like that. Jesse," Gwen says. "Most of the people living in the colony never walk it. It's like the road to their inner sanctum."

"Well, I never made it to the end so maybe I'm still impure."

"Yeah, no doubt, but you didn't aim to get to the end, right?" Gwen says. "You just wanted to see Catalina and you did that."

"And if I strayed from the path?" I ask.

"I don't know, but my guess is something would have prevented you from seeing her," Gwen says.

I let that sink in. The trail did test my self-control, as much as anything has. "Fears and desires," I mutter.

"What?" Gwen asks.

"Fears and desires," I repeat, recalling a teaching from Max. "Max once told me that all of our suffering stems from avoiding or escaping discomfort, and grasping for our desires, or something like that. I think I was walking down the path that divides the two."

"Hah! The straight and narrow," Gwen says. "In a definitely non-puritanical way, that is."

"Yeah, well, I need to crash, kid."

"So what's the plan about the Talfar?" she asks, presenting me with yet another decision point.

"No plans yet," I lie. The last thing I want is for Gwen to freak at the plans for tomorrow night. "I'll come up with something, though."

"You'll keep me in the loop?" she asks.

"Yeah, of course," I say. Lying to Gwen doesn't sit well with me, so while washing up for bed, I decide to tell Gwen about the plan just before leaving for the cannery tomorrow. I hit the bed hard and fall into a troubled sleep of crazed dreams that Salvador Dali would have had a hard time with.

Chapter 48

Incursion

Morning brings another warning from Michelle against breaking into the cannery and a heads up that she'd told Santiago about the threat to his life, which he apparently found amusing. I read Miranda's daily update on Paul and I send her the best words of support I can muster. I think about my encounter with The Grandmother and what I'd felt in the forest on their sacred trail. I think about what I'd heard about their healers and I wonder if they could help Paul. I make a mental note to ask Catalina.

After breakfast I go back to the boat, open my trunk, and select the equipment for the night's mission. Then a thought comes to me: how many times had my father done something similar before his missions, and I wonder what ran through his head the morning of the mission he didn't return from.

I meet Pete at The Kat for lunch, and find Lex bussing tables. We go over the plans, the time we'll meet, the general lay out of the interior of the cannery, and the plan of attack. "You're not serious?" Lex says. We look up and Lex is standing five feet away holding an empty tray; we'd become careless in our secluded corner.

"Lex…" I begin.

"You two really think you're going to pull that off? Michelle's going to love this," she threatens.

"Lexi, sexy Lexi," Pete says in a shit poor attempt to flatter her.

"Lex, you can't tell her. She called the cops the last time…" I begin.

"As well she should have," Lex interupts. "It's a stupid thing to do. With everything that's happening, you're asking for a fuck bomb to go off. Besides, she already thinks you're going to try to get back in there despite your bullshit lies." It takes a good ten minutes of pleading with Lex not to squeal on us before she relents to 'I'll think about it', and then it's time for Pete to bounce.

I spend the rest of the afternoon going over the plan, recalling the inside details, and pondering why Catalina was so complacent about Wingate getting his hands on their most sacred artifact. It didn't make sense, but as I'd concluded the night before by the lantern with Mom and Gwen, the colonials are a hybrid of enigma and contradiction.

Before heading home, I take one last ride up of the coast highway above the cannery and study it from the edge of the road. It's as deserted as it was on the weekend. *No problem.*

At home I'm find two big ones in my In Box—one good and one bad. From Isa's it's clear she intends to meet me at 10:40 tomorrow morning behind The Kat. On the downside, Pete's message was that he was, as he was typing, being dragged by his father up the coast for two days. He assures me that he'll be back by Friday at the latest, and that we could do the deed then.

"Shit," I say. I know I should put the scheme on hold, wait until things can be played out as planned, but my impatience gets the best of me. That's why at 10:30, after the Kat is closed and everyone's gone home, I find myself next to my parked bike by the loading area, starring at the shadowy image of the cannery's gray hulk. They've made it even easier for me; the exterior lights that lit the area around the building are out, leaving the place in darkness.

I toss my pack on my back and take three steps toward the cannery, when a familiar voice speaks out. "Where you going Colorado?"

I turn toward the alleyway. "Lex! What are you doing here?"

"I asked first, cowboy," she says. "Wouldn't be planning to go in there alone would you?" she asks, gesturing to the cannery.

"Well, yeah, what of it?"

"Not going to happen, dear friend."

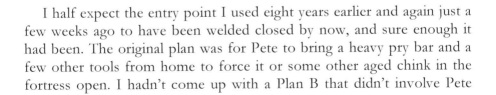

I half expect the entry point I used eight years earlier and again just a few weeks ago to have been welded closed by now, and sure enough it had been. The original plan was for Pete to bring a heavy pry bar and a few other tools from home to force it or some other aged chink in the fortress open. I hadn't come up with a Plan B that didn't involve Pete and his tools.

Lex and I try a few other promising entry points, ever watchful from our exposed positions, but the place has been sealed like a drum. "Fuck," I mutter. There's always the way I escaped the goons with the gun that day, but the shakiness of the scaffolding made it a risk I could not allow Lex to take, and if I went in that way there'd be no stopping her. Besides, that hole in the security was probably sealed as well.

Lex and I sit hunched close to the wall on the gangway, mostly obscured by the old coal silo. We watch as cars drive up and down the grade of the coast highway, and the fact that the occupants can spot us at points along the road if they know where to look makes us both a little edgy. Lex jabs me.

"So what's the plan?" she asks in a hushed voice.

"I'm working on it."

"Hell, Colorado, I thought you had this all sorted out."

"Yeah, right up to sitting here thinking about what to do next." That earns me a punch in the ribs that hurt like hell. "Lex!" I complain, but she's already slipping along the gangway to the stairs that leads to ground level. "Lex!" I whisper as loud as I dare. She is gone and there is nothing more for me to do but follow her.

Rather than staying close to the cannery, Lex makes her way to the strip of scrub between the cannery fence and the buildings lining the road, and then under the fence to the road itself. She looks to be heading home. "Hey, what's up with you?" I ask when I catch up with her. "If you don't want to go with me fine, but I don't want you calling the cops." She'd threatened to do that to convince me to let her come along. "Well, say something." Nothing.

I stop and turn to head back to the cannery, but Lex pulls on my shirt hard enough that I hear a tearing in the shoulder. "Hey, what's with you? If you're still pissed at me then take a clean swing, don't just mess with…" Wham! A strong, clean hook to my chest knocks the wind out of me.

It takes a moment to recover from it. "Okay, I strain. "Feel better?"

"A little," she says, her lips forming a subtle wry smile.

"Got it out of your system?"

"Not yet," she says. "Come on, you want into the cannery don't you?"

She might be stringing me along, part of her payback, and normally I'd have returned to the cannery and tried the coal chute on my own, but it dawns on me that Lex might be working out her hurt—maybe taking me on some pointless jaunt is part of that. I'm willing to go along for her sake; maybe something good will come of the botched venture.

She hikes down to the floating docks and out onto the one nearest the cannery's concrete wharf. It's used by commercial fisherman and is as quiet as a graveyard. Next to an old trawler that's listing badly, sits a dilapidated rowboat. Lex jumps onto the Trawler and makes her way to the rowboat.

"You're kidding." I say.

"You gonna stand there or do you want into the cannery?" she asks.

The boat's gunwale is half rotted away and there's about four inches of water sloshing around the floorboards when Lex steps into it. I'm dead certain it'll sink on us, but I figure we aren't going far and getting wet is no big deal.

After bailing the wreck out with a rusty can, she hands me the larger of two mismatched oars, and unhitches us. "You sure the owner won't mind?"

She gives me a sarcastic glance. "Would you? Besides, it's one of my mom's ex-boyfriend's and what I have on him, he'd give me the boat if I wanted it."

The oarlocks are gone, rotted away, so we sit side by side in the middle and paddle as though it's a canoe. We stay close to the shore and we're surprisingly well concealed by the junk and brush growing there. It is only about 40 feet to the concrete wharf of the cannery and we cross that quick enough. Then Lex steers us between two large pillars and we are swallowed up in the dank gloom of the underside of the wharf.

"What now?" I whisper.

"You'll see." We bump our way between pillars and scrape our way over crap on the bottom. "Works better at high tide," Lex muses when we become hung up on something. We push the boat free and go around it. About 50 feet in we come to a concrete wall, and in it, about 7 feet above the water, a large dark hole gapes at us.

"What's that?" I ask.

"Your way in," she says.

The hole proves to be the end of a large pipe, about 3 feet across, an old outlet for the Cannery's waste. It turns out that before any real concerns about pollution and long before any regulations, the cannery just pumped its waste out into the harbor. Fish blood and guts, and wash water from hosing down the floors, it all went out the nearest, easiest way.

We pull the boat up the wall where it grounds on something hard, and tie the frayed rope to a piece of rebar sticking out of the poorly laid concrete.

"You sure about this?" I ask.

"Yes," she replies.

"How?"

"I've lived here all my life, remember. Besides, you're not the only one who likes breaking into old places," she replies. She stands and can barely reach the edge of the hole. "Shit!" she says. "Like I say, it works better at high tide."

"I'll boost ya." Half grounded, the boat's steady enough that I can stand and push her up from the hips without falling overboard. The moment I place my hands on her hips, however, I feel my skin flush and a surge of energy run through my body. I suppose I hesitate long enough to give my reaction away—she cocks her head to the side and gives me an over the shoulder glance.

"Huh, you feel that do you?" she asks. She places her hands over mine and squeezes them gently, then caresses them. "Feels good, doesn't it?" she coos. I pull my hands from her hips. "Does it suck to know you'll never hold these hips again the way you used to?" she asks in a sultry tone.

"Yeah," I admit.

"Good!" she says bluntly. "Now boost me the fuck up."

I do; on the count of three, I lift while Lex jumps then scrambles into the pipe. She disappears, then her head pops out and she extends an arm for me to grab. A minute later, we're 30 feet into the pipe, crawling on hands and knees with Lex in the lead. We each have a small LED flashlight and neither of us dares talk above a whisper.

I thought the pipe would have been disgusting—wet and filled with rats and bugs and god knows what else. Aside from a few rat droppings, webs, and a bad smell, it's remarkably clean. The bonus is that the bottom of the pipe has a flat area of sediment that has dried smooth and hard.

Lex turns off her light and I do the same. About 20 feet ahead, there's a dim light filtering down from the top of the pipe. She gestures to be quiet and I nod. We creep toward the light and when we reach it I see it's a vertical set pipe, about three feet long, topped with a grating. The light seems to be coming from a dim bulb somewhere high up.

We're beneath the floor of the cannery, looking up at one of the drainage grates in the floor. "I can't believe they missed this," I whisper.

Lex shakes her head. "They didn't," she whispers. "The end of the pipe was capped years ago, something to do with the environment."

"And you removed it?"

She nods her head. "Took weeks. Nearly fell on me when I finally worked it free. Shit!"

"What?"

"It's stuck" she whispers, yanking on the grating.

"Give me a try," I say.

Lex yanks on it a few more times and starts to grunt loudly. I grab the waist of her jeans and pull her down. "Shh!" I caution.

Her eyes are wide and wild and I steel myself for another slug, but her expression suddenly changes to exaggerated yearning. "Oh, god, I love it when you're rough."

"Oh, shut up," I whisper. I push her aside and stick my torso up the pipe. "You're one serious tease, you know that right?"

Lex looks up at me with smug with satisfaction. "You love it."

Truth be told, I do. My attraction to Lex, the chemistry we share, hasn't diminished a fraction. She is a friend, a buddy, an amazing former lover, and a hurt woman wrapped into one tight little package. There's something else as well; I don't understand what but it resonates with something deep inside me. I know we won't—can't—be sexual again, but it doesn't kill the desire.

I grab the rusty grating of rebar and push against it. It's stuck fast. "You sure this was loose before?" I whisper down. Lex pokes her head up the pipe and rolls her eyes. "How long ago?" I ask.

"Last year, after they started all the work over here." She's head level with my waist and almost touching me in the enclosed space. "Hey!" she says conspiratorially.

I whisper, taking my attention off the grate again.

...ow what I can do from here don't you?" Her eyes dart to my crotch then back up to mine with a wicked grin.

"Lex!" I say with a warning tone.

She smiles wider, looks at my crotch, then pats it twice with her hand. "I can see you want me to though."

What she did gives me a sudden jolt of energy and it's transferred to the grating. With a muted snap, the grating pushes free. "It was rusted in place" I whisper down. Lex is hopelessly persistent with sexual innuendos and propositions, but I don't kid myself for a minute that she wants to get sexual; it's her way of putting me back in place as a guy to toy with, but it's also punishment.

With anyone else, it would be fun banter, but with her, it's a reminder of what we enjoyed and would never enjoy again. This is her punishment of me. How long I'll have to endure it, I don't know, but I'm willing to see it through.

"I knew you had it in you, Colorado," Lex whispers encouragingly.

I carefully lift the grating aside and stick my head out of the hole. I do a slow 360 and make out nothing, but I make a silent gesture of being startled and pop my head down quickly.

"What? What do you see?" Lex whispers.

I shake my head. "Nothing."

"But..."

"Just a ruse, in case someone was watching. Want them to think I saw something and bolted. Figure that might force their hand."

Lex's expression shifted from puzzlement to approval. "That's clever. You're a man after my own heart."

"Yes I am," I say. We remain crouched in the muted light together and for the first time since the last time we were together, there's a moment of silent sweetness and connection. Lex's eyes catch mine than look away, and then look back. Her expression dances around and finally settles on sad.

"I miss you," she says softly.

That hit me where it hurt. "Me too you," I whisper.

She buries her head in my chest and we hug tightly. I feel her tremble and hear her sob. "I'm sorry, Lex, I'm so sorry. What we did together means more to me than you can know, and I never want to change that, but I never dreamed you'd get hurt."

"It's okay," she says drawing herself back, tears dripping down her cheeks. "I started it. Be careful what you ask for, they say." I look at her confused. "I asked for a decent guy, someone special, and damn it if you didn't stumble along. I… I guess I just got lost on your doorstep." I was, in a word, speechless. "So was I special?" she asks.

"Yeah," I whisper.

"Really special I mean."

"Totally special Lex."

"And I was good, I pleased you?"

"More than I ever dreamed. You opened a doorway I didn't know existed."

She gives me a bewildered, questioning look. "You really do miss us don't you?" she asks.

I nod my head. "Yeah, I miss us Lex. Miss us like hell."

Her face shifts to a smile that looks a little forced. "Good," she says. Her eyes widen. "Psych!" With that, she is up and out of the rabbit hole before I can stop her.

Shit. I pull myself up and out and join her on the main floor of the cannery. I'm torn between getting angry because she'd yanked on my chain and just feeling yanked. I backhand her softly on the hip. "I don't stumble along," I whisper. She touches her hip where I'd slapped her and gives me a questioning look. "I'm a damned decent guy but I didn't just 'stumble along'." That rekindles her wry smile.

After replacing the grate, we stealth our way across the floor to the south end of the building, keeping a careful watch for signs of habitation and cameras. The first thing I notice when we get there is that the two large containers are missing and the loading chute is partially disassembled. I point that out to Lex and she shrugs her shoulders.

We make our way to the shack in the middle of the floor and do a quick inspection. I place an ear against a shack wall—silent. "Looks deserted," she whispers.

"Yeah, that bothers me. Wonder if they already found what they were digging for."

The door to the shack is closed but there's no padlock. I try the handle and it turns easily, and the door slowly swings open on silent hinges.

Chapter 49

Trapped

"What do you think?" Lex whispers.

"I say I take a look see and you stay here," I whisper back.

"I say you fuck off," she whispers and pushes past me. Inside the shack, the bulky conveyer belt system comes through the roof and disappears into a pit in the floor. Next to it, there's an open hole and ladder steps lead into darkness. There're electrical switches against the far wall, no doubt controls for the conveyer and lighting system. I study them, but I don't touch a thing.

"Down it is," Lex whispers and before I can stop her, she's half-way down the shaft.

"Lex!" I whisper loudly.

"What?" she replies, looking up.

"Don't just bolt off like that."

"Why?"

"Because you might…" She cuts me off by resuming her downward climb. I keep my light on her until she reaches the bottom, then follow. We're 12 feet below the floor level.

"Damp down here," she says in a normal tone.

"We're probably below the harbor's waterline. This close, I'm surprised the tunnel isn't flooded."

The walls are comprised of rock and gravel and in quite a few places water has seeped in, wetting the surface. I touch the wall. "This is the rock and gravel they must have used to fill in the marsh." I shine my light down the tunnel and conveyer system; it slopes downward into darkness. "Must get mucky somewhere down there."

We follow the tunnel down and, as predicted, the rock and gravel walls give way to sand and mud, shored up by wet 6x2 beams. "Why hasn't this place flooded out?" Lex wonders aloud.

"A pump," I answer. I recall the sound of a motor turning on and off when I explored the cannery a few weeks early. "I think they use a sump pump of some sort to keep the place dry."

About 40 feet down the tunnel levels out and takes a hard turn to the right. We're standing in two inches of water and Lex stomps her feet and splashes me with a silly grin on her face; I guess we're well below the low tide line as the ceiling and walls are all beamed with dripping 6x2's and 6x6 braces. The ceiling drips constantly and the tunnel echoes with water drops. "They're letting it flood," I say. "They must be done here."

"Don't you want to see what's ahead?" Lex asks.

"Yeah, maybe we can figure out if my suspicions were right, and if they've found the Talfar."

In another 30 feet or so and we come to a T in the tunnel. It's here that the conveyor system ends. I shine my light around for a clue why. I notice a set of wires running along the ceiling and far wall with what looks like a remote control box attached.

"What are these?" Lex asks. She's shining her LED on a pile or large, rounded rocks near the end of the conveyor.

I step over and examined them. "No idea. They seem too uniform in size to have been dug up down here."

"Look at this," Lex says. I go over to see what she is excited about this time. There, in her the light of her LED, is a curved wooden beam.

"This is it," I mutter.

"What?"

"That's the beam of an old ship." I quickly shine my light down both directions of the tunnel; it's wider down here, about 10 feet across, and stretches 20 feet south on a slight up-slope, and another 30 feet north on a down-slope. Although the floor of the tunnel is flooded, a series of curved beams rise from the water at its edges. "They've excavated the *La Soñadora*."

"You really think it's the ship that brought the colonists here from Spain?" Lex asks eyes wide.

I nod my head. "I'm sure of it."

She steps toward me, trips on something and goes down in a splash. "Fuck!' she blurts, then burst out laughing as I help her up.

"You look like a drowned cat."

"Fuck you," she says, shoving me away. Her smile fades and her face takes on a worried look. "Hey, let's blaze, I'm getting a bad feeling about this place."

"Go ahead, I'll meet up at the shack. I just want to figure out if the Talfar was here and if they'd found it." I start toward the south end, which I assume is the bow of the ship. With my light in one hand, I grope around the bottom with the other. Lex shines her light for me and I use both hands. All I can feel is muck and the rough surface of soft, half rotten wooden planking. At the end, the ship's keel rises out of the shallow water. "Nothing."

"This is freaking amazing but it's freaking me out," Lex says.

I slowly make my way back toward the junction, feeling for anything I might have missed. "I'll be quick about this. I'm getting a bad feeling too." Something is wrong, and it gnaws at the periphery of my conscious thought.

"Yeah, hurry up," she says.

We reach the junction, where the water is a foot deep, and I continue north toward the stern of the remains, groping as I go. The water's 18 inches deep about half way to the far end of the tunnel.

"You think the dark ones set her on fire?" she asks nervously.

My hands feel a set of wooden ridges, and I trace them as they form a two-foot square. Something was set here, maybe the footing for a mast. "I don't know Lex, maybe the ship just caught fire. Shit does happen," I say.

"Yeah, tell me about it," she mumbles.

By the time I reach the end of the tunnel, the water's 2 feet deep. "I don't get it; there's nothing here, nothing that suggest they found anything."

"What's this thing look like anyway?" Lex asks.

My mind goes back to the conversation with Catalina in the woods. "It's a stone tablet, about 18 inches round," I say.

"So a box or something that would hold it," Lex suggest, crossing her arms and shivering. "Or maybe it just sat on a table or wall and in some box that burned or rotted away. Maybe it was just sitting on the bottom of the ship and they took it already."

"The stones," I blurt. "They're ballast stones." I start to make my way back toward the two-foot square ridge on the keel.

"What stones?"

"Ballast stones. They were used to weigh down the bottom of the ship to give it stability," I say.

"I don't know, wouldn't you want a ship as light as possible so it would float better?" Lex asks as she follows me.

"Yeah, but sailing ships are naturally top heavy with the masts and all that rigging. Without a heavy weight along the keel, they'd tip over as soon as wind hit the sails." I find the square outline and feel around inside of it. "Why would they remove all the ballast stones and pile them up like this."

"I don't know," Lex says, shivering, "maybe to get them out of the way. Are we done?"

"Out of the way of what, though?" I feel scoring and crush marks along the inside edge of the wooden square. I pick at a chunk of wood that is nearly torn free and examine it. It is clear that it has recently been damaged.

"Jesse," I hear Lex say.

An image comes to mind, something I saw in the book. I explore the base of the square; there is a slight, circular indentation about 18 inches across. "That's it, it was here, at keel, in the center of the ship. They have it."

"Jesse, we have to leave, I've got a..."

As if on the director's cue in a bad film, the lights on the tunnel pop on. *Fuck! We're trapped.*

"Jesse," Lex whispers as she crouches.

"I know." I look around. There's no place to hide, and given what happened the last time I was found in the cannery, there's no point in trying to fight our way out. "Down here, quickly," I say, moving toward the far north end of the tunnel."

"What are you doing? The exit is that way; there's no way out here."

"I know, but the water is deep enough down here to hide us from view if someone comes down this way."

"Ah, shit," Lex grumbles. "I had a feeling."

"Yeah, I know. I'm sorry."

"You say that a lot," she whispers easing her way into the two-foot deep water at the end. "Fucking freezing!" I move to one side of the tunnel where a beam provides some cover, and Lex moves to the other.

"I'll buy you a hot chocolate at The Kat when we get out of here."

"No you won't," she grumbles. I look at her. "They're closed."

I chuckle. At least she can keep up her sense of humor. "I'm sorry I got you into this, Lex."

"In what universe would you have so much power over me that you could get me into anything?" she asks.

"Sorry anyway."

"There's that word again."

Just then, I hear a faint buzzing and then a series of short beeps. I've heard that before, back in Colorado. "No, no, no," I say, jumping to my feet. I grab Lex and yank her off her feet and run toward the junction. "We've got to get out of here. It's..."

Chapter 50

A Gruesome Death

A blinding light and unbelievably loud bang at the junction throws us both on our backs. My head spins and my body feels like it's been pounded over by a giant sledgehammer. When I open my eyes everything's dark, and I can't find my flashlight. I grope around for Lex and find her just as a wall of wet mud hits.

I stand, stumble, and stand again, pulling Lex up by the shoulders to keep her head above the on-slot of mud. She's dead weight. "Lex! Lex!"

I shout, shaking her. I can't hear my own voice above the ringing in my ears. I take both of her arms over my head, pull her up on my back, and slog through the deepening muck and water. We're trapped, dead most likely, but at least for the moment I can still breathe.

I slog through the darkness with Lex in tow toward where I think the junction is and come to a heap of wood beams. The passage to freedom is completely blocked. Lex stirs to life just as a surge of mud and water hit us from the right side. I lose her and I'm pushed under but force my way to my feet again.

I feel the shift happening and suppress it. *No! Not now, not with Lex my only target.* A blinding light pops on and I look to see Lex, buried past her waist in rising muck, holding her flashlight and moving her lips a mile a minute. She is terrified and crying.

I gesture to my ear, shake my head, and shout, "Can't hear you." She shakes her head and then nods. I grab her arm and pull her up. The muck is watery but still impossible to walk through without something to pull up on, and it's a bitch trying to free her legs from its sucking hold. I make a swimming gesture to her and then pull her by the arms. It takes all my strength and I feel Lex's joints snap and pop in complaint, but I pull her free and push her towards where the water is flowing in. She grabs a beam, sticks the light in her mouth, then reaches back and takes my hand. I wiggle and pull and finally come free.

"I'm sorry!" I see her mouth form with teary eyes. Her voice is muffled and it's less than useless trying to ask her for what. I grab a charred jutting beam and keep myself afloat. I take her light and look around as she clings to my arm so hard it hurts. The tunnel out is completely collapsed and the one we're in is quickly filling up. A damned gruesome death is waiting patiently.

I look to the hole that's been blown open in the west wall a couple of feet beneath the ceiling. Water pulses in through the two-foot gap, like water poured too quickly out of a bottle. That tells me two things: it's water and not mud anymore, and air is escaping. It's a slim chance but the only one I can come up with.

"I have an idea," I shout. I point towards the gap.

Lex looks and her eyes widened. "No!" I hear her muffled shout.

Another glob of muck flows through the gap and the water increases in speed. The rapid flow of water into the tunnel is clearing a path through the mud above us. I don't have a clue how long it'll remain clear and where it actually leads to.

Up to this point I've had no time to panic, but waiting for the tunnel to fill, to drown us, panic begins to set in. As much as I try to center myself, I can't suppress the rampant fear within—I stop resisting it and let it go; oddly, that makes it a lot easier to cope with.

"Do you have a belt? I ask. Lex looks confused and I repeat myself with slow exaggerated mouth movements. She nods. "Give it to me." She slips off her belt and gives it to me. I regain a glimmer of hope when I see it's heavy leather. I slip the end through the buckle and pull it through to make a small noose. I slip it over Lex's right hand and tightened it on her wrist. She doesn't like that. "So we don't get separated," I yell. She looks at the binding on her wrist fearfully, then nods her accent.

We don't have any more time to wait. The tunnel is now filled to within a foot of the ceiling and the water begins to slow. A pocket of air is trapped but it wouldn't remain there for long. "It's now or never," I shout. Lex shakes her head. "Okay, you stay here and I'll check it out.

She shakes her head again and shouts "No." She begins to cry.

I can't afford to wait. I hand Lex the light and take a few deep breaths. I am about the duck under when she pulls on my arm and hands me the end of the belt. "Okay then, on three."

Diving into the water, toward an uncertain end point is the hardest thing I've ever done. I know we'll likely die and panic still threatens from every direction of my mind, but the tugging I feel on the belt as I pull myself through the gap in the wall and kick and paddle upward though a tunnel of collapsing mud, reminds me that someone else is on the other end and she's depending on me to survive. I focus my mind on clawing at the mud, digging my feet into the mud for purpose—one clutch, one step at a time.

As I kick, claw and paddle I have thoughts of my mother, Gwen, Catalina and her people. Then for some inexplicable reason, I think of Santiago. The man's face burns in my mind.

I'm running out of air and I feel the belt yanking harder now. I imagine Lex is panicking now and clawing at the noose around her wrist to get free. The frantic tugging on the belt stops—Lex is gone, and I'm nearly out of energy and completely out of breath. It's all I can do to stop myself from sucking in a lung full of water. Then, with nothing to lose, I let it happen—energy rushes though my body and I feel wild, free, and angry. I hear myself let out a roar and I pull and kick at the mud as though I am ripping it apart, killing it. I so want to kill.

Then my head brakes free of the water and I gasp in a lung of air and let out a haunting, inhuman cry. I draw myself up and throw down the thing in my hand. I am surrounded by tall figures, ready to kill them all, then as fast as it happened, it stops, and I fall to my knees in the hip deep water exhausted.

I look around and find myself surrounded on three sides by wharf pilings. "Lex?" I mutter. "Lex!" I shout in sudden realization. I step back to the churning hole and grope around for the end of the belt. I dive under, grab at something that hits my flailing wrist, and pull on it. I pull with every bit of energy I have left and Lex's body rises slowly to the surface.

"Lex," I cry. "No, no, no. Not like this." I stand, pull her up out of the water, and toss her over my shoulder, belly down, head against my stomach. I shake her and pound her back and her limp limbs flail about. Then I bear hug her hard, trying to force any water out of her lungs. I feel one of her delicate ribs crack. "Fuck!"

I roll her off my shoulder and onto her back and begin to do mouth to mouth. Everything is automatic at this point. I hold her up with one arm and press in on her chest with the other, palm over her heart. After three or four compressions, I blow air into her lungs a couple of breaths, and then repeat the heart massage.

Then it occurs to me to check for a pulse. I feel her neck—a faint pulse flutters beneath my fingers. I am wasting time with the heart massage. I begin a slow and steady train of assisted breaths and will keep it up as long as it takes. It doesn't take long.

Lex coughs, then coughs wildly, and then groans. She breathes a few times and then rolls over and simpers. "Lex." I say holding her back. "We're okay. We're out." I hug her and she hugs me back and begins to cry.

"I was so scared," she says. "I panicked and then everything went black and I thought I was dead."

"It's okay. You're safe." I hold her as she cries and take a look around for the rowboat. It isn't anywhere. We aren't where we entered the tunnel to get into the cannery. As best I can make out, we're on the west side of the cannery, under a narrow section of wharf near the towering mass of Hook Point Head. We went in on one side and broke out the other.

"Hey, let's go." I say in a hushed tone. "Whoever set off those charges might still be around."

A bright light from the water just beyond the pilings hits me straight in the eye and I pull Lex around to shield her body.

"I am thinking you need a lift," Santiago's gravelly voice echoes under the pier.

Chapter 51

Suspicion

Lex sits on Santiago's couch wrapped in a wool blanket but still shivering. Mud clumps her short hair together in places and with her large gray eyes darting around nervously she looks like a cat that just crawled out of a dunk in a swamp. I feel a pang of anxiety when I think about her nearly dying. If I hadn't pulled her through and given her mouth-to-mouth, she'd be dead gone. It's chilling how life can change so quickly.

Santiago comes out of the galley carrying two steaming mugs and offers her one. She looks up at him, then at the mug, then back up at him, and reluctantly accepts it without a word. She's been buried alive in muck, drowned, is chilled to the bone, and likely has a cracked rib, but there's something else in her eyes I've only seen in the flooding tunnel—fear!

Why? Sure, she's heard all the stories about Santiago, but she thrives on edgy and I'd have thought she'd get a rush from being on his boat. Besides, Santiago just dragged our wet asses out from under the wharf and made us comfortable on the Revenge.

He watches her until she takes a hesitant sip from the mug; there's something odd in the way he looks at her as well, but I can't begin to guess what it is. I'm so spooled up I still can't stand still or sit, and Santiago hands me the other mug. It's hot buttered rum.

"Festive spirit today?" I ask.

Santiago ignores the comment. "You should not have been so foolish," he grumbles.

"Probably not, but at least we know Wingate has the Talfar," I say.

"Knowing that is not worth your lives," he counters.

"We made it out," I quip.

"Barely. If the tide was not low you would never have made it."

Lex sips her drink nervously as the two of us argue. Santiago's cat slips out of nowhere, hops up in the couch, and distracts Lex enough to put a faint smile on her face. When she reaches out a hand to pet the tabby, her fingers are shaking. She catches me watching her and looks away quickly. I've never seen Lex so pensive and quiet.

"Someone blew the caisson intentionally," I say to get off the shame game. "We didn't see any sign of anyone else in the place."

"It was probably done remotely," Santiago says.

I thought about the surveillance system that detected me the first time in. They've clearly upgraded it in anticipation that someone might try to do exactly what we had. "So what now?"

"Now you go home and clean yourself up," he says. He throws Lex a glance and her shoulders visibly tense, then returns his attention to me. "Get yourself ready."

"For what?" I ask.

"Anything. Things are coming to a head," he says.

I down the rest of my drink and feel heat spreading through my belly and out my arms, then the gentle buzz of the alcohol as it hits my brain. "I won't be riding anytime soon," I say.

"I'll drive you," Santiago says.

"No," Lex blurts. We both look at her and she shrinks like plastic in a fire.

"Lex, it's okay," I say. "We're out, safe. Let's just get you home." She nervously looks at Santiago then gives me a quick shake of her head. "What's got you so messed up?" I ask—no reaction. "Want me to stay with you tonight?"

That fetches me a brief hopeful glance. "You want Christine to pick you up?" Her eyes brighten and I reach to the inside pocket of my soaked jacket, only to pull out a now ruined cell phone. "Shit!" I just catch sight of the cell phone flying my way in time to catch it. I flip open Santiago's phone. "What's her number?"

Ten minutes later Christine is helping Lex into her car in the parking lot. She gives Lex a worried look and then me an accusing one. She pulls me aside by my sopping jacket. "What the fuck, Jesse?" She says in a subdued voice. "You took her into the cannery, didn't you?" she accuses.

"Well…"

She pounds my chest with a closed fist. "You prick, you selfish fucking prick. You could have gotten both of you killed."

I've never seen Christine this mad, and never want to again. "You might best take her to the hospital, I think she might have a cracked rib," I say against all survival instincts.

Christine clenches both of her fists and I steel myself for the hits I think are inevitable. "Ugh!" she blurts and slaps her thighs. She turns and jumps into the driver's seat and storms off, Lex in the passenger seat hugging her knees and crying into them. I'm so numb I can't even curse.

"Let's go," Santiago says, walking toward his car.

The drive home is silent. Santiago drives without haste and seems comfortable in the quietude. I don't say a thing until he pulls into the drive to let me off. "Thank you," I say. He gives me a long look then nods. "I meant everything I said the other day. I just…" have nothing else to say.

Santiago nods then looks up at the house with the lights shining from the living room. "You are right in what you said and what you decided," he says. "You have no place in my life and I will soon have no more place you yours."

He says this in such a matter-of-fact manner that you'd think things were playing out for him according to some long laid plan. Then it occurs to me that it has been; the slaughter house, the training, the killings—in a few short weeks I've come to know what I am, what I'm capable of; have learned how to tap into the reservoir of the metaphysical; and have made a firm choice against using it to hurt others. Santiago has led me there like a master teacher.

"Muchas gracias, Señor Santiago."

He nods. "Go," he says. "Go before your mother comes out and finds you in your sorry condition and blames me."

He leaves me in the driveway, watching his car disappear down River Road. Through the residual numbness, and the feelings of guilt for nearly getting Lex killed, I feel gratitude. "And what about you, old man? How do we save you?"

I hoof it around the back of the house to avoid being seen but about half way to the boat the kitchen door opens. "Jesse?" Mom calls out.

"Yeah?" I reply, hoping she can't see my sorry state in the darkness.

"Are you alright? What happened to your bike?" she asks.

"Oh, that, yeah, I'm fine mom. I had a hot buttered rum with some of my friends and I thought it best not to ride. I caught a lift home," I said. The truth sometimes pays off.

"Did you eat? Are you hungry?" she asks.

"Yeah, I'm good. Just going to shower up," I say walking backwards. "Everything okay with you and Gwen."

"Yes, we're fine," she replies. "Come in the house before you go to bed."

"Yeah, okay."

I shower up, scrub the grit and mire that is embedded in my fingernails and seems to have invaded every crevice on my body. Images flash through my mind—the blast, the cave in, the desperate crawl through the mud to the surface, pulling Lex's unconscious body into the night air, bringing her back to consciousness—each causing a rush of adrenaline and a racing heart. I also realize had Santiago not taken me out to sea that day and taught me how to dig deep when I needed it, we might not have made it.

I rinse all my clothes as best I can, wash off the knife I'd taken, and rinse the mud from the surface of my phone. If I take it apart and let it dry out fully before trying to turn it on; maybe I can save it. My leather jacket is tough, but it'll never be the same. I rinse water through that as well, but it will take professional cleaning to restore it back to somewhere near it's former self. I'm about done when I hear a voice from the other side of the shower screen.

"What happened?" Gwen asks.

After my heart rate returns to normal, I tell her all about the venture into the cannery, She gives me hell three times over as she helps me hang everything up to dry on a line behind the Therion so Mom won't catch sight of them. "I'll sneak everything into a wash tomorrow if you like," she offers, and then gives me hell a fourth time. "So what do we do about the Talfar?" she asks.

"I don't know. Catalina Ruiz doesn't seem concerned," I say.

"I don't know how she can't be," Gwen muses. "Where do you think Wingate has it?"

"I'm guessing on his boat," I reply.

"You're not thinking of…"

"Sneaking on the boat and taking it? Yeah, it occurred to me," I admit, "but after tonight I'm thinking it's a stupid idea."

"Finally, my brother grows a brain," Gwen says. "Maybe Mr. Santiago will take it back."

"Yeah, that occurred to me as well," I say, and the image of the pearly white halls of the yacht splattered with blood flash in my mind.

It is after 1:00 am by the time I'm finally able to bed down. I don't think I'll be able to sleep well after what happened and I don't. I finally begin to listen to an audio book on my iPod, a sure fire way to put me to sleep, and it works… for a while.

The smell of something familiar and desirable is the first thing I'm aware of as I come to consciousness. I feel the bed against my back and the chill of the night air on my naked skin, and then open my eyes to the darkness of the cabin. I think I'm dreaming, expecting myself to awake in the woods somewhere, but I'm exactly where I should be. I roll over and swing my legs over the edge of the bunk. "Lex!" I say. Lex stands near the galley, her naked form distinct even in the dim light of the cabin. "What are you doing here?"

She looks as though she's trying to speak, mouthing words that won't form. "I'm sorry," she finally says.

"For what?" I ask. I step over to face her, close enough to feel the warmth radiating from her body. Her scent is strong, and I feel an impulse to grab hold of her as I did in her sanctuary just two weeks earlier. I stand back. "Why do you keep saying that?"

"I messed up, Jesse," she says. "I don't mean to, I just do that."

"No, nothing is your fault," I say. "I should never have taken you into the cannery." I extend my hand and she takes it with both of hers and kisses my palm.

"I've ruined everything," she says, tears now flowing down her cheeks.

I step into her and hold her tight and she begins to cry. "It's going to be all right, Lex. Everything is going to be fine."

"I'll make it better," she says. "I promise, I'll fix things."

"Sure, we'll all make it better. You, me, Christine, Michelle, all of us, you'll see. Everything is going to be good again." She stops crying and pulls her head out of my shoulder to look up at me. What I see in her large gray eyes is something I've only seen once before. "What are you afraid of?" I ask. She stares at me, tries to form words that won't. Why were you so afraid at Santiago's? You seem petrified by him. You'd think..." Then it strikes me.

I sit upright in my bunk and slam my fist into the ceiling. "God damn you Santiago," I spit. "You were one of them." I jump out of the bunk and look for my phone. "Shit!" I fire up my laptop and then compose the most vile, venomous email I can think of. I vow to make him pay for what he's done to Lex, and tell him I'll send off an email to child protective services as soon as I am finished my letter to him.

I send the message then search for an eddress to fire off a child abuse report to, but only could come up with phone numbers to call. I wrote two down and was half way across the yard to the house before realized I'm both naked and likely to awaken Mom using the phone.

I want to hunt down Santiago. The betrayal I feel is like nothing I've felt before, even with my father beating my mom and turning on me. The Shadow's in town but I can bicycle in. I check the shed where I keep my bike. "Gwen," I mutter in frustration. She has a habit of borrowing my bike and never returning it where she's found it. I decide I'll walk into town, and go back to the cabin to dress.

Half way through putting my second boot on, I have second thoughts. I'm no match for Santiago, and even if I was, what am I going to do with him? Anger surges through my veins and I want to kill the old bastard, but images of the killings in the warehouse remind me of the sad reality of violence.

I flop myself back on the bed fully dressed minus one boot. "Damn it, Lex. We'll fix this, I promise."

Chapter 52

Revelations

I don't know how much sleep I'd managed during the night but it hadn't been much. I check my email at 8:13 and there's a message from Santiago.

"Calm yourself and think clearly. Don't do anything stupid."

"That's it? That's all you have to say for yourself?" Anger surges through me again.

There are a few venomous messages from Michelle and Christine, all of which I delete without reading then think through my agenda. I'll meet Isa at 10:40, and after that, I'll confront Santiago in person.

I meet Gwen half way to the house. "Mom went to town," she says. "Think I'll get your stuff and wash it now."

"I'll do it later Gwen, you're not my maid," I say.

"It's okay, I'm… god, Jesse you look like shit," she says as she steps up her pace to keep up with me on the way to the house.

"Thanks," I say.

"I mean it I've never seen you like this before. What's happening?"

"Nothing," I say.

"Bull!" she says, grabbing my arm and yanking me to a stop. "What's wrong?" The look of fear on her face makes the rage in my head stop long enough for the rest of my mind to catch up.

"Gwen, I…" I lapsed into silence. What can I tell her?

"What? … What?" she pleads.

The phone in the house rings, saving me from an uncomfortable explanation that I don't think Gwen needs to hear. She dashes in to get it and I follow, and by the time I pour myself a coffee she's passing me the handset.

"What did you mean…" Santiago's voice begins. I hit "end" to cut him off, then dial the only number I've been able to remember since moving to Hook Point.

"Hi, Mrs. Carter, this is Jesse... Yes, I'm okay. I left it there last night because I was too tired to ride home... Yes, I'm fine, thank you. Is Michelle working this morning?... Do you have her phone number?... Thank you." I dial the number right away, gesturing for Gwen to be quiet less I forget. She's vibrating in place.

"Hey, it's me... Yeah, I know. Hey listen, how'd you like to chew me out in person... Well, yeah, I need a ride into town... twenty minutes? Thanks"

"So?'" Gwen asks impatiently.

In the 20 minutes it takes for Michelle to get to the house, I tell Gwen that I think Santiago might have done something to hurt Lex some time ago. She has questions but they're general and I have a sense that Gwen doesn't want to know details.

The ride into town is tense. I let Michelle ream me out every way possible and then some without trying to defend myself. "Well aren't you going to say something?" she asks finally.

"Did Christine take Lex to the hospital" I ask.

"What? Why?" she asks.

"I think I might have cracked one of her ribs pulling her out to safety."

Michelle looks at me as if I have two heads. "You're really... I..." she stammers.

"If all goes as planned. I'm meeting Isa at 10:40." She looks at me long enough for me to become concerned about her driving. "Watch the road," I caution.

"Shit Jesse you are just full of surprises," she says.

We hang out at The Kat and discussed how Lex is doing. According to Christine, she was inconsolably morose when she got her home, had snuck out in the middle of the night and hasn't been seen since.

Michelle wants to know what upset her so much and presses for all the details of our venture into the cannery. I spare no detail, but I don't mention my discovery that Santiago was one of Lex's abusers; I know that would trigger a barrage of warnings and threats designed to stop me from confronting him. Before we know it, it's 10:37 and I intend to be out there waiting when Isa shows up.

"You think I should be there as well?" Michelle asks.

"Ah, no," I say as I stand. "I think that might spook her, but if you want to hang out in the back room I'll call you if she's okay with it."

That is the plan, and I'm out there looking over my bike at exactly 10:40. Michelle has cracked the back door open with a metal milk can as though the back of The Kat is being aired out, but stays out of sight. At 10:43 a car pulls into the alley, but backs out and drives away in the other direction. At 10:47, an old guy walks down the alley and looks at me strangely as he passes. I recognize him as one of our illustrious street people. *No way,* I think. At 10:50 I am beginning to wonder whether she'll show up. At 10:52, old dude wanders back down the alley and approaches me. He stands about six feet from me, looking at me expectantly.

"Isa?" I ask incredulously.

"I what?" the guy asks.

"Ah…"

"This cache is spoken for," he says.

"This what?" I ask.

"Don't play stupid," he says threateningly.

"Listen dumb ass, I work here," I half lie. "You looking for trouble, because if you are the owner is just inside and I'm sure he'll love to call the cops."

He shoots me a look that is supposed to intimidate and points a finger my way. "We'll meet up, kid. Out here," he says gesturing to the alley. "I'll look forward to meeting up with you again."

Anger shoots through me and I feel the stirring deep inside. With all that has happened, it wasn't the right thing for him to have said. I don't know what he sees, but his face blanches and as I step toward him he backs off quickly. I half follow him down the short stretch of alley to the street as he disappears as though his life depended on it. I have no idea how anyone can get a rush out of intimidating another human being, because when my anger subsides, I feel like shit.

"Jesse?" I hear a soft voice call. I turn and there, in the alley on the other side of The Kat's loading area, stands Wade's sister, Sarin.

I walk toward her slowly, looking around for signs of Wade or any of his cronies. "Sarin?" I say when I am about ten feet away. "You're Isa?"

She nods and smiles shyly, then looks back over her shoulder. "Is there some place more out of the way we can talk?" She speaks with a subtle accent I can't place.

I lead her to where my bike is parked behind The Kat's dumpster and catch a glimpse of Michelle's head peaking out from the corner of the door. I lean again the bike's seat. "So," I begin.

She forces a half smile. "So," she echoes.

"So you're Isa," I say.

"Yeah," she says with a shy smile.

"Wow, no wonder you didn't want to be found out." She widens her eyes and nods. "You're accent, why…"

"I was raised in England until I was eight," she replies. "It sticks."

"What about your brother?" I ask.

"Florida," she says. She averts her eyes then gives me a furtive glance. "Different mothers."

"Ah, well." A pregnant silence grows. "Hell, there are so many questions I want to ask," I finally say.

"I bet, only I don't really have a lot of time." She looks over her shoulder and peaks around the dumpster.

"Are you in danger?" I ask.

She tilts her head and shrugs her shoulders. "Maybe, I don't know. I don't know how far he'll go. Sometimes I think…" her eyes go vague with a 1000 mile stare.

"Listen, if you think you're in danger, we can find a place for you to hide out." My mind spins through a dozen bad possibilities without landing any place solid.

"No, it's all right," she says with less than satisfying certainty. Sarin seems like a genuinely decent girl, and I have a hard time imagining what it must be like living in the shadow of Wade and her father. "But I do have to be quick about this. They still think I'm at the doctor's office but it's only a matter of time before they realized I snuck out the back."

"They? Your brother and his goo…friends?" I ask.

"Goons. Go ahead and say it because that is what most of them are, but no. My dad has my brother and I body guarded these days."

"Black Knight security," I suggest.

She nods. "It's supposed to be to protect us because of the deaths of some of his operatives, but I think the real reason is that he suspects my brother or me of having betrayed him."

"My mind races and lands on one possibility. "The book?" Sarin cast me a nervous look and nods. "You took the book from your dad and dropped it at my boat?"

She nods. "He's guarded that more than anything, kept it in the vault at his compound south of San Francisco. When Carlotta brought it up from the city on the yacht, I took it. There aren't many suspects."

"And you gave it to me, why?"

"I heard my dad and Carlotta talking about you. She says you're a key player in something he believes might happen and if it does things will go bad for him and his associates."

Associates. So that's what the vampires call themselves these days, I think to myself. "Who's this Carlotta and how does the book figure into it all?"

"Carlotta is… this may sound strange but she's some sort of mystic or medium he found in Venezuela. She's been with him for a long time." She looks at me as though to gauge my reaction to that.

"Not strange at all," I mutter.

"She's the one who found the book for him about 5 years ago and he's been obsessed with it ever since. He reads it for hours and he and his associates, especially Carlotta, will have long discussions about it. The book seems to be at the center of everything he's done for the past three or four years, and… you're mentioned in it."

I have to do a double take on Sarin to make certain she isn't kidding me. "I'm what? I'm in what?"

"The Book of Prophesies, at least that's what he and Carlotta have come to believe."

"How am I supposed to be in a book written 80 or more years ago."

"That's why it's call the Book of Prophesies," she says shyly.

"Have you read it?" I ask.

She looks at me as though I asked if she was a girl. "Well, yeah, didn't you?"

I have to avert my eyes. "Yeah, well, most of it anyway." Sarin's eyes widen and she gives me an annoyed look. She risked a lot to get the book to me and I haven't taken the time to completely absorb it. She looks at her watch and starts to fidget.

"Hey I have to get back. Read it," she says. "Especially near the end where it talks about the coming together of the Wolf and the Lion. Carlotta thinks you're the Wolf, but I have no idea who the Lion is supposed to be and I don't think they do either."

"Yeah, okay," I say absently, half lost in thought. She turns to leave. "Hey take a coffee with you. If they find you between here and the doctor's office you can say you were jonesing and had to grab one."

"I, ah, don't drink coffee," she says. Her eyes glance upward and her expression shifts to a nervous grimace. "Ah, there's one other thing."

"Yeah?" I ask.

"I wrote that you had a Judas in your midst."

"Yeah, I figured that out," I say. "Bolin, right." Sarin looks glum as she shakes her head. *No? Shit!* Then it strikes me. "Santiago? Señor Santiago?"

Sarin frowns. "No, he's the only man in the world I think my dad is afraid of, freaks at the mention of his name."

And for good reason. "So who's this traitor?"

Sarin looks distinctly uncomfortable. "She's part of your group, I'm pretty sure. Her name's Alexis."

Chapter 53

Betrayal

> ### Journal - Hook Point
>
> *Today, I learned that the greatest wound is betrayal. Enduring an injury at the hands of an enemy is an expected consequence of human conflict. Such wounds can heal quickly and without undue suffering. Enduring the betrayal by a friend, though, is a wound of the soul—one that is slow to heal, and can leave a scar for a lifetime.*

The pressure above my eyes makes me dizzy and my vision fades to gray. My body flushes hot and my mind retreats, but when I remember to breathe I hear my voice blurt, "What? Who?"

Sarin's face is a mask of discomfort. "Alexis. She's about my height, pretty, and has a lot of energy and attitude."

"I know who Alexis is," I growl, "but you're wrong. Alexis is… well she'd never betray us."

"I'm sorry Jesse," Sarin says, nearly in tears.

"Did your dad put you up to this?" I ask. I step into her space and she steps back, eyes wide with fear.

"No," she stammers. "I wouldn't do that. I came here to help you?"

"Why? You helping makes even less sense than Alexis betraying us."

"I'm sorry, I tried to warn you," she says, he eyes tearing up.

"Hey," Michelle calls out from the door. She steps out into the loading area carrying a paper hot cup. "What's going on?"

"You tell her," I grumble.

"Tell me what?" Michelle asks, handing Sarin the cup. "I overheard Jesse suggesting you take a drink from The Kat. I grabbed you a tangerine white tea, your favorite, right?"

"Yes, thank you," Sarin says, accepting the cup.

"Tell me what?" Michelle repeats.

Sarin clears her throat. "I was just telling Jesse that your friend Alexis, is doing things for my father."

"What?" Michelle asks. She sounds as shocked as I feel.

Sarin nods. "I'm sorry, but it's true. I knew he was getting information from someone close to you, someone he called 'Wire' and that's when I warned you. I only found out who it was the other day. I caught sight of her on my father's boat talking to him by the computer, and when he referred to her as Wire, I knew."

"When? When did this start?" Michelle asks.

"It's bullshit," I grumble.

"I can't be sure, but I think last year sometime. I know he was talking to someone here who keeps him up on the local teens and I know he was interested in knowing if anyone new moved into town. I thought for a while it was someone from the old Spanish colony, but when I saw Alexis on the boat the other day, I knew. I think he may have had one of his men bring her down to his compound in the city a few weeks ago."

"What? Why?" I ask.

Sarin blushes and averts her eyes to the ground. "I don't know, but my father—he likes young girls." She looks up, red faced, but an edge of anger shows through her shame.

"Oh, man," I say. I kick the dumpster so hard it startles Sarin and Michelle both, and I feel a sharp pain shoot through my foot.

"It might have been nothing," she says quickly, "and I might be completely wrong. I'm just going by what he used to do to young girls in South America."

"Do to? What do you mean?" I ask.

She stands dead still, then begins to back away. "I'm so sorry. I have to go," Sarin says.

I grab Sarin's arm and hold it firmly. She casts me a fearful look but doesn't try to pull away.

"Jesse!" Michelle says in alarm.

"What do you mean do to? What did he do to them?" I demand.

She blanches and stares off at the pavement. "He has sex with them," she begins in a soft voice, as though recalling a nightmare. "When I lived there with him three years ago I knew his men would bring in a young girl once, sometimes twice a week. They were always taken to a section of the compound I wasn't permitted in, but I snuck in there once and saw him…"

Her eyes widened into a 1000-mile stare. "She couldn't have been more than 12 or 13," she said in a strained voice. "He was rough, cruel, and she was so scared." A tear drips down Sarin's face.

"He raped her?" I ask.

She nods. "I can't be sure, I only caught the profile of her face, but a few weeks later I saw a badly photocopied image of a girl pinned up in a local market and it could have been the same girl. She'd been missing for weeks."

"Oh, my god," Michelle mutters. "You think your father killed her?"

Sarin's face screws up and she begins to cry. "I don't know. There were so many girls and it's so easy to make someone disappear down there."

"Do you think Lexi's in danger?" Michelle asks.

Sarin shrugs. "I don't know. It's hard to get away with that sort of thing here but… there was this girl in Florida… I… I don't know. I've got to go."

"Of course," Michelle says, touching my arm. I release Sarin's arm and she turns and begins to walk away. "Sarin," Michelle calls to her. She stops and looks back "You read the book, you know what your father is then?" She looks down sadly and nods. "What about you?"

She turns sad eyes toward Michelle then me, then back to Michelle. "We make our own choices," she says. "No matter who or where you come from." Sarin shifts her eyes to mine. "I'm so sorry, Jesse. I didn't know the two of you were so close." She looks back to Michelle. "I think my father is arriving later today or tomorrow, and I think he has something big planned. Be careful." With that, Sarin makes an about face and darts back up the alley the way she came.

"It's bullshit," I say. Emotions churn in my gut and I feel like I might explode. *Did she play me from the start?* "Total fucking bullshit!"

"I don't think she's lying, Jesse," Michelle says tearfully.

I lean back against the wall of The Kat and let it hold me up. *No way.* My mind scrambles to piece together my shattered world. New possibilities form; Lex seen with Bolin—the flowers at her sanctuary—her apologies for messing things up—her insistence that she isn't who I think she is—it could fit.

"What are we going to do?" Michelle asks. "If it's true, if she is associating with Wingate…"

"Associating! It sounds like she's been fucking him," I blurt.

"No way Jesse," Michelle says. "I can't see Lexi doing that, but she may be in danger."

I push myself back from the wall and unlock my bike. "We need to find her."

"What are you thinking?" Michelle asks with a worried look. "What do you plan to do?"

"What? You think I'm going to do something to her?" I ask angrily.

"No, of course not. I know how you feel about her. We all do. I'm worried you might do something and get yourself hurt."

Chapter 54

Book Worms

"What's wrong?" Gwen asks. She's standing next to the companionway, staring at me with a concerned look that's hauntingly like our mother's.

I stare down at the phone Gwen let me use and give her a gesture to be patient. Then I make the call I'd contemplated for twenty minutes. Santiago answers. "Did you hurt her?" I ask.

"Hurt who?"

"Did you hurt Lex? Have you ever hurt her in any way?" There is a pause.

"No."

There's an edge to his voice, anger, contempt maybe, and I feel—I know—he's telling the truth. "Did you know? Did you know she's been working for Wingate?" Gwen makes an audible gasp and there is a longer pause on the line.

"I suspected it."

"And you didn't say anything," I accuse.

"No."

I hang up. The way Lex reacted to Santiago after he pulled us from the muck beneath the cannery—it made sense if she feared he was on to her. I look up to see Gwen standing at the edge of the table, tears dripping down her cheeks. Her capacity to empathize, to feel the pain of others is boundless.

"I'm sorry, Jesse," she says.

"Yeah, me too," I say. I let anger trump the hurt I'm feeling. "So what's up?"

Gwen stares at me with a perplexed look. "Um, just wanted to talk; we haven't seen each other much since the start of the festival."

"Yeah, there's a lot to talk about." I stand and breathe in the cabin's air; it feels stale and heavy. I grab my e-reader. "Let's go for a walk."

Gwen disappears into the house for 'a minute' that takes eleven but when she comes back out, she's carrying a pack on her back and her reader in her hand. At the rock in the meadow, she pulls out a blanket and arranges it over the hot surface. I peak into her pack—it's filled with food and drinks. "Thought we might be here a while," she says as I stare into her pack. "Besides, knowing you, you haven't had lunch yet."

It takes a while to get images of Lex out of my head, but as we read together, and with constant prodding from Gwen, my mind finds comfort in the solitary focus of reading and discussing the book. It's sunny and hot but dry, and the pack of drinks and food eventually empty as the hours ticked by.

"Uh!" Gwen grunts. She flings herself back on the rock and lays draped over it, legs dangling over one side and her arms over the other. "My brain hurts."

"Just as well, my battery's about to die." I say. I turn off the e-reader and toss it into the open top of Gwen's pack. I stare out at the open meadow.

"Still thinking about her?" Gwen asks, sitting up from her contorted position.

"No, well not until you mentioned it," I say.

"Sorry," she says. After a few moments of silence she says, "You really don't know what's up with her and Wingate, Jesse, not really you don't."

I look down at my hands; their backs are smooth and brown from the sun, but the palms are as creased and as lined as a man of 60. I feel like 60.

"So, conclusions!" Gwen says in a too cheery voice.

"I have old hands," I mumble.

"Sign of wisdom, Jesse. Maybe you're an ancient spirit." Gwen's tone is only half joking.

"Huh, if anyone's an ancient spirit in this family it is you or Mom," I mumble.

"You're right. You just have old hands," she says.

I try to laugh, to show appreciation for what Gwen's trying to do, but only manage an insincere chuckle. "So what do you make of it all? What's Wingate up to?" I ask.

"Well, he wants to destroy the Talfar, obviously. I mean, if that's supposed to mean the end of the Dreamers, or maybe all of the Seekers of Light, then why wouldn't he," she says.

"Yeah, but… some things don't add up," I say, "like Catalina being convinced there's no danger, and Wingate coming here himself. Why would he risk that if he's so afraid of Santiago? Why not have the Talfar brought to him in the city?"

"Maybe he has to for some reason," Gwen suggests. "Maybe there's something else here that he needs to destroy the Talfar with, or maybe it needs to be done in a special way or place."

"Yeah," I mutter, "maybe." It doesn't make much sense, but it feels right. "Any ideas about that?"

Gwen shakes her head wildly and frenzies up her hair with both hands. "Ayah!" she squeals.

"What?"

She looked up at me through a mat of tangled hair. "Um, just something the women at the colony say." She throws back her hair and grabs her e-reader. "I have an idea… maybe…" She flits through the pages of The Book for a few minutes, then settles on one, reads through it, and rolls her eyes in thought. "Ha!" she blurts.

"What?"

"What do you make of that part on page 73 about the year of darkness?" she asks

"Year of darkness?" I think aloud. "I don't remember anything about that."

"Yeah, well it was an odd reference that didn't make sense so I didn't make much of it when I first read it. Here, listen. *'The year of darkness, one hundred thirty five. It fell upon the people. One and three the number taken, one and three the number lost, and many feared the cataclysm was upon them. But into the earth the Fallen One descended, to the chamber of crucifixions, and with Prometheus' gift, sealed the darkness* within?'

"Huh," I mutter. "What do you make of that?"

"I, ah, I don't know," Gwen says. "I just have a feeling about it."

"Well, it sounds to me like the Spanish Inquisition caught up with them and started to cull the herd," I say. The thought of it chills and angers me.

"Yeah, right," Gwen says, excitedly. "Thirteen of them, and the chamber of crucifixions, that sounds like a cave."

I think about that and an image flashes into consciousness. "Or a mine," I say.

Gwen nods wide-eyed. "What are you thinking?"

"I'm thinking that maybe the Dark Ones finally found the colony, and started abducting members and taking them into the Bender Mine to torture or kill... and now Wingate is busy reopening it."

"Why a mine? Why not just kill them?"

"I don't know, hide their crime, they didn't have a free reign here like that did in Europe."

"Or maybe it is part of a ritual, one that Wingate wants to repeat." Gwen offers.

"Yeah, maybe. Maybe this chamber has been reopened and with the Talfar in hand, he's ready to renew the persecutions," I say, but even as I say it, it sounds far-fetched.

Gwen doesn't say anything to that, but looks to be in deep thought. Finally, she asks, "What about the *Fallen One*? That sounds like their leader. Why would the boss evil dude seal up the chamber and how did he do that, with fire?"

"Fire? Oh, right—Prometheus' gift. Well, maybe that's part of the ritual, maybe he has to burn the victims like the inquisition did. Maybe Wingate has it in mind to do the same." That makes no sense and Gwen's expression tells me she feels the same way.

"Yeah, but…"

"Okay, my brain hurts now too," I say. "Let's go for a ride."

Gwen's eyes open wide. "On your bike?"

"Yeah, why not?"

"Cause I'm not crazy is why not," she says slipping from the rock to her feet. She never wanted to ride on the Shadow, had always been afraid.

"Come on, it'll be fun. I'll buy you a hot chocolate with whipped cream and caramel at The Kat." That makes Gwen take pause, but she shakes her head slowly. "No way."

Chapter 55

Dog and Cat Fight

Gwen's nails dig into my belly as we round the corner. Her arms are wrapped about my waist and she's hanging on so tight it's hard to breath. Nothing I say gets her to loosen her grip and all I can do is tolerate it for the duration. By the time I pull up back to The Kat I'm certain I'll find my shirt stained with blood and equally certain that Gwen will freak once we stop.

"We're good," I shout back when I kill the engine. In one quick smooth move, Gwen bounces off the back of the bike and stares back at me wide eyed. I drop the shadow over on its side stand, step off the other side with my front away from her, and after removing my helmet I glance down at the aftermath. To my surprise, my t-shirt looks puckered and distressed where she dug in to hold on, but there's no blood.

"You can take your helmet off now," I say to her.

"Oh, right," she says. She undoes the strap and slips it off, then stares down at the bike then at me. She has that post-roller coaster look, minus the smile, and I can't tell if she is excited or frightened.

"Fun, right?" I suggest.

"Ah…"

The sound of another bike interrupts her and we both turn to see a figure on another bike pull up. It's Bolin. He stops the bike up to within ten feet of us and dismounts. I take a few steps to place myself between Bolin and Gwen. "Go on in, Gwen. I'll be right with you."

Gwen doesn't move and when Bolin removes his helmet, he's staring at her. "What do you want, Bolin?" His eyes linger on Gwen and I feel the fire light within. I can feel my fingers digging into the edges of the helmet's faceguard. *He's yanking your chain. Stay cool.*

"Very nice," he says with a leer. "New girlfriend? A little young, don't you think?"

"Jesse?" Gwen speaks from behind me. She sounds concerned.

"It's okay Gwen, just go inside the backdoor and see Michelle. I'll be in shortly," I say.

"Ah, you must be Gwendolyn," he says with affected charm. "I'm so glad to finally meet you. I've heard so much…"

"What do you want Bolin?" I repeat.

Bolin finally turns his dark eyes my way. "Such haste, no manners; what is wrong with you, Mr. Benatar?"

I turn my body slightly and flash my eyes Gwen's way for a microsecond, then turn them back to Bolin. He stands only two paces away and I dare not take my eyes off him longer. "Inside, Gwen."

Bolin sneers. "Yes, inside, Gwendolyn, I'll catch up with you later."

Some things happen so fast that if you take the time to blink, you'll miss them—this was faster, so fast that I wasn't certain what was happening until it was nearly over. I'm vaguely aware of moving toward Bolin, the feel of the face-guard in my hand as the helmet moves in an arc over my shoulder, and a jarring sensation as it smashes into Bolin's face.

I'm dimly aware of my body colliding with his and both of us hitting his bike, and a girl's voice screaming, but I only become fully aware of my senses when I feel Gwen pounding on my back with her fists and screaming "You're going to kill him."

We're sprawled on top of his tipped over bike and I look down to see my right hand clenched around Bolin's throat, my fingers digging deep into the flesh around his windpipe. Above that is the bloody mess that was once his face.

"Shit," I shout, jumping to my feet. I stare down at Bolin—he isn't moving. Just then, Michelle slips into my field a vision and bends down over him. "Is he dead?" I ask.

She places a shaking hand over his half-crushed throat and stares wide eyed at his chest. "No, there's a pulse, but…"

Bolin takes in a gasp of air and coughs out a spray of blood. Gwen screams and Michelle recoils and instinctively wipes her face with her hand and checks for blood splatter. "We need to get him to the hospital," she says. "Go," she orders. Bolin starts moving, sucking in air in gurgling heaps.

"No, I'm not leaving you with this," I say.

"You're not," Michelle says. She stands, pulls out her cell phone, speed dials a number, and steps close to me. "Jesse, you need to leave here. With some of the cops in Wingate's pocket, it's not safe for you to stick arou... Yes, this is Michelle Phillips at The Mad Kat. We need an ambulance at the rear. I found a man unconscious and bleeding." She looks at me with wide eyes. 'Go!' she mouths silently.

"Yes, he's breathing and coming to, but I think he had an accident with his bike or something.... Yes I'll stay on the line until the ambulance arrives." 'Santiago!' she mouths. 'Go!' "Yes, I found him by his motorcycle. It's tipped over and he's on the ground... no I won't move him." Michelle put the phone against her chest to block out the sound. "Jesse, you need to take yourself and your sister and go to Santiago. Clean yourself up and your helmet."

"Jesse, she's right," Gwen says to my surprise. I look to see her tear dampened face staring at me with fearful gravity. "He was trying to pick a fight, Jesse—he lost."

"That's not going to make any difference to the cops. I took the first swing," I say.

"That's not what I saw," Gwen says nervously.

"Gwen, you can't," I say.

"She can if it comes to that and so will I," Michelle says. Just then, the sound of a siren starts up on the other side of the inlet. A muffled voice coming from the back of Michelle's phone causes her to lift a finger for us to be silent and places it back on her ear. "Sorry, I didn't catch that... Yes, I hear it now..."

She looks down at Bolin who's blinking open his eyes and trying to get up. "He's coming to now... Yes I will." To my surprise, Michelle places a foot on Bolin's chest and presses down, pinning him to the ground. She shrugs. "Told me not to let him move until the ambulance gets here," she whispers. Now go!"

Maybe it's a huge fucking mistake, but I don my helmet, throw my leg over the Shadow's saddle, and fired her up. With hesitation, Gwen jumps on behind me. "Go," she says. I look to Michelle again and she nods.

We're parked at the marina by the time the ambulance arrives at The Kat. We quickly pad down the gangway and make our away along the floating dock toward the Revenge. "Thank you, Jesse," Gwen says.

I look at her in astonishment. "For what, dragging you into one of my disasters? For exposing you to that shit back there?"

"Yes," she says. She turns her dark eyes up to mine. Replacing the fear I've seen earlier was determination and a touch of anger. "Yes to those and thank you for protecting me."

"You have a weird sense of protection," I say.

"No I don't. I heard what he said and the way he said it. I saw how he looked at me and I felt something from him—it was creepy. He wasn't making an idle threat—I felt... knew he intended to follow through on it, and you didn't let him get away with it."

"Well..." I begin. I feel stuck for words. "Let's hope I didn't piss him off too much."

We reach Esmeralda's Revenge and I call out for Santiago. Gwen walks along the dock toward the front of the boat and stares down at the nameplate. "Bienvenido, Señorita Sanchez," Santiago's gravelly voice calls out. I look to see his torso emerging from a forward hatch near the prow. "Subir a bordo, por favor."

Gwen quickly makes herself at home on Santiago's long couch and his cat, Katherine the Great or whoever, immediately takes to her. For that matter, so does Santiago. He seems fascinated and charmed by Gwen. As tough as the old bastard is, it's clear that my kid sister could have him twisted around her little finger in no time.

Then he turns his gaze to me. "Tell me about it," was all he says. I start right into the details, as few as there are, and Gwen interjects minor details to make certain it sounds like I'm the good guy in it all. Santiago alternates between scowling at me while I speak and smiling an acknowledgment to Gwen when she does. It would have been comical if the situation weren't so serious. When I'm done, Santiago closes his eyes and sits in silence.

"Call Michee," he says at last.

"My, ah, cell's pooched," I say. He tosses me his. With a little prompting from Gwen I call her number.

"Jesse, where are you?" Michelle asks immediately.

I switch it to speakerphone. "We're with Señor Santiago and you're on speaker. So what's happening?"

"They just took him to the hospital, in handcuffs," she says.

"Handcuffs?"

"Yeah. He refused to go with the paramedics and tried to get on his bike to leave and they tried to stop him. A CHP officer pulled up just as he slugged one of them."

"So he didn't say anything about me?" I ask.

"No, not while he was here anyway. I don't know what he'll tell them at the hospital, but I have a feeling he's too angry that you bested him, and maybe too embarrassed."

"Well, maybe hubris will work in my favor for once," I say. I shoot a glance to Santiago and he nods. "Thanks, Michelle. Sounds as though taking off was the right thing to do after all."

"Yeah, but watch yourself, Jesse. If and when they let him free, he's going to be after you."

"Yeah, well let me know if you find out anything else, okay?"

"Of course. Later."

"Bye." I close the phone. "Sounds like we lucked out," I say.

"I would not be so certain," Santiago says. "Let us talk."

Talk we do. We bring Santiago up to date on our thoughts about what Wingate might be up to and the reference to the Year of Darkness. Santiago seems particularly interested in my theory that Wingate is excavating the old Bender Mine because it's there that the dark ones did something to the people of the colony they'd abducted before.

"You think Wingate is the new Fallen One?" I ask.

Santiago shakes his head. "No," was all he says. "Can you please call your mother, Sweetheart," he ask Gwen. "She may be worried." He hands her his cell phone. "A word," he says as he stands and walks past me toward the companionway to the back deck. Once there, with the door closed behind us, he lights one of his cigarillos and scans the surroundings. He settles his eyes on the empty space of harbor where Wingate's yacht used to be anchored.

"You think something's about to happen," I suggest.

"Si," he replies. "I can feel him. He is on his way."

"Wingate? So what's the plan?" I ask.

"The plan is for you to keep your self and your family safe," he says.

"How? I mean, Wingate's has men everywhere and half the cops are supposed to be working for him."

"Take them to the colony, they'll be safe there," he says. Santiago appears to spot something on the hillside in the distance and stares.

"The colony? What are they going to do, fend off guns with good thoughts? They're a bunch of pacifists."

"Santiago loses interest in the hillside, removes the cigarillo from between his teeth and looks at it. He frowns, and then stabs it out in an ashtray built into the gunwale. "Sometimes good thoughts are more powerful than swords," he says. "They'll be safe."

"What about you? What are you going to do?" I ask.

He gives me a scowl and mutters, "I'm going to do what I do best, do what I am destined to do."

That sounds ominous. "I thought you told me we make our own destiny?" I say.

"We do, and I have made this one for myself."

"You're going after Wingate," I suggest. He makes no response. "You can't win that alone, he's bound to have dozens of men guarding him."

"Who says I'm going alone?" he ask cryptically.

"Me? You want to join you? I'm there," I say excitedly.

"No," he says with mild annoyance. "I want you to take your mother and sister to the colony and remain there with them."

"And let you get killed by Wingate and his goons? No way."

"If I had to watch over your sorry ass I probably would be killed."

I don't know why, but that one stings. "Seriously, I can't let you go up against him without helping," I say.

Santiago straightens himself and gives me a look that sends chills down my spine. "You can and you will. You have your own destiny and it is not in what I need to do. Haven't you learned anything from what I've shown you?"

I stand and stare at the old man, wondering if he's foreseen this day all along. Is it possible that everything he's done with me had been choreographed to ensure I don't want to participate in anything so dangerous?

"Well, if there's one thing you've taught me, it's that living your life on your own terms is maybe the most important thing any of us can do. Maybe staying safely squirreled away at the colony isn't living on my own terms."

Santiago takes that in and seems to think about it. Then his attention is drawn to an old, faded blue SUV that's slowly moving through the marina lot. "Your sister needs you in ways you cannot yet see. Work that into your equation."

The SUV slows to a crawl and the driver's window unhurriedly rolls down half-way, more clearly revealing the face of a large man that's almost as hard as Santiago's. "Who's that?" I ask, uncertain whether to hit the deck."

Santiago watches as the SUV leisurely makes its way out of the lot, and then he frowns. "It's time to go."

Chapter 56

Sequestered

I can't follow what Santiago's rattling off in Spanish to my mom, but she immediately stops her protest and tells Gwen and I to pack a bag. Thirty minutes later, the Therion, the sheds, and the house are securely locked and we pile into the two vehicles, Mom and Gwen in her car, Santiago and I in his.

"I don't like this, it's wrong," I say. "You need my help."

"Si, I need your help. I need you to remain with your mother and sister," he says.

"But why?" I protest as we pull out onto River Road. I sound like I'm whining and hate it. "They'll be safe at the colony, you said so yourself. They don't need me there, but you do."

Santiago sighs in clear frustration. "There are considerations you know nothing about," he says. "The consequences of what you do now will affect many for a long time."

"What are you not telling me?" I ask.

"Things that you are not ready to hear," he says.

Santiago may as well have been mute for all my efforts to get him to say more. I notice him scanning our surroundings as he drives, clearly watchful of everything. I begin doing the same when I spot the late model SUV sitting among the trees about twenty feet off the road.

"Hey, I think that's the same SUV we saw at the marina." I say. Santiago doesn't react except to glance back through the rear view and side mirrors. "Who is that guy? Is he one of Wingate's goon?" No reply. "God, you're an ass sometimes," I say, giving up on conversation. That gets a slight smile out of him, and then his face turns deadly serious again.

The SUV doesn't follow us and we pull onto the colony road without incident. The old man at the gate lets Mom and Gwen through without a word, but stands firmly in the middle of the road, blocking our way. Mom pulls her car to a stop beyond the gate and waits, as the old man and Santiago lock eyes on each other, each as defiant as the other.

"This is as far as I go," Santiago says.

"It's not right that they keep you out like this," I say.

"It is exactly right and necessary," he says.

I turn toward him and stare. He hasn't taken his eyes off the old man. "You guys know each other?" He doesn't reply. "There's nothing to hold me here once I leave your car you know."

Santiago brakes contact with the old guardian and fixes his eyes on mine. "Nothing but good sense," he says. "Jesse... you and your sister, your mother too, are important in ways you do not yet understand. You have to trust me on this, but if you cannot, then speak to Señora Margarita Ruiz."

"Any relation to Catalina?" I ask.

"Her grandmother," he says. "Doña Margarita is a very respected elder. Do not embarrass your family."

I step out of the car and lean down through the open door. "When does it all happen?" I ask.

I expect him to blow off my question like he had during the drive, but Santiago stares at his car's instrument cluster a moment, then speaks. "Soon," he says. I feel a surge of frustration. "It will begin within 24 hours," he adds.

"What? What's going to begin? What's going to happen?"

"Retribution," he says, and then nods for me to close to door. "Remain here with your mother and sister. They will need you." With that, he puts the car in reverse and begins backing up, even before I close the door.

I watch the old dodge turn around on the narrow dirt road and disappear along the winding forest road. I turn back to see that the old guardian has returned to his cabin and see Gwen standing beside mom's car. I throw my pack over one shoulder and join them.

———— | ————

"Eat something," Gwen urges.

We sit at the table in the small cabin we've been given to stay in. It's small and cozy, the sort of getaway in the forest I've dreamed I'd have someday, but being here is anything but comfortable. Out there, somewhere, Santiago was preparing to take on Wingate and his teched-out goons, a mission nothing short of suicide. How can I sit back and enjoy a bowl of stew? I push the bowl away. "I can't."

"Sure you can," Gwen says. "Mom will be upset…"

"I can't just sit here and let Santiago get himself killed," I say. I stand up from the table and look down at her concerned face. "I just can't," is all I can think to say. Maybe if Mom were here, she'd be able to settle me down, but she'd left to meet with colony elders soon after we were settled in the cabin.

"What are we going to do?" she asks.

"Go find him, help ou… what do you mean 'we'?"

"Well you don't think you're going to do anything stupid without me there to stop you from getting yourself…"

"No way," I blurt. I step over one of the wooden pegs next to the front door where I'd hung my jacket. "You can help me with one thing, though."

"What?" Gwen says standing and taking her empty bowl to the sink.

"Help me find Señora Margarita Ruiz."

Forty minutes later we're still walking along the forest road. "Where the hell does she live, Oregon?" I ask.

"Come on, it's just up a ways," Gwen says.

"You said that a mile ago. If these people ever get around to modern transportation they'll save themselves a lot of time," I grumble.

"And how would that benefit them?" Gwen asks.

I open my mouth for a quick retort, but nothing comes. How would that benefit them? It would save them time, but time for what? It seems they're already doing what they need to be doing with no rush to get more done or things done faster.

"Here we are," Gwen says. Looking to see a small cabin about 30 yards off the road in the woods. It isn't any larger than ours.

"Doesn't look like much," I say.

"Jesse," Gwen says with concern, "this is her home, don't disrespect it. These people live simply."

"Yeah, but you'd think being the respected elder she's supposed to be…"

Gwen rolls her eyes and slaps my arm. "Just don't embarrass me will you?"

We make our way along the path to the front door, but before we get there, it opens and a young woman in an ankle length dress steps out to face us. "Catalina," I say. "Hi."

She doesn't seem at all surprised to see us. Without a word, she bows slightly to Gwen and I, then invites us into the cabin with a motion of her hands. She steps into the cabin after us, closes the door, then motions for us to sit on cushions arranged around a small low table. "Mi abuela es gone… outside. Come back soon," she says in Spanglish. She seems nervous, or at least uncomfortable. "Want té?"

"Ah, no…" I begin.

"Sí, por favor," Gwen interrupts. "Ambos de nosotros nos gustaría un poco de té."

Catalina looks to Gwen and then to me with a confused look, then nods. She turns toward an open stone hearth where coals glow red and a hanging iron kettle gives off a thin wisp of vapor. She's a living paradox:

at night, when spirit traveling, she is a dangerous beauty, seductress who can shamelessly display her naked body an passions. During the day, she is laughably demure, near purit....

As Catalina makes tea, I manage to take my eyes off her long enough to look over the cabin. It's similar in size to the one we're staying in, but everything is even more ancient in design. No water pump by the sink, and no sink for that matter. Drying herbs hang from the ceiling beams near the hearth, leather and cloth sacs hang in places from the log walls, and several wooden chests are scattered about.

At the other end of the room, a long narrow table by the window is lined with glass jars as though waiting to be filled with homemade jams. There's only one chair in the room, and that's a wooden rocker near the hearth. The place could easily pass for a hermit's or witch's haunt.

"Gwen prattles a slow Spanish, most of which I don't understand, but all of which Catalina encouragingly pays rapped attention to. I can see Gwen fitting in here—well, other than her love of spending hours on the Net studying one thing or another. As we drink our tea, I catch Catalina quickly glancing my way when I'm not watching her, but she won't make eye contact.

We wait about twenty minutes or so, then Catalina brightens, stands, and makes her way to the front door. She opens it and a moment later, an ancient steps into view from around the side of the cabin. Gwen and I stand as the elder enters. She stares at us a moment, then mumbles something to Catalina, who looks uncomfortable and bows her head. She takes the elder's bandolier bag from her shoulder and sets it carefully on the jar-line table.

The old woman gives me a deadpan expression as she makes her way toward Gwen and I. "Hola," I say. She nods. "Hablas Inglés?"

Margarita Ruiz shakes her head slowly and spies an unused cushion on the floor and makes her way for it. "I translate," Catalina says, joining us. She takes a cushion next to her grandmother and a strained silence falls on the circle. Gwen stares down at the top of the small round table, Catalina watches her grandmother nervously, and I feel like I have dozens of times when hauled down the principal's office. The only one who seems at ease is Margarita Ruiz.

After a few minutes, she finally speaks in a low, slow voice. "You here from fear," Catalina translates. "You fear for mother, sister, and Señor Santiago," she continues. "You want help, but confusion."

"Right," I say. "How… why should I not go to help Señor Santiago, why must I stay here?"

Catalina translates and Gwen helps. The old woman speaks without looking my way. "You have fate. If die, then no fate. If die, sister fate not so strong."

I look to Gwen who is busy translating in her own head. "I think she means that if something happens to you, then whatever you are supposed to do won't happen, and whatever I'm supposed to do might not," Gwen says.

"Si," Catalina says. "Sólo así."

"So what are these things that Gwen and I are supposed to do?" I ask. "Why are they so important that I have to sit back and let an old man die who's trying to protect us?"

Catalina stares at me, lips parted, like a deer caught in the headlights. Gwen translates what I've asked as best she can and a very relieved Catalina helps her with the translation. Doña Margarita Ruiz finally looks me in the eye and I feel my skin crawl. It's a look like Santiago has given me more than once, and I feel she can see into me, is seeing things I don't want her to know. She speaks a lot of words but I gap until Catalina begins to translate.

"Fate is only maybe, not certain," she begins. Catalina looks very uncomfortable, and that gets my attention. "World make fate, all life make fate, but also make own fate," she continues.

"Of course, we create our own destiny," I say.

"Si," she says, then hesitates. "Gwendolyn must seek fate, Mi abuela not say what is." I can see Gwen's shoulders drop at that. Catalina drops her eyes and falls mute until her grandmother prods her further. She speaks without looking up. "Mi abuela say Jesse Benatar and me together make fate strong."

"With her?" I say. "What am I supposed to do with her?"

"No," Catalina says shaking her head. "With me," she repeats, pointed a finger at her self.

"Ah…oh!…" My mind flips through several possible meanings and then goes on strike.

"What are the two of you to do?" Gwen asks. Catalina blushes a deeper shade of brown. "Oh!" Gwen says, and goes mute.

Margarita Ruiz speaks again. "She say what happen Señor Santiago, happen before, long time. Is fate," Catalina translates.

"No! Not good enough," I say angrily. I turned to Gwen. "Tell her about the Talfar, about Wingate taking it to the mine, the Cave of Crucifixions. Tell her it's important that Santiago stops him and I need to help. He needs all our help."

Gwen does what I ask, slowly translating what I've said to Margarita Ruiz, all the while the old woman stares at me. In the silence that follows, I become agitated, and at one point, I nearly pick my butt up and leave. I resist the urge and calm myself instead, and when I have, a sliver of a smile forms on Margarita Ruiz' lips and she speaks. Catalina looks at her questioningly, and when her grandmother gives her a firm nod, she looks to me.

"Come," she says, standing. Gwen moves to get up as well. "No, you stay, help Abuela."

Chapter 57

Woodland Passage

> **Journal - Hook Point, CA.**
>
> *It's easy to feel alone. We are born into life alone and I suppose we all die that way as well. Maybe life really is a solitary journey. Yet we are all brothers and sisters, often-reluctant companions on that journey; each has a separate path to follow yet we're surrounded by the river of humanity. In this, we are intimate with everyone who has ever lived or ever will. So are we ever really alone?*
>
> *~ From the Journal of Jesse Benatar*

Gwen throws me a questioning look but all I have to throw back is a shrug and a half-smile. "Later," I add. I stop and bow my head slightly to Margarita Ruiz, the way I'd seen some of the colony men do. It feels weird, but she seems to appreciate it. Then, I'm outside and following Catalina down the path toward the road as she slips a jean jacket over her shoulders.

"So where are we going?" I ask. She doesn't reply; she walks with her head down and her eyes fixed on the dark path. It's almost 11:00 pm and damn hard to see. "Catalina?" She takes in an audible breath and looks up and away. *She's upset, damn it.* "Catalina, stop," I say, taking her by the arm and bringing us both to a stop.

She doesn't resist, but won't look my way. I step in front of her so that we're toe-to-toe, faces only inches apart. "Catalina, what's wrong?" It takes a moment but she gradually tilts her head upward to reveal a tear-streaked face. "What's wrong?" I ask. I'm suddenly aware that I'm still holding onto her arm and let it go. "Sorry."

Her mouth opens and her lips tremble in the pale light of the forest. "All bad now," she mutters. "Ruin."

"What? What's bad? What's ruined?" I ask.

Her large black eyes fix a sad look on mine. "Us!"

"What? You mean that stuff your grandmother said about you and me needing to be together?" She says nothing but her steady gaze is answer enough. "Hey, listen, I don't take that seriously. I…"

"Take serious," she says. The look she gives me sends shivers up my spine.

"Catalina," I begin, but come to a dead end. "Listen, what she says doesn't affect anything."

She rolls her eyes and steps around me. "All change," she says.

I keep abreast of her on the path. "Is that why you were coming on to me the way you did?" She gives me an annoyed, questioning glance. "Those nights you came to me, tried to seduce me. Is this why?"

Her face scrunches up and she looks away, letting out a mournful sound that brings on a wave of guilt. "I'm sorry; I didn't mean to insult you."

She doesn't say anything but I see her lips moving. *She's Translating!* "Ah, insulto. Soy no insulto usted?" I fumble.

Her head perks a little at that and then drops again. "No insult," she says. "No good only." She picks up her pace and I nearly go down when I trip on an exposed root. "I no want seduce. I want you want me," she says through tears. "I try only way."

"No, that's not the only way, why…"

"Soy demasiado tímido," she says passionately. "Only way. No good. You no like and prophecy ruin all."

"Prophesy? What prophesy?"

"No important. I no saber … nunca," she says, reaching what passes for the main road. She turns up it in the direction that leads deeper into the forest.

"Catalina, slow down." She doesn't and I grab her arm and haul her to a stop for a second time. "I don't know what the hell you're talking about," I shout. She looks at me with frightened eyes. "Sorry," I say as I let her arm go, and I realize I'm getting pretty fucking tired of saying that. "I'm really not having a good day here—in fact it's probably about the worse day of my fucked up existence, so just please just stop and talk to me… please."

Catalina looks up at the sky and another tear flows down her cheek. She looks down at the ground to the right of us then brings her gaze back to mine. "Si," she says. "Okey-dokey."

"Okey-dokey?" That puts a grin on my face. "So what's wrong? Why are you upset; your grandmother embarrass you?"

She seems to think about that a moment then speaks slowly, as though carefully selecting each word. "I hear prophesy when child," she begins looking down at my chest. "I think, maybe, wolf come for me, be muy strong, muy guapo… ah look good?"

"Sure?" I say. "Entiendo."

"When I see you…" she hesitates, "… I like. When I see you is wolf… I muy feliz… happy. Pienso que el sueño es verdadero…"

"Catalina…" She stops me short by placing her fingertips on my lips.

The movement seems to embolden her as her eyes dance between my lips and eyes. She gives me a sad smile. "I hope you want me… también. I see other girl want, two girl. I come, make you see. No good? No success? Ah, I come make you like, ah, entiendes?"

"Si, entienndo." I do understand and feel sad. She thought I was this wolf she was to mate with and tried to make herself known to me, to get me to like her, to want her. The ironic thing is, I do like and want her.

"I not know way to this…good way to you." She struggles for her words. "We not like others, like you, like Gwendolyn. We no cortejan, ah, date?" I nod. "We not know how you do, but know life, know nature way, know spirit strong." Her face changes, takes on a glint of the passion and power she showed when she'd visited me in the night. "This I do," she says with gusto. "Only way know, and do good, do strong... but no good; you no like."

"Catalina, I ..."

"You want, but no like," she says defiantly. "My sad." Her jaw muscles tightened and she breathes out a heavy breath. "We go."

"Wait," I say. "You have to know this, Catalina. I was attracted to you the first day I saw you. I just rode into town for the first time, and there you were, in the back of that old yellow pickup truck. I searched around for the truck, for you, but you were gone. It was as though something connected us, compelled me to seek you out."

I'd rattled on at normal speed but caught myself. "Entiendes?" She looks at me cautiously, but nods. "Catalina, I think you're amazing, and I feel something pulling me to you, and no, it's not just your wicked ways, either." That seems to confuse her. "I like you, I like you a lot, and yes I want you, but... not like other girls." *Fuck! How do I explain?*

"Listen, you are one seriously beautiful girl, and there is something very special, very powerful about you. Deep down I know that getting involved with you is serious business, it will not be just for fun, and I'm just too confused about everything now to make that jump."

A very thoughtful look comes over her face, then she gives me an odd look that is part smirk and part glower. "Stupid boy," she says. "We go now." She continues up the road.

"Yeah, stupid boy," I mutter and follow.

We walk together in silence, the serenity of the primal forest contrasting with a tension between us—part concern, part frustration, and part excitement. I think about that; I am drawn to Catalina in a way that's totally new on me. Were we somehow destined to be together? That thought annoys me—I don't believe in karma or destiny for one; for another, it implies there are forces messing with my freedom.

Lex certainly puts off the sexiest vibe of any girl I've met and can stir my passions into a frenzy, but I know I can shut that off if I want to, make myself immune to the effects of anything she might try. Catalina— she's a whole different animal. She triggers my desires—subtly, powerfully, and undeniably—but there is something about her that compels deference as well.

It's unassuming, not at all demanding, and maybe that's what makes it so powerful. It is more a feeling that you don't want to disrespect her in any way because that would just be... wrong.

We walk for a good 10 minutes with me obsessing about who and what this girl is to me, and then I become irritated with myself; I feel distracted from my purpose and I have only myself to blame. "Where are we going?" I ask irritably.

She walks on as though she doesn't hear the question or doesn't intend to answer it, then she breaks the silence. "Go see mi tatarabuela," she says without looking my way.

"Your tatara what? Who's that?" I wish Gwen were here to translate.

She looks up toward the darkness of the tree canopy as she walks, then holds out a hand and touches it to her chest. "Catalina," she says. "Madre, ah, mother es Maria Ruiz," she says gesturing with her hands as though removing something from the palm of one with the other. "Entiendes?" she asks, giving me a questioning look.

"Yes. Your mother is Maria Ruiz," I reply.

"Si. Maria mother es Margarita Ruiz. Margaritia Ruiz es mi abuela," she says, repeating the gesture.

"Your mother's mother, your grandmother, is Margarita Ruiz," I offer.

"Si. Margarita Ruiz mother es Issabella Ruiz es mi bisabuela.

"Your great grandmother," I mumble.

"Isabella mother es Rosalyn Ruiz es mi tatarabuela," she says.

"Your great, great grandmother? Holy shit," I blurt.

"Holy shit?" she repeats doubtfully.

"No, nothing. We are going to see your great, great grandmother?"

"Si," she says with a nod. "Ella es La Abuela."

That stops me in my tracks. *Fuck... The Grandmother? The one Gwen was so freaked about... her great grandmother?* I swallow hard; it feels as if we're walking to Judgment Day. Catalina hasn't stopped and I have to jog to catch up.

We leave the road for another footpath, but instead of leading to a house, it just leads deeper into the woods, then into a valley. We take two small bridges over the active stream as we snake our way up the

sides become steeper as we go. It eventually becomes a
between rock faces, a shallow canyon. It must be close to
ʊᴜ and it's so damn dark that even with my eyes accommodated, I
can barely see where we're walking.

"You guys ever hear of lanterns or flashlights?" I mutter. Catalina
ignores the comment; she seems to have no trouble finding her way. I
make out a faint hissing sound in the distance ahead that grows ever so
slightly louder as we walk. Suddenly, as if materializing from nowhere,
two large cloaked figures block our path. Catalina rattles off something
in light-speed Spanish and a deep male voice barks back something in
obvious displeasure. She says a few words in a gentle tone and the two
figures slowly recede back into the darkness.

When we round the next bend, I'm looking at a large open area the
size of a basketball court, surrounded by forty-foot cliffs on all sides.
The shallow canyon has dead-ended, and the stream, the source of the
hissing sound, cascades down a step rock face on the far side, forming a
pool at it's base. Next to the pool stands a large, solitary tree, a live oak
or madrone. What really grabs my attention though is the large, dark
opening of the rock face to my left. It looks like the opening of a cave,
four feet above the floor of the canyon, and about ten feet around.
Beside it, one on either side, stand two large figures like the ones we
encountered on the way in, cloaked in black robes.

Chapter 58

Purification

Catalina pauses and bows towards the cave, muttering something
softly. She steps into to the stream, squats, and then slides her hands
into the water. She gently rubs the wrist of her left arm with her right
hand, as though washing it, then repeats it on the other side. Then she
takes her wet hands and gently rubs her temples, then her forehead, and
then holds her hands to her heart and mumbles more indiscernible
words.

She stands and turns to me. "You stay," she says, pointing to the
open area on the opposite side of the stream from the cave, where a few
large logs sit close to the cliff face. There's a distinct firmness, a hint of

power in her voice, and her eyes meet mine without hesitation. Catalina is in her element.

"Okay, I'll wait here, but how long it this going to take? Santiago…"

"You wait," she says with finality, then turns, and walks into the stream. She stops half way and turns her face back to me. "You no cross!" she commands.

"Yeah, I no cross," I mutter. I watch as she crosses and makes her way up to the rock shelf at the mouth of the cave, then disappears into the darkness. I'm left in the dark—literally and figuratively—staring at the black opening of the cave and the two figures that I know are watching me. *So what would you guys do if I crossed?*

I wasn't in any position or mood to push buttons so I wander over to the logs and sit. Despite the ominous maw of the cave, there's something undeniably beautiful and serene about the place. After a while, the white-noise hiss of the tumbling waterfall, the curved elegance of the tree's limbs against the cliff backdrop, and the pinpoint lights of the stars overhead lull me into a quiet state of mind.

My concerns for Santiago are there and very real, but rather than the impatient imperative to do something about it, I feel a strong need to just be where I am, doing what I'm doing. In this quiet space, things begin to sort themselves out in my head.

Sometime later, my attention is drawn to the cave entrance— Catalina's standing there, looking my way, holding a bundle in her arms. She makes her way down to the stream and crosses it as I make my way over to her. "Come," she says, then turns and walks toward the pool of water beneath the falls. Rather than give voice to the questions in my head, I follow her, and when we reach the pool, she sets down the bundle that now looks to be two folded robes. "We wash."

"Ah, I had a shower today… I think," I mumble.

Catalina takes off her jean jacket, turns her back to me, and loosens her dress. The light cloth falls away from her shoulders, revealing the richness of her dark skin. I look up at the guards by the cave, but they seem to pay no heed to what we're doing. Catalina squats and picks up the robes, then slowly walks in to the pool. When she's knee deep, she looks back to me. "Come, Jesse Benatar. We must wash."

Go figure. I'm in the middle of a colony of people that seem lost in time, people who could give the Amish a run for their money, yet this? They're supposed to be backward, near puritanical; what's one of their young women doing inviting me to join her naked in the pool, and in front of others?

I strip off and find myself knee deep in the coldest water I've felt since Colorado; the stream has to be spring fed. Catalina reaches a large flat rock on the other bank and places the robes up on it then turns to face me.

Here we are, in the buff for real this time, and she looks all the more beautiful for it in starlight. Her teeth flash briefly in the darkness, a quick smile, then she wades back towards the middle of the pool. She turns toward the waterfall and I follow. The pool grows deeper until I'm up to my neck, while Catalina is forced to breaststroke. She swims under the tumbling cascade and I follow.

I open my eyes to darkness on the other side, the dim starlight barely penetrating the tumbling water, and I find myself in a small grotto. I move forward a few feet, hands held in front, until I touch something warm and smooth. "Sorry," I say. She remains silent. I inch forward and find the rock ledge four feet beneath the surface that Catalina's standing on. I stand next to her. "What are we doing here?"

"We wash," she says in a voice just loud enough to be heard over the sound of the falls.

"I know, but…"

She reaches forward and places a finger on my lips, the universal sign for 'shut up'. "We wash," she repeats. Then she scoops up a palm of water and brings it to my face and rubs the side of it, paying special attention to my temple. She repeats that on the other side, then gently washes the center of my forehead. They're the same places Gwen paid attention to when she prepared me for the spirit calling.

Her hand trembles and I hear her breath quivering in the darkness—she's shivering from the cold. She takes my left hand and rubs its palm beneath the water. As she's doing that, my eyes wander to the mounds of her breasts just above the water surface. Between them something flashes a faint sparkle of light and I use my free hand to touch it; it's hard and cold. "What's this?" I ask.

Catalina frees my left hand and takes my right and begins to wash it's palm. With my left I touch, then lift from her skin, a small spiral of gold that's dangling from a fine chain. I can barely make it out but I know it's a spiral with a line through it's center; I'd seen the image in the book, somewhere near the end.

"Es mi talismán," she says finally as she let's my hand free.

"Should I do yours?" I ask.

"No," she says simply. "Do back?" She turns around and I begin sliding my hands over her back. Her skin has become cool but it's still warmer than the water and still electrifying to the touch. I feel myself thinking things I ought not to just then. I slide a hand down over one of her butt cheeks and leave it there to get a rise out of her, but all I get in return is a slow glance over her shoulder. That sends impulses up my spine.

"You're done," I say as I quickly remove my hand.

She turns and motions me to turn around. When I do, she rubs my back with long slow strokes, as though she is giving a massage. Then she slides her hand down and grabs one of my butt cheeks and holds on tight, just long enough to get a reaction from me. Despite her demure nature in the light of day, she's clearly able to dish it back. "Do all," she whispers. "leg, foot, chest… all."

I turn to see her stroking her arms and shoulders as though soaping herself up. "You want some help with that?" I joke. She ignores the comment.

As we wash in the quiet darkness, my body becomes comfortable with the cold and my mind becomes calm yet alert. All carnal thoughts and excitement about standing next to Catalina, naked, give way to something else—I feel connected to her, a gentle sense of intimacy without any sexual overtones.

It's… sweet, pure. Ha! Imagine that. It's similar to the way the gang and I can hang out together on the beech without lust or embarrassment, only this has become totally devoid of any sexual feelings. Catalina was simply a fellow human being, and no longer an object of my sexual desires.

We finish the scrub down and she steps off the rock ledge and dives under the cascading falls. I follow and find her breast stroking toward the rock with the robes. Once there, she wades out of the water and steps up onto the rock. From where I am in the water, her body is silhouetted against a sky of pinpoint stars. It's pure magic as she squeegees the water from her body.

I make my way out of the water and do likewise. She slides a crimson robe over her head and I slide on a brown one she hands to me. She steps close and whispers, "Make head clear, make thoughts good."

"What's wrong with the thoughts I'm having about you?" I whisper back. "Does that mean I can't think of you and I under he waterfall?"

She hesitates, then whispers, "No hurt thought, no violent."

At the mouth of the cave, the two guards don't budge as we pass them and are swallowed up by the darkness.

Chapter 59

The Cave of Prophesies

Catalina takes my hand and leads the way, which is damn fortunate because it's so dark I literally can't see my hand in front of my face. The cave seems to bend left then right, and then, about 50 paces in, I make out a faint glow in the distance that steadily grows until I can see enough to walk unguided. The lighted walls of the cave flicker and I can smell burning wood and incense. Then, the passage opens up and we are standing at the edge of a large chamber, lit by a single fire in the center.

It's about 60 feet across with a ceiling around 20 feet high, and the floor of it is about 10 feet below where we stand. The flat walls of the chamber are painted with a maze of pictures and symbols, and sitting by the fire is The Grandmother, staring at the pictures.

"The cave of prophesies," I whisper. "Poor Gwen is going to shit when she hears this." That draws an angry look from Catalina, whose eyes prove to be a lot bigger than I'd thought. I hold up my hands in surrender. "Sorry," I whisper.

Catalina pads down the cold natural steps in the rock, worn smooth by countless bare feet over the years. I know I'm supposed to follow her, but something holds me back. There's something in the air, something palpable, and it holds me back as well as the guards outside could have. Catalina pads over to her great grandmother and kneels beside her quietly. After a few moments, she leans her head toward the ancient and appears to speak words I cannot hear.

The old woman does not respond in any way I can see, but the thing that's holding me back gives way, and I feel drawn toward them. When I'm three paces away, the force returns and I feel compelled to stop. I have an impulse to force my way forward, but I remember Catalina saying keep my thoughts and feelings good. As soon as I let the impulse go, I feel released from the force.

I take another step forward and stop. The two women—one so young and the other so very old—kneel side-by-side staring at the far wall. I look to where they're gazing and see a muddled mix of signs, symbols, and badly drawn pictures. *Huh! This is the cave of prophesies?*

The mural is chaos itself—nothing seems related to anything else. My eyes dart from picture to picture, symbol to symbol, like someone trying to find his way out of a maze, but there is no escape; nothing makes sense. They may be important to the gods, but details bore and frustrate me; my mind struggles to grasp the big picture, the essence of it all, but it become hopelessly lost.

My eyes begin to hurt and my mind grows numb with fatigue. *How long have I been here?* I want out, want to break away from the wall's clutches, but am compelled to remain... no, to surrender.

I become aware of the odor of incense; cedar, sage, and something unfamiliar. It seems to surround me, uplift me, and whatever it is, I want to breathe it in and let it infuse me. My mind shifts down, and the anarchy on the wall changes, as if the symbols were rearranging themselves. I know nothing has changed yet pictures begin to form obscure links with other pictures and the symbols begin to assume vague meanings. Is something really happening here or is my mind playing psychedelic tricks on me? Then I notice it.

To the far left, near the bottom of the collage, the symbol of a spiral with an arrow transecting it seems to radiate on its own. It's the same symbols worn by Catalina and as I stare, the spiral begins to move. Is it really doing that? My attention shifts to another symbol and I feel bliss, the next symbol radiates belonging, and the next love. That leads me to anguish, then anger, and as my attention is drawn from one symbol to the next, my emotions run the entire gamut of the human heart.

I feel my body jolt violently and pain radiates from my knees but my mind won't leave the wall. Pictures turn into epic tales, daytime years compressed into dream-time seconds, and in the millennia that pass before me, I witness the history of humankind, and the efforts of the Enlightened Ones to save us from our own folly. It's exhausting, exciting, painful, and ecstatic and I don't want it to end, but it does. When my attention is finally drawn to another symbol of the spiral near the right end of the mural, I see Catalina dancing in my mind, see us together, and then...

Something touches my shoulder and I'm yanked back into physical reality. I'm down on my knees, have fallen there I imagine, and sense Catalina standing to my left, and The Grandmother to my right, each with a hand on my shoulder. I lean forward and let out a long, feral cry that frankly scares the shit out of me, and then I hurl.

Catalina has a large pail waiting and slips it in front me to catch everything that comes up. "Sorry," I gasp between hurls. "Sorry!" The old woman pats my back, mumbles something, then walks back to her cushion by the fire and sits, facing the wall.

With my gut empty, my attention is drawn to my knees; I've collapsed onto them and hit the rock floor of the cave and now they throb with pain. I roll over on my butt and straighten them out on the floor. The thick robe cushioned the blow and saved my skin, but from the look and feel of them, I am going to have a nasty set of bruises.

"Apologies," Catalina says, kneeling next to me. "You see muy rapido. No tiempo. I no think you fall. Leg good?"

"Yeah, leg great," I grumble. My head is still numb from the psycho-trip. "What's in that incense?"

Catalina glances down at the abalone shell sitting on the floor, still letting off a trail of smoke from the smoldering ashes. "Salvia, cedro, e osha," she says. "Is good only; clear thought, help see."

"Yeah, you think?" From the confused look on Catalina's face, I know the sarcasm's lost on her. I slowly get to my feet and Catalina pops up and holds my arm to steady me. "Thank you." She keeps hold of my arm and leads me to the side of the fire and motions for me to sit on a cushion next to The Grandmother. "So what happens, how can..."

"Shhhhh," The Grandmother hisses gently.

I look her way but she doesn't take her eyes from the wall. She sits with perfectly straight posture, and so still that if not for a blink I catch, she could pass for a too-real mannequin. She suddenly shifts her eyes to mine and it all comes back—the dream, the old women in the dream who taught me in that meditation weeks earlier—it had been The Grandmother. *Jesus!*

I take my seat while Catalina scurries around the fire to the other side of her, and in a smooth graceful move, lowers herself to another cushion. Then... nothing happens, and nothing is exactly what I need. I closed my eyes and the countless images and symbols continue to flash through my mind.

A voice says something and I open my eyes to see if it's being directed at me. The Grandmother gives no indication that she's said anything. I look to Catalina and she glances my way and motions with her eyes for me to pay attention to the wall. I return my eyes to the wall and feel the rush of confusion again. I close my eyes and do as I had in the dream when The Grandmother taught me the meditation.

I breathe deeply, let the air permeate every part of me, and recall the feeling of my body sinking into the earth. I breathe in, then out, then in, then out, and once again become enraptured by the countless sensations throughout my body, of the sounds and smells of the fire, and then those other senses come alive, the ones that emerge when I shift and I find myself floating into the blissful world of pure, peaceful awareness.

I open my eyes and the wall comes alive again but with greater clarity and meaning. It replays the story, the passion, and drama of human history, and the ceaseless dedication of The Enlightened Ones—The Dreamers—to counter our darker potentials, to make a difference, and perhaps, despite odds against, save us from ourselves. Their work begins at the first symbol of the intersected spiral—the unbound and the restrained, the endless and the linear—and weaves its way through the fabric of humanity like a thread of golden sanity, holding it all together.

When the tale reaches the second symbol at the far end, images of Catalina and I flood my mind, a difficult union opposed by many, resisted from within, but giving rise to something that remains obscured. Whatever it is… it's important, and while many pray for it, many curse its very possibility.

I struggle to see through a mist that seems to obscure the end, but only manage to weaken my detached calm. Then I feel myself disconnect from the wall and its tale. "Why can't I see the end? What is supposed to happen?" I ask.

The Grandmother looks down at the fire and sighs. She mumbles something in Spanish and Catalina translated it. "Not see all. Not good see all. Not freedom yes?" she says with a confused but hopeful look. I understand what she's trying to say though. If I were able to see into the future, to see what's supposed to happen, then I'd lose my ability to choose my actions freely.

"Entientdo," I say nodding. I look back at the wall and reflect on a thousand generations of struggle depicted there. "What if I want to do the right thing? What if I want to do what's best?" I ask her.

I don't know if I make myself clear, and I can't translate what she speaks to her great, great grandmother, but her translation of the old woman's response is, "Follow heart."

Seriously? Maybe the most important decision I ever make and I get a Hallmark moment. I think about what Mom would advise and decide it would be the same. I know Gwen would tell me I have to make the best decision for everyone, that my destiny would be found in doing that. Then I think about what Santiago would say. *Santiago!* "Santiago!" The Grandmother closes her eyes and Catalina looks giving me a puzzled look.

"I've been so stupid," I berate myself. "I came here to get help for Santiago, to know what to do for him, not for myself," I blurt. "Ask your... The Grandmother what I need to do to help Santiago." Catalina frowns and doesn't say anything. "Señor Carlos Santiago is in danger," I say slowly. "How can I help him?"

She translates this and the old woman sits in still silence for so long I wonder whether she heard her. Then she speaks in a voice that sounds disembodied. I look to Catalina who says, "Señor Santiago is Fallen One. He do what must. He do like before, he do destiny."

"What?" I ask. "No, no. Santiago isn't the fallen one, Wingate is, he's the one."

The Grandmother speaks and Catalina translates on the fly this time. "Los Oscuros come many years ago. Take, kill, want destroy all good. Fallen one no walk, ah, el camino de la luz," she says, gesturing with her left hand. "Fallen one no walk el camino oscuro," she says, gesturing with her right hand. Then she put her hands together between where they have been. "Walk here, no good, no bad. He do what must do, he do like before."

"What do you mean like before, what happened before?" The old woman looks over her shoulder towards a portion on the wall to our far right and begins to speak. That section of the wall is detailed, and in the dim light of the fire, there are features I have a hard time discerning.

Without thinking, I stand and walk over to it. It's a depiction of events after the Dreamers came to California, and as I stare at it, listening uncomprehending to her words, it begins to retell its tale.

Major events—the initial landing at the site of Hook Point and the peaceful alliance with the native tribes, establishing a permanent colony inland, the mysterious burning of the La Soñadora—were all woven together with symbols that set off emotions and resonant thoughts within a single minded commitment to ascend into light, beyond the darkness that was overcoming humanity.

Threads link references to the continued struggle of The Enlightened Ones in Europe and Asia in a failing attempt to hold back the influence of the Dark Ones. Then, five generations of peaceful striving are broken by the year of darkness.

I recall what Gwen read to me from the del Baca's book—thirteen colonists taken, thirteen lost. The wall speaks to me in detail—the Dark Ones abducted colonists and took them deep within the earth, to a place to be forever known as the Chamber of Crucifixions. There they were tortured and killed in an attempt to end the quest of The Dreamers once and for all.

Then comes the Fallen One, not from the ranks of Los Oscuros, but from their own, one who chose to leave the colony, never allowed to return. One who takes it upon himself to do what the Dreamers cannot do for themselves—a Black Knight of folklore, he moves against the Dark ones... *And does what? What did he do? Something about Prometheus' gift? Sealing...*

Then it comes to me: this ex-patriot, rejected by his people, uses fire to seal the Dark Ones in the Chamber of Crucifixions, a chamber that becomes their tomb. I then know what Wingate is doing at the old Bender mine, and what Santiago plans to do about it.

I turn to the old woman who casts sad eyes on me. "You know what's about to happen," I say. I walk toward her and Catalina. "You know what Santiago is going to do and that he'll likely be killed doing it." The old woman's eyes make it clear she doesn't need a translation— she knows exactly what I'm talking about. "So what are you going to do about it?" I ask angrily. "He's out there now, trying to save you and your cause, and you're sitting here staring at walls?"

Tears streak Catalina's eyes as she opens her mouth to speak but says nothing. "Come on," I urge. I kneel down in front of the old woman. "We need to do something; you can't just... I can't just let him die."

The old woman speaks, never taking her eyes from me, and Catalina translates. "Señor Santiago es free. He do what want do. Stop do, not our way."

"What, so you'll let him 'stop do' the fucking Dark Ones from hurting you and your cause, but you'll not do anything to help him?

That's bullshit," I grumble, popping up to standing. Catalina cringes and casts a worried look toward her great, great grandmother. To hell with keeping my thoughts good.

The old woman doesn't seem the least bit phased by my anger. She stares up at me with nothing but sad understanding. "Well, I'm not one of you, and I'm not going to sit by and let Santiago die for a bunch of people who won't do anything to help themselves."

I turn and storm from the chamber, leaving Catalina chattering away at her grandmother in a high, anxious tone. I trip once and bounce my shoulder off the rock walls of the passage twice before I spot the tell-tale glow of the entrance. On my way out, I stop and glanced back at the two guards; they look so formidable it's laughable. "You guys are pathetic," I quip. "What will you do if someone tries to force their way in, OM them to sleep?"

I stomp over to the stream and slosh through it to the other side, find my clothes by the pool, and change. I stop once to look at the mouth of the cave and find myself hoping that Catalina will emerge and offer to help. "What the hell can she do," I grumble as I follow the path that leads me out of the canyon.

There's no sign of the two guards at the entrance to the canyon and I soon find myself lost in the forest beyond… seriously lost. I know the direction I have to follow to get back to our cabin and once there I'll know how to make my way out to the highway.

To my frustration, the path we'd taken there that seemed like clean single track, branched once, then twice, where other paths leading to the cave from difference parts of the colony joined it unseen by me earlier. "Shit," I mumble looking at the barely visible third fork in the path. "Fuck!"

I kick the ground and clench my fists. I know working myself up won't help so I try walking it off in a circle. That's when I notice the shadowy rock in the forest. It's large and still and… familiar. The smell of the night air comes back in a rush. That first dream, when I'd run down the cloaked figure who turned out to be Catalina. I spotted the tree that I'd hid behind to watch the procession of hooded figures pass. I recalled how exhilarating the dream had been and how I'd run free… like a wolf. "Come on, Jesse. You're supposed to be part dog, you can do this."

I kick off a shoe and take a good smell of it, then get on all fours and sniff the ground. All I can smell is dry earth and the piney scent of the forest, and I feel stupid. "Not like this." I think back to the time Santiago had taught me to track those drug dealers. It wasn't by smell, exactly… it had been something else, a different sense, part smell, part intuitive feeling, and part… something… .

I slip my shoe back on and sit on my haunches. I think about Catalina, about how she looks and smells, and it slowly works it's way onto my awareness, an essence like the air after a spring rain—that's Catalina, that's her scent. I stand slowly and breathe in, I can smell it everywhere, strong, but it is stronger on the path to the right. Without hesitation, I start down that path, first at a walk, then at a jog, and then a run, the feral sense of freedom growing stronger by the step.

The path, ferns, and trees seem so distinct to me, like a highway marked with reflectors; I can run full tilt in the dark. The run is exhilarating, jacked up by the anger I feel toward the colonists for being so willing to let someone die for them without lending a hand. I won't do that, can't do that, and as I run my anger grows into a craving to rip into Wingate and his goons. Santiago warned me about this, about the feral blood lust that he said was our greatest weakness, only this feels like an incredible strength.

Chapter 60

Flight From Safety

Journal - Hook Point, CA.

I've learned the hard way that when we embark on some journeys, some courses of action, we can too easily cross a line, after which there's no turning back. Then—for better or worse—we're committed, and can only hope that things will turn out. That hope, I've learned, can be a very thin thread to hold, and regardless how things turn out, you have to be willing to face the consequences of your decision. Bottom line—In all you do, choose wisely.

~ From the Journal of Jesse Benatar

"Where are you going?" Gwen calls out as the door closes. I'd only stuck my head in the door of Margarita Ruiz' cottage long enough to say I was leaving. I hear fast footsteps on wooden floorboards and see the dark path flooded with light as Gwen flings open the door. "Where are you going?" she shouts, emotion cracking her voice.

"Where I have to," I call back.

"What are you going to do?" she cries.

"What I have to," I shout then brake into a run.

"Jesse, wait," Gwen shrieks. In the distance, I hear the door close and a moment later open again, then hear footfalls on soft earth. "Jesse," she calls out, but I'm gone.

The hike out is a long one and by the time I reach River Road, I figure it's well into the dead zone, somewhere between 2:00 and 4:00 am. I look east, the direction of the bender mine, then west, the direction of home and my bike. I decide on west. Home is miles away and I am tired and hungry so running isn't an option.

Traffic is light, it's the dead zone after all, but I decide to hitch a ride if I can. Hope is born every time a rare car's headlights approach from the east, then dies as it passes and the taillights recede into the distance.

I'd all but given up when I hear an approaching vehicle slow, and turn to see dim round headlights. It's old and slow, but I stop and wait with a hopeful thumb in the air. As it draws closer, I recognize the sound of the engine and the shape of the cab; the antique yellow pickup pulls up next to me and stops.

"Jesse you stupid idiot," I hear Gwen say from the interior. She flings open the door and piles out. "What do you think you're doing?" she blurts with pent-up emotion. Then she steps up and slugs me. "You ass!"

Things become surreal after that, and I lose my shit again. I hear the driver gasp, Gwen's face turns from anger to shock, as inner world shifts from disbelief to anger. Maybe it's my frustration with The Dreamers, my concern for Santiago, or the adrenaline that's been pumping through my system since I'd left the cave, but I grab Gwen by the shoulders and ram her up against the doorframe of the truck. She lets out a sharp grunt when she hits and her face screws up in pain. "Jesse!" I hear Catalina scream.

I jump back in shock at what I've done. "God, god, oh god, I'm sorry, Gwen. Are you okay?" I blurt. I reach out to touch her shoulder and she shrugs it off. "Gwen I'm so sorry, I don't know what…"

"Shut up," she says, tears streaming down her face now.

"Gwen…"

"Just shut up and get in," she says.

"Jesse?" Catalina says. The fearful look on her face shining in the dash lights.

I'd shifted so fast it caught me off guard. *Did she see me that way?* It's then that I realize I have tears flowing as well. "This is nuts," I say. I turn away and face the forest. "Totally fucking crazy." I feel like bolting into the woods, away from everything. How had everything become so insane?

"Come on," Gwen groans. I feel her hand touch my arm and I flinch. I have to step back quickly and that makes me feel even more like a shit bag.

"I'm sorry," I say, turning to face her. "I didn't mean to…"

"I know," Gwen says. "I know what happened, I know how worried and angry you are."

"No excuse," I blurt.

"Hitting you was stupid," she says.

"Yeah, it was," I admit. That brought a glimmer of a smile to her face. "I'm not going back, Gwen," I add.

She gives me a sad look and nods. "I know."

"I can't. Someone has to do something."

She nods again. "I know, but it's not safe to be out here at night hitch hiking."

The absurdity of the statement makes us both look at each other and pause, then we both crack up, a welcome release of the pent up emotions I'm feeling. It is good to see Gwen laugh, but by her eyes and a grimace she tries to hide I know she's in pain. My laughter stops and she sees the concerned look on my face. "I'm okay, just get in." I motion for her to load in first and as she does, she quips, "Just hurts when I laugh."

We start down the highway and I notice Gwen squirming in the seat. "I think we need to get you to the hospital," I say.

"Don't be stupid, I'm okay…" Gwen whines.

"Gwen, I pushed you hard, I felt it, you could have broken something…"

"I take," Catalina says. I look at her as she drives, staring ahead with both hands on the steering wheel. She takes her eyes from the road just long enough and nods at me. "I take doctor."

"No you won't," Gwen protests.

I place a hand on her knee. "Yes—yes she will, and she'll take you to a doctor that can have your back and ribs x-rayed," I say directed at Catalina. Catalina's eyes, flick between the road and me a few times and then she reluctantly nods.

"This is perfect. First you cheat me out of seeing the Cave of Prophesies, now this," Gwen complains.

"I didn't… I had no say in that, Gwen," I protest.

"I know, but I have to be mad at someone," she says.

The banter's relaxing, but my mind doesn't venture far from my purpose: to find Santiago and stop him from getting himself killed. I have no idea if I can do that or even how to try, but if it comes to it, I plan to be at his side.

"I hope this doesn't get you into trouble," I say to Catalina. Gwen translates and Catalina shakes her head. "No es importante."

"She said…" Gwen begins.

"I know," I say, 'but yes it is. After you drop me off and take Gwen to the hospital, I want you two to get back to the colony."

Gwen translates again but Catalina says nothing and gives nothing away in body language. Then Gwen turns her head to me and says, "No!"

"Gwen…" I begin.

"No," she snaps. "We stay together. Whatever you're up to, I'm in whether you like it or not."

I don't argue with her. I know once I get to my bike they're history; they couldn't keep up in this antique and they wouldn't have a clue where I was going. I try my cell again. I tried a half dozen times to call

Santiago once I reached River Road, but nothing was going through. Maybe my phone is finally pooched after the soaking it took or maybe he's off the grid now. I try texting him as well—same nothing.

As we approach the house I tell Catalina to pull in. "No way, Jesse," Gwen protests. "Once you're on your bike we'll never see you again."

"Gwen, I need something from the boat." Catalina pulls into the drive and I pop out and closed the door. "Get her to the hospital," I tell Catalina as I shut the door.

"Jesse!" Gwen protests. She tries to force her way out of the cab but I hold the door shut. She's crying again.

"Gwen, I'll join you at the hospital, I promise."

"Yeah, after you get yourself killed."

"No, right away. I need to go to Santiago's boat anyway to see if he's there." It takes a bit of convincing, but a minute later, the old yellow pickup pulls back out on to River Road on its way to town. "Time to gear up," I mutter to myself.

Chapter 61

Preparations

The ride into town is a blur. Speed being irrelevant, I soon find myself running along the floating wharf toward The Revenge. Before I even get there, I know I'll find him gone. I have no sense of his presence, and when I reach the dark yacht, I feel it's completely void of life. I sense something else as well—there's an aura of danger around it, and a subtle scent, but of what?

It's cloying and bitter-sweet, and it rekindles a memory of sitting over a burial cairn I'd built on the mountainside in Colorado. *Death!* Someone has died here; I know it—feel it in my bones.

"Santiago?" I whisper, heart racing. I begin to step up onto the deck, but a surge of adrenaline stops my foot mid-air; I sense stepping aboard is dangerous, perhaps deadly. "Santiago?" I call out. The boat sits in dark silence but for the clear call of a Mockingbird echoing from across the harbor.

———— | ————

The hospital is quiet; being midweek and the middle of the night, the only person I spot in the waiting area is Catalina. She stands when she sees me and walks toward the examination wing, motioning me to follow. "Doctor see now," she says when I catch up to her.

A nurse at the entrance to the suite looks at Catalina and then at me. "You the brother?"

I nod. "How's my sister? Is she okay?"

"Where's your mother? We haven't been able to reach her. Something about being at the colony is it?" she asks.

"Yes, she'll be hard to get in touch with without driving out there. How's my sister?" I ask.

"You'd best go in and talk to Dr. Jamieson. It's been all we can do to stop your sister from leaving," the nurse complains.

Great, just my luck it would be Miranda's dad again. He's going to think we're a pack of Neanderthals. The look on his face as he peeks out from the curtains around an examination bed confirms my suspicions. He ducks back behind the curtains and says something I can't make out, then emerges again. He holds up a hand to stop me from going behind the curtain.

"How's Gwen?" I ask.

"I'm okay, I told you that," she says unseen.

"You're sister is not fine," Jamieson says. "At least I'm not certain yet. She has a contusion across half of her back that transects the spine and one of her shoulder blades." Gwen grumbles something incoherent. "I don't think there are any broke bones but I've ordered an x-ray series to make certain," he continues.

"How long will that take?" I ask.

"The technician is on short call but the radiologist won't be in until morning," he says.

"What? No way am I staying here," Gwen says. I hear movement behind the curtain and she sticks her head out through a gap, holding the sheets to protect her privacy.

Jamieson makes on a very stern look and orders her back onto the bed. I add my support; "Gwen, get back into bed," I say. "If you do have something broken in your back…" I gave her my best 'man, it would really suck to be you' shrug. In the meantime, one of the attending nurses gently eases Gwen back behind the curtain and signals to another who joins them.

I listen in shock as the two nurse's work to get Gwen back into bed without bending her spine in any way. My mind goes in a dozen places I don't want it to go before I realize Jamieson is talking to me.

"What?"

"I said you need to tell me exactly what happened," he says. "I've delayed calling child protective services out of deference to your mother, but I can't delay it any longer.

"Child protective… No, no, it's nothing like that. It was me, I did that to her. We were horsing around and I grabbed her shoulders to scare her but tripped and we both kinda crashed into the door frame of Catalina's truck."

Before I'd finished saying that he had already started to shake his head. "Sorry Jesse, it won't wash. The bruise across her back is just too severe for that. Only a very powerful person using all of his strength could do that, and you just aren't that strong."

"You'd be surprised," I mumble.

"I'm not joking Jesse. I need to know who did this to your sister. If I can't identify a culprit then CPS is going to do a full investigation and I don't think you're mother will like that," he warns. "Who really did this and why? Was it one of the men at the colony?"

"Shit, no!" Gwen spat from her bed. "I told you. I fell scrambling over rocks tonight."

Huh! No wonder he doesn't believe us. Gwen never was good at lying or making up stories. I thought about Santiago out there, possibly dead already and breathe deeply into that burning fire. I hear Catalina gasp and sense her step back. Even Jamieson seems to notice something because his face pales a shade. "You want to know who really did it?" Let me show you. My right hand shoots out and grabs his shoulder cap and digs deep.

"Jesse, no," I hear Catalina and Gwen utter in unison. Jamieson's face contorts with pain as he tries to pull his shoulder free but my grip is too tight.

"Jesse!" Catalina shouts.

I let go of his arm and he immediately begins rubbing it with the other. He gives me a hurt, questioning look but I don't have time to feel like shit. "There, believe me now? So you go put that in your report and let the cops' arrest me, but right now I have a life to save."

I turn and storm out of the examination area while Gwen wrestles with the nurses and Jamieson. Catalina follows me out of the room and I turn my attention back to her. "Listen, Catalina. Thank you. Thank you for tonight, for taking me to the cave and for picking me up on the road. I want one more huge favor from you." She looks at me with a panicked look in her eyes, a look that's not lost on the nurse at the station.

The nurse clears her throat and grabs our attention. "Señorita Ruiz, Permiso por favor," she says, then rattles off something that seems twice as long as what I have said to Catalina.

"What?" is Catalina's reply.

"Go back in there and convince my sister that she needs to stay in bed," I begin with the nurse translating on the fly. "Convince her I'll be okay, lie if you have to, tell her the prophesy sees me as a happy old man someday." That brings an irritated look from Catalina and a firm shaking of her head. "Just reassure her and tell her I'll be okay and that I'll come back here as soon as I've talked Santiago out of whatever he is planning to do." She nods and then I am gone—out the door—on my bike—racing up River Road.

Chapter 62

Into the Fray

By the time I reach the fork in the road that leads to the Bender Mine, I can just read the sign in the dim light of the eastern sky. I try to smell the air, to taste the vibe, but everything's awash in emotion. Santiago's different—he can stay calm and dispassionate in the face of all the shit of the world. He'd tried to teach me that—tried.

Now, I'm a boiling pot of adrenaline, anger, and fear. It tortures me that I'd hurt Gwen, and that feeding the desire to rush blindly—mindlessly—into the fray. Take me down three or four levels of consciousness and add 100 pounds of bone and muscle, and I'd be no different from a berserker.

"Think Jesse, think," I urge myself. "What would Santiago do? Hell, he'd probably just stroll up there and kill them all." Thoughts run around my head, possible courses of action and resulting scenarios. Problem is I never had much patience for this sort of thing. "Don't think, just do it!" I flip the MacGyver to run dark, kick the bike into gear, and head toward the mine.

Before I'm half way up the narrow road, I can make out the glow of lights from the mine through the foliage; they're making no attempt to stay dark and concealed—not good. Then I hear a single shot ring through the air. It's a sound I know too well from growing up on military bases—someone is firing a Barrett 50 cal sniper rifle.

I stop the bike and remove my helmet. Another shot breaks the deathly silence that follows the first, and then small caliber automatic fire echoes through the forest from the area of the mine. I pop on my helmet and accelerate up the hill, going as fast as running dark will allow on the old road.

Sporadic gunfire continues to ring out, small caliber automatic fire punctuated by the cracks of the big gun. The lights from the mine blink out but the gunfire continues. I'm nearing the last few bends in the road when the deep thwopping of a helicopter clutching at air in a hard climb echoes around me and a moment later the sleek silhouette of the bird screams overhead and arcs downward into the valley below. I expect it to crash, but it disappears and the sound of its rotors fades and becomes drowned out by the continued gunfire above.

A bend later, the lights of a vehicle race around a corner on the road ahead and I brake to a stop. I have seconds to get off the road or turn around and run for it. Automatic gunfire and muzzle flashes blaze from the vehicle as it rounds the last bend before it would be on me, but the section of road I'm on is a rock face on one side and a shear drop on the other. Trapped!

Another single shot rings out and a blink later the vehicle careens off the edge of the road and catapults out over the drop off. I stare in morbid fascination as the dark mass of the SUV bounces off the steep slope, flips over, and lands with sickening finality on its roof on the forest floor below. Unlike in the movies, nothing but darkness and silence come up from its final resting place. The effect is more sickening than any special effect Hollywood could think up.

No more gunshots rip through the early dawn air—hell has become placid, cool, and fresh. Heart pounding, I continue up the road to the

t incident, and when I reach the spot where I hid the
γ first excursion to the mine, I pull over again. This time I
 ..s far off the road as the hillside will allow, and tuck it
between a young redwood and a rock outcropping—no one could
possibly see it from the road.

It's only a quick hike up over a ridge and I'll have a good view of the
mine workings below. What I find when I reach my vantage point isn't
like a flood-lit scene from a movie after a fire-fight; the mine's work
yard is bathed in the palest light of early dawn, the blind point where
night vision fades and color vision has yet to kick in. I crouch and
struggle to make out what lay before me

The shipping containers are both sitting next to the dirt piles from
the cannery excavation and the mine-tailings along with one of the
hauling trucks. Three large, black SUVs are parked near the main
building, and a fourth sits where it came to an abrupt stop against one of
the large rocks that border the lot. Its doors are open and around it, four
dark figures are sprawled in contorted, grotesque shapes. I begin to
make out other, more distant bodies scattered about like tossed dolls—
five... six... seven.

The carnage is sickening, obscene—the ugliest thing imaginable and
my mind goes numb staring at it. It's exactly the sort of shit my father
had witnessed, had done. "No wonder you were so fucked up," I
whisper. *This would seriously fuck-up anyone.*

As true as that is, even now I know it was no excuse for what the old
man had become. Max had experienced such things, others I'd met as
well, but they'd somehow transcended the horror, dealt with their
demons. Santiago had said something about my dad being an asshole to
begin with, that his trauma had only made that worse.

I give my head a shake. I can see why The Dreamers would never,
could never, partake in anything so vile. I know now that I couldn't
either... but someone has.

I take out my monocular and scan the scene Santiago, first among the
bodies and then within the shadows. "You must be Benatar?" a rough
but hushed voice grumbles behind me. I turn to see a hulk of a man
standing only six feet behind me, brandishing a Barrett M82. He's scary
as hell itself, and I'm shocked that someone so large could have snuck
up behind me without a sound, but I sense no menace from him.

"Who are you?" I ask.

"Keep it down," he warns. "Carlos said you might show up. Asked me to make sure you don't get your ass fragged." The man says as he scans the open space below.

"Santiago? He's… he's okay?"

That brings me a scowl from the man. "Down there rooting out the last of them," he says. He takes a few steps and kneels next to me, then sets the bipod legs on the ground and hunkers down.

"You killed them?" was all I can think to say.

"No kid," he says. "They killed themselves." He carefully adjusts the sight on the gun and begins peering through it. "They're no better than Mercs, walking dead."

I look at the man, at the deadly weapon he's preparing and find it insanely humorous. "So what are you?" I ask.

The guy doesn't flinch, just adjusts his sights, bolts another round into the chamber, then says. "He warned me you were a little shit!"

"I need to go help him," I say as I scan the area for a way to sneak down there.

"No you don't," the giant grates out.

"You don't understand, I need to…" what can I say, that I need to save Santiago from repeating what's been done in the past, the fallen one sacrificing himself for the good of all?

"No you don't," he says.

Old dude is seriously pissing me off. I pop up on my haunches and turn to say something. The last thing I see is a massive fist about to connect with the side of my head.

Chapter 63

Retribution

Out of the void, a groan. Movement... pain... dim light... then another groan. I flutter open my eyes to see fading stars against a murky blue sky. My head feels like it's been split open and my shoulders are tight and cramped. I try to sit up but find myself unable to swing my arms or legs freely. I let out a grunt and roll over on my side. By the feel of it, my wrists and ankles are bound with zip ties.

"Son of a bitch," I mutter. "Prick." I roll over on my stomach, lift my lower legs vertical, and shake them. The clip that's holding my Tanto to the inside of my boot holds fast. I arch my back and pound my knees against the ground as hard and fast as I can, and only managed to tire myself out. "Fuck!" I spit into the dirt.

I roll around and with a little effort manage to sit up, and find myself where the big guy had dropped me. I inch over to the edge of the ridge and peer over it carefully; everything below sits silently in the growing light. I see more details but nothing of movement, of life.

I try to wriggle off my boots but the zip ties hold them too, tied around my ankles. I look around, see what I hope to see, and roll back over on my side. I snake my way over to the manzanita bush and maneuvered my legs into position with a thick broken branch between my ankles and above the tie.

It takes about five minutes but I manage to snag the edge of the knife clip on the branch and work it free. It takes another couple of minutes to fish it out from underneath the manzanita, get my hands on it, and cut through the ties, but in short order I'm up and looking for a way to approach the mine under cover.

I decide on a route that will take me around to where the shipping containers and tailing piles sit. It's the longest route of those considered, but it promises the best cover. While I'm scrambling across a hillside that's hidden from view of the mining buildings, a short burst of automatic fire rings out; the place is still hot and Santiago is still in danger. I listen for a return fire but nothing comes. I speed up my pace.

Sneaking between the two tailing piles to the container truck, I crawl beneath it and scan the yard. Aside from the main mining building, there's a smaller office building, a half dozen work sheds, vehicles, crates, barrels, a large water tank, and bushes around the perimeter. It's a nightmare of places for a gunner to hide in wait of an unwary soul. My mind goes back to a conversation I had with Santiago during my training…

"So, like, does this mean it will take a silver bullet to kill me or something" … *"No. A lead one will do fine."*

I feel exposed, even hidden where I am, so I crawl back the way I came and nestle myself into a spot between the tailings were I can see nothing but sky and the tailings themselves; that means no one me either. Somewhere out there I hope Santiago and King Kong are still alive and well, but I fear there are more goons as well.

The air still carries the acrid stench of gunfire mixed with the sweat scents of early dawn, but it's devoid of sound. Even the calls of awakening birds are absent. I close my eyes and explore the silence. Surely something… a faint shuffle sound from near the main mine building. I focus on that area but hear nothing. I begin to feel something, however. *Santiago!*

I probe further, wider, and pick up on one more presence, then another. I sniff the air—dust, manzanita, oak, sage, bay, pine, redwood… death. More subtle than death, the now familiar scent of corruption wafts across my face on an early morning breeze. If I only studied more, worked harder, I might be able to sniff out the remaining goon or goons. *Then what?* I ask myself. *Serious—What the fuck am I doing here?*

Then things happen fast—too fast. I sense tension in the air and feel Santiago's presence grow stronger. I leave my safe spot and move toward the buildings. I see nothing when I pop my head over the edge of the tailings, but I feel a sudden surge of concern from Santiago and I bolt in that direction. I just reach the space between one of the abandoned SUVs and the office building, when Santiago steps out from behind the structure and fires two quick shots over my shoulder with an assault rifle.

I dive to the ground and spin around to see the dark-clad goon slumped over next to the water tank. I look back to see Santiago pick up the two ejected casings and pocket them while scowling at me. He mutters something but doesn't look my way; he's talking into a com system. I slowly rise up. "Is that it?" He doesn't reply but begins to walk toward the main mine building.

I do a 360, looking for signs of danger, and notice the guy who tied me up moving toward us across open space from a far shed, cradling the M82. The guy's freaking King Kong—at least six foot six and three hundred solid pounds. I catch up with Santiago who marches with an unwavering stare.

"You were supposed to remain at the colony," is all he says.

"Yeah, well, plans change," I begin. "I went to the cave with Catalina and saw The Grandmother, saw the prophesies, learned about what the last outcast had done back in the 1800's and figured you were off on a suicide mission."

We reach the mine building and he takes and cursory look inside. He hands me a pair of blue nitrile gloves. "Put these on and don't touch anything," he says, then steps in. It's a massive room with a large, decrepit conveyor system that disappears into the floor at a 45 degree angle. It looks to have been run by an old boiler system similar to the one in the Cannery and it's clear it hasn't been used in at least eighty years. Santiago makes his way over to a much newer elevator system. "So you decide to come and die with me?" he asks at last.

"No, I came to save your ass," I say.

"And nearly lost yours instead," he grumbles.

"No, I know, felt you were in danger so I…"

"I was alarmed for you because you were in danger," he interrupts. King Kong strolls in just then. Both men pause to listen to their ear buds but I can't make out what is being said on the other end.

"How long?" Santiago asks.

"Okay, pack it up and go to stage three."

"Twenty minutes isn't a lot of time," King Kong says.

"It'll have to do," Santiago replies.

"Do for what?" I ask. "Let's get out of here, you did what you came to do."

"No, there remains one more task," Santiago says gravely.

"Wingate took off in his helicopter, what more is there to do?" I ask.

"The helicopter was a decoy. Adam Wingate buried himself below like a rat in a burrow," Santiago says.

"So what—you going to get yourself killed making certain he dies?"

Santiago gives King Kong a scowl. "I thought you were supposed to take care of this," he says, gesturing toward me. The big guy scowls and shrugs.

Santiago slips on a pair of blue nitrile gloves and hits the button that will bring the lift to the surface, but nothing happens. He hits it again. "It must be locked out from below," King Kong growls. "Let me take a look." *How does it not hurt to talk with that voice?* The guy puts on a pair of gloves as he moves into a small shed next to the lift and shoots a glance back at us.

"Hey, I recognize you now. You're that guy in the marina parking lot, the guy with the old blue Pathfinder. He ignores the observation. "So you were never in this alone," I say to Santiago.

"A man is never alone who has friends," he says while rummaging through a satchel he swings from his shoulder.

"Well, true, I just never thought of you as having any friends." He pulls a bundle of brick-sized blocks and wires from the satchel. "Is that? Where'd you…"

"A gift from Wingate," Santiago says. "Special delivery to *The Esmeralda* by way of underwater courier."

"And you're returning it to sender," I say. Santiago nods. "But why, he knows we're onto him. He won't do anything like they tried in the past."

"He already has, Jesse. He won't stop," he replies.

"Get him later," I suggest.

"No!" A sharp crack rang out from the control room the large wheel that controls the lift swings into action. "It has to end now. The police will be here in less than 20 minutes and if he's not dead and buried by then, he'll just squirrel himself away where he'll be hard to dig out."

"Looks like a shallow mine," King Kong says. "It'll be up shortly."

Santiago moves to the edge of the cage-enclosed shaft and looks down. "Move back," Santiago says and he and King Kong move to the far side of the room and take up firing positions. "Step outside," he orders. There was no mistaking that was meant for me.

"I ah…" I begin.

"Now!" he demands.

I do what he says, but I stay just outside the door and keep an eye on the elevator. An empty elevator cage rises to the surface and the whine of the electric motor spools down. Santiago approaches the cage as though it might explode, then lifts a trap door in the floor near the lift and hops down into the crawl space beneath. King Kong gives every inch of the visible cage a thorough look over and then climbs up a ladder to a nearby gangway and does the same thing with the top of it.

"Looks clear," Santiago says as he climbs out of the crawl space.

"Less than sixteen minutes, King Kong spits."

"Wait," I shout. "You can't just send that bomb down the shaft; you don't know who's down there." Santiago ignores me, pulls out a touch-screen phone, and taps at icons until what looks like an image of intersecting lines pops up. As he uses his finger to manipulate the image, it becomes obvious it is a 3D map of some sort. "Is that the mine? Where'd you manage to dig that up?"

"Let's get her moving," Santiago says. He moves over the to elevator and slides the outer cage door open, stepping in, then monkeys his way up the framework until he is perched atop the cage. With his satchel over his shoulder, he loads his M16 with a fresh clip.

"You're not..." I start.

"You are right about this one," King Kong grumbles, gesturing to me. "You certain he's related?" He hits the control button and the cage begins its decent.

"If I'm not on my way up in ten minutes, extract yourselves through the back door and we'll meet up as planned," Santiago says gravely.

"Hey, if you're not on your way up in ten minutes I'm not leaving you here," I say. Santiago ignores that and disappears down the shaft. I walk over to the edge and peer down. I catch his eyes looking up and they convey an unexpected thank you. "Oh, shit," I blurt.

"What?" King Kong blurts.

"My bike. I hid it in the trees at the last bend down the road. If the cops are on their way up here, they'll find it for sure if they look around, which they will."

Kong looks at his watch. "You have just enough time if you beat it now to make it to the first junction and hide out until they pass."

"I'm not leaving," I say.

"Then you'd best come up with a good story why it was left... Say again..." he says into his com-piece. "Yeah, down the road, last bend, maybe 200 yards."

It's then that automatic gunfire rings out from bellow and Kong pulls me back away from the shaft and possible ricochets. There is no M16 fire. Santiago has either been hit or is playing a smart but dangerous game. A deathly silence follows, then it's interrupted by gunfire again.

Still no sound of an M16. Then all hell brakes loose. Kong listens intently to his com-piece.

"What's happening?" I ask.

"Shut up," he says quietly in two very distinctly punctuated words. The gunfire stops. "…Right," he says into the air, his com-piece picking up his voice. "…Signal fading."

"Is he okay?"

"…Right! … Yes!" Kong stares blindly at the ground, as though visualizing what is happening below. Then he shoots a look my way.

"How much time?" I ask.

He glances at his watch and scowls. "Less than 14 minutes."

"We're not really leaving him in four minutes, right?" I ask.

"Don't make me have to carry you kid," he warns.

I'm antsy and step outside to listen for sirens. Even if they were sounding I doubt I'll hear them until they were one or two hills away. I'm tempted to run for my bike and hide it someplace more secure, but there's no time, and I can't leave while Santiago is down below somewhere. I stare at the body of one of Wingate's goons, or what is left of it after it had been hit by a 50 caliber round. It's horrific and sickening.

Despite all the negatives of being a Wingate goon, he was someone's child, someone's brother, perhaps someone's father. How would they react to seeing him there like that? It's nothing like the movies, nothing like anything on YouTube or some of the sick-fuck websites out there, and nothing I could have imagined—it's real—hear and now—and I can smell the iron in the splattered blood. It's obscene—true horror in its most sickening form.

I know why The Dreamers will never participate in anything like this, know they would rather die clean than kill or injure another, but what of Santiago? He's doing what they cannot and will likely be killed doing it. Is it wrong? Will he be damned for that? I always thought that I could kill to protect myself or my loved one's, but now, I don't know if I'd choose Santiago's path or that of The Dreamers.

I stepped back into the building. "Time?"

"Just under 10 minutes," Kong says solemnly. He's giving him more time.

I run over to the cage. "What's taking him. I should have gone with him to help." We both watch and at the 5-minute mark I can just make out the first hint of a siren in the distance. "We can't leave him." I say, more question than statement.

Kong's head twitches to the side a little. "Say again," he spits into the ether. A surge of hope wells up inside of me. "Signal weak…"

Then, the ground trembles and a gust of dusty wind shoots up the elevator shaft. I look at King Kong and catch a grim look on his face. "Is the bomb supposed to go off with him still down there?" He doesn't answer but with the look on his face he doesn't have to. "Just one more minute, please?" I ask. Kong hesitates. A siren suddenly grows louder. "Must have rounded the last hill." I blurt. "How long will it take for the elevator to get up here?"

"Too long. Time to go." Kong turns to go and when I don't follow he grabs me by the arm and starts to escort me to the door. "How fast can you run across the yard to beyond the tailings?" he asks as he storms toward the door, dragging me.

"Fifteen or twenty seconds maybe. Why"? I ask, trying in vain to pull free from his grip. "Let me the fuck go."

He turns his hard face to me. "Because we barely have that long before the cops arrive—we're out of time."

I try to pull away but it is no use. I become angry and try to shift but the guy snorts and squeezes my arm so tight I think the bone will snap. "I wouldn't do that, kid—I'll have to hurt you."

He's a shifter; he has to be. "You too?"

"Yeah." He shoves me out the door and the sirens sound as though they're just a bend away. Instinct takes over and my resistance dies. The two of us dash across the yard and between the tailing piles. We just make it over the lip of the hill and start down into the bush when the blast of a siren erupts in the yard and car tires biting into gravel tell us the first of the cops have arrived. The carnage must have been a shock to them because it isn't until two more vehicles come to a skidding stop that we hear a car door close.

I follow King Kong down the hill as he steps quickly from rock to rock as nimbly as a goat. We hit a trail a quarter mile later and then we're running at top speed, like two wolves on the hunt. I follow him along 4 miles of complex trails that end at a gravel road where his old Pathfinder is parked. We pile in and he fires up the engine.

A half-mile later we're tooling at an easy pace along R
only then that the full impact of what just happened si
elbows on my knees and bury my face in my hands. "Santiago,

After a few moments of silence, King Kong speaks. "One thing ı
learned a lifetime ago, kid, is to never underestimate that man. If there
was any way to survive the blast and escape the mine, Carlos will have
found it."

There's an edge of doubt in his voice and his hard, weather beaten
face betrays subtle signs of distress. As much as I want to believe him,
to grasp at that thread of hope, I know better.

Chapter 64

Aftermath

Hook point is just stirring to life when we pull into the hospital
parking lot. Catalina's yellow pickup is still there where she'd parked it
hours earlier—not a good sign. "Remember! Don't go anywhere near
Carlos' boat and don't do anything outside of your normal routine,"
Kong says. "I'll call you on this when I learn more," he says, handing me
a cheap cell phone. "Don't make any calls on it and after I call you, get
rid of it unless I tell you otherwise." I slip out of the truck and close the
door, giving him a look that was probably as vacant as I felt. His
hardened face softens slightly and his eyes shift downward to in a blank
gaze. There's always hope," he finally says, and then he's gone.

I stare at the yellow pickup as my mind struggles to comprehend how
everything had changed so quickly. The morning air is cool and fresh,
but it feels oppressive. There are more cars and people out on foot now
then just a few moments before, as though a master alarm has awakened
the town to the new day. I imagine they're awakening into the same
Hook Point they went to sleep in, and look forward to another day like
the day before. To me, the world's different; everything has changed—
everything.

The hospital waiting room is empty when I drift in, but I no sooner
begin to talk to the nurse at the intake station when the door to the
examination area opens and Gwen and Catalina walk through.

"Gwen!" I mutter.

She walks slowly with Catalina close by her side, and looks to be in pain. She smiles when we make eye contact, as though to say, 'See, I told you I was okay.' She must have read something in my expression because her smile shifts to sympathetic sorrow. When Catalina sees me, she brings a hand to her mouth and stares at me, wide-eyed.

"Hey Gee, how badly you broken?" I ask.

"What happened?" she asks, tears beginning to form in her eyes.

"Not here," I say. "You okay, you free to go?" She nods. "Then let's go." We begin the slow walk toward the exit, Gwen clearly uncomfortable with each step. "So?"

"What?" she asks uncomfortably.

"Did I break you?" I ask?

"You wish," she manages to say. "Just stiff."

"Doctor say pain, pero no bone break, no ah, peligro," Catalina says, barely taking her eyes from Gwen to make contact with mine.

"I'm sorry, Gwen," I mutter before we get through the doors. Those words are enough—a damn broke somewhere inside of me and I'm flooded with a torrent of emotions. Guilt, grief, anger, fear, sadness—it all coalesces into mind-gapping and anguished sobs.

Somehow I manage to get them into Catalina's pickup and to pile in beside Gwen, then mutter, "Go!" I bury my head between my knees and hold on tight. Images of Santiago ravage by mind—our training, his guitar playing, his tortured life, and it all leads to the carnage at the mine. They are interrupted by images of dad—the alcohol and narcotic violence, my love and hatred for him, and the funeral.

Gwen holds me tight and I can hear her voice reassuring me, but can't make out the words. After a while, everything becomes still and I finally manage to raise my head up and see that we're parked at Hook Point's main beach.

Without a word, I fling the door open and slide out. I want to run but turn and help Gwen ease out of the cab. With Catalina on her other side, we begin a slow stroll to the water's edge. After Gwen reassures me again that she's only bruised and that her muscles will be stiff and sore for a few days, I let it all out. I explain everything that happened since I ⸻ a at the hospital, and Gwen translated as much as she could to ⸻ When I'm done, we sit down in the sand and watch the ocean ⸻ e.

——— | ———

We park on the side street next to The Kat and Catalina insists that she go in to get our drinks. Gwen and I sit looking at the cannery, silently brooding, until I say, "Everything can change so fast."

"Yeah," she croaks at length, "we know that."

"Yeah."

A few minutes later, a flurry of activity in the side mirror draws my attention. Catalina's approaching the truck carrying a cardboard tray with three drinks, but so are Michelle and Jeffrey. I dry my eyes quickly and slip out of the cab. Michelle takes one look at me and slows as she reads my expression. "What's happened?" she asks.

I shake my head—I can't go over it all again. Understanding flashes on her face and she gives me a hug. "Are you okay?" she asks.

"Yeah, I'm good," I lie.

Catalina hands me my coffee and Gwen her tea and gives me back the ten I gave her to buy the drinks. She then turns away and talks to Jeffrey in Spanish. We hang around the sidewalk for 10 minutes, while Catalina conveys enough to them to make Michelle cry and Jeffrey angry. As nice and gentle a guy that he is, when he is angry he has a surprising edge.

We make plans to get together at the Therion as soon as I'm back from the colony, and then the three of us slowly make our way back up River Road. The mood is beyond somber, but before long we're approaching home. "Pull into the house for a minute please," I ask Catalina. "I need to pick something up." She does so, and Gwen and Catalina go into the house so she can pick a few more things up to take to the colony while I make my way to the Therion.

Halfway there, my emotion-addled brain registers it once, then twice—my bike—it's parked next to the Therion. I bolt to its side and stare down in disbelief. I check it over, as though expecting that somehow it wasn't really my bike, then I dash up into the boat, too fearful to trust hope.

There, sitting on the table beneath my helmet, is a slip of paper and my spare key. I draw the sheet out and read it.

Thanks for the ride. Spare key wired in place under the gas tank? Too easy. Go back to the colony. Talk to no one. ~ S

"Santiago," I blurt through tears. "You crazy wonderful son of a bitch."

Gwen's so happy when I tell her Santiago's alive, that she tries a victory jump and nearly falls over from a back spasm. Then I suggest that she and Catalina get back to the colony.

"You're not staying here alone," she says.

"Gwen, there are a couple of things I need to do here," I retort. "Mom's probably worried sick about us by now and someone has to tell her we're okay." It takes a lot of arguing, but she finally leaves with Catalina and vows to be back that night with Mom's blessing.

"Fat chance," I mutter to myself as I wave bye.

I'm exuberant. He'd somehow made it out of the mine and pulled off an escape with what must have been dozens of police around. I clearly have a lot more to learn from him and it was looking like I might just get the chance to do just that. I dash back to the Therion and jump on the Net. No word has yet hit the news feeds about the slaughter at the mine, but I imagine the police can't keep something like that under wraps for long.

Lack of sleep and emotional exhaustion finally catch up with me and I throw myself on the bunk for a power nap. I set me alarm for an hour, but never hear it go off.

Chapter 65

Loose Ends

I'm blissfully aware of the nothingness around me, the proverbial and eternal void, when a disturbance shimmers in the distance. I've heard about this place, the source of everything, have read about it, but never thought I'd experience it until after I died. The disturbance grows, draws closer, and it's only a matter of time until I'm pulled from this place of profound peace. Then it happens…

A chiming fills the space around me. *I know that sound, I've heard it… A cell phone? It doesn't sound like… .* I open my eyes and sit up. I feel drugged as I grope around for the source. I pick up my cell but it sits silently in my hand when the chime sounds again. Through my hypnopompic haze,

I spot the cell that King Kong gave me sitting on the table next to my laptop. I grab it and flip it open.

"Wha?" I mumbled hoarsely.

"What are you doing at home still?" Santiago asks.

My mind rallies. "Santiago, you are alive, I started having doubts that it was…"

"You are supposed to go back to the colony."

"Yeah well I have a few things to do first," I grumble. "Wait, how did you know I was at home?"

"The phone's track-able. You need to get out of there now and get to the colony," he says. There's urgency in his voice.

"Why, what's up? I thought the danger was over? Didn't you get Win…dows 10 yet?" I say, nearly blowing it.

He hesitates on the other end, likely angry that I'd nearly used Wingate's name. "Yes, but it's not over. We're still cleaning up the hard drives," he says. "There are viruses to clean, and these ones are like creatures that go bump in the night. Get yourself to the colony."

"I, ah, can't. I have friends coming over around seven, and it's only…" I look at the time on the phone then do a fast take on the clock across the room—it's quarter after six. "Shit, how'd it get to be so late? I just laid back for a nap…"

"You've slept the day away. Get to the colony. Your friends will understand," he insists.

"Do I destroy the phone?" I ask.

There's a pause at the other end. "No," Carlos says. "Since you're not going to do what you're told, maybe you can do something useful."

"What?" I ask.

"Your friend Alexis; she may be in danger."

I swallow hard, then manage to blurt, "Lex? Why?"

"She helped us. Yesterday morning she brought me a map and intel on resource placement." I recall the map of the mine on Santiago's phone. "She also gave me the heads up on a gift someone was to deliver by underwater courier, the one I returned. She did it at great risk and if they even suspect she's responsible they will be looking for her."

It occurs to me that Wingate doesn't act alone, that he's only one of many, one of the People of Darkness. Others like him and their corrupted followers are probably trying to continue his plans without him, or wreak vengeance. So that's why Santiago and King Kong are cleaning up; it didn't end at the mine. "I'll find her," I say.

"Not alone," he warns.

"He who has friends is never alone," I reassure him.

"Then stay together and stay alert. Remember everything I taught you but most of all, trust your instincts."

Santiago hangs up and I turn my own phone on—it works. I try to call Lex, no answer, then call everyone in the gang to bring them up to speed. Christine's working at The Kat and it's Thursday, one of their busiest nights. I tell her she needs to help find Lex even if it means quitting her job. I suggest we all meet behind The Kat as soon as possible.

I strip off; use the toilet, splash water on my face, then put on a fresh t-shirt and jeans. My stomach groans loudly as I pass the fridge. I haven't eaten in over 20 hours and I've used a billion calories. With my metabolism, I could waste away to nothing if I didn't fuel up. I take a quick look around for something to shove in my face but decide to grab something at The Kat.

I've developed a few brutal blisters running in my boots, so I slip on my runners instead. I stare at the tanto still clipped to the inside of my boot top—I don't think I could ever use it to injure or kill, maybe not even in self-defense, but I did free myself with it at the mine. A tool is a tool and after a rock and a stick, a knife is the most elemental and ancient of all.

I pluck it from my boot and clip it inside my front pocket. Grabbing my helmet, I'm out, down the steps, and at the side of my bike before I take notice of something in the air. An alarm goes off in my guts and I freeze and sniff the air.

"Mr. Jesse Benatar," a smooth voice says slowly from the trees beyond the Therion.

Fuck no! I turn to see Bolin walk into view.

He's dressed in his leathers and walks with his normal slow swagger, but most of the left side his face is clad in bandages. He looks to be alone, but from what Santiago said, there could well be someone else in the woods with a bead on me. "Surprised to see me?" he asks.

"Yeah, I am," I admit. "I didn't sense you there at all."

He shrugs as he moves close. "A difference between cats and dogs—we're more subtle."

And deceptive. "Uh huh," I say as I scan the trees and shadows. "I thought they arrested you."

"Friends in high places," he says.

Fucker's buried beneath a mountain now. I'm mindful of Kong's instructions—I know nothing about anything. "And they let you out of the hospital as well. Guess I was all worried about you for nothing." Bolin chuckles but a strained look comes over the right side of his face and he stops. "What, only hurts when you laugh?" I ask.

He stands still about 12 feet away and stares. "No," he says. "It hurts constantly." There's no anger in his voice, and a subtle wave of regret washes over me.

"Sorry to hear that," I say truthfully.

"What is it they say—live by the sword... something or other... No, I left against doctor's orders. They wanted to send me down to The City right away. Seems I need a little reconstruction work," he says gesturing to the left side of his face with one hand, "but I have a more pressing matter to tend to."

Here it comes. I feel my muscles tense and a flame ignite within. I think of the blade in my pocket—another moment of truth? "Is that why you're here, Bolin? You here for pay back?"

He gives me a look I can't interpret then takes a few steps closer and stares down at my bike. "I've been told to find your little friend, Alexis."

"Don't even think about it," I warn.

"Seems she betrayed the boss man, stole something and turned it over to the other side. I'm ordered to find her and... well..." There's something odd in his voice. Is it remorse? Then I realize what he might really be saying, that he's already found Lex. The flame roils into life, but I can't bring myself to ask.

He squints at me with his one un-bandaged eye, and I sense he sees or feels the turmoil, the rage and fear I'm burning up with. "I didn't," he says at last. "I, ah, couldn't."

The fire within diminishes, and a sense of relief washes over the embers. "So then why are you here?" I ask.

"I've been given instructions that must be carried out," he replies.

"You don't have to do shit for him anymore," I say.

"Why, because he's likely dead? Doesn't end there, Benatar."

"It does if you want it to," I say.

Bolin turns his back and looks up at the trees and stars. "He threatened my family, my sister," he blurts. "Told him I wanted no part of hunting down your friend. He said it was her or my family."

"Like you threatened my sister," I remind him. He drops his head and nods. "Well, if he's dead, as you say, then why worry about it now?" I ask.

Bolin turns to face me. "Because his reach is long, perhaps even longer than the grave. He has plans; backup plans, and back up plans for the back up plans. Right now there're over a dozen men out there following through on his contingency plans, dead or not."

"I, ah, hear that there are some people taking care of that," I venture to tell him.

"Santiago and his pack," he muses. "Yeah, they're known to us… my kind. Once they start hunting you down, there's no escape. Especially the big one from Canada."

I'm confused. "So, why exactly are you here? I ask.

Bolin turns his shattered face up to mine. "I need your help."

Huh? "My help? You're kidding right?" I ask.

"Make certain my parents and sister are safe?" he asks.

"You really think Wingate's men will hurt them now?" I ask.

"If I fail to do what I was ordered," he says.

"But if Santiago's pack is so effective, is there really any danger to them?"

"Would you be willing to take that risk with your mother and sister? It only takes one man," he points out.

"But you're more than one man, Bolin, you can protect them," I suggest.

To his clear discomfort, Bolin chuckles. "You don't get it yet dead man," he says. "Santiago's pack is coming for me, I can feel them, like wild wolves closing in for the kill. They'll soon have me treed and then…" He shrugs.

"I'll talk to them," I offer. "If Santiago knows how you feel, knows you refused to hurt Lex…"

Bolin closes his eyes and shakes his head. "No good; even now you don't fully comprehend what they're like and how they work."

"And maybe you don't fully comprehend what Santiago is really like. He's not the heartless killer people think he is," I say.

Bolin chuckles but looks more shaken with emotion. "I just want my parents and sister to be safe. They don't deserve to pay for anything I've done."

I stare at the guy I've despised, the one I apparently tried to kill and would have if Gwen hadn't stopped me. Perhaps he wasn't the monster I pegged him as either. "How can I help?"

Chapter 66

Crucible

> ### Journal - Hook Point, CA.
>
> *Today I learned that if you truly love someone, cherish them for all their faults, then forgiveness comes easy even—after the most bitter betrayal.*
>
> *~ From the Journal of Jesse Benetar*

At a few minutes before 7:00, Michelle, Jeffrey, Miranda, and I are standing around at the back of The Kat waiting for Christine. I give them a quick version of why it's important to find Lex, and mention that Wingate might be gone but nothing else—there isn't any point in making them all accessories to what the law will no doubt consider acts of murder or terrorism.

At a few minutes after, Christine slips out the back door and joins us. "Bill's not happy about this but I still have my job," she says in a worried tone. "So what's the emergency?" When I tell her, she looks panic stricken. "I haven't seen her since yesterday. I looked everywhere

last night and this morning before work. It's not unusual for her, but…"
She didn't need to finish the sentence.

"So what's the plan?" Jeffrey asks.

"We split up, comb anywhere and everywhere she might have been
and ask anyone we find there." I say. "If we come up with anything,
make the call, let's stay in the loop." Everyone nods and instinctively
checks their cell phones. "I'll take the east side of Main, check out the
houseboat and the side streets."

Everyone identifies the area he or she will search and we split. I ride
immediately to Lex's sanctuary, hopeful that she'll be hiding from the
world there. I'd asked Bolin if he'd looked for her or if he knew of
anyplace she might be, not giving up a hint about the sanctuary, but he'd
said nothing to suggest he or Wingate knew anything about it.

I'm hopeful… until I spot the patrol car parked on the street not a
hundred feet from the hidden entrance to the warehouse. Unpleasant
thoughts run through my head—the Sheriff's department could be
investigating the finding of Lex's body—a Sheriff's deputy's working for
Wingate to track her down.

I do my best to ride normally—a little too fast and carefree—and do
a quick sideways glance toward both the car and the building. The patrol
car's empty and the building looks as vacant as it always does. I can only
catch a glimpse of the old iron sheet that acts as the doorway, and it
looks to be in place. I stop at the corner and look both ways as though
deciding which way to turn. "Now what?"

I turn left and keep an eye on the building and an eye out for the
deputy, but after I pass the sanctuary without seeing anything
noteworthy, I'm not certain what to do. If the deputy's in there with Lex
and working for Wingate, he could be killing her right now. On impulse
I gun the bike and race down to where the houseboat listed at the river's
edge. I no sooner dash down the gangway and reach the front door
when my phone goes off.

"Jesse!" Christine blurts. "I just got a text message from Lex and I'm
scared." It shows in her voice.

"Why, where is she?" I ask. I pound on the door to the houseboat.

"She didn't say but it was a good-bye. She sounds… well, like she
does when she's not doing well."

"Did you try calling her back?" I ask.

"Yes, right way but her phone's off now."

"What did she say?" Christine read through what sounds like the brief but confused ramblings of someone drunk and sorrow filled, her voice trembling and breaking as she reads. The ending makes the blood pulse in my ears.

"Earth, air, water, and fire make us all, and on scorched earth, the ashes of sin purify, and make way for rebirth. Good-bye love. Sorry for all the shit."

I hear Christine saying something in the background as I kick in the door of the houseboat. She's nowhere to be found. By the time I get back to Christine she is crying. "Christine, listen. I have an idea. Do you know the old boat repair warehouse on Dillon between First and Second..."

I dash out of the houseboat and turn back to make the door look as though it's locked again, then jump on my bike and make for the warehouse. I'm contemplating what I do if the Sheriff's car as still there, and have all but decided to break in on the other side of the building, when I see the cruiser is gone. I ride around the block quickly to make certain and there's no sign of it.

I slow to a stop in front of the boarded up doors and stare at them. *What if...* Then I hear faint music and feel her presence wash over me like a warm summer breeze. I pull around to the side of the building and behind the rusting dumpster, muscles shaking from adrenaline, and still feeling nervous anticipation. I'm comforted to know she's there, but it's unlike Lex to play music or do anything that might lead someone to think the building's being used.

I kill the engine, and take off my helmet. The music is loud and I give the street a quick nervous glance in both directions. No one's around, but I know it'll only be a matter of time before someone hears the music and becomes curious. *What are you up to, Lex?*

I quietly pull back the corrugated iron, and slip in, leaving it propped open a few inches for the others to find it. The sound is even louder inside, and fills the space like an organ in a cathedral. I find Lex in the center of the building's open floor, dancing by herself. Off to one side a set of portable speakers boom out the music from her iPod—steady, smooth, and sensual, while Lex moves like she's part of it.

I'm mesmerized; her movements are slow and smooth, wild and gyrating—she dances the same way she makes love, and my heart races wildly as I watch, barely able to stop myself from stepping out and making myself known. As I stand back in the shadows against the far wall and watch, her face and movements exude joy then sadness, triumph then defeat, agony then ecstasy; wherever the music goes, she's there within it.

She embodies it all—the human experience—life itself displayed in all its sadness and grandeur, like some offering to the gods on hallowed ground. I'm witnessing perfection, the spirit of life incarnate, and in the light of that, none of the shit of the past few days means anything. It is a perfect point in time and place.

Lex is so lost in her dance, eyes barely open; she doesn't notice me observing her ritual—it's just that, a ritual, something deeply spiritual. I have no idea how long she's been at it, but her clothes look to be soaked with sweat and her face glistens with it. I lose track of time as I watch her, and only slowly become aware of a shift in the atmosphere.

The music has grown faster with each piece and is now more chaotic. More striking, is the change in Lex; her body keeps in step with the music, a perfect enactment of the increasing frenzied and harsh sounds, but her face has become a mask of detachment. With every shift in the music, her body responds in kind, but her face grows impassive—dead.

Lex's movements slow and her facial mask takes on a quality of bitter determination. She steps over to one of the large support posts, and stagers a little as she does—she's been drinking. *How could you possibly dance like that half corked?* She picks up a couple of liquor bottles, and dances back to the center of the floor. To the mad rhythm of the music, she begins to move in a slow spin like a dervish, a bottle in each outstretched hand.

It looks as though she is praying, making some sort of offering to the gods, but then she turns the bottles up over her head and begins poring the amber liquid over herself. She must have been drinking some of it before I arrived. It makes me smile and want to join her, to pour booze all over myself and immerse myself in the beautiful insanity of her moment.

With the bottles empty, dancing in a large puddle of liquor, she chucks them aside and makes her way back to the post to pick something up. That's when the smell of the liquid wafts over to me and sets off all the alarm bells everywhere in my universe.

"Lex!" I shout. I sprint towards her. She almost stumbles at my voice and gives me a stunned look, but picks up what she was after and leaps back to the spreading puddle of fluid. I stop just outside of it and stare in horror as Lex stands in the middle of a small lake of gasoline, holding a road flare in one hand.

"What the fuck are you doing?" I shout.

She has trouble focusing on me but when she does, her eyes convey more hurt than I'd believed possible. Despite the dim lighting, her pupils of tiny dots of black against gray—she's high. "I'm fixing it Jesse, fixing everything," she cries.

"No, no you're not. Give me that," I demand, gesturing to the flare.

She looks at the flare and pulls the safety cap off. "No, dear friend" she says, tearing up. The smell of gas is eye watering and her hair and clothes are dripping with it.

"Are you crazy?" I shout.

She gives me a surprised look. ""Ha!" she blurts, eyes flashing wildly. "Um, yeah!"

"Lex, please," I plead, "just give me the flare." I take a step closer, right to the edge of the gas.

Lex steps back and makes ready to light the flare. She looks pained again and begins to cry. "I'm sorry, Jesse. I'm sorry for everything. I told you I wasn't what you thought."

"You're everything I thought, Lex, and more." I begin to cry. "You're the most amazing girl I've ever met, your smile, your fire, that crazy fucked up head of yours—everything, everything about you. If you'd only seen yourself dancing just then you'd have seen something incredible, someone unique, special…"

"I'm no good," she cries.

"You're perfect," I shout. "Your…"

"That's…" Lex clenches her fists and screws up her face. "That's such a fucked thing to say. Why are you saying that?"

"Because it's true. You're perfect in all your bullshit and chaos. You're, like a one-of-a-kind flower, outrageous colors, powerful scent, perfect, thorns and all, and now someone wants to rip you up by the roots and burn you."

Lex slowly shakes her head. "No. I'm so sorry. I'm no good, Jesse, never have been. I hurt everyone I care for, fuck over everyone who's ever trusted me."

"So have I," I cry. "God, if you only knew… if you could only see what I've… I don't know why, Lex, but hurting those closest to us… it's just what some of us do. But when you're loved, really loved, then those people stick by you."

Lex stares wildly at the pool of gas and her hands tremble. "Lex, you're important, you're one of us, you're family."

"Family sucks, Jesse," she cries, tears flowing, "haven't you figured that out yet?"

"No it doesn't, Lex, not this one, not us. Maybe those men hurt you, maybe your mother didn't protect you, but we're standing by you regardless of what's happened." I step into the puddle of gas, within two feet of Lex. "I'm here, now, standing with you."

Lex stares at me with a lost, searching look. "Get away," she shouts. She holds the igniter cap just inches from the live end of the flare. She is a flick of the wrist from ignition. "Not you! I don't want to hurt you."

"Too late, dear friend. You hurt yourself you hurt a part of me. You kill yourself, you kill a part of me." I cry.

"I'm here too Lexi," I hear Michelle's strained voice cry over the music. Lex's eyes dart off to the shadows on her right, toward the secret entrance, but I don't take my eyes from Lex. "I'm here for you," Michelle's voice quavers.

"I'm here too Lexi," Jeffrey says. "We all are."

"Lexi," Christine's voice cracks with emotion. "I'm hear honey."

"Me too, Lexi, I'm here," Miranda's voice calls out with obvious emotion.

"Go away all of you," Lex cries. "Get the fuck away."

In my periphery, I notice the figures slowly approach.

"Can't do that Lexi, you're one of us and we love you."

"I'm standing right here, Lex," I say. "For you. We all are. We're here for you."

"I'm standing by you Lex," Jeffrey says, stepping next to me, into the pool of gas." Lex's eyes grow wider, wilder.

"I'm standing by you Honey," Christine says with barely contained tears. She nervously steps into the pool just to the left of Lex, hands shaking, lips trembling.

"No," Lex cries, stepping back from Christine. "Go away, all of you. Get the fuck out of here." She holds the igniter cap against the end of the flare.

Michelle looks down at the pool of painful death and steps into it, to the right of Lex, knees shaking. "I'm standing with you too, Lexi," she says, crying. Her tears drip onto the floor and mix with the gas. "I'm not going anywhere, Sweetie."

"What the fuck are you doing?" Lex cries, searching our eyes for an answer.

"Loving you, Lexi," Miranda says, voice trembling with anguish. She slowly approaches Lex from behind, causing Lex to look over one shoulder, then the other, and scan the circle forming around her. Miranda trembles as she stares down at the gas and then bites her quivering lip, and with a look of desperate determination, steps into the pool of gas behind her. "Nothing you've done or will do can change that," she says.

"Nothing," Jeffrey echoes.

"Nothing," Michelle says.

I reach a hand toward Lex. "Please Lex."

With gasoline still dripping from her hair and tears from her eyes, Lex slowly moves the flare toward my hand. I gently take it and toss it well away from the gas. We all draw in tight around Lex and embrace her and she sobs long and hard. In those dear moments, we learned something special about ourselves and each other, felt the power of family, and in that crucible of heart, experienced what it is to heal.

Chapter 67

Closure

In the days that follow, life seems to slip back into some measure of normalcy. I even have a surprise birthday gathering of family and friends who remember it when I don't. Hook Point reels at the news of the gun battle and carnage at the mine, but basks in the light of national news coverage about it. It'll likely be the main topic of conversation for years.

Speculation runs wild—from a drug war, to a battle between rival extremist groups, to a sanctioned hit against a terrorist training camp that the government is denying. Finding the bodies of two scuba divers in Hook Point's harbor who apparently drowned with nearly full tanks of air steals some of the gossip, but no one seems to notice or care about the quick departure of the Wingate Yacht the day of the mine incident. In fact, the Wingate presence in Hook Point seems to fade overnight.

I haven't seen Santiago for nearly a week, when he shows on the back deck of the Therion early one morning during the last week of summer break. The first thing I'm aware of is the odor of his cigarillo. I stagger out through the companionway in jeans and stare at the man sitting on the edge of the gunwale.

"Hey," I say. I make my way to the back deck and lean on the opposite gunwale.

He looks around and nods. "You're uncle did a good job with her, except for those Christmas lights," he says, gesturing to the string of lights I put up around the hoist rigging and radio mast. "She should be in the water though."

"I'm, ah, not sure the engine even works anymore." I venture. He says nothing. "So where have you been, or should I ask."

"No," he says looking down at the deck. "You shouldn't"

"Wingate?"

He doesn't answer at first, only stares at the deck. "Last I saw of him he was ducking into a back chamber under the cover fire of his guards. The explosion nearly collapsed the whole level."

"So he could till be alive?" I ask, troubled by the thought.

"If he survived the blast and the initial cave in, he wouldn't have lasted long. They're not re-excavating the mine; they have no reason to believe anyone is down there," he says.

The thought of Wingate and some of his men having suffocated in the mine isn't a pleasant one, but the thought of Wingate alive and free is even more unpleasant. "So, are things cleaned up then?" I ask.

He nods. "For the most part. Still have a few loose ends in Florida, but the rats have fled to their South American haunts."

"What about Sarin and Wade?"

Santiago gives me a solemn look. "They haven't been seen since the yacht left for Mexican waters."

"You don't think…" Santiago shakes his head. I think about Sarin, how she just didn't fit the rest of the family. She isn't one of the Dark Ones, doesn't belong with them, and it saddens me to think of her as living among them. "And Bolin?"

"His family is safe," Santiago says.

"And Bolin?"

"Officially missing with enough clues to suggest he succumbed to whatever feud took place here a week ago."

"But…"

He nods. "Safe, though I don't think he's going to like the cold when winter hits up there."

"He went back up north with King Kong," I guess aloud.

Santiago gives me a stern look. "His family must never know. It's hard on them but if they ever come to believe he's still alive and the wrong people find out about it, it could endanger them."

"That's rough," I say, thinking about what it would be like to be alive but knowing Gwen and mom thought I was dead.

"It was his choice," Santiago says.

"Yeah." We're silent for a few moments as I mull things over.

"You never told me how you escaped the mine," I realize aloud.

Santiago gives me what I think is a faint smile. "Conveyor system. It was blocked up, but I managed to clear things enough to crawl up it."

"Then you somehow managed to sneak past a pack of cops in broad daylight, steal my bike right under their noses, and make it back here undetected."

"Something like that," he says.

Another pause falls on us. "So is it over?" I ask finally.

"For now."

"And what now?" I ask.

"Chop wood, carry water," he says, quoting the Buddhist saying.

"And my training? Am I done?" I ask.

ne a look that is something between 'are you kidding' and
ish' then says, "When you're ready." He looks over his
...ards the house. A light comes on in the kitchen; mom's up
and no doubt staring on breakfast. "How is your mother?"

"Settling down," I say. "She still hasn't forgiven me for nearly
breaking Gwen's back... ah, long story... but she's okay. Some of the
people at the colony have been inviting her there, making her welcome,
and Gwen too. I think the seeds of change have taken root there."

"Good," he says with a sad smile. "It's time."

"Perhaps they'll even invite you back," I suggest. Rather than a mood
booster, the comment darkens his further. "Sorry." Santiago stands and
looks to be ready to leave. "Listen, You wanna stay for breakfast. Mom
makes the most amazing..."

"No, but thank you." He turns and steps over the gunwale and takes
the steps to the lawn.

"Thank you," I call after him. He stops and looks back. "For
everything." He nods slightly, but before he can turned away I add,
"You're not who you think you are you know. I see you for who and
what you really are." I am hoping he'll ask, but he doesn't. Another time.

He looks over toward the name of the boat. "It is a good name; it
should never have been changed." I nod in agreement. "Take care of
her, she always did me, but get her back into the water; she's like a caged
wolf like that."

The Therion had been his and somehow it all fit and felt right. I
watch him walk out to the road and get into his car and drive away. I
feel sad for him, but I have time, Gwen, and Mom on my side, and
there's the gang.

After breakfast I ride into town but instead of dropping by The Kat,
I go straight to the sanctuary. It's the last week of summer break and
everyone is there fixing up the place. Pete and Jeffrey are working on the
floor where the gas had soaked into the thirsty old wood. They're
cutting out and replacing the affected lengths of plank and replacing
them with ones salvaged from other parts of the building. Michelle and
Miranda are cleaning the windows while Christine and Lex are
rummaging through a pile of boxes and barrels in the far corner.

"You could sell a lot of this stuff at the flea market," Christine says,
then they look up and see me approach.

"Hey," I say.

"Hey," Christine replies. She glances at Lex, who looks away. "I'll be right back," she says without explanation and then disappears, leaving Lex and I to our selves.

I haven't spoken to Lex since the incident with the gasoline; she's refused my calls and manages to duck out whenever I come around. This time, she just stands with her side to me, moving the contents of an old box around aimlessly. "Hey," I say.

She stops her rummaging for a fraction of a second then resumes. "Hey," she finally says.

"So how are you feeling?" I ask.

A grimace shows on her face. "You mean do I still want to off myself?"

"No!" I say quickly. "I mean, how are you feeling? I've been worried."

A quick smile crosses her lips and her eyes dances like they do when she spits out one of the retorts, only she says nothing. She shoves something down into the box with a thud and steps away from it. "Stupid," she spits, shaking her hands as though flinging water from them. "Really, really stupid."

"Well, you were high on booze and some of your mom's Oxys, but yeah, it probably wasn't the smartest idea you've come up with," I say, hoping it'll ease her mood. It doesn't.

I don't have to ask her why she worked for Wingate; she already explained to Christine how it had begun two years earlier, informing a woman in Wingate's employ of things going on in town under a guise of marketing. By the time she realized what was really happening, she was in his clutches, fearing for the safety of both her mother and friends. She didn't make excuses for herself, though; she took the full load of self-recriminating blame.

"You scared the hell out of me." I say.

Lex snorts and rolled her eyes. "Yeah, you and everybody else." She folds her arms and bites her lip. "Sometimes I wonder... Huh! I guess I scare the fuck out of myself too."

I give the sanctuary a quick look over. "Place is looking different. You sure you want to do this, fix it up and live here I mean? I kinda liked the Gothic squalor look."

Lex gazes at the floor and nods. "I, ah, decided there's no more hiding away. Bad things happen in the dark."

"Yeah," I say.

"Besides, there'll be loads of gothic squalor left when we're done," she says with a hesitant smile

Silence follows that for just a little too long for both of us. There's so much more to talk about; so much unfinished business, but it's a start. "Well, I best make myself useful here, or the owner might fire me."

Lex is, in fact, the owner. Christine filled me in on that one as well. Lexi's father had bought the old warehouse for a business scheme before abandoning Lex and her mom. He'd been killed five years earlier, but had left it to her in trust, along with just enough money to keep up on the taxes until her 21st birthday.

When Lex turned 16, she'd legally emancipated herself, with the aid of the estate lawyer, and had only been living with her mom to keep an eye on her. Girl is full of surprises.

"Jesse?" Lex says as I turn away. I face her. "I ah, really am sorry," she says, tears welling up in her eyes. I take a step toward her but her body stiffens just enough to notice so I stop.

"So am I," I say.

Another silence falls on us but she breaks it this time. "I don't regret anything that happened," she begins, "between us I mean."

"Me neither," I say.

"I just, can't go there again," she says apologetically. I nod, torn between relief and disappointment. "I just hope it doesn't make things to weird."

"Me too," I say. What she and I shared was amazing in ways I'll take years to appreciate, but like an uncontrolled flame, we'd both been burned by it. The scars may linger and keep us a safe distance from each other, but I know we both feel the warmth of that fire even now. "I think we've both had enough weird for one summer."

She nods sadly.

Chapter 68

Destiny

I stop in the woods at the edge of the meadow and see her by the rock. She stands luminescent, waiting. She knows I'm there, but the choice to engage is mine. I feel her, know the scent and feeling as she approaches, and hear the voiceless call. This time I look back to see myself sleeping, a tangled mess of limbs beneath a blanket. I don't awake then, nor do I awake when I hike over the ridge and down through the forest.

I step into the meadow and slowly approach her through the tall grass, then stand only a touch away. Her eyes watch mine, wide and bright, but betray nothing of thought or feeling. "I don't know if we'd ever meet like this again," I say finally. "Not after the cave."

Her eyes dart to the ground and back to mine. "All different," she says. "Not same."

"How? Why?"

"I want…" she begins, then falters. With a look of suppressed frustration, she speaks too quickly for me to follow. "Te quiero a ti, pero tú no me quieres." she says. She looks at me, then looks around nervously.

"Catalina, I don't, I don't… Listen, there is something between us," I say gesturing with my hands. "I don't know what it is but I feel it and it's strong," I continue, watching the confusion grow on her face, "and I know you don't understand a damn thing I'm saying, but I can't be with anyone right now, and I don't want to be with someone just because…"

She reaches forward and places her fingertips over my lips. "Shhhh," she soothes. "Prophesy true, pero you, me," she says, bring the tips of her fingers together, "because prophesy say, I no want."

I let that sink in. "Right, exactly. I don't want to be with you just because of the prophecy and I don't want you being with me for that reason either."

She nods. "Si, es good."

"So who knows, right?" She nods hesitantly. I am definitely going to have to learn Spanish.

"You come colonia soon?" she asks.

"Yeah, soon." She nods and smiles just a little sadly, then closes her eyes and begins to fade."

"Wait! The Talfar. It's gone," I say with gestures.

She nods. "Si. No es importante."

"Not important? But I thought…"

"El Talfar es sólo piedra, ah only stone."

"But I thought if the Talfar was ever lost, your people would cease to be."

She takes time with this and then speaks slowly. "Talfar stone," she says touching the saddle rock, "only stone; no es importante. Talfar," she says, holding both hands to her heart, "es muy importante." She touches her head. "Good, ah, pensamientos… good here."

"Good thoughts?"

"Si! Good thought." She makes a universal gesture for speech. "Good speak," then reaches over and strokes my shoulder. "Good, ah, actos. Eso es Talfar. Es muy importante."

"Okay," I said doubtfully.

Catalina holds up a finger. "I practice," she says slowly. "Talfar say, 'Love all people, all is precious, part divine.'" She searches my eyes for a clue if I understand. I nod. "Talfar say, 'Respect all creature—they are elder. Honor all plant—they are caregiver. Cherish earth—she es mother to all.'" She watches me with anticipation.

"Right," I say. I get it, finally. "Yes!" I nod. It isn't the tablet or even the words that are important; it was how they live. If they ever lost that simple way of being, or their respect for life, they would cease to be who they are. "Si. Entiendo."

She smiles brightly and closes her eyes, then utters, "Buenas noches, Jesse Benatar," as she fades away.

Chapter 69

Epilogue

The cool breeze wafts up the cliff's edge, smelling of salt and kelp and hot sand. A horn draws my attention, and that of its intended audience—a largish middle-aged lady with white legs and a camera. She looks back at the hulking RV and waves an annoyed gesture at the driver, then turns and takes another picture.

The scene takes me back to that first day riding into Hook Point near the start of summer. "Great entrance, Benatar," I chuckle to myself, recalling how I'd nearly ended it all on the back end of an RV. So much had happened since—too much—enough for a lifetime of summers, and everything's different now. "Everything."

The horn blows again and the woman snaps another picture and gives in. I watch as she disappears around the other side of the beast that soon pulls back onto Highway 1 from the viewpoint. "Gotta love a gorby," I mutter with a smile, thinking about how I might have reacted just a few months earlier. I chuckle to myself. "What a sorry bastard you were."

I look back out over the gleaming Pacific and spot a white cruiser moving through the gentle swells. It's nothing compared to Wingate's yacht, but it sets off a recollection of seeing Wade the day before...

He drove into town in his Audi and parked it across from The Kat. A text and 20 minutes later I was there, and followed him as he drove away slowly. He parked at the main beach, leaned against the hood of his car, and stared out at the crowded beach and ocean beyond. We both stood in silence a good 5 minutes, him like that and me leaning against the seat of the shadow six feet away.

"I loved him, you know," he finally said. I couldn't think of anything to say to that. "...and, hated him," he muttered just audibly. "He did some things..." he lapsed into silence and I tried to fill it.

"I know," I said.

"You know nothing," he spat with contempt and I knew then that I'd not been invited to make amends. He began to laugh to himself in a way that made my skin scrawl. "You know nothing," he repeated.

"Your sister, Sarin, how is she?" I'd asked.

He stopped his rattling and closed his eyes. "You think it's over? You think this ends it all?" he asked. "You and that old man think it's the end of my father's plans?" He opened his eyes and smiled up at the sun, then turned his face toward me. I don't believe in devils or demons, but the look of utter hatred and malice that Wade exuded nearly made me a believer.

He pointed a finger at my face and made a trite gesture of pulling a trigger, then he was in his car driving away. As I watched him disappear, I thought to myself, 'He's turned. He's one of them now,' and I wondered when Santiago or perhaps even myself, would have to deal with him.

I stare down the waves rolling in below. "Yin Yang," I say, then take in a deep breath and stretch. It's the last Friday of summer. School starts on Tuesday, but this weekend is another celebration for Hook Point, and my tribe. We have plans for Redline Beach at sunset tonight and Gwen, Mom, Uncle Frank, and myself are invited to something at the colony that no one will say anything about. So much has changed and I feel happy.

I look down into the helmet on my lap and spot the edge of a piece of paper tucked behind the padding. I pull it out, thinking it's another $5.00 bill I'd hidden there and forgot, but found a page from my diary pad I'd tucked there during my journey from Colorado. On it, I wrote something one night while lamenting under desert stars. It's the closest thing to poetry I'd ever attempted.

I will die, as I have lived... alone. What personal trait, what trick of fate, has left me... forever... alone?

The words bring back the feeling of utter desolation I'd felt that night and I marvel how I'd steeled myself to it, how willing I'd been to accept that fate. I shake my head then smile. I read the words again then lift the paper up by a corner and let it flutter precariously in the breeze.

We may come into this life alone, and we may leave this life alone, but in that, we are all united and share the same fate. In between those two great moments, however, alone is only an option. I lower the paper and fold it carefully and slip it behind the lining once again; a reminder that I am no longer alone.

Journal - La Colonia de los Soñadores, CA.

I've been told more than once I'm a dreamer and I've never disagreed. But what is a dreamer? According to the dictionaries, a dreamer is one who is asleep dreaming, an idealist, one given to fanciful ideals without regard to practicalities, or an escapist. It's sad that something so beautiful and important is denigrated, for it's the dreamer who has always found the path to a better way, and the dream that gives us hope.

We all start out as dreamers, idealists with an instinctive sense of real possibilities, and then we falter. At the boundary between the dream and the physical, we encounter inevitable challenge, but more lethal to our souls, we encounter all those who went before us who have lost the dream, who have accepted things as they are and now cling desperately to false promises and momentary pleasures. For those sad ones, the dreamer is a laughing stock, the brunt of jokes, but deep down, the dreamer is a reminder of all they have lost.

I thought I'd lost the dream, but it turns out I'd only misplaced it. Moving to Hook Point and all that took place that summer helped me find it again. 'I was lost, and now I am found' were some of the words of a dismal hymn I once heard, but now I understand at least one meaning for them, and my gratitude is boundless.

I am a dreamer! It is a noble and profoundly gratifying existence, and it is my intension to remain such until I pass from this world. To be less, is to have lived a hollow existence, to be less, is to lose one's soul.

~ From the Journal of Jesse Benatar

45440178R00203

Made in the USA
Charleston, SC
23 August 2015